HOW
TO
SAVE
THE
CATHOLIC
CHURCH

Andrew M. Greeley and
Mary Greeley Durkin

HOW
TO
SAVE
THE
CATHOLIC
CHURCH

Preface by David Tracy

ELISABETH SIFTON BOOKS
VIKING

ELISABETH SIFTON BOOKS · VIKING
Viking Penguin Inc., 40 West 23rd Street,
New York, New York 10010, U.S.A.
Penguin Books Ltd, Harmondsworth,
Middlesex, England
Penguin Books Australia Ltd, Ringwood,
Victoria, Australia
Penguin Books Canada Limited, 2801 John Street,
Markham, Ontario, Canada L3R 1B4
Penguin Books (N.Z.) Ltd, 182–190 Wairau Road,
Auckland 10, New Zealand

First published in 1984 by Viking Penguin Inc.
Published simultaneously in Canada

LIBRARY OF CONGRESS CATALOGING IN PUBLICATION DATA
Greeley, Andrew M., 1928–
How to save the Catholic church.
"Elisabeth Sifton books."
1. Catholic Church—United States.   2. Church renewal—
Catholic Church.   3. Catholic Church—History—1965–
4. Catholic Church—Doctrines.   I. Durkin, Mary G.,
1934–   .   II. Title.
BX1406.2.G725   1984   282'.73   84-40261
ISBN 0-670-38475-5

Grateful acknowledgment is made to the following for permission to reprint
copyrighted material:
  Doubleday & Company, Inc.: Selections from *Song of Songs* (Anchor Bible),
translated by Marvin H. Pope. Copyright © 1977 by Doubleday & Company, Inc.
  Harcourt Brace Jovanovich, Inc., and Faber and Faber Publishers: A stanza
from the poem "Objects." Copyright 1947, 1975 by Richard Wilbur. Reprinted
from Richard Wilbur's volume *The Beautiful Changes and Other Poems*, published in Great Britain under the title *The Poems of Richard Wilbur 1943–1956*.
  The New York Times Company: "American Catholics: Going Their Own
Way," by Andrew M. Greeley, from *The New York Times Magazine*, October
10, 1982. Copyright © 1982 by The New York Times Company.
  Penguin Books Ltd: An extract from St. John of the Cross, from F. C. Happold,
Mysticism (Pelican Books, Revised Edition, 1970). Copyright © F. C. Happold,
1963, 1964, 1970.

Printed in the United States of America by
R. R. Donnelley & Son, Harrisonburg, Virginia
Set in Sabon

For Jack Durkin,
who has to put up with both of us

Preface by David Tracy

Once upon a time everyone—friend and foe alike—thought he or she knew where the Catholic Church stood on every possible issue. That time is no more. However accurate these nostalgic or bitter memories of the great "monolith," the "Marine Corps of churches" may be is a theme for historians. The central fact is that once—and not so very long ago—the Catholic Church *seemed* solid, clear, distinct, immovable, and permanent. And then it moved. Everything seemed to become suddenly and inexplicably pluralistic, self-reforming, self-questioning. Once permanent fixtures of Catholic life seemed to evaporate with dizzying rapidity. The Catholic people became either exhilarated or confused—or, more likely, both. The foes of the Church no longer knew where to shoot, for the once immovable target kept moving.

Nowhere was this sudden change more rapid or more effective than in the Catholic Church of the United States. As European observers correctly insist, the American Catholic Church has become the major self-reforming church of our era. The future of Catholicism now seems clearly to lie not with Europe but with the reforming movements of the North American Church and with the great explosions of hope in the "small communities" of Third World, especially Latin American, Catholicism. The future relationships of the American Church and those "Third World" churches has become a major concern on anyone's future agenda for world Catholicism. But before that conversation can occur fruitfully we all need to have a little distance and a better perspective on what has and has not happened in American Catholicism itself.

We need theologians and sociologists with the kind of historical knowledge and religious sensibility who can see the forest for the trees. We need some daring proposals informed by a larger perspective than last week's controversy. We need a book that is not written just for theologians or sociologists or historians but for everyone. Better yet, we need a book not only for but *from* everyone—a book that takes seriously the concrete, day-by-day struggles of the American Catholic people and recognizes that struggle as a major resource for all our reflections and much of our hope.

In this work by theologian Mary Jule Durkin and sociologist Andrew Greeley we find the kind of book we now need. For each of them, in this as in their former work, has been deeply concerned with the actuality of the concrete, everyday struggles of Catholic individuals and communities in the midst of vast and unnerving change. Each of them, as the reader will soon discover, is deeply informed by the long, rich, and pluralistic Catholic heritage. They know that the Church of our childhood memories—the Church where doctrinal propositions and ethical norms often seemed to be the heart of the matter—was but one moment in a wider and richer history of spirituality, imagination, story, and community. They know that a primary responsibility of any serious Catholic is to recover that heritage in all its pluralistic power for the different needs of today.

They also know that theology is too important to be left to the theologians alone, just as sociology and history are too important to be left to their experts alone. For theology, sociology, and even history are important and illuminating abstractions emerging from a study of concrete communities and returning, to be transformed by those same communities.

This book, in sum, is a work deeply informed by contemporary theology, sociology, and history but just as deeply transformed by a sense of the concrete—of imagination, everyday experience, working symbols, and living communities. It will be read by some as a series of radical proposals. And yet it is, in fact, a profoundly conservative book—one that attempts to retrieve long-neglected, even forgotten and repressed dimensions of the Catholic tradition: art, imagination, pluralism, symbol, sacrament, story, analogy and small communities. These are the principal resources of the Catholic heritage in all its rich, even wild, plurality. These are the resources through which the Catholic people live and die. These are also the central resources which the Catholic people today need to hand on to future generations and need to render available for the questions and probings of a wider public.

And precisely these same realities, as the authors make clear, are the religiously empowering forces of the drives for self-reform in the Catholic Church in the United States. This does not mean, as Durkin and Greeley also make clear, that every experiment is good. It does mean that we must experiment and reform for the very resources of the tradition demand no less. There is a fine American pragmatic sense that theologian Durkin and sociologist Greeley bring to this study. There is an even finer Catholic religious sense for the everyday, for imagination, for art, for story and sacrament that infuses their entire work.

This book will inevitably stir controversy—what worthwhile book has not? But, above all, it will provoke the reader's imagination to try new possibilities, retrieve old and too long neglected dimensions of the tradition, and refine criteria for thought and practice alike. It endorses neither reaction nor revolution, but retrieval, reform and the risk of imagining new possibilities.

This work, in sum, is deeply experiential, pragmatic, imaginative, sacramental, pluralistic, and communal: which is another way of saying this book is both very Catholic and distinctively American. By being so distinctively American in pragmatic concern and experiential tone, this book should aid the struggle of the worldwide Catholic Church by offering some peculiarly American resources to that wider discussion. By proving so clearly Catholic in both imagination and content, the book should render available the resources of that classic tradition to the concerns of the wider public. For both these contributions, the authors deserve the wide readership that this book should command.

Acknowledgments

Co-authorship demands a system. For this book we each prepared initial drafts of certain chapters that we then submitted to each other for suggestions, additions, and corrections. Andrew Greeley wrote the initial draft of the introduction and chapters 1 through 6 and 12 through 15. Mary Greeley Durkin drafted chapters 7 through 11. In addition, the final draft, revised by Mary Greeley Durkin, incorporates ideas, critical comments, and suggestions from the following: Lawrence Cunningham, Eileen Durkin, Dan Herr, Martin Marty, David Riesman, John Shea, and David Tracy, who reviewed the initial draft. None of these worthy persons is to be held responsible for the use we made of their ideas, but we wish to thank them for their gracious cooperation. In addition we want to thank David Tracy for his kind preface and our editor Elisabeth Sifton for her careful editing.

Contents

Contents

Introduction

The Catholic Church in America seems to be in serious trouble. Despite his personal popularity, Pope John Paul is not able to command agreement from many Catholics who do not accept the principal doctrinal propositions and ethical norms of their Church. With the "Englishing" of the liturgy, the democratization of parish and diocesan structures, and the popularity of ecumenism (which tends to minimize differences among religions), there seems nothing distinctive left in the Catholic Church, no reason save the accident of birth to be a Catholic. The powerful structure of faith and morals, standing steadfast against the turbulence of the ages, which so appealed to converts like Evelyn Waugh, for example, seems to have collapsed. By the turn of the millennium, will there be anything left of Catholicism in the United States, except perhaps some ethnic customs, to distinguish it from other Christian Churches, say, Methodism?

Can the Catholic Church be saved?

And if it can be saved, how?

Some Catholic commentators, most notably James Hitchcock (always a conservative) and Michael Novak (a turncoat liberal in Church matters as in civil and economic ones) advocate a return to the structure of Catholicism as it was before the Second Vatican Council began in 1962, a reassertion of ecclesiastical authority and discipline. However, it is not clear that such an attempt (which many attribute, without reason, we believe, to the present Pope) would have any hope of success even if Church authorities had the stomach for it. If the Church seriously imposed sanctions for disobeying its teaching on birth control, for example, it would empty the churches of four-fifths of the weekly communicants—assuming that it could indeed impose such sanctions and have them taken seriously, a highly dubious assumption. Once authority itself is in question, it no longer has the ability to reestablish its power by asserting that it has the power. It merely makes itself appear ridiculous.

Others think that Catholicism can be saved if it "identifies with the poor" or "becomes an advocate of the poor." Often this means merely a wish that Catholics would echo the latest radical or Marxist political and social party line, with little regard for any specific religious content in their social activism (save for a spurious correlation of Marxism with the Gospel) and no regard at all for the possibility that Catholicism might have a contribution of its own to make to social justice. Such a search for "relevance" (what Paul Tillich might have called "cheap grace") is bound to be unsuccessful, both because it reduces the Catholic tradition to extremely concrete and specific social causes and movements (and hence to what Tillich would have called idolatry) and because it writes off as the "enemy" most of the Catholic population, who are neither "poor" nor "oppressed" as the social crusaders define such terms.

Social justice (which Marxism rarely seems to bring) should be a consequence of a religious vision and not a substitute for it, a healing power that binds humans together instead of dividing them into warring classes.

We believe that the Catholic Church will be saved and must be saved, and this requires us all to understand two truths:

1. Many of the changes in Catholicism today are *not* incompatible with the Catholic tradition. On the contrary, such modifications as a vernacular liturgy, democratic structures, extensive and amorphous

boundaries, and pluralistic forms were part of the Catholic tradition for millennia—long before the Reformation. They seem to dilute the Catholic tradition only to those who know little of the history of that ever-responsive, strong tradition.

2. The question must be reformulated. It ought not to be, Can we save the Catholic Church? but, Is the Catholic Church worth saving? What is Catholicism good for? Are there elements in the Catholic heritage that represent, if not an absolutely unique Catholic contribution to the human condition, then one that Catholicism is better able to make today than other religious and cultural groupings? The answers to these questions would indicate the kinds of policies that Catholics in the United States—lay, clergy, and hierarchy—would be wise to pursue for the rest of this century, policies that will not seek ways to be different, but make contributions that are unique.

Our purpose in this book is essentially conservative, in two senses of that word. We propose no doctrinal or ethical changes, but focus, rather, on policy, that is, on the methods and approaches and styles of Catholic behavior. Such policy matters at most times in human history are far more important than the theological issues that preoccupy the elites. And Catholicism knew implicitly, long before its brilliant son Marshall McLuhan, that the medium is the message: the style in which a message is communicated delivers the message more powerfully than the actual words of the message.

But this policy focus is also conservative in that it demands a reexamination of the Catholic tradition. The principal obstacle to a serious consideration of Catholicism is the equation of the "Catholic heritage" with "what we were taught in school" or "what Sister told me in sixth grade." One hears this equation from both liberals and conservatives, the former rejecting "what S'ter said" and the latter endorsing it, from bitter fallen-away Catholics, and from non-Catholics, who apparently honestly believe that the length and breadth, height and depth of the Catholic tradition is what "S'ter" said to their Catholic friends in grammar school. Common to "left" and "right," to "orthodox" and "heretic," to "insider" and "outsider," to "neoconservative" and Catholic Marxist is a sadly deficient sense of Catholic history, a woefully inadequate awareness of even the outlines of the development of Catholic history.

For example, most Catholics and many non-Catholics imagine that:

Catholics have always been obliged to marry in the presence of a priest.

The Church has never tolerated remarriage after divorce.

The Pope has always been thought of as the Vicar of Christ.

The Church has never been tolerant of masturbation and fornication.

The Church has never thought that human life did not begin at the first moment of conception.

The Church has always taught vigorously and forcefully that artificial birth control was seriously sinful.

None of these propositions is true in the form in which it is stated here. Yet most Catholics, good, bad, and indifferent, think they are true because "S'ter said so."

Even a cursory study of the Catholic heritage will show that the form of Catholicism that has prevailed in this country for the last 200 years has stressed (though not without some vigorous dissent and criticism) the propositional and the disciplinary aspects of its heritage (as embodied in lists of doctrines, moral rules, and canonical requirements) and has not emphasized enough the Church's experiential, imaginative, narrative, and communal dimensions. A new policy—a new set of emphases and concerns—is now required. And it is precisely their dim awareness of those de-emphasized components of their heritage that holds Catholics to their Church even when they seem to reject much of what it stands for.

In an earlier time experience and imagination were considered to be essential dimensions of Catholic life. In the present-day American Church they are considered luxuries, even dangerous luxuries. In earlier stages of Catholic history, religion and art were inseparable, both because religion was thought to deserve the very finest art and because art was perceived as one of the most effective means of passing on a religious heritage. These notions were completely lost to those who designed what one expert called the "hemorrhoidal Gothic" of immigrant parish churches or the late nineteenth century Jesuit Ugly of most Catholic college campuses, or the stark modern barn-like churches of the post-war suburbs. The airplane-hangar-modern church—lacking statues and stained glass, in a mistaken gesture to ecumenism—represents the logical conclusion of this modern "policy." If a responsive new Catholic policy will once again recognize the enormous religious importance of experience and imagination, it will preserve Catholicism's distinctive contributions to the human condition. This is not to deny the importance of doctrine, philosophy, catechisms, ethical principles, laws, rules, and authority. But in human religion, experience, imagination, and community are also important, and in these areas Catholicism can make its most important contribution to the modern world and can find the policies that will enable it to save itself.

By way of another illustration, saints, angels, and souls in purgatory were recently dismissed from Catholic life because liberals found them irrelevant, ecumenists thought them offensive to Protestants, humanists found them opposed to science, and Church authorities found some of them incompatible with scholarly history. But if one views them not as doctrines to be insisted on but as narratives responding to religious experience, stirring religious imagination, and imparting religious meaning, then there is a good case for bringing them back.

To dismiss such saints as Nicholas, Christopher, and Catherine (the three most popular of the nonbiblical saints) because they may never have existed is to miss the point that they are characters in stories of God's love as it affects everyday life, and, as such, they are legitimate figures in "religious historical fiction."

Moreover, to neglect the symbolism of Mary the mother of Jesus— the most powerful cultural artifact in 1500 years of Western history, according to Henry Adams—for feminist or political reasons or on ecumenical grounds (when Protestants like Harvard's Professor Harvey Cox are discovering her as a revelation of the womanliness of God) shows imaginative naïveté. Whatever doctrinal propositions may have been used about her, Mary's poetic function in the Catholic tradition, as one can see in many great poems and paintings, is to represent the womanliness of God—the life-giving, nurturing, healing aspects of God's love.

There is a Catholic "sensibility," i.e., a Catholic religious "style" at the core of the Catholic heritage. This "style" is *not* something that exists in addition to, much less over against, Catholic doctrine and ritual, ethical principle, and canonical norm. Rather, it is the essence of the Catholic religious "stance" or "instinct" or "insight," which the doctrines and rituals, ethics and rules articulate and codify (more or less adequately in different times and different places).

The Catholic religious experience is sacramental: it encounters God in the events, objects, and persons of every day. The Catholic imagination is analogical: it pictures God as being similar to these events, objects, and persons. The Catholic religious story is comic: it believes in happy ends in which grace routs both evil and injustice. The Catholic religious community is organic: it is based on a dense network of local relationships that constitute the matrix of everyday life.

This sensibility is what keeps Catholics in the Church even if they have problems with doctrines and ethics and rituals and rules. It represents a unique Catholic contribution to ongoing human religious experience. And it points in the direction of ecclesiastical policies that can guide Catholicism into an era of fruitful growth and development. Does this approach to religion seem odd? Doesn't religion consist of doctrines and rules and rituals? Religion is a set of cognitive propositions; it explains to people what life means and how it should be lived, doesn't it? Have we not all been taught to think of religion this way, whatever our religious heritage—in our schools, in our instruction classes, in our sermons, in our adult education programs? Do not these statements—the twelve tenets of the Apostles' Creed, the 2000 canons of the Code of Canon Law, or the various essential remarks from the ecumenical councils contained in the Enchiridion—constitute the essence of our faith?

Yes, the propositions are indeed essential to intelligent understanding, reflecting, and codifying religion, but no, they do not *express* the religious heritage. Catholicism existed before the Code of Canon Law, indeed, even before canon law, before the Nicene and the Athanasian Creeds, even before the Apostles' Creed. Christianity existed before the Gospels were written, indeed even before the first book of the New Testament. Christianity was first of all an experience of Jesus, who had died and yet still lived. Images of the risen Jesus were taken from the Jewish religious tradition and transformed in the early Christian imagination—Adam, Moses, Messiah, King, the Son of Man. Then Christianity became a series of stories proclaimed to people— "the leaders put Him to death but He rose again from the dead"— and finally a community in which the stories were told and to which members came with their own stories of the experience of redemption and liberation in the risen Jesus.

In an earlier era this kind of presentation of the truth of the Christian experience might have occasioned little surprise. In most of human history, people have thought of religion as a collection of stories and a community in which the stories were told. Perhaps a few central doctrines codifying the stories were dutifully memorized, but long and detailed checklists of regulations were both unknown and unnecessary.

The equation of religion with an extensive list of propositional assertions is probably the result of the accidental combination of the development of the printing press and the theological arguments of the Reformation and the Counter-Reformation. Theologians abstracted and digested catechisms for easy memorization. The churches widely distributed such books to ordinary folk, who committed them to memory and clung to them tenaciously even though they did not always understand what they meant and frequently saw little relationship between such memorized religious truth and their daily lives.

But the ordinary person is born into a religious heritage whose elementary components are absorbed from parents, through stories and behaviors only vaguely related to catechetical propositions, which would not be learned until one was of school age and which would never fully articulate one's commitment to the heritage.

When we were growing up we learned early on that we were Catholics and parishioners of Saint Angela's (or perhaps the reverse is true: we learned first our parish, then our religion). We were taken to the old wooden church and were introduced to God, Who apparently lived behind the tabernacle veil and whose presence was signified by the burning red light, and to the saints, especially Joseph and Mary, who were represented by statues. We were frightened by the crucifix and the Stations of the Cross but were impressed by how much God loved us.

We were, of course, brought back to the church at Christmas to see the crib. Wide-eyed, we stared at the scene of the Mother and the Father and the Baby and the Wise Men (one of whom was in an early form of "quota-integration" black) and the oxen and the sheep and the shepherds and the angels. We were flattered when the parish priest noticed us, intrigued and a little scared by the nuns and their strange habits, captivated by the changing colors of the liturgical season, eager to join the big kids in the parochial school, and vaguely aware, through pictures in the Catholic papers (there wasn't television in those days) of such important, almost sacred Church leaders as Pope Pius XI and George Cardinal Mundelein. We learned from our mother to say the prayer "Angel of God, my Guardian Dear," and welcomed Santa Claus and the Easter Bunny, both of whom seemed to have some kind of vague religious connection.

Then we went to school and learned from S'ter and the Baltimore Catechism that we were made to know, love, and serve God in this life, and be happy with Him forever in the next. The point seemed unobjectionable, but also not to have much to do with the experiences, the images and stories, and the people we had encountered so far. Moreover, the life of the parish community, with its cycle of feasts (Halloween, Thanksgiving, Christmas, Little Christmas—it was important in those days—Saint Patrick's Day, First Communion, grammar school graduation), its personnel (parents, brothers, sisters, friends, monsignors, priests, sisters), and its angels and saints and souls in purgatory continued parallel, but unconnected, with the catechism. It never occurred to us to ask why the relation between the catechism and our daily, weekly, and yearly religious life was so inadequately clarified.

The inadequacy became more obvious in our lives when Pope John opened his famous window and convened the Second Vatican Council. The Baltimore Catechism disappeared and a host of new catechisms appeared, some of them easier to understand and some of them harder but few of them having any more connection with either the lives we lived or the religion we knew from personal experience than did the Baltimore Catechism. Moreover, the religion we knew from personal experience also underwent enormous changes. We Catholics now ate meat on Friday, we no longer fasted during Lent, and it seemed less obligatory to go to church on Sunday. The souls in purgatory, the angels, the saints, and even the Blessed Mother disappeared from our sermons and sometimes from their accustomed places in many of our churches. The sharp distinctions between us and the Protestants seemed to diminish, and Pope Paul VI summarily dismissed many of the truly important saints, like George or Christopher or even Patrick, from our calendar. And, of course, on one Septuagesima Sunday (a Sunday that itself was shortly to be abolished) the Mass shifted from Latin to English and priests began facing the people instead of the wall. We learned little of the new theology and the new catechetics, but what we did hear of it sometimes seemed very reasonable and at other times sounded more like Marxist politics or Freudian psychology than religion.

The lack of articulation between the new popular religion and the new propositional religion that was a tolerable, indeed hardly noticed, problem before the Vatican Council has now become both serious and obvious. Typical Catholic lay people, befuddled because some things have changed (in the liturgy) and others have stayed the same (in sexual ethics), ignore the strain and continue to root their religious life in the popular religion of parish and family experience, having chosen perhaps implicitly and unself-consciously the Catholicism that they feel is at the core of their religious commitment.

If indeed the religion of daily life, the religion of family and parish, needs to be criticized and corrected by the formal cognitive and reflective norms of propositional Catholicism, so too the latter needs to be criticized and corrected by the insights of primordial, experiential religion. Our emphasis in this book is on the religion of experience and image and story and community, but we are not Modernists reducing religion to inkblot symbols that can be interpreted *ad libitum*. This is not a book about Catholic doctrine, which we respect and accept. No one should look in these pages for a compendium of such doctrine, which other books provide. This is rather a book about the Catholic sensibility, the Catholic poetic intuition, the Catholic religious imagination—a subject on which few books are written.

No pejorative comparisons with the other traditions of the great Yahwistic family of religions are intended. The notion that Catholicism is more sacramental and analogical than Protestantism (or Islam or Judaism) is frequently advanced as much by Protestant theologians like Langdon Gilkey, Martin Marty, and Paul Tillich as by Catholic theologians like David Tracy, Lawrence Cunningham, and Richard McBrien. But this is not to say that the Catholic way is better than the Protestant (or Jewish or Islamic) way, but merely to assert that Catholics and the Catholic Church must understand what is special to their tradition if they are to speak fruitfully with members of other traditional religions. Catholicism has a different style of religion than Protestantism does, but not completely different, not totally different, not different to the point of mutual exclusivity.

Not all Catholics at all times in all places share the same religious sensibility. A person's religious style is affected in part by the religious heritage itself, but also by his or her family, ethnic group, education, and life experiences in the secular world. The Catholic sensibilities of a Maronite Christian in Lebanon, an Irish Catholic in Derry and a Liberation Theologian in Peru are clearly very different—though not totally different, not completely different, not different to the point of mutual exclusivity.

Perhaps some readers will think that these preliminary qualifications about the subject matter of this book are both unnecessary and tedious. But it has been our experience that many people are all too eager to misunderstand when the subject is religion and particularly when the aim is to present an alternative (but not contradictory) perspective or model for considering it. To fend off this misunderstanding we feel constrained to say at the very beginning that we are not attacking Protestants, that we are not attacking Catholic doctrine, and that we are not attempting a universal portrait of Catholicism. Rather we are examining the uniqueness of the Catholic sensibility, maintaining that when popes, Curia members, bishops, priests, and laity appreciate this sensibility, the Catholic Church will be saved and will make a "saving" contribution to human existence.

Part One

. . . .

GROUNDWORK

Chapter 1

. . . .

THE RISE OF
SELECTIVE CATHOLICISM

Shortly after the beginning of the Second Vatican Council in 1962, Pope John XXIII told a visitor that he intended to open the window and permit fresh air to blow through the Roman Catholic Church. In the United States, the papal breeze turned into a tornado. The turbulence in contemporary American Catholicism is on the whole healthy, for the obvious vitality of the Catholic community in the United States can be a matrix for richness and growth. But it can also, over the long run, exhaust itself if it is not rooted in the historical Catholic sensibility.

Unfortunately, both the leaders and the intellectuals (real or self-anointed) of the American Catholic community are, for the most part, singularly innocent of any understanding of their heritage. Evidence of the devastating effects of the post–Vatican Council turbulence can be seen in the rubble strewn around the once sedate and stable American Catholic Church. Weekly church attendance rates among the 53 million members declined almost immediately from around 70 percent to approximately 50 percent after Pope Paul VI issued the birth control encyclical in 1968. Massive numbers of Catholics dissent from official teaching on divorce and birth control and act accordingly. As many as a fifth of the priests in the country have left the active ministry, and a high proportion of nuns have withdrawn from the religious life, while the number of young men enrolled in seminaries is less than a third of what it was twenty years ago. Bishops can no longer count on pastors to obey them. Pastors can no longer assume that their religious associates will do what they are told. And many parish priests have learned that they must consult with, not command, the laity about what needs doing. Only Pope John Paul II seems to think that issuing edicts is an effective governmental style. And while the Pope may be personally popular, few American Catholics are attentive to what he says (in part because the complexity of his thought frequently causes him to be misunderstood).

In direct defiance of Rome, many parish priests permit women to act as acolytes at Mass. ("If the Pope comes to our parish, we won't use them that day," says one pastor.) Elected parish councils challenge the authority of pastors. Local church school boards demand the right to set policies and budgets, even to hire staffs. "Do-it-yourself" liturgies, sometimes tasteful but often not (Ry-Krisp and whisky instead of bread and wine at Communion), are taken for granted in many places. Order, neatness, discipline, stability—all were swept away by Good Pope John's storm.

Careful empirical studies suggest, however, that the whirlwind has been more benign than not and that, all things considered and despite the confusion and uncertainties, Catholicism in America is more healthy today than it was before Vatican II. And alive. In truth, never more alive.

Catholicism before the Council was not so stable, perhaps, or so monolithic as nostalgia portrays it. The Church appeared to be solid, rooted and unchangeable: fish on Friday; Mass on Sunday, in Latin, as it had been for more than 1300 years, with the priest facing the altar instead of his congregation; bishops who ruled like unquestioned Renaissance lords; priests supposedly immune to temptation; Catholic schools staffed by nuns dressed in clothes from past eras; marriages with non-Catholics barely tolerated; Protestants barely trusted; and the Pope a holy old man in the Vatican with whom no one dared to disagree in public because it would be almost like disagreeing with God.

Then, almost overnight, it was all right to eat meat on Friday, Mass was said in English with the priest facing the people, the laity could receive a Communion wafer in their own hands instead of having it put in their mouths by the priests and minister it to themselves, or take bread and wine from the chalice as the clergy had always done; women became lectors at Mass and even ministers of Holy Communion; priests resigned because they wanted to marry; nuns doffed their all-encompassing habits and marched on picket lines; Protestants lost their status as heretics and schismatics and became separated brothers and sisters; and Pope Paul VI issued a birth control encyclical whose instructions were promptly rejected by outspoken Catholic scholars and then by almost nine-tenths of the laity.

Perhaps the most important observation that must be noted about the changes that were initiated by the Second Vatican Council (ecumenism, for example) and those which unexpectedly followed (such as the political involvement of priests) is that they were extremely popular among the lower clergy and laity. For the first few years, good Catholic liberals—of the sort who write for and read *The Commonweal*—were convinced that ordinary folk in the parishes were bitterly opposed to the changes. And that sentiment was shared by many bishops, who, not quite sure of what they had wrought, came home from Rome to reassure the laity that "nothing had really changed"—only to discover that few wanted that reassurance. But reactionary opposition to the transformations, though loud and articulate, is numerically insignificant compared to the widespread endorsement of change: an astonishing 87 percent of the laity, for example, approved the changes in the Mass, while 68 percent approved all post-conciliar changes.

The pace of change was breathtaking. But you cannot change practices that have been immutable for 1500 years without raising questions about what else might be changed. If you could eat meat on Friday, could you not practice birth control? If priests could say Mass in English, might they not marry? If Protestants were now separated brothers and sisters to be loved and cherished, might you not cherish a Protestant spouse or a divorced and remarried Catholic?

Indeed, the gradual modification of the norms for annulments in Catholic marriage tribunals has created a quiet revolution in the practical response of the American Catholic Church to divorce. And if priests could not marry and continue an active ministry, they could at least receive official permission to resign, marry, and still work within the Church, at duties not unlike many performed in the ecclesiastical bureaucracy.

While the 1960s were a turbulent time in American life, they did not significantly affect the upheavals in the house of Catholicism, though churchmen now made headlines by boycotting lettuce and nuclear weapons, not films and books, and the National Conference of Catholic Bishops moved into the forefront of the movement favoring arms control. Yet even the most politically conservative Catholics were caught up in changes within the Church. The conservative syndicated columnist William F. Buckley, Jr., for one, became a lector at Mass and expressed some doubts in print about the Pope's birth control encyclical.

The window, once opened, could not be closed.

And Pope John XXIII did, after all, set up a commission on birth control; most clergymen and many members of the Catholic laity assumed a change would occur in the Church's opposition to all forms of birth control—otherwise why set up the commission?—and they behaved accordingly. Between the beginning of Vatican II and the Pope's final encyclical six years later—which dismissed the commission's majority argument that a marriage, not each individual marriage act, should be open to the possibility of conception—the Pill replaced the rhythm method as the typical Catholic method of family planning in the United States.

But Pope Paul VI's encyclical on birth control (*Humanae Vitae*) shattered the euphoria that had flourished after Vatican II. Despite enthusiastic, if often two-faced, endorsements of it by the hierarchy (one cardinal went to Alaska when he heard the papal document was on its way), the laity turned massively against it. Today nine out of ten American Catholics do not accept it, including four out of five weekly communicants.

Sophisticated mathematical models developed by the National Opinion Research Center to sort out the "Council effect" from that of the encyclical showed that the encyclical canceled out the positive results of Vatican II and sent the Church into a sudden and dramatic decline: priests refused to endorse its ban against birth control in the confessional; Sunday church attendance dropped off sharply; church collections diminished; resignations from the priesthood increased, while priests who remained in the Church lessened their efforts to recruit young men for the vocation, and family support for religious vocations also eroded; acceptance of papal authority declined dramatically.

(Moral decisions ought not to be made by majority vote, and when one reports the sociological implications of a negative effect of a papal decision, one is not saying that the decision was wrong, or that one is opposed to the decision. One merely notes that the encyclical has failed to win acceptance with either the laity or the lower clergy, and the resulting disappointment and anger led to a dramatic decline in devotion.)

Vatican II also produced a psychological state that enabled Catholics to turn against the birth control decision with more ease of conscience than would have been imaginable a mere decade before. Would Pope Paul's decision have been accepted more readily if the Church had not been swept by the winds of euphoria and enthusiasm that followed Vatican II? The question is without meaning. If it had not been for the environment of Vatican II, the issue of birth control would not have been raised, the commission would not have been established, and the encyclical would never have been issued.

As for Pope John Paul II's thinking on the birth control issue, it is more complex than is generally realized. While he strongly endorses the teaching of his predecessor, he generally refers only to the need for marriage to be open to procreation—as though he were deliberately avoiding the question of whether every individual marriage act should be.

Religion, an explanation of the purpose of life, is not the same thing as ethics, a prescription for how to live, although one has considerable implications for the other. However, it would be a mistake to think that Catholics' rejection of their Church's birth control teaching presages a systematic abandonment of Catholic ethics. Rather, the laity and the lower clergy seemed to be saying that Pope Paul did not understand the issues in this particular matter—and were appealing the decision of a Pope "badly informed" to a Pope "better informed,"

7

not the first such appeal from the laity and lower clergy in the history of Catholicism.

By the early 1970s, then, the positive and hopeful environment of the first post-conciliar decade had been considerably diluted and the American Church was in decline according to almost every available measure of loyalty and devotion. But then a third major event was added to the dyad of Vatican II and encyclical—one which might be called, for want of a better term, reappraisal. In ever-increasing numbers, American laity and lower-echelon clergy came to realize what their European confreres had known for some time: as long as you define yourself as Catholic, no one is going to throw you out of the Church or refuse the sacraments to you, regardless of what you do in your bedroom or what reservations you have on doctrinal matters. Make your peace with God, in other words, and don't worry about the Pope or the bishops—at least so the reasoning went.

Weekly church attendance has recently increased somewhat. And many "lapsed" Catholics looking for a religion to pass on to their children, to reinforce their marriage, or to prepare them for old age and dying are drifting back to regular church attendance. They return on their own terms, however, and find that many of their fellow Catholics are Catholics on the same basis. (Not that they had ever stopped defining themselves as Catholics. As the writer John R. Powers remarked, "It's almost as hard to stop being a Catholic as it is to stop being a black.")

"Selective Catholicism," "Do-It-Yourself Catholicism," "Catholicism on Your Own Terms"—whatever one calls it—infuriates conservatives. But the alternative, which conservative theorists would approve of but which would horrify pastors, bishops and, one suspects, the Vatican, would be a Catholic Church minus four-fifths of its communicants. In effect, the boundaries of the Church, once narrowly and precisely defined, or so it seemed, are now vague and comprehensive. Peter H. Rossi, the distinguished sociologist at the University of Massachusetts who began the research tradition on which this chapter is based, observed: "I left the Church when I was twelve. At forty-two, I woke up and discovered that I was a Catholic again. I didn't change, but they modified the boundaries without warning me."

The rigid, often oversimplified, unquestioningly self-confident American Catholicism of the first half of the twentieth century was the result of an effort to provide poor and frequently uneducated immigrants with a simple and serviceable religious response to the trauma of adjusting to an unfriendly—and frequently anti-Catholic—host society. But by 1960, even though roughly half the American Catholic population were still immigrants or children of immigrants, Catholics under the age of 30 were as likely as other Americans to graduate from college and enter white-collar and professional careers. Almost without warning, and largely unnoticed by the hierarchy, Roman Catholicism was becoming a religion of the well-educated suburban, professional-class American.

By the early 1970s, the Irish were second only to Jews in annual income, and the Italians were close behind them, with the Poles fifth, after German Catholics. Hispanics, who account for a little less than one-fifth of the American Catholic population though their numbers increased by 61 percent in the last decade, have not yet fared so well financially, but they have begun to be visible in government and in the Church hierarchy. In another quantum leap, Catholics turned to academia and now total one-fifth of the younger faculty at the nation's top colleges and universities (they are not as well represented at the elite private campuses). But as two Canadian sociologists have observed, while Catholics are now very much part of the intellectual life of America, Catholic universities are not. Many of them may be excellent undergraduate institutions, but none of them ranks among the nation's great intellectual centers.

While the Catholic intelligentsia is expanding rapidly and Catholic culture is flourishing, Church leaders and many of the clergy are scarcely aware of this phenomenon; they avoid artists and intellectuals whenever they can—mostly, it seems, because they are afraid of them. Despite the observation of the great Canadian Jesuit thinker Bernard J. F. Lonergan that the storytellers are where the official Church and its theologians will be in twenty-five years, there is little disposition on the part of the Church or its theological and journalistic elite to take the Catholic cultural resurgence seriously. And yet during recent years there has been an outburst of fiction by authors with Catholic backgrounds (among others, Mary Gordon, Walker Percy, Joyce Carol Oates, John R. Powers, Joseph Wambaugh, Eugene C. Kennedy, Jimmy

Breslin, James Carroll, and Walter Murphy), of Catholic drama, and of films made by Catholic directors (most notably Martin Scorsese and Francis Ford Coppola), in which religious symbolism abounds. The relationship of some of these artists to the Church may be vague and their works are often angry, but they appear to be concerned, preoccupied, even obsessed with Catholic themes.

Similarly, the Church shies away from intellectuals and thinkers who are Catholic. Thus, when the Bishops' Committee on Nuclear Disarmament was holding "hearings," it did not ask for testimony from the senior senator from New York, despite Daniel Patrick Moynihan's thoughtful article on the subject in *The New Yorker*; one had to wonder if the bishops were even aware of it.

Amazingly enough, given its severe institutional problems, the Catholic school system has survived the crisis of the past decade better than might have been expected, with enrollment increasing in many parishes, mostly because of an influx of black and Hispanic students, who do extremely well in these schools. But Catholic religious education is in sad disarray, as those responsible for it leap from fad to fad in an attempt to recapture the old certainties. Some of the best theoretical Catholicism in the world is to be found in the work on the religious imagination done by John J. Shea, of Saint Mary of the Lake Seminary in Mundelein, Illinois, and in the philosophical theology of David Tracy, of the University of Chicago. But little of this excellence is to be found in grade-school religious instruction.

Though the mass media may focus on the Church's doctrinal concerns such as birth control and on the personalities of leaders such as popes and cardinals, the Church for most of the laity is the parish and the pertinent Church figure is the parish priest. The identification of lay persons with their parish and the impact of the parish priest's preaching is infinitely stronger than the impact of the Church's doctrine on divorce, the ordination of women, and papal authority put together. (Regrettably, the proportion of Catholics who find Sunday preaching "excellent" has declined from almost 50 percent in the 1950s to less than 20 percent at the present time—possibly because lay expectations have risen and not because clerical skills have declined.) With the decline in importance of institutional structures, Catholics increasingly look to their faith for comfort and challenge, for inspiration in life and consolation in death. Few take seriously any more the Church as a teacher—on either moral or social-action matters. The Church, as they see it, is not for ethics; it is for religion. Ironically, many of the clergy, and more recently the hierarchy, have turned away from religion toward ethics.

With hierarchy less important and parish clergy more important, the most serious problem facing the Church is the increasing shortage of priests. Some estimates suggest that there will be half as many priests in the United States in the year 2000 as there are today. The evidence suggests that celibacy is not the reason for the shortage, but, rather, the lack of support among priests and parents (enlightened mothers, especially) for recruitment.

Almost as bad as the priest shortage is the suspicion of many Catholic women under 45 that church leaders are committed to keeping them in narrowly defined gender roles. This suspicion may not be justified—especially not in the case of Pope John Paul II, whose obscure but important audience talks, when properly understood, are far more pro-feminist than American Catholics realize (thus his harsh words against men "lusting" after their wives in context meant that men should not treat their wives as sex objects)—but it is strong and dangerous. Church leaders persist in thinking that feminism (with a small *f*) is popular only among a small group of nuns who want to be ordained priests. The "good Catholic wife and mother" so beloved in clerical homilies is, on the average, madder than hell at Church leadership. The ban on the ordination of women, while an excellent symbolic issue, infuriates them far less than more ordinary issues. College-educated mothers, who do not want to be priests and who may even oppose the ordination of women, are driven to bitter anger when their daughters are excluded from acolyte training. "Why is my daughter inferior to my son?" they demand. The Church hasn't figured out a good answer to that one yet; indeed, there is no sign that its leaders realize there is even a need for it to do so.

Pope John Paul II's announcement that women would be banned as ministers of Communion during his American tour made many Catholic women livid and precipitated the sharp decline in his popularity in this country. At a recent meeting of priests and nuns, the women were told, halfway through Mass, that their role as distributors of Holy Communion had been canceled—on orders of Archbishop Pio Laghi, the Apostolic Delegate to the United States. As one angry nun remarked, a woman could carry the body of Jesus in her womb for nine months but is not deemed worthy to hold the Eucharist in her hands for even a few minutes during Mass. This is an issue on which the American Church leadership seems utterly insensitive. The hierarchy, concerned mostly with its influence and reputation in Rome, seems unequipped to deal with the problems of Catholic women.

In fact, the Church leadership in America is not particularly impressive overall, especially when one considers that one of its primary activities today may be representing the Church in the media. Just after Vatican II, the Roman Curia appointed to American dioceses men who could be counted on to slow down the pace of change. But in the last decade—especially while Archbishop Jean Jadot was the Apostolic Delegate—many more open and sensitive men were appointed to bishoprics. Nonetheless, they, too, continue to be caught in the structural dilemma of having two constituencies—the Curia which appointed them, and the priests and people they are supposed to serve. Rarely does the Curia lose in conflicts created by such dual allegiance (despite the ancient Catholic custom that the election of bishops by anyone other than the local clergy and people is immoral). Many American bishops and archbishops are good men, open and democratic in their style, deeply concerned about their people. They would only lie, as the Jesuit John Courtney Murray once put it, for the good of the Church. They try, but few of them are heroes. However, with the Church caught up in the kind of whirlwind it finds itself in today, the times require not only good men, but brave men; not only genial men, but honest men; not only sympathetic men, but courageous men.

No careers in the American Catholic Church are risked by standing up to the American government on nuclear disarmament. But this kind of resistance to entrenched policy only becomes credible when the bishops also stand up to Rome on the rights of women and on sexuality in marriage.

Two developments show both the vitality of American Catholicism and the dangers it faces if it continues to ignore its historic tradition: the conversion of the national Catholic hierarchy to social and political liberalism on issues of "peace and justice"; and the "witch hunt" (in the strictest sense of the word) that the Vatican has launched against women and to which the American bishops seem powerless to reply.

The American bishops have received extremely favorable press coverage because of their pastoral letter speaking out against nuclear weapons, even though most of the laity and many priests have not plowed through the 150 pages of its obscure and turgid prose, and though public-opinion polls show that the bishops are not leading the laity on this issue but following them. (Read *Living with Nuclear Weapons,* by the Harvard Nuclear Study Group, which takes essentially the same position as the bishops did, and compare the clear-thinking, well-informed, and incisive presentation of the Harvard group with the bishops' prolix, obscure, and often uninformed effort.) Basking in media praise for a document whose position is not so heroic as it is made out to be (there are footnotes in it—rarely cited by the media—praising bellicose statements by President Reagan and Defense Secretary Weinberger), many bishops are apparently persuaded that social liberalism will be an adequate replacement for their lost credibility in the area of sexual ethics. It is reported that they will commit themselves in the years ahead to the cause "of the poor and of peace."

Surely it is admirable for bishops to speak out on both subjects, but the nuclear weapons document suggests that the bishops do not realize they need to know what they are talking about before they pontificate on either subject. Nor do they understand the importance of competent and honest staff. The final draft of the pastoral letter on nuclear weapons was dramatically different from the earlier drafts. At first the bishops rejected the doctrine of deterrence as immoral and found little difference between the United States and the Soviet Union. They were clobbered, even by the moderate Jesuits on the staff of *America* magazine, for making this comparison of the superpowers and roundly criticized for endorsing unilateral disarmament. Many of them replied that they were not unilateralists but were opposed to deterrence. When asked what possible middle ground there was between the two, they seemed unable to answer. Others pointed out that the Vatican had, in a letter from Cardinal Casaroli, the Vatican Secretary of State, taken the position that deterrence was tolerable as a conditional position while disarmament was pursued—a position with which even the Reagan Administration could not have disagreed (at least in public). The bishops reworked their pastoral to differentiate sharply between the United States and Russia and to bring their position on deterrence in line with that of Cardinal Casaroli (perhaps under pressure from the Vatican and from West European hierarchies).

These flip-flops were not much noted by the media and hence no public explanation was required. But the bishops were ill-served by their peace and justice staff, which either wrote the draft for them that was unilateralist and anti-American in tone (which, it is fair to say, accurately represents the staff's position) or did not protect them from using indiscreet language. In most organizations, staff personnel who bungle so badly would not last five minutes. But Catholic bishops apparently ask not for competence or even integrity from their staffs, only docility.

The simple truth is that the "justice and peace" staffs of the hierarchy are committed to the hazy anti-Americanism of the 1960s and use models of social criticism that are soft and fuzzy manifestations of a vague "vulgar Marxism." As long as the bishops look to such men and women for guidance in their attempts to be politically and socially relevant, they will make fools of themselves. Pop liberal answers to intriçate social problems may win the bishops many friends in the media. The question they must ask themselves is whether such brave stands are not in fact a form of "cheap grace" by which they cover up for their failures as leaders of their own institution by responding with clichés to the leaders of other institutions.

In fact, the truly brave stands they take are often missed or misunderstood. Thus when Cardinal Bernardin insisted that future Catholic pro-life efforts must be consistent—that is to say, must oppose not only abortion but also capital punishment, maltreatment of the old and the needy, and the nuclear arms race—he was attacking the one-issue approach to abortion that characterizes many of the Catholic anti-abortion enthusiasts. This required far more courage than the nuclear pastoral letter because many of the "one-issue" anti-abortionists are the meanest and nastiest people in the Church, while the nuclear pastoral represents the position of most American Catholics and stirs up no organized animosity. It also wins plaudits and prizes from the national media. The pro-life consistency issue is misunderstood by the national media and evokes animosity from vicious and vindictive opponents.

"Cheap grace" through easy social liberalism that offends no one in the Vatican leaves the leadership of the American Church open to the charge of hypocrisy when it fails to face the problems of the terrible discrimination against women within the Catholic Church. In the last decade and a half a broad consensus has developed in American society about what is "fair" in the treatment of women. While the consensus is still inchoate and vague on specific details, there is no doubt that, measured against its fundamental assumptions, the Catholic Church is monstrously unfair to women. Most Catholics rarely evaluate the Church against the standards of this new consensus on equity for women unless the Church calls the matter to their attention. But each time the Church takes a stand against the ordination of women, support for this reform *increases*. And whenever a bishop repeats the Vatican's insistence that young women may not assist as acolytes at Mass (as Cardinal Bernardin did in the summer of 1983), an overwhelming majority of Catholics (men even more than women) are furious to discover once again how unfair the Catholic Church currently is in its sexism.

Yet, many, perhaps most, Catholic bishops are unaware of the fury that this issue is creating even among their most loyal members. When social researchers report that over a million (perhaps as many as a million and a half) Catholic women no longer go to church because they believe the Church is trying to keep them in their old and narrowly defined gender roles, most bishops dismiss the evidence as incredible.

A few bishops are aware they have been handed a hot potato and have persuaded their colleagues to work on a pastoral letter about the rights of women. They are, one hopes, well aware of how worse an already bad situation can be made by a poor pastoral, one which can be interpreted as either reaffirming the old gender roles or arguing from history and scripture (despite the testimony of the best historians and scripture scholars) that Jesus excluded women forever from the priesthood, that women cannot be priests.

Most Catholics are not affected by the positions of Church leaders. They stay in the Church and pay little attention to what their leaders say—a continuation of do-it-yourself Catholicism, with even more vigor and a clearer conscience. Others will stay and fight, more furiously and more bitterly, doing all in their power to make the lives of bishops and pastors as miserable as they can. The Catholic population has grown skillful at that in recent years.

The media paradigm of Catholics leaving the Church in disgust ought to have been abandoned after the birth control encyclical, but somehow it persists even though it does not fit the data very well. In 1963, before the effects of the Council, 9 percent of those who were raised Catholics no longer identified with the Church. By 1970, in the wake of the birth control encyclical, the proportion had risen to 12 percent, and there it has remained ever since. Such a small increase in attrition despite the highs and the lows, the ups and downs of the past twenty years is remarkable. The pertinent question is why, despite the ambitious toadies on the one hand and the uneducated ideologues on the other, Catholics still identify with their Church, why they are able to ignore so effectively both the ideologues and the toadies. The answers to that question will point the way to appropriate strategies and tactics for American Catholicism in the future. Perhaps some day even Rome, finally hearing the truth and taking it seriously, might see some utility in an approach to American Catholicism that re-examines the implications of the authentically and distinctively Catholic religious sensibility.

Perhaps the brightest spot on the Catholic horizon is to be found among those who have reached maturity since Vatican II. These youths may turn away from the Church's sexual ethic, or they may reject by majorities of more than four-fifths the Church's birth control teaching, and they may reject the concept of papal infallibility; yet they remain solidly Catholic in their fundamental convictions about life and death and about the nature of God and God's love, and they are firm in their intention to stay in the Church, though on their own terms.

American Catholics under 20 display a new religious sensibility, and are much more likely than Catholics only a few years older to have warm, tender, and affectionate images of God. (A quarter of those between 14 and 30, incidentally, imagine God as a woman at least some of the time. Since the womanliness of God is hardly something that is preached in Catholic churches or schools, it would seem such images must come from satisfying and religiously important relations with wives and/or mothers. Women, in other words, are "sacraments"—revelatory agents—of the womanliness of God for their men.) This new sensibility correlates positively with social generosity, religious devotion, marital fulfillment, a willingness to consider a life of service to the Church, and even chastity. The Second Vatican Council, the encyclical, and the dawn of "Catholicism on One's Own Terms" seem to have combined to produce a new generation of Catholics who are admirable by almost any Christian standard.

It is enough to make you believe that someone is drawing straight with crooked lines.

A Rembrandt landscape after a storm: ineffective, confused and conflicted, if sincere, Church leaders; poor religious education; disheartened priests; unenlightened preaching; angry women; a vigorously independent laity; a moribund sexual ethic; economic success; cultural resurgence; distinguished theologians; increased religious devotion; shortages of priests; democratization of local institutions; fads; conflict; shouting; anger; hope; a new religious sensibility among the young—thus American Catholicism twenty years after Pope John XXIII's breeze became a whirlwind after crossing the Atlantic.

There is no reason to think that the storm will stop blowing for the next two decades, though there may well be a re-evaluation of some aspects of the heritage that were thrown out with the bath water. The American Catholic Church will continue to be a noisy, contentious, disorderly place.

No one will mistake it for a mausoleum.

Chapter 2

. . . .

A MODEL OF
RELIGION

We now understand enough about the ordinary working process of the human mind to know that human intelligence does not proceed either by the logical, deductive methods so admired in the old courses in scholastic logic in which many of us were trained, or by the pseudo-empiricism of the so-called scientific method, but rather by a process of "mental model" testing. In the process of knowing and learning, human ingenuity starts out with a hunch, an intuition, an instinct about the way things are, and then it tests this instinct, hunch, or intuition against the data from reality, refining and reformulating the mental model as it examines the data from the real world.

The fundamental assumption of this book is that there is a mental model for religion: image, experience, story, and community. The model has been derived from the work of theorists—Max Weber, Rudolf Otto, William James, and Clifford Geertz—and the work of contemporary Roman Catholic theologians such as David Tracy and John Shea. We have found it useful as a perspective for examining religion and make no claim that it is the only way or necessarily the best way to look at religion. It is simply something between a useful way of organizing reality and a tentative, refinable description of reality. A model-builder says, in effect, I find this a useful way of organizing the data I have found in the real world, a convenient summary of how I understand the real world in the present state of our knowledge. If you have an alternative model, it can either serve to correct and improve this one or co-exist and even be complementary to it (as in physics, where the wave and quantum models co-exist in relative amity).

We begin with a series of propositions and then illustrate these propositions with an example.

1. In the human personality there exists a propensity to hope.

2. There also exists the need periodically to validate this hope.

3. In the human organism there is a capacity to validate hopefulness in a wide variety of experiences, which are believed to be occasioned by objective realities.

4. These experiences are perceived as an encounter with goodness that exists in the objective realities but also exists in some fashion apart from or even beyond them.

5. The "goodness experience" is perceived as overwhelming and yet ambiguous. Because of its utter gratuity (it is there but it need not be), it may be called "grace."

6. These propensities, needs, and experiences are all functions of the pre-rational or pre-conscious part of ourselves, where free-floating images, pictures, and stories exist independent of direct control by the conscious self.

7. Almost any external reality is capable of triggering an experience that will reinforce hope. Because of their power and importance, certain realities are especially likely to do so—sun, water, night, mountains, fire, birth, sexual differentiation, food, drink, and so forth. The language welling up out of our "creative imagination," which articulates our experience with these realities, is likely to be as ambiguous as the experience itself.

8. A symbol—a picture or an image that re-presents the experience of grace—may also be used to share this experience by re-presenting to others parallel experiences of their own.

9. The experience of grace promises salvation by validating the purposefulness of human life: it affirms that our existence is not a

series of random, unconnected events but has, rather, a beginning, a middle, and an end.

10. Implicit in the experience of grace is the linking of an individual's story with a Great Story. The meaning of the individual life is related to the overarching meaning of the cosmos.

11. The images that re-present experiences of grace are stories linking my story to a cosmic story, linking the purpose of my life to higher purposes.

12. There is an enormous variety in the religious stories that humans create for themselves. A person's story is shaped by biological, cultural, educational, psychological, ethnic, and biographic factors.

13. That which is encountered in the experience of grace is perceived as "other."

14. Otherness (the Wonderful) is undifferentiated and yet complex. Its initial effect on the creative imagination is plastic and fluid, so there are many symbolizations of otherness.

15. The symbolization of a grace experience is the result of both the experience itself and the background of the experiencing person (or group).

16. The available repertory of symbols affects not only the symbolization of our present experiences, but the nature of that experience itself.

17. Some persons, places, times, and behavior are especially likely to reveal otherness because the images of them are especially suitable for re-presenting our experiences of otherness. Whatever reality discloses grace to us may be called a "sacrament." Those realities that are especially likely to do so (water, fire, food, drink, sex) are the sacraments par excellence.

By way of illustration, let us suppose I am walking down Michigan Avenue in Chicago on a gray day in December, feeling melancholy, partly because I am Irish, partly because it is December, partly because I'm not as young as I used to be, partly because the sky is gray, the lake is gray, the city is gray, the people are gray, and I'm feeling gray. As I pass by Tribune Tower (which is always gray), I notice a young mother, several parcels in one arm (multicolored wrappings peeking out of the bags hinting Christmas presents) and a squirming boy-child in the other arm as she tries to board a Chicago Transit Authority bus.

She is unable to climb on the bus and at the same time restrain both her armful of packages and her armful of son. I walk over to the bus stop, take the boy-child in my own arm and help the mother into the bus. With a sigh of relief, she drops her packages in the front seat and turns around and stretches out her arms for the boy. He hesitates, having found me a temporarily intriguing custodian. On the other hand, I'm no match for Mama, so he quickly wiggles from my embrace to hers. Once she is certain that she has a firm grip on the squirming young ruffian, his mother turns to me and smiles her gratitude. It is a dazzling, multicolored, three-dimensional, radiant smile in Dolby multichannel sound.

The door of the bus closes and it pulls away. I look around Michigan Avenue and discover that all the gray has been exorcised and the world exists once again in technicolor. In the radiance of the young mother's smile, life takes on meaning and purpose once more, for in a world where that sort of smile is possible, there simply must be meaning and purpose. I don't reason to this conclusion: I intuit it, I experience it, I am overcome by it, for her smile need not be there: it is totally gratuitous, i.e., gracious, i.e., graceful, i.e., grace. I meet friends for supper that night (let's say at L'Escargot) and begin the conversation by telling them the story of my experience. "Today I met a Madonna."

Now, it is in experiences like this that religion begins—sometimes spectacular experiences of the sort that William James wrote about in his classic, *The Varieties of Religious Experience* (and which, surveys tell us, about one-third of all Americans have, 5 percent of them frequently); sometimes in the great experiences from which religious traditions arise—the sense of peoplehood that possessed the Hebrew tribes in their Sinai encounter with Yahweh, the sense of liberation and rebirth that the Apostles experienced in their encounter with the risen Jesus on Easter; and sometimes in the more mundane and ordinary experiences of grace that fill our daily lives—reconciliation after a quarrel, the touch of a friendly hand, a glorious sunset, the smile on the face of a little child as she toddles across the floor for the first time, a Christmas dinner in which all the members of a family are happy, a moment of silent prayer in a church, a smiling face in a busy crowd.

Note what happened in this very simple, commonplace religious experience of mine. First of all, I was in an interlude in which my hope was weak. While renewal experiences may occur at times when hope is strong, it is the nature of human nature that we are especially open to renewal of hope when hope seems to be fading. Second, I am caught up in an encounter with a person whose goodness is utterly contingent: it is there, but it need not be there; it is a given, but it doesn't have to be given. It is a grace in the strict sense because there is no necessity that it happen. It is a surprise because I have no reason to anticipate it, no reason to expect it, and certainly no grounds on which to claim it. It is a hint, not a proof, an experience, not an argument, an encounter, not a theorem.

Third, there is a hint of "otherness" in this experience, a suggestion of an *Umwelt* (as a German philosopher calls it), a loving and protective envelope embracing both this creature/grace that comes into my life and me. In this hint of otherness, humans begin to suspect that there is a God. Voltaire was wrong when he said that humans fashion God in their own image and likeness: he would have been closer to the truth if he had said, "Humans fashion God in the image and likeness of the grace that they intuit in life experiences that renew their hope."

Fourth, I encode my experiences of the woman's smile in my memory. I have seen many other women's smiles in my life and this one goes in the memory bank along with the others, but it has a special flag on it signifying that this is no ordinary smile but a smile that gave direction and purpose to my life at a time when I needed direction and purpose; it is an image of a smile that was more than a smile, but was also a grace. The smile has become a symbol, an image with a meaning beyond its own immediate meaning. Precisely because the woman's smile has been grace to me, she has become sacrament. Or, to put it the other way around, which is also accurate, because she has been sacrament—sign of grace—to me, she has brought me grace.

Fifth, in making her smile a symbol, I have perhaps employed an image from my own repertory of religious images. It may be only at supper with my friends that I think of her explicitly as Madonna, but the "Madonna" images that have stayed in my memory perhaps since the first day I saw the Christmas crèche in Saint Angela's or even

Saint Lucy's Church in the 1930s are there to shape my experience of the woman and her smile.

Sixth, I recount my experience to my friends at L'Escargot in a story. I do not tell them the woman's height (about 5'8"), age (about twenty-four), socioeconomic background (probably North Shore, and most likely elite woman's college), hair color (light brown), eyes (blue). Nor do I guess about her occupation or her husband's, or her child's weight at birth, or her I.Q., or her place of residence, or her score on College Board and Graduate Record exams. Rather, I tell them the story of my encounter with her, and of her effect on me. Christmas is coming, a time when we think of the Holy Family in Bethlehem, of Mary and Joseph and Jesus and of those who came to the cave to see the Madonna and her child. My friends are prepared to understand someone who has had a Madonna experience, who has encountered grace masquerading (or perhaps only revealing itself) in the guise of a mother's affection and love. My purpose in telling the story is to stir up in the imagination of those who hear it, the memory of similar experiences they have had; then they may share, however transiently, and in terms of their own images and experiences, the experience I had. Because I am part of a community of people who understand what a Madonna is and to whom I can go afterward and describe what has happened to me in Madonna terms, I am especially likely to interpret a random smile on Michigan Avenue as a sacrament and to experience grace in such a smile. Of course, somebody who is not part of a heritage in which there is a Madonna might well have a similar experience. But I am especially likely to experience the renewal of hope in such an interlude because I am part of a storytelling community that will understand what that experience of hope is like when I briefly summarize the experience in the simple story, "Today I met a Madonna."

If you want to know what someone's religion is, you should try to ascertain what the pre-existing paradigms in that person's imagination are, for they are likely to shape and encode his or her experiences of hope renewal. The potential story lines people carry around in their imaginations are likely to pre-dispose them to hope-renewal experiences that they can share with those who have similar story lines in their imaginations.

To put it differently, if I ask you who you are, you are very likely to tell me your story—where you come from, what you are doing here and now (and why you are doing it), and what is likely to shape the future of your life. If I then ask you what this story means, you are likely to tell me—if you trust me—the major experiences that have renewed hope in your life. Moreover, these experiences will likely have been at least implicitly expressed (and probably shaped by) the overarching story lines (symbols) of your religious heritage. If we share this heritage and have been explicit about it, then you will probably use explicit story lines from our joint heritage when you tell me your story, for, under such circumstances, we belong to the same storytelling community.

In day-to-day life these stories are our religion. If I ask you what your religion is, you may tell me the name of a denomination and then list doctrinal propositions to which you are committed—the Trinity, the divinity of Jesus, papal infallibility, indissolubility of marriage, the Immaculate Conception, and so forth. If I ask you what your life means, you may tell me about the rejuvenation of your life because of an experience at the time of a serious illness or the death of a parent or child or of a reconciliation after a bitter marital quarrel. You may not see much connection between the doctrinal propositions of your religion and the story line of your principal grace experiences. But that is unfortunate. Proposition and story line should be closely aligned instead of existing in separate worlds. You are committed to accept the doctrinal propositions of your faith because you have elected to be part of the storytelling community whose symbols enable you to organize your hope-renewal experiences. These propositions originated in and still derive their raw power from the stories that existed before them and will continue to exist even when the propositions may be reformulated.

The religious experience, symbol, and story come into existence in that dimension of the personality which may variously be called the imagination, the poetic faculty, the creative intuition, the pre-conscious, or even, in Aristotelian terms, the "agent intellect"—that restless, fertile, endlessly active "scanner" that arranges and rearranges and then rearranges again the images and pictures and stories we store in our memory banks. Religion occurs, at least primordially, in that dimension of ourselves that produces dreams, poems, stories, myths, and great or lesser works of art. Religion is a right-hemisphere activity, an altered state of consciousness before it becomes left-hemisphere behavior, before it becomes an ordinary state of consciousness. The poetic and imaginative dimensions of religion come before its propositional, cognitive, and theological dimensions. The Apostles had to experience the risen Jesus and tell their stories of that experience to others before kerygma, theology, philosophy, catechisms, and creeds could appear. These later developments can and should not be dispensed with. They are essential because humans are reflecting as well as experiencing creatures, philosophers as well as poets, scientists as well as storytellers. It is regrettable that so few people realize that the propositional religion is the same thing as, and intimately related to, the stories, the hope-renewal experiences they tell when they are asked what their lives mean.

Let us take, by way of illustration, one of the great hope-renewal experiences in English-language literature (though the experience is patently Irish and not English). In *A Portrait of the Artist as a Young Man,* Stephen Dedalus is walking along the beach at Clontarf (where Brian Borou routed the Danes a millennium before), agitated and disturbed by the turmoil of his life, affronted by the dry, narrow, rigid pieties of the Jesuit retreat, but yearning still to forge, as he would later say, "the uncreated conscience of his race." He encounters a girl on the shore as the tide goes out:

A girl stood before him in midstream, alone and still, gazing out to sea. She seemed like one whom magic had changed into the likeness of a strange and beautiful seabird. Her long slender bare legs were delicate as a crane's and pure save where an emerald trail of seaweed had fashioned itself as a sign upon the flesh. Her thighs, fuller and softhued as ivory, were bared almost to the hips where the white fringes of her drawers were like feathering of soft white down. Her slateblue skirts were kilted boldly about her waist and dovetailed behind her. Her bosom was as a bird's, soft and slight, slight and soft as the breast of some darkplumaged dove. But her long fair hair was girlish: and girlish, and touched with the wonder of mortal beauty, her face.

She was alone and still, gazing out to sea; and when she felt his presence and the worship of his eyes her eyes turned to him in quiet sufferance of his gaze, without shame or wantonness. Long, long she suffered his gaze and then quietly withdrew her eyes from his and bent towards the stream, gently stirring the water with her foot hither and thither. The first faint noise of gently moving water broke the silence, low and faint and whispering, faint as the bells of sleep; hither and thither, hither and thither: and a faint flame trembled on her cheek.

—Heavenly God! cried Stephen's soul, in an outburst of profane joy.

He turned away from her suddenly and set off across the strand. His cheeks were aflame; his body was aglow; his limbs were trembling. On and on and on and on he strode, far out over the sands, singing wildly to the sea, crying to greet the advent of the life that had cried to him.

Her image had passed into his soul for ever and no word had broken the holy silence of his ecstasy. Her eyes had called him and his soul had leaped at the call. To live, to err, to fall, to triumph, to recreate life out of life! A wild angel had appeared to him, the angel of mortal youth and beauty, an envoy from the fair courts of life, to throw open before him in an instant of ecstasy the gates of all the ways of error and glory. On and on and on and on!

Note first of all how closely Joyce's description fits our paradigm: a troubled, anxious man whose hope is waning encounters another creature whose gracefulness envelops him and renews his hope; the experience is recorded in images which pre-exist from the man's heritage, an angel from the halls of light, a creature of hope, a promise of life; a story of that experience is recounted to us in order to explain the troubled pilgrimage of Stephen Dedalus's life. In the story Joyce sings of the glory and desperation of the human condition, and in such terms that readers in the same storytelling community—in this case, Western culture—can share in the experience because they, too, have had similar and parallel experiences.

Joyce's experience was profoundly Christian and shaped by the powerful strains of woman-as-sacrament that abound in the pagan and Christian Celtic cultures in which he was steeped. The young woman on the beach at Clontarf was God—or, if one wishes to be less bold, a sacrament of God, a sign of God, of God's womanly love, a revelation of a generous, life-giving, nurturing, healing love. The tragedy from the point of view of Catholicism is that she was a far more accurate reflection of the Irish Catholic heritage than the aridities imposed on Joyce by the well-meaning but insensitive Jesuits at his college.

We would dearly like to persuade our readers that hope-renewal experiences of the sort that occurred on the beach at Clontarf are not only not incompatible with but have been fundamentally shaped by the Catholic heritage. The Church must be concerned to help future Stephen Dedaluses to understand that the Angel from the Halls of Light is in fact an angel of Yahweh.

The purpose of this book is not to sweep away propositional religion but to encourage the Church to develop policies that will integrate more decisively imaginative religion and propositional religion—the religion of the experience, image, symbol, story, and storytelling community on the one hand, and the religion of theology, creed, catechism, and institutional Church on the other.

This is a reactionary suggestion in the sense that it argues for a return to a condition of things that would have been taken for granted in the past. The Abbot Suger of Saint-Denis, who thought of his church as a *portacoeli,* a gate of heaven, contended that by participating in the creative light of the Church one would be led more surely to the light of God. (Note that he mentions, almost assumes, almost in passing, that the craftsmanship of the work should be of the highest.)

The modern Catholic, particularly the modern Catholic bishop, is uneasy about assuming the role of the *magisterium* (an idea borrowed in the early nineteenth century from Lutherans). The bishop, conscious of his magisterial powers, might wonder who will be empowered to say which is more important, the religion of imagination or the religion of intellect, the religion of experience or the religion of thought, the religion of storytelling or the religion of theology.

But the Abbot Suger or Dante or Michelangelo would not have understood the question: he would have seen no opposition between intellect and imagination, between prose and poetry, between symbol and doctrine, between reflection and imagination. In any religious experience the whole human personality is affected.

Obviously those who preside over the community to which a heritage has been entrusted must define the boundaries beyond which certain experiences, images, and stories cannot claim to be part of the heritage. The official teachers must determine what is compatible with the heritage and what is not. At its best periods, the Catholic Church defined the boundaries as widely as possible. Yet not everything could claim admission. What, for example, of the various voodoo-like cults that have become part of the popular religion of Brazil, the most populous Catholic country in the world? The teaching authority quite definitely excludes these experiences and images and stories from the Catholic tradition. Yet even well-educated and devout Brazilian Catholics will insist that there is no incompatibility between the *macumba* of Bahia and Catholicism. The official Church condemnation falls on deaf ears, perhaps because in earlier generations the Church in Brazil rejected elements of what might have been good, true, and beautiful in African religion, instead of Christianizing them.

Perhaps the lesson for religious leaders is this: You will only be effective in defining the outer boundary of your religious heritage when you have absorbed all you can from the world around you. If you try to take away the stories of the people, then the stories will come back to haunt you. Much better that you modify the stories, if you can, so that they are compatible with your heritage and take an honored place in it.

Those who founded the Church in Brazil, if they had been in fifth-century Ireland, would have surely thrown out good Saint Brigid—after all, didn't the ignorant people believe she was the Blessed Mother reincarnate? (Reincarnation was taken for granted in pre-Christian Ireland.) And we would have all lost the saint of spring and storytelling and poetry and new life, devotion to whom is still commemorated in churches and chapels in whatever part of Europe Irish monks visited 1500 years ago.

To put the matter differently, the theological discussion of who Jesus is that preoccupied the first four councils of the Church (Nicea, Constantinople, Ephesus, and Chalcedon) still has a place in the Catholic heritage, but so, too, does the experience of the risen Jesus that launched the Christian movement on Easter in its trajectory toward Chalcedon and its further trajectory toward the present moment. Now, through the images and the sensibility of the Catholic heritage (and the Protestant heritage, too) men and women still have hope-renewal experiences of death and rebirth shaped by their antecedent images of Jesus and recounted to members of the Jesus storytelling community in story lines that have lurked in the Christian imagination for almost two millennia. There are, in other words, two trajectories— one of theological reflection and one of image, symbol, and story line. There is no need for these trajectories to diverge, though for unfortunate historical reasons they have tended to do so in the last several centuries. The challenge is to bring the storytelling trajectory and the theological trajectory back together.

Part Two

. . . .

THE
HERITAGE

Chapter 3

· · · · · · · · · ·

SACRAMENTAL
EXPERIENCE

A sacrament is a created reality that discloses to us Uncreated Reality. It is a sign of goodness, a hint of an explanation, an experience of otherness, a promise of life, a touch of grace, a rumor of angels.

In the Catholic tradition, Jesus is the sacrament of God, the Church is the sacrament of Jesus, the Church's sacraments link us with Jesus, and we are sacraments for the Church to the rest of the world.

The Catholic idea that God is experienced in and through created realities is backed up by the philosophical explanation that God's normal operation is through "secondary causes"—that in the ordinary course of events God does not intervene directly but works out His plan through the laws of nature and with the cooperation of the objects, events, and persons of daily life. This position leaves open the possibility that God can on occasion dispense with the secondary causes and deal directly with us. But the Catholic Church has always been suspicious of those who claim to be the recipients of such direct encounters and of those whose religious life is preoccupied with the extraordinary to the exclusion of the ordinary. The philosophy of "secondary causes" is central to Catholic philosophy but it is not, we think, at the origin of the Catholic sacramental sensibility.

To cite two examples of Catholic piety that reject the "secondary cause" theory and the sacramental instinct:

During the conclaves of 1978 a number of American cardinals rhapsodized to the media about how the Holy Spirit intervened to influence their voting—an intervention which, to judge from the descriptions, went beyond the conclave's discussions and the ceremonies and the awe and the reverence and the hard-nosed politics and the intricate compromises. More sober analysis of the secondary causes of the elections of the two John Pauls suggests that the Holy Spirit works most effectively through the coalition-builders, and that those who thought they heard the voice of the Spirit were simply voting with the crowd. One does not want to exclude the possibility that the Spirit might sweep aside the ordinary processes of a papal election and intervene directly. Yet to rely on this is to expect God to do the work that we should—and to raise the question of where the Spirit was when Rodrigo Borgia was elected Pope.

One of us tried to explain the theme of his first novel to a group of priests: the four principal characters were sacraments of God's love for one another through thirty years of their lives, drawing one another to God, often through very crooked lines. "God doesn't need to draw us to Himself through humans," snapped one of the priests, "especially when they're sinners."

What God needs is beyond human speculation. But the Catholic heritage has always assumed that in the ordinary course of events God does indeed work through created realities. Both the cardinals who heard the Spirit whispering into their ears and the priest who wanted God to dispense with sinful human intermediaries failed to understand their own tradition in the name of a piety which, if not quite heretical, is at odds with the Catholic sacramental instinct and the Catholic philosophy of secondary causes.

We Catholics knew sacraments long before we knew what the sacraments were. We were baptized, of course, usually at an age when the experience could not mean anything to us. Perhaps we saw younger brothers and sisters baptized. We went to Mass and watched the grownups walk down the aisle to Communion. Perhaps our older brothers and sisters made their confirmation. Parents occasionally or frequently went to Church to go to confession. We may have been invited to weddings, perhaps even participated in them as confused but "adorable" flower girls or ring bearers. We certainly knew about priests and shared our parents' admiration and respect for them and maybe even, though it was unlikely, we knelt at the sickbed of a member of our family while the priest anointed him or her.

The names have changed. Baptism is now the Rite of Christian Initiation; confession is now the Rite of Christian Reconciliation; Extreme Unction has become the Sacrament of the Sick (after being called for a time the Last Anointing); Holy Communion has become the Eucharist. Most of us ignore the liturgists and still use the names from our childhood.

We also knew about statues and rosaries and holy candles (which were lighted at home during thunderstorms) and holy water (which was sprinkled about the house during thunderstorms and perhaps even used to bless ourselves before we went to bed at night) and Saint Christopher medals and other charms to ward off evil or attract good. We were baffled perhaps by the fact that our Protestant friends seemed to have none of these things and viewed our possession of them as a form of idolatry. (And we were baffled if there were no pictures of God or Jesus or Mary in the stained-glass windows of their churches—if the churches were God's house, we asked, why wasn't God's picture there, or His Son, or His Mother?)

Then we came to catechism class and were told that a sacrament was an "outward sign instituted by Christ to give grace."

"Fine," we probably said. It was a definition that was relatively easy to memorize, and we could recite it quickly and proudly when the pastor came to question us before Holy Communion or when the bishop, having nothing else to do, would spend a few moments asking questions before confirmation. The definition was acceptable—unobjectionable—and unrelated to the wonderful ceremonies and signs that marked our life. Holy Communion was an outward sign instituted by Christ to give grace. Fine. The crucifix and the rosary and the crib and the statue of the Blessed Mother were only "sacramentals"; they didn't automatically give grace but they were a help with the giving of grace. Fine, too. We weren't sure what grace was, but if S'ter said it was something we needed, we weren't going to argue.

Nor was the definition wrong. On the contrary, it is a nice synopsis of the religious experience of the kind we discussed in chapter 2. Only no one told us that; no one explained the link between the definition and, say, the purple veiling of the statues during Lent (a practice, alas, abandoned in the post-Vatican era. It followed into the ashcan of history another and even more spectacular Lenten ceremony, the breaking of the Alleluia. In medieval and early Renaissance Catholicism, a wooden carving of the word *Alleluia* was thrown from the steeple of the Church at the beginning of the pre-Lenten season to indicate that the Alleluia would not be heard again in Church until the end of the triumphant first Mass of Easter). Hence we did not comprehend that the definition represented a profound religious intuition about the relationship between created reality and Uncreated Reality, an intuition that had produced the purple statue coverings, the Ash Wednesday ashes, and indeed the whole rich and complex custom of Lent as sacred time. No one told us that the theology of sacraments (as digested in the catechisms) was not the *cause* of the Catholic view of created reality disclosing Uncreated Reality but rather the *result* of it. But the truth is that we Catholics have a highly developed theory of the Seven Sacraments because we are the kind of people who are already disposed by our heritage to drape statues, plunge fire into water, impose ashes on one another's heads, turn the midwinter solstice into Christ's Mass, sanctify place with great churches of wondrous stained glass, and sanctify time with such seasons as Advent and Lent. Even today, when many Catholics, well educated in their catechisms, hear the word "sacrament," they think only of the Seven Sacraments and resist the wider use of the term.

We illustrate with a story.

A decade or so ago one of us was in New Delhi visiting the then-ambassador of the United States of America to the Republic of India. The ambassador, very much a storyteller, told us about a recent experience of his (it is regrettable that we cannot have a recording of the now senior senator from New York telling the story himself and on himself). Late one afternoon he glanced at his desk calendar and saw that it was Ash Wednesday. He was dismayed and a little guilty because he had missed the penitential ashes of Lent. It would have served no purpose to assure Ambassador Moynihan that the Lenten ashes were not obligatory nor to tell him that perhaps the Ash Wednesday symbol was more appropriate in the fourteenth century, in the wake of the Black Death, than in the twentieth century when we have a more highly developed theology of the Resurrection. The ambassador would have doubtless agreed that it is both more encouraging and theologically more accurate to say, when the ashes are imposed, "Remember, person, that thou are destined for glory." He would have added, however, that the words *"Memento homo quia pulvis et in pulverem revertis"* are far more dramatic. A Ph.D. in international relations, sometime professor at Harvard University, ofttimes public servant that he was, Ambassador Moynihan still would have asserted that the penitential ashes were an important part of his personal religion, however old-fashioned or out of date or nonobligatory they might be in the official religion.

Then he remembered who he was. After all, there are certain privileges that come with being the representative of the United States of America. So he clapped his hands (or whatever ambassadors do these days) and the ambassadorial Lincoln was summoned. The Marine guards saluted, the America flag was attached to the front of the car, the two Indian police inspectors whose job it was to protect the ambassador climbed into the car, and the ambassador directed the chauffeur to bear him to the papal nuncio. Upon arrival the chauffeur announced to the usher who opened the door of the chapel that the ambassador of the United States of America was without, requiring his penitential ashes. With all due ceremony, the ambassador was conducted into the nuncio's personal chapel, candles were lighted, and the nuncio, clad in stole and cope and accompanied by two chaplains, appeared solemnly to remind the ambassador of the United States of America that he was made of dust and to dust he would return.

We're not sure, but perhaps afterward, in the finest traditions of Catholic sacramentality, Ambassador Moynihan and Archbishop Gordon (in Dublin born) had a small drop of something or other and, well aware that they were dust and to dust would return, discussed the problems of India and Ireland and the United States and the world—and probably the cosmos too.

The story has a certain amount of Moynihan-ish charm but there is more to the story than charm, for in its own way it is a classic manifestation of the Catholic religious sensibility. "For the ashes,

damn it all, Andy, are important!" They are a minor, perhaps mis-
leading sacramental in the official religion, but to the ambassador/
senator and to hundreds of millions of Catholics all over the world,
terribly important. The imposition of ashes is an experience/image/
story/community event of enormous artistic and poetic power. God
is revealed in the ashes, a God of Death and Judgment at the beginning
of Lent, but a God of promise and glory at the end of Lent. The
season of Lent itself is also an experience/image/story/community event
which shapes time, defines space, and provides meaning.

It is difficult to imagine any phenomenon in the Protestant tradition
of comparable importance to the Wednesday Ashes in the Catholic
tradition. Some of the ceremonies of the High Holy Days in the Jewish
tradition have parallel importance for Jews, but they are integrated
in a much longer, more complex and elaborate, and somehow (in our
experience at any rate) less solemn event.

On Ash Wednesday, you come into church and walk down the
aisle, the priest smudges your forehead with ashes and murmurs some
words, and you go out of the church with the unpleasant realization
that someday you're going to be buried in a tomb in which you will
be considerably less attractive than you are now with the ashes on
your forehead. A quick ritual, but oh, how effective! If one wants a
single example which says virtually everything that needs to be said
about the Catholic religious sensibility, one can point to Ash Wednesday. Where is God on Ash Wednesday? God is in church reminding
us of our mortality, as we should be reminded.

The fundamental issue in the debate about sacramentality is precisely that: where is God? All the world religions are forced to insist
that God is both "out there" and "in here," that is, God is both
transcendent and immanent, God is the "totally other" but also our
good friend. God is the God beyond the gods for Paul Tillich, but
He is also the fellow wayfarer of Alfred North Whitehead.

But in practice a religion must choose where the emphasis ought
to be. In Catholicism, as in certain forms of Hinduism, there seems
to be little fear of a God that is too immanent, too much "down
here," too much the fellow pilgrim. Protestantism, Islam, and Judaism
all have a horror of idolatry and a holy fear of identifying God too
closely with nature, of anything that smacks of pantheism. They em-

phasize the distance, the otherness of God, the decisive difference between God and nature, the absolute transcendence of God, or, as Tillich called it, the Ground of Being. Catholicism certainly acknowledges the transcendence of God, and some Catholic theologians echo Tillich's insistence on the God beyond the gods. They observe, not without data, that if one identifies God too closely with nature, one ends up, if not with pagan superstitions, at least with a tendency to create culture gods, i.e., domesticated idols modeled in our own image and likeness, comfortable, reassuring gods who reflect our biases and our prejudices, if not our superstitious fears.

In the ecumenical dialogue of recent decades, the two positions have crossed on the theoretical level. Protestant scholars such as Langdon Gilkey, Martin Marty, and Paul Tillich will confess their respect for Catholic sacramentality, and Catholic thinkers will criticize Catholic folk religion and culture religion and any other forms that have lost their sense of the "totally otherness of God." Yet, in the mild Protestant envy of Catholic sacramentality there is also, if one reads carefully between the lines, a continued fear of and dislike for Catholic propensities to superstition and idolatry. And if some Catholic scholars have cheerfully given up angels and saints and the Blessed Mother and the souls in purgatory as excess ecumenical baggage, few of them seem able to muster the passion of their Protestant counterparts for intermittently erupting in violent—and it seems to a Catholic—almost obsessive proclamations about the "otherness" and transcendence of God. Catholic writers, on the contrary, are more inclined, when push comes to shove, to quote that quintessential statement of sacramentality, "God's Grandeur," written by that most Catholic of poets, Gerard Manley Hopkins:

> *The world is charged with the grandeur of God.*
> *It will flame out, like shining from shook foil;*
> *It gathers to a greatness, like the ooze of oil*
> *Crushed. Why do men now not reck his rod?*
> *Generations have trod, have trod, have trod;*
> *And all is seared with trade; bleared, smeared with toil;*
> *And wears man's smudge and shares man's smell: the soil*
> *Is bare now, nor can foot feel, being shod.*

And for all this, nature is never spent:
There lives the dearest freshest deep down things:
And though the last lights off the black West went
Oh, morning, at the brown brink eastward, springs—
Because the Holy Ghost over the bent
World broods with warm breast and ah! bright wings.

In the Catholic experience of God, and in the Catholic sensibility that helps to shape the repertory of images predisposing the individual Catholic to his own hope-renewal experiences, "God's grandeur" inheres in the world. God may be "out there" but He is also most certainly and most definitely "down here." It is our opportunity and our obligation in the course of our life to encounter Him "down here" while at all times acknowledging, of course, that in addition to being "down here" God transcends all that is down here and only begins where our imagination and our experience leave off. Or, as the medieval writer Allen of Lille put it, "The created world is for us like a book, a picture in a mirror."

Or as the American poet Richard Wilbur, here very Catholic in his orientation, says, in his poem "Objects":

...Oh maculate, cracked, askew
gay pocked and potsherd world
I voyage, where in every tangible tree
I see afloat among the leaves, all calm and curled,
The Cheshire smile which sets me
fearfully free.

The sacramental principle means that the natural world is a sign of God, not merely because God created it, not merely even because God created it as good, but because God, somehow actually is *in* it. God is not, indeed, totally identified with the world and is surely greater than the world. Doubtless God transcends the world but is nonetheless accessible to us in it, and not merely through Her/His work but also through His/Her reality. The Catholic sacramental tradition asserts that God is known through signs, both natural and ecclesiastical. As Lawrence Cunningham puts it, "It is possible to think of the entire Christian reality in terms of sacramentality. Jesus is a sacrament in the sense that his incarnation was a visible sign in the world that God is real and concerned with the world. The Church, in turn, is also a sacrament because, as a visible reality mediating the invisible grace of God, it is a sign/extension of the presence of Jesus in the world. The Church is the sign that Jesus gives us to guarantee His work in history. The Church in turn makes concrete the presence of Jesus through visible signs that the Church numbers as seven."

The Catholic theologian Richard McBrien says, "The Catholic vision sees God in and through all things: other people, communities, movements, events, places, objects, the world at large, the whole cosmos. The visible, the tangible, the finite, the historical—all these are actual or potential carriers of the Divine Presence. Indeed, it is only in and through these material realities that we can encounter the invisible God."

Neither Judaism nor Protestantism nor Islam would deny that God is at work in the world, but these religious traditions dislike identifying God with the natural world (see, for example, Paul Tillich's anguished and twisted chapter, "Nature and Sacrament," in his book *The Protestant Era*). All right, the Protestant imagination says, nature is sacramental, God is in the world, but for the love of God, be careful that you don't *identify* Him with the world. Live in fear and trembling that in your love of sacraments you do not taint God, you do not degrade Him, you do not drag Him down to the corruption of worldly things and events. As Martin Marty puts it in his book *Protestantism,* his heritage has been "uneasy about objectification of the Divine Drama in images which might themselves draw the devotion of the supplicant from the invisible God beyond the gods. It has often and maybe even usually been uneasy about unrestricted bodily attention and has rather constantly feared the ecstasy of the dance for most of the years of its history."

(It is not only Protestants who have been fearful of dance: Cardinal Casoria, the head of the Vatican Congregation of Divine Worship, not so long ago wrote a letter warning against dance during Eucharistic liturgy. "Dance," observed the Cardinal, who may be the biggest damn fool to sit in a key position in the Roman Curia in the twentieth century, "might remind people of love." Patently, one can't have people thinking of love during Divine Worship!)

The Protestant theologian Langdon Gilkey notes that there is, "especially to a Protestant, a remarkable sense of humanity and grace in the communal life of Catholics," and he praises the fact that "the love of life, the appreciation of the body and the senses, of joy and celebration, the tolerance of the sinner, these natural and worldly and 'human virtues' are far more clearly and universally embodied in Catholics and in Catholic life than in Protestants and in Protestantism." Indeed, Gilkey writes that the Catholic principle of sacramentality "may provide the best entrance into a new synthesis of the Christian tradition with the vitalities as well as the relativities of contemporary existence."

The sacramental instinct sees the things and the events of this world as signs of God's grandeur, presence, activity, as the continuation of God's work in the world, and finally as revelations of God's love. The Protestant critique of the principle of sacramentality may well be valid—it opens the way to superstition, to corruption, to idolatry, to culture religions—for Catholicism all over the world and in all times has been dangerously vulnerable to appropriation by nature religions. Mixtures of Catholicism and paganism seem to have existed from the beginning and to persist even today in, for example, Latin America and Africa, where pagan cults and pagan gods seem to exist side by side with, and are even integrated into, Catholic doctrine and worship. Protestantism has been able to avoid such corruption. There are few if any manifestations of "folk Protestantism" in missionary countries, while "folk Catholicism" seems to flourish. But one must reply to the Protestant critique by saying that while some forms of folk Catholicism do stray over the line and become more pagan than Christian, other forms of folk Catholicism represent, rather, the "baptism" of good pagan customs, practices, ceremonies, and beliefs, and their absorption into the Christian tradition. In fact, God can probably take care of Himself/Herself and does not need our protection from the corruption of this world. After all, God did create the world and did create it as good, and it is a matter of His/Her taste and not ours that S/He wishes to inhere in the world.

To illustrate with the vivid and indeed loaded example of sexual love: despite Cardinal Casoria and despite the anti-sex themes of much patristic and medieval Catholic theology (not including Thomas Aquinas), and despite the obsession with sexual ethics that preoccupies Catholic church leaders today, the Catholic religious sensibility has to believe that sexual passion is sacramental. Not only does Saint

Paul say so, but marriage (of which sex is an essential component—however offensive that might be to some Catholic popes and bishops) is a sacrament, i.e., a sign that causes grace. Although Rome may warn of the dangers of "unbridled passion," the Catholic religious sensibility still must insist that the more unbridled the passion between two lovers the more effectively is revealed the enormous passion of God's love for us. Sexual passion, in other words, is a sign and a hint of God's passion. God is turned on by us in the same way, except far more so, that we are turned on by one another. Moreover, God not only reveals Himself/Herself to us through each other in sexual love; S/He is somehow present in the body of the lover in the act of sexual love. We make love to our lover and at the same time we make love to God (because, to be philosophical about it for a moment, the other's being participates and inheres in God's Being). The "Other" who we sometimes sense has enveloped us in His/Her *Umwelt* at the height of sexual ecstasy is merely God, present not as a voyeur (though doubtless God enjoys the heights of our love) but as a fellow lover. All love affairs in the Catholic tradition of sacramentality are *ménage à trois*.

Such a statement may horrify some Catholic laity and offend some Catholic clergy and certainly make some members of the Teaching Authority of the Catholic Church nervous. Such images, they would say, are not "prudent." But they would not deny the truth of the description and certainly not be theologically offended by the suggestion that the God beyond the gods might be lurking as a third party in the marriage bed. The Catholic religious imagination says that God lurks *every* place. How are we then going to keep Her/Him out of the bedroom? A Protestant teacher/leader might react with horror to that suggestion, and not because he feared sex and hated women (as many Catholic bishops do). On the contrary, in practice, a Protestant teacher/leader would be much more open and sympathetic and flexible on matters of sexuality. But he would be horrified at the possibility of idolatry contained in the suggestion that God was intimately involved in the sexual satisfaction of two lovers. His taste and sensibility would be offended by the old Polish wedding night practice of the bride and groom rising after their first union to sing together the Magnificat, a hymn of gratitude to God and Mary for their joy and their pleasure. (And that such a custom offends some modern Catholics shows how dim the Catholic religious sensibility has become on matters of sexuality.)

While it is relatively easy to define and describe the Catholic experience of God in and through sacraments, it is rather more difficult to explain the origins of the Catholic sacramental sensibility. Catholicism emerged out of a matrix of prophetic and Pharisaic Judaism that had sternly rejected the idolatries and the superstitions of "folk Yahwism" (which apparently was widespread among the ordinary people of Palestine and the Diaspora even in the time of Jesus), and had insisted vigorously on the utter transcendence of God.

Writers of epistles in the tradition of Saint Paul had indeed described the whole of material creation as "saved." Some of the early Fathers of the Church had said that anything that was good or true or beautiful was therefore Christian. Nevertheless, in the early years of the Church, most theologians shared the profound pessimism of their pagan contemporaries about the material world, and were heavily influenced by the anti-world, anti-matter, anti-body theories of neo-Platonism and Stoicism. Yet, in the ordinary practice of the early Church, the resources of the nature religions, as inherited by the dying paganism of the Roman Empire, were enthusiastically absorbed. Pagan art, customs, devotions, and ceremonies were taken over and baptized en masse just as the armies of kings converted to Christianity were baptized en masse.

Patron saints replaced patron gods and goddesses. Angels and devils and souls in purgatory replaced spirits and demigods. In Ireland, Dagda became God the Father, Lug became Jesus, and Brigid became the Blessed Mother. The Celtic Cross, an Indo-European fertility symbol representing the union of the male and the female, was said to represent Jesus and Mary. The Brigid Cross, an Indo-European sun symbol, became Christ, the Light of the World. The pagan goddess Brigid (or Bride) was replaced by the Christian Saint Brigid (who was also identified with Mary to the extent of being called the Mary of the Gales) and assigned the same shrine at Kildare and the same responsibilities: spring, poetry, new life, storytelling—and, more recently, the Irish radio and television network!

The Roman midwinter festival of Saturnalia was baptized and became the feast of the Lord's birth, Christ's Mass. The pagan spring fertility festival, in which a lighted candle was plunged into water—clearly and patently representing sexual intercourse—was transformed into part of the Church's Resurrection liturgy with the interpretation that when Jesus arose from the dead He consummated His marriage with His bride, the Church, and that those who would be baptized with the Easter waters are the first fruits of this union. (Cardinal Casoria clearly was not consulted about that symbolism, though his mentality is certainly in the new liturgy, which translates the old phrase "May this candle fructify these waters" into harmless words about the Holy Spirit "visiting these waters.") That pagan customs were baptized and made Christian, and that this was done enthusiastically, if erratically, in the first centuries of Christianity, is beyond question. *Why* it was done is less clear, and the historical research that could explain the enthusiastic sacramentality of early Christianity has yet to be attempted. Perhaps in the optimistic enthusiasm of the Easter experience the early Christians felt confident that they could appropriate anything that was good or true or beautiful or useful or appealing in paganism and put it to their own uses. Christianity turned favorably toward the pagan and nature religions from which its prophetic Jewish predecessor had turned away in horror. The prophets and the rabbis after them were terrified of the possibility of idolatry. Early Christianity did not share that terror and was, on the contrary, confident that both intellectually and devotionally it could defeat paganism.

The issue still remains in doubt. Iconoclasts in the Orthodox tradition and reformers in the Western Catholic tradition both revolted in part against what they saw as a Catholic surrender to idolatry and superstition. Catholicism itself, flexible enough to adapt to Slavic customs in the time of Saints Cyril and Methodius, was not flexible enough, some seven centuries later, in the time of the Jesuit missionaries Matteo Ricci and Roberto de Nobili, to adapt to the customs of China and India (with horrendous and fateful results for the history of humankind). While the Catholic sacramental instinct was broad enough to tolerate pagan admixtures in Latin America and Africa (complete with an informal, married clergy and an informal, polygamous hierarchy—based on the custom that chiefs have many wives), it was not comprehensive enough, particularly in the Orient, to distinguish between conversion to Christianity and conversion to Western culture.

Is Our Lady of Guadalupe, for example, really Mary the Mother of Jesus (one never sees Jesus with her in the pictures) or is she an Indian goddess whose meaning as a political and social symbol is more important than her meaning as a religious symbol? Or is the Madonna of Guadalupe a combination of Mary and the pagan goddess in which the component elements are impossible to sort out? And is it Christianity that her devotees celebrate as they come to the great church at Guadalupe? What components of their devotion are Christian and what components are pagan?

The Easter ceremonies of the Yaqui Indians are vaguely connected in form with what happens in Catholic churches, but in substance and meaning they seem profoundly different. To what extent can these be said to be Christian? Or the Jesu Christo and San Pietro folktales that the Yaquis tell: are these not American Indian trickster tales, in which Jesus and Peter become stereotypical characters with rather little connection to the New Testament personages whose names they bear? Catholicism's sacramental sensibility inclines it to draw the boundaries out far and to include as many people and as many customs as possible. Catholicism at its best does indeed try to mean "Here comes everyone." While the Vatican itself may be much more stern in its announced and pronounced policies, in fact it too is remarkably tolerant of a wide variety of customs and practices whose origins are clearly on the other side of the line that must be drawn somewhere to separate Christianity from paganism.

All persons must decide for themselves whether the greater risk is to involve God too much in nature, and hence run the risk of mixtures of Christianity and paganism that end up as more pagan than Christian, or to isolate God too much from nature, and run the risk of desacralizing nature and isolating God from the human condition. That abuses of Catholic sacramentality run wild is all too evident. The abuses are less obvious in a bloodless, lifeless religion deprived of all sense of sacramentality, all sense of awe and wonder and mystery, all feel for the transcendent because the transcendent has been so thoroughly removed from the world in which humans live, but the abuses are there. Writers like Gilkey and Tillich and Marty are envious, each in his own way, of the Catholic sacramental sensibility, precisely because they are aware of what the reformers lost as well as what they gained. But as the ecumenical trajectories continue, and the churches come closer together, the "Catholic Principle" and the "Protestant Principle" will be better able to criticize and complement one another, and a better balance may be achieved between the transcendental and the incarnational emphases. Yet it is perhaps healthy that a certain amount of stress and strain between the two sensibilities remains. Those who defend the Catholic sensibility must offer as their final word the observation that the Word of God did take on human flesh, did pitch His tent and dwell among us, and that this shows a reckless sacramentalism on the part of God, a reckless disregard of the dangers of identifying God with nature, and in retrospect seems very Catholic of God. Paul Tillich might well have advised Him not to try it.

The devotee of nature religion sees spirits and gods lurking in wind and rocks and water, in sun and moon, in sky and stars, in the fruits of the field and of the flocks, in the fertility of men and women and the structures of family and community, of village and tribe. The sacred is everywhere for such a person, especially perhaps on the sacred altars and the sacred places and at the sacred times. But if the sacred lurks with special power and special danger in certain places and times, it does so because it is to be found, perhaps with less power, in all times and all places. Most of the world religions pull back from such seeming pantheism. God is above and beyond the energies and powers of nature; God is everywhere, perhaps only because He can be identified as being nowhere. Alone in the Western religions, Catholic Christianity disagrees. The sacred remains everywhere. If some times and places and events are especially sacramental, the reason is that everything is potentially sacramental.

Saint Thomas Aquinas's analogy of being is the philosophical argument that articulates and defends this instinct. Lesser beings participate in the Being of that which is Being-in-itself (*ens a se,* as we used to put it in the mother tongue). God exists in Himself (and nowadays we'd add Herself), and creatures (*ential ab alio*) exist not in and of themselves but in and of the Being, which does exist in and of itself. But the analogic instinct came long before Aquinas. When Karl Rahner, the contemporary transcendental Thomist theologian, writes "Grace is everywhere," he not only reflects Thomistic theory but also a much more ancient Catholic instinct. There may not be

47

gods and demons and demigods and spirits in the sticks and stones, the sky and the stars, the caves, the dances, in conception, birth, growth and death, but God is still there—not totally encompassed by these material realities but nonetheless totally present in and among them (because their being is sustained in His Being).

Paul Tillich speaks of the God beyond the gods and the Being beyond the beings and calls God the Ground of Being. The words "Ground of Being" are thoroughly compatible with the Catholic imagination, even if Tillich would scarcely have put such an interpretation on them. Because all beings are grounded in God's Being, God reveals Herself/Himself through all beings (more through some than through others). Does God reveal Himself/Herself through sexual love? How better might She/He reveal the intensity of His/Her passion, a passion as a sacrament of which human sexuality is too weak and not too strong? Oddly enough, there is empirical evidence to sustain such a position: the more frequently a husband and wife pray, the more satisfactory their sex life. And the correlation runs the other way: the more satisfactory their sex life, the more frequently they pray.

The sacramentality of the everyday is not and has never been lost on ordinary people. Some modern sensibilities may be immune to the mystery, the wonder, the awe of the everyday. There is a "modern man" sensibility of which divinity school theologians frequently write—for example, the Protestant theologian Rudolf Bultmann's "modern man," who thinks that because he controls electricity with the flick of a light switch, he no longer needs to stand in awe of a thunderbolt. But the rediscovery of nature that spawned the contemporary ecological movement is at least in part a revolt against the modern loss of respect and reverence, the sense of wonder and awe for the ordinary, the everyday, the commonplace, and the natural. Despite Saint Francis of Assisi and its own sacramental tradition, Catholicism has not been involved in this rediscovery of the importance of nature and the revolt against irreverence for nature. It was also, by and large, unaware that some polemicists were charging that the Christian tradition, and especially the Catholic tradition, were somehow responsible for the modern desanctification of nature. There are many ironies in the fire. Catholic Christianity, which presided over a sacramental tradition for a thousand years, was not involved in the rediscovery of wonder and was blamed for the loss of wonder, yet it was unaware of both. Greeley's second law: when Catholics abandon something, others discover it.

However poignant the ironies, sacramentality is back in fashion and the Catholic religious sensibility, rooted in an awareness of the revelatory power of the natural world and natural events and fortified with a philosophy of analogy that supports this awareness, ought to be able to contribute to the ongoing discussion about nature and grace, and to strengthen the awareness of its own people of the richness of the sacramental tradition.

Other aspects of the Catholic sensibility—the analogical imagination, the comic narrative, and the organic community—are almost inevitable consequences of the Catholic insight that God is signified and encountered in the ordinary, the everyday, the natural. For if the world is a sacrament, then it is possible to imagine God and our relationships to God as being rather like (if also rather different from) the phenomena and the patterns of this world. God is rather like our lover, if also very different from the lover; hence the lover is, in some sense, an analog of God (an assertion that makes Protestant thinkers very nervous); if we live in the sacramental world most adequately encoded in analogical images, then the stories we tell must finally be comic, stories about love affairs with a God Who has both the power to save us and the passion to want to save us. Even the endings in this life that seem unhappy will in fact be transformed. Finally, if the ordered patterns of relationships that mark the human condition reveal our relationship with God—some of the time, at any rate—then our organic communities, in which order triumphs, though just barely, over disorder, are the most appropriate places to do our storytelling. Once one opts for sacramentality, in other words, analogy, comedy, and organic community follow logically if not quite inevitably.

Some Catholic readers will doubtless say the respect for the sensual, the ordinary, the everyday, the commonplace, the natural, the worldly, which we contend is at the core of the Catholic religious experience, was singularly absent in their own religious education, which, as they recollect it (or as they may still hear it on Sunday) was anti-sense, anti-body, anti-matter, anti-emotion, anti-feeling, anti-art, and anti-intellect. "Fair enough" is all we can say in reply. Catholicism is, as a result of its basic sacramental commitment, necessarily pluralistic, and in some times and in some places (especially on the East Coast of the United States in the middle decades of this century), the sacramental dimension of Catholicism received short shrift, especially because, with the Holy See's recent obsession with sex, anything that was sensual or physical or material was swept away on the grounds that it might give people erotic thoughts. Enjoying music, or literature or art, or even the changing seasons, not to mention enjoying one's lover (too much, the Curia would add), was to run the risk of putting oneself in the "occasion of sin."

We do not mean to defend what has in some times and some places passed for Catholic education. To those critics who say they never heard of sacramentality and were certainly not taught in the sacramental mode, we reply, "Your teachers were wrong, that's all!" and invite them to display the maturity that will enable them to transcend the limitations of their education and discover what the heritage, of which they are part, truly stands for. If they do not wish to make this investigation, of course it is their privilege not to do so, but it is our privilege and obligation to deny that what they experienced in their Catholic education was an adequate expression of the age-old Catholic religious sensibility. Obviously no form of Catholic education is sufficiently free of the limitations of time and place to articulate the Catholic heritage adequately, but any form of Catholic instruction that is unaware of sacramentality, either in theory or in practice, is so inadequate in its expression of the Catholic heritage that it deserves to be dismissed as fundamentally false.

Chapter 4

. . . .

THE ANALOGICAL
IMAGINATION

I f someone asserts that his or her lover is Godlike, or makes the correlated assertion that God is a lover, he or she is engaged in an act of metaphor, comparing God and the human lover. An enormous literature has developed through the centuries, and has doubled and quadrupled in the last decade or two, one suspects, on the subject of metaphor—a literature so complex, intricate, and oftentimes befuddling that one is often tempted to conclude that only those with Ph.D.s in English or, even better, in semiotics are capable of metaphor. At the risk of enormous oversimplification, however, we will say that a metaphor is merely a statement that something is something else.

Juliet is the morning sun, for example. Patently, Romeo knows that Juliet isn't to be totally identified with the morning sun. She has a number of characteristics in common with the morning sun—for example, she brings light and warmth and clarity; and she is, of course, substantially different from the morning sun—she is on the balcony and not in the sky, her temperature at 98.6° Fahrenheit is substantially lower than the sun's, she is capable of knowing and loving and the sun is not. In any metaphor, then, two different things are being said at the same time but are in tension with one another: A is B and A is different from B. Juliet is the sun and Juliet is different from the sun. God is the lover and God is different from the lover.

The critical question in the Yahwistic heritage about the religious imagination is, which aspect of metaphors about God is more important—the one, for example, that asserts that God is a Mother (which is at the basis of the Mary metaphor), or the assertion that God's life-giving power is radically different from human maternity? The normal propensity of the Catholic imagination is to opt for the former choice and of the Protestant/Jewish and Islamic imaginations to opt for the latter.

Catholic theologian David Tracy calls the Catholic imagination "analogical" and the Protestant imagination "dialectical" (and most Protestant reviewers of Tracy's classic *The Analogical Imagination* agreed with this distinction). The Catholic religious imagination, and the theological systems emerging from it, tend to emphasize the similarity between God and objects, events, experiences, and persons in the natural world, while the Protestant (and Islamic and Jewish) religious imaginations and the theologies emerging from them tend to emphasize the difference between God and objects, events, experiences, and persons in the natural world. The tendency of the Catholic imagination is to say "similar" first and the Protestant imagination to say "different" first. The Protestant imagination stresses opposition between God and World; God is the totally Other, radically, drastically, and absolutely different from His creation. The Catholic imagination responds by saying that God is similar to the world and has revealed Himself/Herself in the world, especially through the human dimension of Jesus.

In a satisfactorily balanced Christianity the dialogue between analogy and dialectic is useful and creative. One of the harmful effects of the Reformation is that the dialogue broke down for 400 years. Father Tracy comments that, while both imaginations are necessary, the analogical imagination is prior to and subsumes the dialectical imagination, because it is in the nature of metaphor that similarity be noted before difference. If you assert the similarity between Juliet and the sun, there is still time to say "but, of course, Juliet is different from the sun." However, if you begin by saying that Juliet is radically

different from the sun, you certainly have an unobjectionable statement but you don't have very interesting poetry and you certainly
don't have a functioning metaphor.

The difference between these two imaginations, which as Tracy has
shown, permeate the classics of the two religious traditions, is not
something the ecumenical movement has removed, or even effectively
dealt with. Not so long ago the great Protestant theologian Karl Barth
denounced the metaphysical principle of the analogy of being as "the
work of the devil." Barth was perhaps the most influential of a group
of German theologians who between the two wars engaged in what
is called, appropriately enough, dialectical theology and whose influence, perhaps somewhat muted, persists even to the present. To such
thinkers, there is but one sign from God available to humankind, and
that is the sign of Christ crucified: all cultural forms of Christianity
are at best a corruption of that sign.

The dialectical theologians had so much influence and continue to be
important precisely because they give radical statement to a fundamental and crucial Protestant instinct. One cannot imagine a sensibility more
opposed to the Catholic sensibility, which sees signs from God everywhere, than one that sees God in only one sign and that one sign in
constant peril of corrupt misunderstanding. Catholicism will, of course,
admit that the crucified (and risen) Jesus is the sign par excellence, but
it does not let the rest of the world, including human culture and human
relationships, be deprived of all religious meaning.

In theological conferences, one need only murmur the words "radical monotheism" to stir up conflict between these Protestant and
Catholic worldviews, and it would seem that the Reformation and
the Counter-Reformation are still going strong.

For the Protestant imagination, the most effective sacrament of God
is the "Word," the "Word" of the scriptures and the "Word" who
is Jesus, and especially the "Word" that is the crucified Jesus. To a
Catholic it seems that when the Word as sacrament is divorced from
nature as sacrament, it all too easily becomes an abstract, deracinated,
and lifeless Word, and Jesus as Word becomes a person so rarefied,
transcendental, distinct from the rest of us that He almost ceases to
be human. The propensity of the Protestant religious imagination is
to stress Jesus as God's Word while the Catholic religious imagination
stresses Jesus as God's Sacrament. Both, of course, are acknowledging

that God reveals Himself in Jesus—the former through the things that are said, the latter through the things said and actions that are taken by someone who shares a human nature with us.

The issue here is not doctrine, for both the Catholic and the Protestant believe that Jesus is human *and* divine. The issue is rather image and language. Is your fear that you might identify the sacramentality of Jesus too much with the natural world, or is your fear that you might isolate the Word of Jesus too much from the ordinary human condition?

The difficulty is even clearer when one considers the image of Mary. Catholics see no risk to the radical otherness of God in imagining Mary as a sacrament of God's life-giving, nurturing, healing, maternal love. To the Protestant (and also the Jewish and Islamic) religious imaginations, this smacks of identifying God with the natural fertility processes or at least of not maintaining a sharp enough distinction between God and natural fertility. The Protestant imagination can accept Jesus as sacrament of God because He is God's Word (whereas the Catholic imagination would put it the other way around: Jesus is God's Word because He is His/Her sacrament); but Mary clearly is not God's word and therefore it seems inappropriate and even dangerous to compare her motherhood with God's motherhood. Have we not had enough evidence, the Protestant argues, from the Old Testament conflicts between Yahwism and fertility rituals and from the corruption of folk Catholicism by pagan fertility rites to realize how enormous is the danger of not distinguishing between human and divine fertility? Isn't Mary the functional equivalent of pagan fertility goddesses like Astarte and Venus? Perhaps the classic Catholic response to this critique is, appropriately enough, not theological but poetic, one of the great exercises in the analogical imagination of the last two millennia, Gerard Manley Hopkins's "The May Magnificat":

> *May is Mary's month, and I*
> *Must at that and wonder why:*
> *Her feasts follow reason,*
> *Dated due to season—*
>
> *Candlemas, Lady Day;*
> *But the Lady Month, May,*

The Analogical Imagination

Why fasten that upon her,
With a feasting in her honour?

Is it only its being brighter
Than the most are must delight her?
Is it opportunest
And flowers finds soonest?

Ask of her, the mighty mother:
Her reply puts this other
Question: What is Spring?—
Growth in every thing—

Flesh and fleece, fur and feather,
Grass and greenworld all together;
Star-eyed strawberry-breasted
Throstle above her nested

Cluster of bugle blue eggs thin
Forms and warms the life within;
And bird and blossom swell
In sod or sheath or shell.

All things rising, all things sizing
Mary sees, sympathising
With that world of good,
Nature's motherhood.

Their magnifying of each its kind
With delight calls to mind
How she did in her stored
Magnify the Lord.

Well but there was more than this:
Spring's universal bliss
Much, how much to say
To offering Mary May.

The Heritage

When drop-of-blood-and-foam-dapple
Bloom lights the orchard-apple
    And thicket and thorp are merry
    With silver-surfèd cherry

And azuring-over greybell makes
Wood banks and brakes wash wet like lakes
    And magic cuckoocall
    Caps, clear, and clinches all—

This ecstasy all through mothering earth
Tells Mary her mirth till Christ's birth
    To remember and exultation
    In God who was her salvation.

The Protestant imagination is capable of becoming analogical when it deals with Mary. Henry Adams, in his "Prayer to the Virgin of Chartres," understood Mary's sacramentality:

Simple as when I asked her aid before;
Humble as when I prayed for grace in vain
Seven hundred years ago; weak, weary, sore
In heart and hope, I asked your help again.

You who remember all, remember me;
An English scholar of a Norman name;
I was a thousand who then crossed the sea
To wrangle in the Paris schools for fame.

When your Byzantine portal was still young
I prayed there with my master Abelard;
When Ave Maris Stella was first sung
I helped to sing it here with Saint Bernard.

When Blanche set up your gorgeous Rose of France
I stood among the servants of the queen;
And when Saint Louis made his penitence,
I followed barefoot where the King had been.
For centuries I brought you all my cares,

And vexed you with the murmurs of a child;
You heard the tedious burden of my prayers;
You could not grant them, but at least you smiled.

Finally, that very dubious Catholic and incorrigible sinner François Villon also understood:

Lady of Heaven and earth, and therewithal
*   Crowned Empress of the nether clefts of Hell,—*
I, thy poor Christian, on thy name do call
*   Commending me to thee, with thee to dwell,*
*   Albeit in nought I be commendable.*
But all mine undeserving may not mar
Such mercies as thy sovereign mercies are;
*   Without the which (as true words testify)*
No soul can reach thy Heaven so fair and far.
Even in this faith I choose to live and die.

O excellent Virgin Princess! Thou didst bear
*   King Jesus, the most excellent comforter,*
Who even of this our weakness craved a share
*   And for our sake stooped to us from on high,*
*   Offering to death His young life sweet and fair.*
Such as He is, Our Lord, I Him declare,
*   And in this faith I choose to live and die.*

Peculiarly enough, at the beginning of the ecumenical era, when some Catholics were only too willing to abandon Mary as an ecumenical encumbrance, some Protestants began to discover her as a sacramental advantage. Harvey Cox notes in his *Seduction of the Spirit*: "Our overly spiritualized sentiments about immortality reveal yet another way in which our curious blend of technology and Victorianism has removed us from our own bodies. If pressed to a choice between symbols, I vastly prefer the Assumption to Ethical Culture.... If God is dead, Mary is alive and well and she deserves our attention."

Our purpose here is to locate the Mary phenomenon in its broader

Catholic context. The Catholics Hopkins and Villon and the Protestants Adams and Cox both understand the context to be the sacramentality of nature. If nature is truly good, and if God reveals Himself/Herself through nature, if nature images are appropriate to give us some hint of what God is like, then it follows that bearing of life, which is so very much a part of nature, is a legitimate metaphor for the life-giving activity of God.

The problem, in other words, is not Mary worship; the problem is analogy. If you concede the appropriateness of an analogical approach to God, then you have no difficulty in accepting the Mary image as part of that approach. If the Mary image is legitimate Christian poetry and language, then angels and saints and holy souls and processions and rituals and stained-glass windows and statues and holy cards and medals and blessings are also legitimate. But if you think that a scapular medal (or a Celtic cross) around somebody's neck runs the risk of superstition and idolatry because it calls into question radical monotheism and challenges God's "total Otherness" and Jesus as God's "Unencumbered Word," then all of the rest of the paraphernalia of Catholic devotion and imagery, from incense to the Sistine Chapel, from Guadalupe to Lourdes, from the rosary to Ash Wednesday, must also be called into question. Doctrine is not the issue, at least not primordially.

Catholics must be clear about it: if they wish to rejoice in the Mariological genius of Gerard Manley Hopkins and in the dazzling stained glass of Notre Dame de Paris, they have to run the risk of the multiplication of indulgences and medals and inane private revelations and devotions and the ever-present possibility of pagan contamination. Protestants on the other hand must also be clear about their risks: if they throw out statues and stained-glass windows and images of all kinds, if they strip their churches (physically as well as psychologically) of everything but cross and candle and book and the proclaimed Word, they may also strip the churches bare of people.

For Catholics, the risk is that if you permit nature unlimited access to your religious imagination, you may find that you're stuck with altogether too much of human nature. For Protestants the risk is that if you exclude nature as best you can from your religious imagination, then you may find that you have a religious tradition that is not very appealing to those who possess human nature.

Unrestrained analogical imagination may open the way to corruption, and unrestrained dialectical imagination may open the way to sterility. Which one you opt for is very likely to be a function of which one you acquired very early in your maturation process. The point is that whatever its weaknesses and frailties may be, and however open to abuse it has been in the past (particularly when not corrected through ongoing dialogue with the dialectical imagination), the Catholic religious imagination is analogical: it is more willing to say "God is like" than it is to say "God is unlike."

The Mary image, attractive to elite Protestants at the same time, oddly enough, that it is becoming unattractive to elite Catholics, is an excellent touchstone. Do you rejoice that you are able to say "God is like Mary," or are you, in the depths of your personality, shocked and not a little offended by images that suggest that such commonplace and even messy human activities as giving birth, nursing, diaper-changing, and nose-wiping might be acceptable hints of who and what God is and how S/He behaves? Some radical Catholic feminists reject the validity of the Mary image because, they argue, the emphasis on her virginity turns her into a negative sex goddess and the emphasis on her fertility is an attempt to freeze woman forever in a narrowly defined gender role. One can hardly deny that some churchmen have used the Mary image for these purposes. But one need merely to read a book of poems or walk through a museum or glance at the spires of a cathedral to know that the image transcends such misuse. Sociological research done at the National Opinion Research Center on young Catholic adults shows that, despite post–Vatican II neglect of the Mary image, the image is still extremely powerful, and none of these negative connotations has any effect on the religious imagination of young Catholics. One wonders whether the Mary image was not similarly uncontaminated in the Catholic past. The analogical imagination is much deeper and richer and more durable than theological attempts to explain, interpret, or exploit it.

If we want to know what Catholics in any time and place believed, we would properly explore the imaginations of the laity and not the teachings of the theologians. In a religious tradition dominated by the analogical imagination, the fine arts (and such popular arts as endure) are at least as valid an indicator of what the faith was as the theological treatises. Catholic philosophers and philosophical theologians have attempted to validate the analogical imagination with intricate philosophical arguments based on Saint Thomas Aquinas's teaching on the analogy of Being. These arguments are effective and not implausible: if creatures take their Being from the Creator, then it is reasonable to assume that some of the Creator's nature is revealed in the creatures and that one can know the Creator, at least in part, from them. But, especially if one has been trained in the aprioristic Catholic philosophy that used to be taught in Catholic colleges, one should keep in mind that the analogical imagination is not something that has been deduced on logical grounds from a theory of the analogy of Being. Rather the reverse is true: the analogy of being is a philosophical argument that has resulted from reflection on the workings of the analogical imagination.

It is interesting to read the Catholic David Tracy and the Protestant Paul Tillich on the subject of God. Tillich's existential philosophy has much in common with Father Tracy's transcendental Thomism, and the German philosopher Martin Heidegger peers over both their shoulders. Tracy has no difficulty in proclaiming an orderly pattern of relationships involving self, world, and God, whereas Tillich, whose Ground of Being is not all that different from the Thomists' *ens a se*, is forced to maintain a radical disjuncture between God and world. It is a disjuncture to which he seems committed because of theological rather than philosophical presuppositions. Solid Protestant that he was, Tillich had to insist on radical monotheism, even if his philosophical position inclined him on occasion in the direction not only of sacramentality but even of pantheism. Father Tracy, on the other hand, almost gleefully protects and promotes the Catholic imagination with an argument that says, in effect, if creatures exist at all, they have to be at least a little bit like God. Note well, however, that the philosophical argument between Tracy and Tillich (in which, to our prejudiced Catholic eyes, Tracy seems to have the advantage) is in fact an argument about what kind of imagination is appropriate for God. Tracy, at any rate, acknowledges this: all classic theological controversies are fundamentally rooted in classic differences in the religious imagination.

The other great Protestant prophet of the twentieth century, Karl Barth, may have pursued a better strategy once he dismissed philosophical arguments and rejected the analogy of Being as the work of the devil. God is radically Other because in His own Word, he says that's the way He is. According to Barth, no other argument is either required or suffices. One stands for the dialectical imagination (though Barth would not have used that term) not because there are solid philosophical reasons for doing so but because, damn it all, that's the way God has told us in the Bible that we should imagine Him. The attractiveness of this defense is that it forecloses the possibility that an ingenious New York Irishman like Father Tracy will be able to subsume dialectic under analogy, difference under similarity, radical monotheism under metaphor, the totally Other under the Cult of the Virgin with the clever—and to Barth and the other dialectical theologians, wicked—argument that once you've said that two things are similar you must immediately add that of course they're different.

The sacramental experience needs always to be corrected by the experience of "negative transcendence" lest it degenerate into pagan superstition. We need you, Father Tracy says in effect, to keep us from going off the deep end, from permitting an analogical imagination to run amok. Such an argument, which Barth would have considered diabolic, has insidious appeal to such post-Tillichians as Martin Marty, Harvey Cox, and Langdon Gilkey, who are prone to embrace sacramentality and even analogy but realize that they can't quite beat the David Tracys of the world at their own game. It is very useful to say "Yes, but Juliet is really very different from the sun," which is the role in Father Tracy's paradigm assigned to the Protestant dialectical imagination and its insistence on the radical discontinuity between the world and God. But such a literalist caution is at most a useful but distinctly secondary contribution to the imaginative process.

Moreover, and here's the rub, one cannot turn the tables on Father Tracy and say that the proposition "Juliet is kind of like the sun" is a useful corrective to the proposition that "Juliet is radically different from the sun." Similarly, once we have been told that God is radically Other, it is rather an anti-climax to be informed that in some corrective sense nature also is His sacrament. It is precisely such Jesuitical word tricks that scared Karl Barth away from philosophical dialogue with the Papists long ago.

The more sophisticated Protestant theologians know that David Tracy has backed them into a corner where their imagination either is reduced to playing a secondary or corrective role (and thus bringing to an end the Reformation) or is forced to the Barth-like retreat of the scholar who embraces metaphor but denies analogy. Moreover, if they listen to the fierce debates raging about metaphor and narrative and if they take modern literature and art seriously, they realize that the alternative to the Catholic analogical imagination is a world of absurdity where one does not imagine God because there is no God to be imagined. The choices, at least in modern high culture, are now either the analogical imagination, which sees God lurking everywhere (with His/Her Cheshire cat smile that makes us fearfully free), or the Modernist imagination, which sees only phenomena in which nothing meaningful or purposeful lurks or can lurk.

In the ordinary lives of people, the dialectical imagination has yet to be subsumed under the analogical imagination and it has yet to make common cause with it. Differences in the ordinary daily experience of Catholics and Protestants are the result not of the Reformation's theological disputes or today's philosophical ones, but rather of different imaginative approaches to religious reality. Those Protestant denominations that continue to oppose drinking, smoking, gambling, dancing, and excessive festivity do so—whatever ethical or doctrinal reasons might be advanced—because these things are all of the world and the world is radically different from God. And Catholicism tolerates these things. ("Where e'er the Catholic sun does shine/There's always music and laughter and good red wine/At least I've always found it so/*Benedicamus Domino.*")

At meetings of church groups under Protestant auspices, work sessions go on all day and evening, whereas under Catholic auspices, the work is much more likely to end in middle or late afternoon and the evening be devoted to festivity or at least informal conversation. The most industrious form of the Protestant work ethic results from an imagination that views the world as such a dangerous place— radically alienated from God as it is—that only by staying busy can we stay out of trouble. Even the denominational magazines are different. The Jesuit magazine *America,* for example, animated by the analogical imagination, calmly and cooly speaks of rational and orderly wisdom in a world where indeed there is much wrong but where there are still fundamental principles and basic forces that make for stable social structure and just societies. However, a Protestant magazine like *Christian Century* (and a fortiori *Christianity and Crisis*) feels obliged to confess, denounce, prophesy, and recoil in horror from the chaotic and ungodly confusion of the social world; and to confess one's guilt (time and time again, *ad nauseam,* it would seem to the Catholic) does not mean what it would mean in *America* or *The Commonweal.* There one confesses one's guilt to acknowledge the confusion and the horror, the ugliness and evil of a world radically alienated from God (necessarily so), not to assert that one has personally performed actions that have caused the existing evils. For a Catholic, a protest against a social injustice does not require that one assume personal responsibility for having caused that injustice unless one could have done something to alleviate it and did not—unless, in other words, one has shirked one's obligations to restore the social order so that it might more adequately reflect (be a sacrament to, a metaphor of) God's loving goodness.

In the Protestant imagination we are all guilty of evil in the world because we're all part of the world, and the world fundamentally alienated from God is basically depraved. For the Catholic the world is not so fundamentally alienated from God and while it might lack all the patterns of justice that it ought to have, it is not totally evil. We are responsible for the world's disorder—which is not pervasive— to the extent that we either personally caused it or refuse our responsibilities to do anything about it.

Robert M. Brown, a Protestant theologian, at a meeting of the World Council of Churches in Kenya, confessed the guilt of all Americans for the Vietnam War and other atrocities, much to the displeasure of many of us who had hardly delegated him to speak for us, but his rhetoric was perfectly consistent with his imaginative heritage. If American Catholics respond with a complicated casuistry about who was responsible and who wasn't, and who was more responsible and who less, they do so not because they are trying to shirk responsibility but because they believe that the social order, however imperfectly, is reflective of God, is a sacrament, and does participate in a natural world from which God is not absent.

Yet another manifestation of these differences is to be found in the different emphasis on political reform. Catholics are more tolerant, for example, of machine politics, not because they invented political machines to come to power in the great immigrant cities of America (the machines antedated the coming of Catholics—Saint Tammany, for example, was an English Protestant response to the Society of Saint Nicholas, a Dutch Protestant political organization in early New York City), but because, believing that social order is in part reflective of God, they are wary of reform movements which, in the name of purging the political world of corruption, may in fact do more harm than good to the always fragile sacrament that a political order is. If you can help it, you don't let gambling casinos or off-track betting into your city if your background is Protestant because these institutions offer one more opportunity for the evil that lurks in the world, whereas, if you're a Catholic, you might be inclined to tolerate them (being all the while aware of their addictive dangers) because they are not evil in themselves, the society needs the revenue, and people are going to gamble anyway.

The Protestant doctrine of the depravity of human nature is not a theory that gives rise to a different religious imagination but, rather, a doctrine that results from a different religious imagination. Why the division among Christians in the sixteenth century should have occurred precisely on the religious-imagination axis is a question that is yet to be answered, and is outside the scope of this book. But it has been necessary here to contrast the Catholic with the Protestant experience of God and the Catholic analogical imagination with the Protestant dialectical imagination—not as we have said repeatedly, to score points against our separated sisters and brothers, much less to win arguments with them, but to try to persuade Catholics to reflect on the nature of their own heritage of experience and imagination. A proper conclusion to such reflections is that Protestants have been true to their religious imagination to the bitter end, whereas Catholicism as an institution and Catholics as Christians have been unfaithful to their own experience of God and the images that contain memories of that experience. There are all too many places in the world where the Catholic sun does indeed shine but there is little music, only hollow laughter, and virtually no red wine—and what red wine there is is not of the best vintage either. Catholicism, particularly in the United States at the present time, has come dangerously close to abandoning the sacramental experience and the analogical imagination.

There are two reasons for this flirtation with infidelity, one common to Catholicism in most nations, and one especially prevalent in the United States and other English-speaking countries.

The worldwide, long-term, and fundamental failure in Catholic Christianity has been its inability to take seriously the sacramentality of sex. If God is experienced in and through nature, and if the objects and energies and events and persons that constitute nature are appropriate sacraments of God and symbols to memorialize our experience in those sacraments, surely sexuality—a powerful process, a dramatic event, and an encounter with the total personality of another person—ought to be considered a sacrament par excellence. If Mary, as Woman, is a sacrament of God's womanly love, then women ought to be sacramental persons. But, in fact, despite some occasional abstract theorizing (such as Saint Thomas Aquinas's assertion that sexual love is sacramental), Roman Catholicism, in its institutional theory and practice, in its "moves" and instincts, its programs and its policies, has feared sexuality when it has not deliberately repressed it. It is afraid of women when it is not fundamentally anti-woman. Fear of sexuality and hatred of women are not a result of Catholicism's absorbing some of the dialectical imagination of the Reformation, for these attitudes antedated the Reformation (and generally speaking, infected the reformers as well as the counter-reformers). The historical reasons for both positions are clear enough in broad outline. Catholic Christianity matured in a world in which Neo-Platonic and Stoic philosophies were exceedingly suspicious of everything in the material world, yet the Church overcame these suspicions and made peace with the wisdom and symbolism of pagan nature religion in every other area but sexuality. Historically, the Church's repression of sexuality has been, it is much to be feared, the result of its leaders' and theorists' strong suspicion that sex makes men vulnerable to women and that to "lose control" because of women is grievously sinful for celibate males and unmanly for noncelibate males. Virtue and manhood are, somehow or other, lost when one permits oneself to be subjected, however transiently, to the wiles of a creature so clearly inferior as woman.

Obviously this failure of the analogical imagination has not been universal. The Church's marriage rituals and the "handbooks" for confessors and marriage counsellors down through the ages give a very different perspective than do the theological tradition and the institutional practice so heavily influenced by that grim hater of women, Saint Augustine (who never did recover from the fact that he thought he had once loved them too much). And the sacramentality of sexuality has survived explicitly or implicitly in the fine and the folk arts. Mystics like John of the Cross and Teresa of Avila had no hesitation about using erotic imagery in their descriptions of their encounters with the Deity. Yet the Church as an institution did not effectively question the notion that the bodies of women were like tombstones, painted on the outside and filled with corruption inside, the memorable image of the fourteenth century English Dominican John Bromyard. Marriage was indeed a sacrament but it was a sacrament that had precious little, if anything, to do with sex. The less sex a husband and wife had with one another, the more a sacrament their marriage was—the equivalent of saying that the more passionless a relationship is, the more effective it is as a sign of God's love, hardly what Saint Paul had in mind.

One Roman bureaucrat who, in drafting a working paper for a meeting of the synod of Bishops a few years ago, urged the bishops to warn married people in their churches of the dangers of "unbridled passion" between husband and wife, had very much the same idea on his mind and he was saying in effect the same thing that Bromyard said in the fourteenth century. He was urging the bishops to warn married men not to lose control of themselves in their relationships with their wives lest they be pulled into a tomb of filth and corruption. Manly love of your wife, in other words, means being as passionless as possible in your relationships with her and having sex as infrequently as possible. The piety and practice of Catholicism has conceded to men the necessity of occasionally losing control in sexual relationships with their wives but only in order to discharge passion and only to conceive children. Any other reason somehow defiled the sanctity of the sacrament of marriage.

Unfortunately, many of those trained in the Catholic schools of the mid-twentieth century only too willingly acknowledge that the above description is not a caricature; indeed, it is not fundamentally a caricature of the position of the Roman Curia today (which does not understand the revolution in Catholic sexual theory accomplished by

John Paul's "Audience Talks on Human Sexuality"). Moreover, if passion is to be avoided, then anything that might "inflame the senses so as to stir up a passion and to ignite sexual fires" must also be avoided whenever possible. The anti-sex theory of the institutional church and of Catholic piety, given half a chance, cancels the entire sacramental imagination and produces a practical, if not a theoretical, disjuncture between God and world as radical as anything Karl Barth could have hoped for. The Irish Catholicism against which James Joyce was revolting (very different from the sensuous and erotic Irish-language Catholic heritage, which was virtually wiped out in the mid-nineteenth-century famine) was a cultural form of Catholicism that almost totally denied sex (no mean feat for Ireland, whose archaic cultural tradition may be the most erotic in Europe) and inevitably came to reject anything that pertained to the senses, the physical world, human passion, and human art. Irish Catholicism of the late nineteenth and early twentieth century, imitating, perhaps, the dialectical imagination of the British Occupying Army, outdid in its anti-analogy, anti-sacrament sensibility anything of which the English or Continental dialectical imaginations would have conceived. It was not the true Catholic imagination against which Joyce revolted but a perversion and negation of that imagination. Joyce's revolt was not against sacramentality but in favor of it.

In much of the religious training that many generations of Catholic immigrants in the United States have received (and the Irish had no monopoly on the perversion of the analogical imagination into sexual repression), the fear of sex and the hatred of women were so strong that young men and women grew up with a disintegrated religious imagination, shaped in part, of course, by the rituals and the ceremonies and the statues and the stained glass but also, in part, by extraordinarily repressive sexual orientations. The world was good, we learned from our stained glass and our incense and our candles and our Midnight Mass and our May crownings and our First Communions, but the world was also bad, we learned in our classrooms and sermons and confessional because, alas and alack, sex was terribly important in the world and sex was, most of the time, at any rate, evil. Its slick and subtle temptations had to be resisted wherever they manifested themselves—and that was practically everywhere! Catholicism was fully prepared to make distinctions about the use and abuse of liquor, the use and abuse of gambling, the use and abuse of money, the use and abuse of political power. It was even prepared to admit, under duress, that you could make a distinction between the use and abuse of sex. But it promptly added that sex was usually abused and that the only way to prevent its abuse was to use it as little as possible.

If Catholicism had been true to its own sacramental and analogical instincts, it would have said that the only way to prevent abuse of the sexual dynamisms is to use those dynamisms as well as possible, as brilliantly, as imaginatively, as creatively, as passionately as one can. For Catholicism, fidelity has almost always had to do with staying out of other people's marriage beds and not with developing the pleasure, the power, the creativity, the ecstasy—and hence the sacramentality—of what goes on in one's own marriage bed.

Whatever is to be said for the past justifications of Catholicism's sexual repressiveness (and, heaven knows, the pagan world into which Catholic Christianity emerged was a dissolute one in which the personhood of one's sexual partner was virtually unimaginable), it is clear that Catholicism can no longer justify excluding sexuality (and women, because of sexuality) from the domain of sacramental experience and analogical imagination. On the level of high theory, the integration or reintegration of sexuality into the analogical imagination has already been accomplished with John Paul II's brilliant audience talks—the implications of which have yet to filter down to ordinary Catholic practice and piety and perhaps even to filter down to the Pope's daily decisions in the institutional church.

Suffice it to say that the failure of the analogical imagination to subsume sexuality is the most grievous failure in the history of Catholic Christianity, a perversion of the best Catholic instincts and the most authentic Catholic sensibilities, and a perversion that has done, and continues to do, enormous harm to the Catholic Church, the Catholic heritage, and the Catholic faithful.

It is especially remarkable that this perversion has been possible despite the critical position of the Mary image. Catholic institutional practice has been able to achieve the feat of being anti-sex and anti-woman while at the same time being pro-Mary. One must, for example, admire the ingenuity and the skill with which Saint Bernard warned against women on the one hand and sang the praises of Mary on the other. He was not a hypocrite, and certainly not a bad poet. He was, rather, inconsistent and self-deceptive, as are most members of the human race at least some of the time. Fortunately, for Catholic Christianity, the faithful, many of the lower clergy, and most of the great creative artists have been true to the analogical imagination. They have celebrated Mary as a sexual creature and as a woman and paid no attention to the curveless stone statues which the ecclesiastical institutions often imposed on their churches (and, more recently, the faithful and the lower clergy have paid no attention to the attempts of some fanatics to impose measures of neckline and hemline on the dresses of young women in the name of Mary).

American Catholicism has been infected by the fear of sex and hatred of women found in many other Catholic countries and even to some extent affected by the virgin/tramp imagery and the ethical double standard that has accompanied this sensibility in other countries. There has been all too much of the "good girl/bad girl" or "mother/temptress" imagery in the piety and the education of young Catholics in the United States. However, perhaps because the United States is not, after all, a Latin country, and perhaps because the Anglo-Saxon and especially the Irish traditions take women a good deal more seriously, American Catholicism has been substantially less anti-sex and anti-women than, let us say, Italian Catholicism and especially the Roman Curia. If one tells the typical American Catholic priest or lay person today that sex is a sacrament of God's passion and that women are sacraments of God's love, the reaction is very likely to be, "Who the hell ever said they weren't?" The era when women and sex were excluded from the domain of the analogical imagination has ended abruptly in the American Catholic Church, save among a few older clergy and laity, and the majority of the hierarchy (at least on the public record).

Just as sex and women have become appropriate analogies for God, American Catholicism seems to have abandoned many of the traditional bastions of the analogical imagination and to have become vigorously low church, precisely at a time when Protestants are most seriously attracted by the high church and tempted to make their peace with sacramental experience and analogical imagination. With the abandonment of Latin almost all sense of mystery (which is not the same as mystification or obscurity) has also slipped away from Catholic church services (though in principle, a vernacular liturgy, while less mystifying, ought to be capable of greater mystery than a liturgy in a language that no one understands). In many new Catholic churches, statues, the Stations, and the stained glass have either been swept away or reduced to diagrams or abstractions that would not offend even the most fundamentalist Protestant. Reverence and awe have been replaced by often cloying informality; solemnity by "letting-it-all-hang-out" manners. Great music has been replaced by bad, pseudo-folk music, punctilious precision of movement by semi-literate lay readers stumbling through the difficulties of the Psalms or the Pauline Epistles. None of this need be so. Liturgical dance—Cardinal Casoria to the contrary notwithstanding—need not profane the liturgy but can easily make it more sacred. It need not diminish mystery but can enhance it. Popular hymn singing does not have to be limited to forms appropriate to strumming the guitar or the bow tie or the six-shooter. Spontaneity need not conflict with dignity but can, in fact, reinforce it, and the spirit (whether one spells it with a small *s* or a capital *S*) need not be constrained by forms and structures but, on the contrary, normally flourishes the most effectively within flexible structures. Nor is mystery or sacramentality recaptured by slowing the Mass down and by inserting long and usually maddening pauses (the genius of the Roman liturgy is that it does not drag, it moves) of the sort that a priori historicist liturgists try to impose on their congregations.

There was a time when Catholicism had blessings for almost everything, and it was assumed that almost every Catholic carried the rosary and wore at least one religious medal. Empirical evidence shows that many Catholics still consider the rosary an important artifact in their religious devotion, even if they don't recite it very much. But the institutional church, led in this instance by most of the lower clergy, seems to have abandoned blessings and medals and holy objects and holy cards and pictures and sought for "relevance," either in the social activism of Liberation Theology (borrowed in substantial part not from Catholic social theory but from Marxism) or the emotionality of the Charismatic Renewal (borrowed in substantial part from Protestantism). There can be no objection, of course, to the Catholic heritage's learning from either Protestantism or Marxism unless that learning process involves rejecting the heritage itself. But the sacramental principle and the analogical imagination are so little perceived in the education of the typical Catholic cleric that he is like the character in Molière's play who discovered that he had been speaking prose all his life.

Theoretically it should be possible to integrate both the Charismatic Renewal and Liberation Theology into the analogical imagination. In Latin America, at any rate, attempts have been made to link Liberation Theology with "popular religion" (attempts which do not seem to have been very successful). And our friend and colleague Virgil Elizondo has written effectively on the relationship between devotion to our Lady of Guadalupe and a variety ("non-Marxist") of Liberation Theology. Yet in the United States both the theorists and practitioners of Charismatic Renewal on the one hand, and Liberation theology on the other, have been indifferent to the need for or even possibility of integrating these two movements into a Catholic heritage that is both sacramental and analogical. Typical of the mindless pragmatism of American Catholicism at its worst, they much prefer to be prisoners of a past they don't understand.

Are we suggesting that medals and rosaries should be brought back, even Saint Christopher medals, even though Saint Christopher was tossed out of the Church calendar by Pope Paul VI? You bet your life we are! The trouble with the customs of the Church of twenty-five years ago was not that they were tried and found wanting but that they were not understood, interpreted, or explained. Could not a ceremony for the blessing of automobiles (every year, perhaps) and even the distribution of Saint Christopher medals (or you name the kind of medal you want—design your own patron saint of automobiles) be an occasion for a powerful sacramental lesson on the dangers of drunken driving? But then, sermons are never heard on drunken driving, so how can one expect there to be any sense of the symbolism that might experience God's power reflected in the power of an automobile engine, God's agility in the mobility that a car makes possible, and God's responsibility and affection experienced and reflected in courtesy and responsibility and affection at the wheel of a car?

No, indeed, the analogical imagination has not been tried and found wanting by American Catholicism. It has been found hard—i.e., impossible to undeveloped imaginations—and it has not been tried.

Some of the most creative dissents from the anti-sex, anti-woman traditions in the Catholic heritage are to be found in the medieval and Renaissance blessings for a marriage bed, blessings which do not deny the utterly secular activities that will occur there but also affirm that these activities are graceful, in the sense of being full of God's grace. Without necessarily advocating a return to blessings for the marriage bed, ought not the Catholic analogical imagination to be able to find ways to validate and reinforce the sacred nature of the bedroom, which married people do comprehend despite and indeed because of its utter secularity? Few places more effectively refute the artifical opposition between secular and sacred. How can we ignore the religious importance of this most analogical—because most creative—of places?

There may also be a social-class factor involved in the flight of American Catholicism from sacramentality and analogy. For many years we absorbed from the culture beyond the Catholic community the impression that there was something ignorant and superstitious and immigrant and working-class about our holy water and lighted candles and incense, and our old women fumbling with rosary beeds, and our priests dressed up in funny clothes, and our murmurings and blessings and obscure devotions that no one quite understood. They were the ecclesiastical equivalent of ethnic neighborhoods and organization politics and communal loyalties outside the church doors. As part of the final phase of our acculturation into American life, it became appropriate to abandon the whole mess, to dismiss neighborhood loyalties, and eliminate all the murmurings and the mumblings, the mysteries and medals, the invocations and pieties, the blessings and rosaries, the May crownings and the mumbo jumbo.

Our research evidence shows that Catholics have not abandoned Mary or the rosary, enthusiastically support May crownings, and try to create neighborhoods wherever they go. Nor is there any evidence that they would be opposed to a reconsideration of angels and holy souls and patron saints, the blessings of automobiles and rings and Christmas presents and newborn babies and new homes and old friendships and family reunions and dinner parties and dances and everything else that is natural and human and thus a potential sacrament and a possible analogy of God's nature and action.

One carries a Saint Christopher medal in one's car, for example, not because the saint (who may or may not exist) is going to protect us from our own or others' irresponsibility, but because he will remind us that we live in a world which, as Rahner has put it, everything is grace, everything is a possible revelation of God's love, and everything a possible image to remind us of God's love. A blessing or a medal or a rosary need not be superstitious, much less magical. It can, quite simply, be sacramental, i.e., a sign of God's love and an image to remind us of that love.

Doubtless there were superstitions and abuses in years gone by; doubtless the exercise of the analogical imagination had deteriorated. But to flee from it, to reject it is mindlessly to throw out the baby with the bath water—an exercise in which contemporary Catholic elites are exceptionally skillful.

The world outside the Church, particularly the world of serious scholarship, is in the process of one of its most important revolutions in the last several centuries. It is rediscovering the importance of symbol and story. Many scholars have come to believe that the model and the narrative are the typical, paradigmatic exercises of human knowledge and speech, of human knowing and communicating. The sign and the metaphor, in other words, are at last recognized as being not enemies of science and knowledge but rather the way science works in its ordinary pursuit of knowledge. Sign, image, and story have been rediscovered as critical and decisively human activities at the very time American Catholicism is trying to de-sacramentalize and de-symbolize itself. The myth of "modern man" is being abandoned just as Catholic theologians and preachers are trying to speak to him. The myth of a world without mystery is being rejected at the precise time American Catholicism is trying to shake off the last remnants of its own sense of mystery. The enormous power of symbol and story has been rediscovered at the very time that Catholicism is shedding its last symbol and forgetting its best stories.

Chapter 5

. . . .

THE COMIC STORY

The favorite Catholic story is the crib; the favorite Protestant story is the Cross and judgment. The favorite popular Catholic feast has always been Christmas; the favorite elite Catholic feast has always been Easter. The most successful of Catholic festivities is the Midnight Mass of Christmas and thus far, despite its brilliant symbolic possibility, the least successful of Catholic feasts is the Easter Vigil.

Such assertions are by way of prelude to a discussion of the Catholic story, which, we contend, is comic. When a Catholic after encountering grace in a sacramental interlude wishes to share his story with others, his story will almost necessarily be comedy, i.e., its trajectory toward an ending will be in the direction of happiness. If one wishes to imagine a typical dialectical Protestant story, the ending would have the naked and lonely soul shivering before the Cross of Christ, which is also serving as God's great judgment seat. If one wants to imagine a typically Catholic religious story, it would end with the Wise Men and the shepherds slipping into the cave to admire the newborn babe and then going home to eat a Christmas dinner. A favorite Protestant ending would be that of Saint Mark's Gospel in which the women leave the tomb, uncertain and afraid. The typically Catholic ending would be Saint Luke's Gospel in which the Lord departs with the promise that once again he will eat the evening meal with His followers in the kingdom of His Heavenly Father.

The nature of the Catholic story was described to us vividly by our friend and colleague Father Leo Mahon, who said (we paraphrase): "Look, Easter is important. Jesus rose from the dead. We will rise from the dead too. There is life after death. I believe that. So does everyone else who is a Catholic. But we've never been there. We've never seen a dead man rise. We've never experienced life after death. All right, it's there, but we've never seen it. A newborn child in the arms of its mother, with family and friends looking on? We've all been there and we all understand in some fashion that God is there, too: God is present in the new life of the baby, God is present in the love of the family for the baby, and God is present especially in the embrace of the Mother and the Child. Christmas tells us that once upon a time there was a special little boy, a special mother, and a special intervention of God's love, which transformed the human condition and promised us that the mystery of life revealed in the boy-child and his mother is infinitely stronger than the mystery of death. We converted Europe with the Christmas story."

Like many of Father Mahon's insightful remarks, the last sentence (which we do quote precisely) is both unfalsifiable and unverifiable. Surely scholars would want a more elaborate and nuanced description of the conversion of Europe. Yet, on the level of a story about a story, it is surely true that Europe was converted by Christmas.

If there ever was a comedy, it is the Christmas story—a tale asserting that in the middle of the darkness there will always be light, in the middle of loneliness there will always be friends, in the middle of rejection and insensitivity and stupidity and cruelty there will always be love. The crib scene, with the star in the sky and Mary and Joseph and the angels and the shepherds (including the little shepherds), the oxen and the sheep around the baby, is the world's all-time happy ending. G. K. Chesterton captures the comedy of the Christmas story perfectly in his Christmas Carol:

The Christ-child lay on Mary's lap,
His hair was like a light.
(O weary, weary is the world,
But here it is all right.)

The Christ-child lay on Mary's breast,
His hair was like a star.
(O stern and cunning are the kings,
But here the true hearts are.)

The Christ-child lay on Mary's heart,
His hair was like a fire.
(O weary, weary is the world,
But here the world's desire.)

The Christ-child stood at Mary's knee,
His hair was like a crown,
And all the flowers looked up at Him,
And all the stars looked down.

Christmas is now the feast of all Americans, offending only a handful of non-Christians. One of our Jewish colleagues celebrates both Hanukkah and Christmas, arguing, quite correctly it seems to us, that feasts of lights and trees and little children and new life are for everyone. We refrained from suggesting to him that it was an act of the analogical imagination and the comic narrative instinct—maybe the most ingenious such act in history—to take the trees and the lights and the fruits and the gifts and the little children and the new life and say to all, "Hey, this is what our religion is all about!"

However, it has not always been so. One wing of the Reformation vigorously opposed Christmas celebrations on the explicit grounds that the holiday was a "popish" feast of disgraceful revelry and superstition, and on the more implicit and fundamental grounds that it identified the "totally other" too much with ordinary and everyday events. In the United States during much of our history, Puritan New England tried to abolish the feast of Christmas and to replace it with Thanksgiving, a more dignified and stately feast in which the family gathered around the table, heads bowed in reverential gratitude, acknowledging a distant and radically different God. Such a celebration was much more compatible with the Puritan worldview than a feast in which the family gathers around a crib scene and points admiringly and even laughingly at an infant God, at—to use John Henry Newman's words—"Omnipotence in bonds." As recently as the 1870s, public schools in Boston were open on Christmas day as evidence of the stern and sober refusal of the Commonwealth of Massachusetts to respect the frivolity and the comedy of popish Christmas.

When we were in grammar school, the nuns used to insist that Easter was a more important feast than Christmas. We didn't believe them, because the Easter Bunny did not hold a candle to Santa Claus and the Easter Parade was no match for Midnight Mass, and Easter breakfast (those were in the days before brunch) was not nearly as much fun as Christmas dinner, and pictures of Jesus rising triumphant from the tomb were not nearly so compelling as pictures of the Mother and the Child. Easter was a nice holiday but kind of dull—not nearly so colorful or vivid or exciting as Christmas.

From the wiser perspective of adulthood, we understand—in perhaps a not altogether unconscious attempt to twit the nuns—that the opposition between Christmas and Easter is inappropriate, for the Christmas story and the Easter story are the same, the story of love that is stronger than hate, of life that is stronger than death, of goodness that is stronger than evil, of light that is stronger than darkness. The angels of Christmas and the women at the tomb of Easter are the same—light shatters darkness, whether it be the light on the hillside at Bethlehem, with the angels announcing the coming of the Savior, or the light from the star guiding the Wise Men, or the light of the morning of the first day of the week when the stone was rolled back from the door of the tomb. New life is new life, whether it is the renewed life of the human race when a new child is born, or the renewed life of the human race when the Son of Man is reborn; and love is love, whether it is among the band of friends—shepherds, Wise Men, Mary and Joseph—around the Infant or the Apostles around the risen Jesus. Christmas and Easter are but two versions of the same comedy, two scenarios of the same happy-ending story, two variants of the insight that the new life—which is promised when the days grow a bit longer, at the end of December, and given with the coming of spring several months later—is one of the best hints we have of how God deals with the world and with us human creatures, who, for unaccountable reasons, S/He seems to love.

To agree with Father Mahon about the awesome importance of the Christmas story is not to say that the Easter story does not have the potential for being equally important but merely to say that, after two thousand years of Christian history, we have not been able to be creative and imaginative enough to make the Easter story as vivid an experience for the people as the Christmas story is. It may well be that theological and apologetic arguments about the resurrection of Jesus, preoccupations as far back as the time when the Gospels were set down on paper, inhibited the freedom of narrative and imaginative creation. It may also be that Catholic tradition has shied away from the sexual implications of the three Passover narratives that are combined to create the matrix for the Easter story: the Feast of Unleavened Bread was the spring fertility ritual of the Semitic agricultural peoples; the Feast of the Paschal Lamb was a fertility festival of Semitic pastoral peoples; and the Feast of Light and Water—hinted at in the Exodus story—was a very explicit fertility rite of ancient Rome that was early integrated into the Christian Passover celebration. These fertility images of Easter are obvious and doubtless could be made into the material of a very powerful and attractive Christian spring festival. Nonetheless, despite the fact that those who created the raw materials of the Church's Easter liturgy were well aware of the fertility significance, Catholic Christianity has been hesitant to make the most of, indeed even to mention, the sexual aspects of the merging of the fire and the water at the Easter Vigil. It was somehow or other easier to "baptize" the pagan festival of the Saturnalia in the middle of winter—even if baptism was, in fact, an element of the Christian counterpart to the pagan spring fertility festivals.

(In the English-speaking world, there is, incidentally, a fourth Anglo-Saxon overlay to the Semitic pastoral and agricultural and Roman urban levels of meaning. The very word "Easter" is the name of a pagan spring festival in honor of the goddess of the dawn Easterne, the goddess who reigns in the East and whose familiars are eggs, lilies, and rabbits, all symbols of fertility!)

In terms of symbolic raw material and artistic creativity, the new Easter Vigil of the Catholic liturgy ought to be a powerfully effective pedagogical tool and an increasingly important element of the sacramental life of Catholics. Perhaps more time will be required for the Easter Vigil to become a popular service, and perhaps, too, the Church will have to make its peace with sex and women before it can make a springtime sexual festival (commemorating the marriage between Christ and His church) an important and impressive Christian experience, image and story.

A number of reasonable objections could be made to the "popish" feast of Christmas and to extending the ethos of that feast to the celebration of the Christian Passover:

1. By bringing God so dramatically down into the cave, Catholic Christianity runs the risk of corrupting the radical monotheism of the prophets and of the "Word of God."

2. It does so as part of an unsuccessful attempt to baptize the pagan midwinter festival. Today there is perhaps more paganism in the festival than there is honor to a God who is, after all, "totally other."

3. It also promises too easy a happy ending, leaving out the need in the Christian life of uncertainty and judgment. A cozy, consoling Christmas too readily reassures the Christian that he need not be anguished when, in fact, in the absence of anguish and alienation the Christian will not be able to face his or her own radical sinfulness, liability for judgment, and need for salvation.

4. Where in the "Christmas spirit" is there to be found any hint of the singlemost important Word God has spoken to us—the crucified Jesus?

The first two criticisms pertain to Christmas especially as experience and image, and the last two apply to Christmas especially as story— it is too sentimental, too warm, too soft, too cuddly. That isn't the way the world is and that isn't the way humankind is saved. Such criticism would be sound Reformation theology. The New England Puritans who fought Christmas knew what they were about. Even from the viewpoint of some Catholic critics, Christmas is dangerously sentimental and devoid of serious social and political criticism. Christmas, they would contend, needs a thoroughgoing reformation. Perhaps, as one Catholic critic suggested, the Saturnalia ought to be turned back to the pagans and the more theologically pristine Eastern Catholic celebration, the coming of Jesus as an Epiphany on January 6, might be more appropriate. If Christmas has been lost to the pagans, perhaps Epiphany can be salvaged from Twelfth Night.

Such objections, whether from self-critical Catholics or from the remnants of the Reformation, simply won't work. Doubtless there is a danger of excessive sentimentality and self-deception in the Christmas festival. Doubtless, too, it needs to be modified so as to tie it more closely to the rest of the year and to social and political commitments and obligations. But if the narrative is abused, that does not mean that the story is to be rejected, only that the story needs to be retold. A Christmas story that leaves us easy and complacent is a false Christmas story, but a Christmas story that does not bring hope and consolation and light and love and laughter and joy is a false Christmas story, too. While there may be much in the family dinner at Christmastime that does not reflect the relationship between God and humankind, the prior insight of the analogical imagination is that there is something in the family dinner that *does* reflect God and something in the happy ending of love renewed on Christmas night that does reflect the purpose and destiny of the cosmos.

Object as much as you want, in other words, to the abuse of the Christmas narrative, but don't object to the happy ending, for if there is no happy ending then there is no purpose. If there are no reasons for hope, then there are precious few reasons for human life. The glow of Christmas does not fend off the misery, the anarchy, the uncertainty, the anxiety, the confusion of the world. Catholic Christians have never really thought it did. But because of God's love, the ultimate ending, the last word will be happy instead of sad, joyful instead of despairing, comic instead of tragic.

American Catholicism might do well to consider the religious imagination of the newly discovered migrants in our midst, Catholic Christians of Hispanic origin. If you press Hispanic-American Christians as to what their religion means, they will repeatedly tell you about its festivals—birthdays, name days, First Communion days, Confirmation days, saints' days—a yearly calendar filled with excuses for parties. Press them again and they will tell you about the parties in greater detail—the people who are invited, the kinds of foods prepared, the delicious cakes served at the end, the new relationships that are established with the various patrons, this-worldly and heavenly friends entertained at such parties. Finally, if you push once again as to how this all relates to the purpose and destiny of human life, the

Hispanic Catholic is very likely to look at you in some confusion and respond that it means that God loves us and celebrates our life with us and comes to be with us and our families as we celebrate the passage of life and the fact of His love. The Hispanic Catholic does not feel called upon to make this theological explanation very often, presumably because it is so obvious. Alas, in a curious twist of Greeley's Law, just as some of the clergy who are ministering to Hispanic Catholics are discovering the wisdom of their religion of festival and celebration, upwardly mobile Hispanic Catholics are themselves sending their children to Catholic schools, as one remarked to us, so that they will "learn all the religious rules that you Irish know already."

Comic narratives not only have a happy ending but end on a note of celebration. The Catholic Christian story, for weal or woe, is a celebration story. Even though many of our Eucharists are anything but celebrations, the phrase "to celebrate Mass" or, more recently, "to celebrate the Eucharist" is a giveaway to the comedy-loving propensity of Catholic Christianity. To those who prefer a story of Cross and judgment, the Catholic Christian must respond: "Sure there is Cross and judgment; we know that, too. But how can one be expected to face Cross and judgment unless one knows already that something wonderful has happened already that demands celebration and that, at the end, when Cross and judgment are over, there will be yet another celebration?"

The principal foe of Catholic comedy is not the dialectical imagination or even the Catholic puritanical tendency (especially prevalent among the Irish) to tone down the celebration lest people think salvation is too easy (as one nun explained it a long time ago, if people knew how much God loved them, they might relax more than was good for them). The real enemy of the comic narrative is the imagination that denies the possibility of a happy ending or, more recently, denies the possibility of any ending at all.

A sophisticated modern reviewer can quickly dismiss a film or novel on the grounds that it has a "happy ending," for of course, the reviewer implies, life does not have happy endings. Fairy stories, the psychologist Bruno Bettelheim has written, are powerful attempts to impose meaning on life when there is no meaning. Popular fiction, writes a University of Chicago English professor, panders to the reader's desire to find purpose in life when there is no purpose. Even ending a story, according to the critic Frank Kermode and his followers, is intellectually and epistemologically dishonest. An ending imposes a structure that does not exist in the real world. Happy endings, even faintly happy endings that hint at a smidgen of hope, are merely concessions to those who are not tough-minded enough to recognize wishful thinking.

The point about wishful thinking is not whether it's wishful but whether it's accurate. The point about tough-minded rejection of purpose in human life is not whether it is tough-minded but whether it is valid. Hope can require as much toughness as despair. Pessimism that is too easy may be as wishful finally as optimism that is too easy. As the novelist Stephen King says of horror stories, their appeal finally lies in the fact that at the end of them there remains a little bit of hope. In *Cujo* things get better for the bereaved mother and father, not much but a little better. (They don't get much better for anybody in *Pet Sematary* but that story seems to have been written before King concluded there were perhaps minute grains of hope in the cosmos.)

The successful novelist, we were told by a very wise publisher, begins with violence and ends on a note of hope. "They all live happily ever after" becomes a naïve fairy story only for those readers who don't realize that living happily ever after means perhaps two or three fights a week, days when the prince and princess don't speak to one another, and all kinds of conflicts with parents and children and neighbors and friends. Hope, as G. K. Chesterton remarked, is only a virtue when the situation is hopeless. The note of hope in a realistic "they all lived happily ever after" is merely a reasonable bet that the good days will outnumber the bad days and that whoever is responsible for the cosmos is better known in the good days than in the bad days. Many of the critics of the comic narrative persist in thinking that those of us who are committed to comedy are naïve fools, unaware of the tragedy, the suffering, the anarchy, the anguish, and the frequent futility of life. Perhaps some of us who have tried to tell the Catholic story have sounded like naïve fools (though innocent children die in the Christmas story and they die because of political oppression). Yet we are at least as well aware as they of evil in the world, and all our comic stories and our happy endings say is that good is marginally stronger than evil, life marginally more durable than death, and that the erratic trajectory toward a happy ending in this life must necessarily end on an uncertain note. It is not an effective response to a comic narrative of the Christmas story, for example, to say that it is soft-headed because it tries to impose on life structure that is not there. Such an argument begs the question, which is whether indeed there is structure. On that issue the evidence is inconclusive and one must make a leap of faith in either direction, though as transcendental Thomists, following Father Bernard Lonergan, would argue, the very fact that we have a passion for structure and purpose, for form and meaning stamped on our personalities means that there is already some form, structure, and purpose in the universe.

Critics who think that the ending of a narrative is false because it imposes structure on reality when no such structure exists do serve to point up the central issue about religious narrative: humans enjoy hearing stories because they love to tell stories and in both the telling of and listening to stories they can bring some order out of the chaotic phenomena of their existence. The child's plea, "Mommy, tell me a story," is, as Nathan Scott calls it, a wild prayer of longing, a cry for meaning. Indeed, this is a primal religious cry, and the child wanting to hear a story before facing the end of the day and the oblivion of sleep (and the terror of dreams) will survive into adulthood looking for stories which, however temporarily, organize the phenomena of life and point toward its further development.

We like to read novels because we are all novelists, all of us telling a story in which we are the narrator, hero/heroine, and principal character. Even those who believe that there is no order in the cosmos and that their lives are merely concatenations of random chances will nonetheless have a story to tell that shapes the events of their life into a beginning, a middle, and a trajectory toward an end.

We listen to stories and we read them because we are searching for paradigms into which our own story will fit. Even if we do not believe there is any purpose in *our* story, and even if we rebel against the propensities of humankind and demand that our novels end on a note of something close to despair, we still expect the heroes and heroines in the stories we read to act bravely, to act as if there is purpose, as if there is hope, as if second chances do occur even if, in fact, such behavior is mere existential bravery, a refusal to "go gentle" into Dylan Thomas's "good night." One only rages "against the dying of the light" if in the rage there is at least a demand for hope and perhaps a hint (à la Stephen King) that at the last moment hope might not be impossible.

So the real question is not whether stories may be comic but whether there are any stories at all. (Students of Greek drama point out that even the tragic cycles often end on a note of hope for the future.) The alternatives are not comedy or tragedy, not celebration or judgment. Finally, the alternatives are, on the one hand, comedy and celebration, and, on the other, chaos and despair. The human passion for narrative, for narrative with endings, and for endings that have at least a trace of hope is either self-deceptive, the last trick of a cruel and absurd universe, or revelatory, either a trick structured into our personality by a mindless evolutionary process or a hint of an explanation. There are only, in other words, two kinds of stories: Macbeth's "tale told by an idiot, full of sound and fury, signifying nothing," or Pierre Teilhard de Chardin's notion that "something is afoot in the universe, something that looks like gestation and birth." Every time a child is born the question arises again: is this new birth part of an idiot's tale or is it part of a narrative that has meaning because it has a plot and the plot is a conspiracy and the conspiracy is love? The gestation and birth celebrated at Christmas tell a simple and profound story, finally as unsentimental as the light of an acetylene torch, that asserts that the mystery of gestation and birth is anything but an idiot's tale.

The Catholic imagination can afford to be comic because its religious experience is of a God who is Love, revealed most powerfully through and represented most effectively by human love. God's love in the Catholic religious sensibility is hinted at by a natural order which, for all its faults and failings, must be more good than evil if God inheres in it and is revealed by it. Catholic Christianity could afford to take over and "baptize" midwinter nature festivals because it believed that the same God who disclosed Himself at Bethlehem also discloses Himself each year in the return of the sun after the winter solstice—and in the renewal of human familial intimacies as the days grow longer in the middle of winter. The comic narrative becomes a celebration precisely because the Catholic Christian sees in the world of nature cause to celebrate—evidence of God's goodness and love, evidence not so radically distinct from God as to be totally deceptive.

But is not the Catholic comic narrative finally too easy? Does it not refuse to face the mystery of evil in the world? Does it not duck the really hard questions about evil that have been asked, without effective answer, since at least the time of Job?

The Holy Innocents are slaughtered at Christmas and the Child who is born will someday die on the Cross. Even if the One who died on the Cross could not be kept in the tomb, still there is the horrendous evil of the execution of an innocent man and the continuing separation of that man, even though He was still alive, from His friends with whom He no longer walked the lanes and the hills and no longer ate the evening meal. If the sacramental experience, the analogical imagination, and the comic narrative cope at all with the problem of "evil," how can they account for sin and suffering in the world? Must not one turn away from comedy to sin and judgment or to absurdity? Does not the Catholic religious sensibility find itself forced to yield, in the last analysis, because of the problem of evil, to either the Protestant or the atheist religious sensibility? Must we not concede, ultimately, that either the world is a profoundly wicked and perverse place, totally depraved and radically distinct from God, or a thoroughly absurd and meaningless place in which the question of God (and the questions of endings to a narrative) cannot even legitimately be raised?

Catholic Christmas festivities may very well celebrate the fact of birth but such comic festivities cannot survive very long when faced with the fact of death. What does the Catholic narrative sensibility have to say in response to the problem of pain and of evil?

As a preliminary response, one must note that if in the name of the problem of evil one denies the possibility of purposeful narrative and meaningful life in the face of the fact of death, one is still faced with the necessity of accounting for the fact of birth and for the problem of human hope. If the universe is truly absurd, then hope can be written off as a cultural/genetic adaptation in the evolutionary process of the only creature we know of that is conscious of its own mortality. But such an explanation for hope is really no better than the believer's explanation for evil. If you yield to evil and say that life is absurd and hopeless, then you still have to explain the human experience of goodness. In terms of the argument you are in no better position than the person who decides that goodness is more revelatory than evil, that birth is more of an explanation of what life means than is death.

For the mystery of evil there is no solution, no philosophical explanation. In the battle between good and evil in the world, there are neither solutions nor satisfactory philosophical explanations but, rather, stories with a trajectory toward a conclusion. The Catholic story, at its best, tells us that the worst evil in the world is fear—the only thing we have to fear, in Franklin D. Roosevelt's words, is fear itself. We can cope with suffering so long as we are not afraid of it. If we can keep our fear under control we can absorb the pain and anguish and protect others from being hurt by our suffering. Our fear finally is existential terror, the fear of non-being, the fear that we will cease to exist. Christianity does not deny the power or the plausibility of that fear. Jesus was afraid in the Garden of Olives.

We know from the secular psychology of death and dying that the acceptance of death is a partial defeat of death. At least it meets death on its own terms. In this frame of reference Jesus came to teach us to die, to accept death with the kind of courage that puts death on the defensive. Jesus showed how those who know of God's love respond to the injustice and the tragedy of death. By giving us a new paradigm for dying and death, Jesus transformed the possibilities of our response to death. His example of how to die provided both salvation and redemption, or in modern terms both reintegration and liberation. Jesus caused our liberation by showing us how free and integrated men and women could die. In His case, because of Who He was, his partial triumph over death by the courage with which He accepted death became total triumph in the validation of Easter. The Heavenly Father confirmed on Easter that sin and death are finally defeated, especially by those who, since they know how to die, also know how to live.

In this story line, the Cross does not stand as the ultimate word. At most it is the Word before the final Word. It discloses to us not so much the absurdity of the world and our own powerlessness as it does the way one can respond in the face of seeming absurdity and as a victim of powerlessness. The Cross reveals a response to death that is appropriate for those who fear death but who believe that life is stronger than death and are confident that, somehow, in some way—they do not know how or when—this belief will be validated.

This religious story line does not provide answers to intellectual questions but rather practical hints on how to live in the face of unanswered questions. It is not the only Catholic story line that is a map for how to live with evil. But whatever Catholic story about evil might be told, it must end with life being stronger than death, love stronger than hate, light stronger than darkness, good stronger than evil, laughter stronger than tears, Easter stronger than Good Friday, the empty tomb stronger than the Cross.

In the Catholic narrative, then, the happy ending may occur not even on the last page of the book but on the page *after* the last page of the book, not with two out in the last of the ninth, but after the third strike has sent the Mighty Casey to the showers. The comic celebration, the reconciliations, the renewals of hope, the second chances, the endings that hint at new beginnings: all these experiences in the human condition are—according to the Catholic story—hints of an explanation, sacraments of God, images of what God is like and subplots that reveal the key themes of the Big Story.

One may dismiss such comic celebration as absurd, or self-deceptive or wishful. Our only point here is that they are Catholic. Of all the world religions that have emerged in the last 2500 years, none has a story line so blatantly and militantly and romantically hopeful as the Catholic Christian story line. Many Catholics, alas, do not understand this and do not realize that the principal weakness of their own story line is that it is *too* hopeful, comic, celebratory. The hope and celebration and comedy of the Catholic religious narrative has not been communicated explicitly to enough Catholics, and the failure is not of the Catholic religious sensibility but rather of those whose mission it is to preach and to teach the Catholic story.

Chapter 6
· · · · · · · · · · ·
ORGANIC
COMMUNITY

Catholic friendship networks are like the spokes of a wheel en-
closed by the rim; and Protestant friendship networks are like
the spokes without the rim, according to a brilliantly designed social
research project executed in both the United States and in Germany.
Or, to describe it differently, if I am a Catholic and John and Peter
are my friends, it is very likely that John and Peter are friends, too;
but if I am a Protestant, John and Peter do not necessarily know one
another. Moreover, if a young Catholic married couple have a strain
in their marriage, they will probably increase the amount of interaction with family and friends, while their Protestant counterparts
decrease interaction with those who are close to them.

Neither style of community relationship is superior to the other.
Both have positive and negative aspects. But the "organic community," spokes plus rim, is a specifically Catholic style, a product of
the Catholic religious sensibility that sees the storytelling community
as an "organic" and local-interaction network.

Many Protestant writers, including Paul Tillich and Langdon Gilkey, insist that the principal difference between Catholicism and Protestantism is that Catholicism sees salvation as a phenomenon provided by a hierarchial institution, the implication being that in the Protestant heritage salvation is primarily a matter between the individual and God and that no other individual or community or institution could dare to interject itself between the person and God. Traditional Catholic catechisms have seemed to confirm this description, presenting salvation in such a way that it seems that the Church has a monopoly on it. Even the liberal Catholic theologian Richard McBrien suggests that the principle of the Church's "mediation" is part of Catholicism's genius. "The universe of grace is a mediated reality: mediated principally by Christ and secondarily by the Church and by other signs and instruments of salvation outside and beyond the Church."

McBrien's formulation at least excludes the old impression that the Catholic Church has a *monopoly* on the means by which grace is revealed and salvation is transmitted (both are, of course, the same process). But his formulation is still open to an aprioristic interpretation: it might easily seem that mediated grace is the beginning of a religious journey instead of the end of one, an option for salvation chosen by God among many such options (and preferable in principle to the one of an immediate relationship between God and creature defended by Protestants) but not structured into the nature of the human experience of grace. We're the ones you have to come to if you want to be saved, Catholics seem to be saying, because salvation, or grace, is a mediated matter and we're the only ones around even offering the mediation.

In fact, the Catholic theological principle of mediated salvation (the phrase "communal salvation" is perhaps better) is not a theological premise from which everything else flows but rather a theological explanation emerging from the Catholic religious sensibility. If your religious experience is sacramental and if your imagination is analogical and if your story is comic, then it follows that salvation comes to you in the storytelling community that has shaped your experience, provided you with the repertory of images to articulate those experiences and the story line with which to describe them, and is waiting for you to present yourself in order that you might tell your story.

Grace comes in and through community, because religious experience and imagination and narration occur in community context. If God is disclosed sacramentally, i.e., through the objects and events and persons in daily life, then how else can this self-disclosure occur save in community? To remove God from the community context would be, in the Catholic religious sensibility, to remove God from the human condition. A "nonmediated" or "immediate" relationship between God and the individual person seems an artificial construct developed in a religious heritage so profoundly suspicious of the natural world and of the nature of human nature as to feel that social groups, communities, and the institutions that hold them together are almost inevitably corrupt and evil. Catholics concede that human communities are flawed; the Protestant religious heritage suspects that human communities are mostly, if not entirely, depraved. But the doctrinal articulation of these differences, and theological argumentation about them, are the *end* of the process of religious reflection, not the beginning. The Protestant and Catholic differences about community originate on the level of experience, image, and story.

Catholicism quickly adds that of course individual human persons must make their own decisions (or to use the more recent jargon, "exercise their own fundamental options"). No one can constrain another person's religious choice or prevent it, though we can certainly impede or facilitate it. But because religious choice is individual, it does not follow that experience, imagination, and story are purely individualistic phenomena. If one can isolate a human from community in all the other aspects of his life, then one can isolate that person from community in the religious aspects of life because, ultimately, the other aspects of life are the source of his experiences of God, the images that code those experiences, and the stories he tells about them. Only if you so radically separate God from nature as to minimize the workings of grace in and through nature can you imagine grace being communicated in ways that are not communal. One goes to the community to tell one's story because in the community one has already heard the stories (as well as broken the bread) and, by hearing the stories, developed the images and the pictures for sacramental encounters that facilitate later repetition of the stories.

If grace is encountered in passionate love with one's spouse, that is in part because one has already heard the story (however badly told because of the Catholic Church's anti-sex, anti-woman bias) that the spouse is a sacrament of grace and because one knows that one can repeat one's own story of God encountered through spouse—if only by attending church together with the spouse—in a community that will understand. A religious heritage that sees the community as somehow intervening invalidly between the self-revealing God and the individual almost seems to require the individual to face God without story lines and without images and indeed, quite possibly, without the spouse as a story line par excellence and an image par excellence of what occurs in the encounter with God.

The Protestant religious sensibility tends to imagine society as a collection of isolated individuals interacting with one another on mutually agreed terms. Whether the paradigm is Hobbes's jungle or Rousseau's social contract or Marx's class conflict or Adam Smith's market economy, social order is imagined as something imposed from the outside and inevitably, or almost inevitably, oppressive in the long run. Such paradigms are logical enough if one imagines nature as radically separate from God, and the world of nature, because separated from God, as a place where anarchy and evil and depravity and sin abound.

On the other hand, if you imagine God engaging in self-disclosure through nature, then you are likely to imagine society rather differently. In such an imagination, there is no such thing as a state in which everyone is free from everyone else and against which social contracts and social obligations and social order must be imposed. Quite the contrary, humans come into existence as participants in ordered patterns of relationships which, while they impose responsibilities and obligations, also facilitate creativity and freedom. To reject social structures because they sometimes become tyrannical is one more example, in the Catholic perspective, of throwing out the baby with the bath water. You come into a world of pre-existing relationships; you are born a son or a daughter, most likely a brother or a sister, a cousin, a niece, a nephew, a grandchild, a member of a community or a tribe or a city or a nation. What you are is in substantial part the result of those relationships. Because the relationships may be disorderly, either collapsing into anarchy or rigidifying into oppression, it does not follow that the relationships themselves are inherently evil. Just try to live without them, the Catholic religious sensibility says emphatically.

Moreover, these ordered patterns of relationships, governed by justice and love, which are distinct and yet related (certainly not opposed to one another), fundamentally good yet open like all good things to deprivations and flaws, are in themselves a powerful analogy and an intense sacrament for human relationships with God. The "Totally Other," in other words, reveals Itself, however incompletely and imperfectly, through the patterns of human relationships. The Catholic heritage would not go as far as the sociologist Émile Durkheim in seeing the origins of religion only in moments of a collective, religious ecstasy. But it would say, somewhat more modestly, that in the best, most generous, most loving, most rewarding of our human relationships, we do enjoy our most powerful encounters with grace. A social structure made up of such relationships is obviously sacramental— even though, like all other sacraments, it can be degraded, corrupted, perverted, and destroyed.

The Catholic instinct that society is sacrament points in two directions: first of all, it shapes the Catholic paradigm for the storytelling community; second, it imagines a social order that both reflects God to the storytelling community and *represents* the dynamics at work in the community. Thus Catholic political and social action places enormous value on the "natural," "organic," pre-existing social structures. The Catholic social activist does not believe that one wipes the slate clean, eliminates existing social structures, whether in the name of "reform" or "development" or "revolution." You cannot pretend that there are no existing friendship networks in a large American city; you cannot pretend that there are no informal relationships in a factory environment; you can't pretend that there are no pre-existing competing and conflicting social classes in a Third World country. Social reform that does not respect the existing and pre-existing patterns of a society—family, neighborhood, work group, rural community, church—is bound to fail. You can impose a nation-state, capitalist or socialist, on an African society, for example, but if that state ignores the resources, the strengths, the inertia, the commitments, the values, and the energies of the native village, then it is bound to fail disastrously.

To say that society is an organic community and that the storytelling church both reflects and is a model for the organicity of society is merely to say that neither church nor government nor social reformer nor parish priest can afford to believe that pre-existing structures are unimportant. No one can begin again as though nothing has ever happened before and as though no existing relationship pattern need be taken seriously.

If human relations are indeed sacraments of God's presence in the world, then their patterns are of the essence of human community and they cannot be ignored or dismissed by those who wish to preside over the community—to direct or change or reform or renew it. The storytelling community itself must be the model of respect for the pre-existing and more or less ordered patterns of human relationships. An ecclesiastical institution that pays no attention to the existing relationships in the community of its members is, from the Catholic viewpoint, a contradiction in terms. (Which does not prevent many parish priests and some Vatican officials from ignoring completely such wisdom.)

Considering its own internal experience of community, its observation of community in the world beyond its boundaries, and its experience of community as sacrament of God's relationship with humans, the Catholic heritage insists that human community (including ecclesiastical community) must be both "pluralistic" and, for want of a better word, "decentralized." This commitment to variety and diversity is less a theological principle than a result of sacramental experience and analogical imagination. If God's self-disclosure is in and through nature, through objects, phenomena, events, and persons, then it is bound to assume many different forms. Catholicism is committed to variety and diversity because of the variety and diversity of the human condition, which it sees as the flawed and imperfect revelation of God.

In the Vatican's canonical ideal, everything is neatly ordered and effectively disciplined. There is one line of authority, one set of rules, one collection of approved customs and rites; the issue of variety and diversity does not arise. However, the Vatican has never tried to impose such uniformity in practice, in part because it really doesn't believe in it and in part because it knows it wouldn't work. The Curial pose, brilliantly summarized by Pope John XXIII—"See all things, ignore most things, correct some things"—is marvelously skillful at tolerating what it does not approve of so as to avoid greater evils.

The Curial bureaucrat will tell you with a sigh that ideally a certain custom should be eliminated, a certain "abuse" corrected, certain practices punished, certain attitudes and behaviors eliminated, but he will say with yet another sigh that human beings are weak, materialistic, and sinful, and that an attempt to correct abuses would probably do more harm than good to the faithful. It's a great excuse for laziness—and one should never underestimate the laziness factor when dealing with the Roman Curia—and it also dispenses authority from impossible tasks demanded by its own fanatical supporters, like reimposing its birth control teaching on the American Catholic laity. But in their own dim way the Curial bureaucrats probably realize that the Catholic religious sensibility not only tolerates variety and diversity, but celebrates them, that customs, styles, manners, and cultures of different parts of the world are not merely compatible with the Catholic heritage but are different ways of God's revealing His/Her loving goodness to humans. The essence of Catholicity, whether one spells it with a small "c" or a capital "C," is to leave as much freedom as possible to the Holy Spirit and to the self-disclosing God.

Catholicism has been better at embracing diversity in some eras than in others. Its failure to adjust to the possibilities of India and China in the seventeenth century has already been noted. Many missionaries contend that a similar failure is taking place today in Africa. (How the Church could be expected to tolerate and even approve polygamous marriages involving not only the laity but the clergy and hierarchy may be difficult to understand, but it managed this in Ireland until the late Middle Ages!) Catholicism's best instincts, most powerful traditions, and greatest wisdom incline it not only to tolerate variety but to celebrate it. In its best moments, the Church realizes that its role is one of discernment rather than of regulation. When it is operating most effectively, Catholicism uses its own revelatory tradition, sacramental system, and authoritative structure as a sounding board, a touchstone for testing the experiences that are to be found within its boundaries. And it draws its boundaries as far out as possible to make certain that the Spirit that has spoken to it through its own revelation is not unintentionally excluded when wishing to speak to the experiences of the faithful. If you draw the boundaries too rigidly and exclude too many people, the Catholic heritage realizes, in the process you may also exclude God's Holy Spirit.

The Catholic principle or, perhaps better, the Catholic instinct for social pluralism is based on the Catholic experience of God's self-disclosure in the variety of nature and the human condition and its image and story of a Holy Spirit that blows where It pleases. Its philosophical and theological principles of social pluralism are derivatives of its own pluralistic experience. An immediate consequence— not necessarily logical, but psychological and existential—is Catholicism's instincts for "localism," "decentralization," "subsidiarity." In its final philosophical elaboration by Pope Pius XI in his encyclical *Quadragesimo Anno,* the "Principle of Subsidiarity" states that in human institutions nothing should be done by a higher and larger level of authority that cannot be done just as effectively by lower and smaller institutional structures. If the Catholic principle of localism does not quite say "Small is beautiful," it does indeed say "No bigger than necessary." Human nature operates most effectively when the maximum amount of freedom is granted to the individual person and the intimate small communities that constitute his or her interpersonal network.

Among the great social philosophies and mystiques that compete for our attention, only anarchism shares with Catholicism this concern for the local, interpersonal network—for the family, the neighborhood, the small community. Both capitalism and socialism think that such networks can be disregarded or eliminated if they stand in the way of social progress. Catholicism and anarchism believe that if you destroy them, you deprive humans of freedom and dignity and you deprive yourself of effective social control. Even though the controlling political institution may abolish the local networks, it does not follow that they will go away. The higher authority will either articulate itself with them or find itself struggling with intractable opponents.

It should be carefully noted that the Catholic instinct does not favor a pure free-market society imbued with the simple naïve optimism that "that government governs best which governs least." Committed to the vision of ordered human relationships reflecting God's relationship with nature and humanity, the Church thinks of social authority not as a necessary evil but as a positive good. Social authority exercises its proper role most effectively neither by making all the decisions nor by making no decisions. Rather, in the words of *Quadragesimo Anno,* social authority "guides, watches, protects and promotes." In particular, it intervenes to protect the rights of the individual against oppression by intervening structures and to protect some intervening structures from oppression or exploitation by others.

In its best moments, Catholicism believes that the role of ecclesiastical authority is the same as the role of political authority in human society. Indeed, Pope John XXIII in his encyclical *Pacem in Terris* explicitly applied the teachings of Pius XI's *Quadragesimo Anno* to the Church. In canonical theory and in mass media image the Church is a large multinational corporation with the Vatican acting as top management, the local bishops as middle management, and the parish priests as grass-roots management. Doubtless, many bishops and parish priests, to say nothing of Curial bureaucrats, accept this paradigm, but in philosophical theory and in imagination and experience it is invalid. Catholicism is a community of communities, and the role of its authority figures is to maintain communication among communities rather than merely to pass down orders.

When we were preparing the first draft of this book, the Cardinal Archbishop of Chicago was absent from his diocese for more than a month at an international meeting of bishops in Rome. We both heard considerable complaints about this absence. What was the Cardinal doing in Rome when there were so many problems to attend to in Chicago? In fact, the Synod of Bishops on Reconciliation, which was taking place in Rome, *was* a waste of time, yet the Cardinal was right to be there. Just as he represents Rome in Chicago, so too he speaks for the local community in the international community of Catholicism. The institutional structure of the Church is designed more for communication than for management, more for discernment than for regulation. Doubtless it has managerial and regulatory functions and doubtless these have sometimes overwhelmed the essential functions, but discernment and communication are not forgotten.

In actual practice, local bishops have enormous autonomy and are likely to be reprimanded or removed by Rome only in extraordinary circumstances. Similarly, local pastors have enormous de facto independent power and will be replaced by the bishops only after the most severe provocation. And the ordinary Catholic lay person in his or her personal religious life is not likely to be harassed by his parish priest unless he gives the priest permission and power to do so.

One of the most interesting stories of Catholicism in the nineteenth century is the response from the Vatican to the Church in France during the demographic revolution in that country. Birth rates had climbed rapidly because of improvement in public health and living conditions; death rates declined more slowly. When the population of France "exploded," and French married people responded to this "crisis of overpopulation" with coitus interruptus as well as abortion and infanticide, French bishops wrote discreet letters to Rome asking what was thought of the practice. Although Rome did not approve of coitus interruptus as contraception, it urged the French bishops not to "trouble the consciences of the faithful"—in other words, to leave them alone if they were in good faith. The advice was echoed by the famous Curé of Ars, Saint Jean Baptiste Marie Vianney, who, in the many conferences he gave to confessors, urged priests not to pry into the marital relationships of their penitents. In effect, the sainted Curé of Ars said, if they are practicing birth control in good faith, leave them alone. Indeed, so much had this approach become Church policy that when Pope Leo XIII wrote his encyclical on Christian marriage, he ignored the contraception issue entirely, though he and his advisors were well aware of the situation in France. The point in the present context is that this nineteenth century experience illustrates how the Church exercises authority: leave people alone unless you have absolutely no choice.

Similarly, on the same subject of birth control, the American Catholic laity made the decision in the mid-1960s that their contraceptive practices were no business of their clergy or hierarchy. In overwhelming numbers they stopped asking their clergy about contraception and ceased to mention it in the confessional. With few exceptions, the American clergy and hierarchy made no attempt to dissuade them. Almost overnight, the American Church returned to the practice of Jean Vianney and Leo XIII, in substantial part because ecclesiastical leaders knew, whatever the pressure was from Rome, there was not much they could do once the laity had made up its mind.

This is not to say that oppression does not exist in the Catholic Church at every level, especially oppression of women, nor that there are not tyrannical and oppressive Church leaders. It is simply to make two modest assertions: (1) the Catholic heritage believes in pluralism and localism and in its best moments puts those beliefs into practice, however inadequately; (2) out of indifference, out of incompetence, out of laziness, but also out of principle, Catholicism leaves more practical day-to-day decision-making power in the hands of its grass-roots leadership than does any other large corporate institution.

Abuses are possible under such governmental structures—particularly financial abuses at the diocesan and parish levels. The Vatican has no uniform accounting procedures that will give it any notion of how money is spent in American dioceses, and no bishop has effective control over how a parish priest uses his money. (A sometime auxiliary bishop of Chicago estimates that during the last years of Cardinal Cody's administration, tens of millions of dollars were invested by pastors in secret bank accounts [certificates of deposit, mostly] in order to safeguard the parishes' money from confiscation by the Cardinal. One suspects that most of these funds are still in hidden accounts, however popular and trustworthy the new archbishop is.)

This local power can facilitate and promote spontaneity, creativity, and freedom; it also can produce dishonesty and corruption. At its best moments and perhaps at its most cynical moments too, Catholicism knows that, if you have to choose, the risks of corruption are preferable to the risks of oppression, and the risks of too much control over local leadership are far worse than the risks of too little control.

In the Catholic religious sensibility, the storytelling community is always local. It is in the local parish that most of us hear the stories for the first time, and it is in the context of the neighborhood parish that we relate our own stories to the overarching ones. Indeed, in the life of most Catholics the only ecclesial community that matters is the parish. The diocese, the national hierarchy, and the Vatican are abstract entities existing at a distance, staffed by personnel one never sees. One might read with mild interest front-page newspaper articles about them, or even watch television clips just before the sports and weather. And the larger institutions exist, Catholics will admit if

pushed to it, to make sure that the traditional stories are retold accurately, and that there is a discerning authority to determine, if need
be, that one's own story or one's friend's or neighbor's correlates with
the tradition. But it is the parish priests, the family, and the neighborhood that constitute the meaningful religious environment for most
Catholics. Judging by the enthusiasm with which Catholics in the United
States rebuild the old immigrant neighborhood parishes in their new
upper-middle-class suburbs, the neighborhood parish has been benign.
Whatever may be wrong with it—and every parishioner and pastor could
write a book of complaints—it is still where Catholics feel most at home
and whose support they most insistently demand.

The local storytelling community is the most basic relationship
network in our life, when that network orients itself toward sacrament
and grace and celebration. The storytelling community consists of our
most primal relationships, oriented toward God.

In these chapters we have contrasted the Catholic religious sensibility most frequently with the Protestant sensibility and on occasion
with the Marxist and the atheist sensibilities. We have used these
comparisons not to make points or to win arguments but to illustrate
by contrast what the Catholic religious sensibility is. It may well be
that a sacramental, analogical, comic, and local religious sensibility
is defective or inferior. It may not be what you want (though religious
sensibilities are frequently shaped before people know what they want,
and maturity often consists not so much in rejecting one's sensibility
as in making peace with it). The sensibility we have described thus
far is not necessarily for you nor is it unquestionably the best. But it
is Catholic, and the competing religious sensibilities would not even
claim sacrament, analogy, comedy, and localism for themselves. This
is what Catholicism is. All human heritages are flawed when imperfect
human beings try to live these heritages in their daily existence. Criticize the practitioners of a heritage, if you will, in the name of their
failures to live up to the heritage. And reject the heritage, if you will,
because its experience and image and story and community are not
compatible with your own sensibility, do not strike you as being true.
But if you reject the heritage because of the flawed way it is lived,
realize that you are using an inappropriate criterion. In other words,
reject the Catholic heritage if you will because it is false or deceptive
or the work of a devil or wishful thinking or too Thomistic or too

celebratory or too sacramental or too analogical. But don't reject it because individual Catholics and the ecclesiastical institution live it imperfectly. What else would you expect but imperfection? Find a perfectly lived heritage and ally yourself with it, realizing, of course, that the moment you join it, it becomes something less than perfect.

We are all painfully aware of the perversions and subversions of the Catholic religious sensibility. We have all heard the stories about inappropriate birth control sermons at the Christmas Midnight Mass, abortion sermons at Easter Vigil, and both at funeral liturgies (perhaps a certain kind of clergyman preaches these because he has nothing else to preach about). These are insensitive corruptions of the Catholic sensibility, but that is all they are; they are not the essence of the Catholic tradition.

Reject Catholicism not because some Catholics are obsessed with negative sexual ethics, but, rather, because we believe that sex is sacramental, human passion revelatory of Divine passion. Reject us not for the birth control sermon on Christmas but for the incredible, almost unbelievable hopefulness of the Christmas comic celebration. Reject us not because of the idiocy of your pastor but because Catholicism believes that the primary religious experience is to be found in the primary networks of human life. Reject us for the idolatry of suggesting that God is like a father or a mother, a brother or a sister, a husband or a wife, a child or a neighbor, a parish priest or a lover. Don't throw us out because a pope sold indulgences to build Saint Peter's but because we suggest that God is encountered especially in sacred places. Reject us for the notion that God can be revealed in stone and stained glass and not for the hypocrisy and dishonesty, the frailty and self-deception, that may infect fund-raising practices by which we pay for these structures of stone and glass.

To conclude this section of the book: we feel that we have given what is basically an accurate and fair description of the Catholic religious sensibility. We have shown the manuscript of this book to a number of competent Catholic theologians and while they themselves might have preferred somewhat different wordings, and certain minor changes of emphasis, they have pronounced our efforts as an adequate description of the Catholic religious sensibility. Sacrament, analogy, comedy, and local community constitute a fair and adequate outline of the Catholic religious sensibility.

But we suspect that most priests and many Catholics who received advanced religious education will have read thus far in the book with increasing bafflement and impatience. The words "sacrament" and "analogy" they have heard before but they are not sure we use them in the same sense in which they've heard them. The word "comedy" for the Catholic story seems frivolous. Our emphasis on the local storytelling community does not correlate with the emphasis they acquired in their education on the infallibility of the ecclesiastical institution.

Indeed, we suspect many priests and more conservative Catholics will read this book with a checklist of doctrinal propositions in the back of their heads and will in fact be so eager to examine us against this checklist that they will have little patience for what we are saying and little sympathy for our goals. The doctrinal checklist will have become so obsessive that they will not understand what we are saying and not comprehend our goals.

This book is concerned not with doctrine but with sensibility. Doctrines are important because they codify sensibility and provide a criterion by which it may be criticized (a propositional reflection against which the appropriateness of stories might be discerned), and because they codify and make a cognitive summary of religious sensibility reflecting on the raw material of experience, imagination, and story.

If the clergy and laity reading this book can take our word for it that we accept the doctrinal checklist and will put the checklist aside and try to relate what we are saying to their own experiences of Catholic Christianity before and after and outside the classroom, then they will realize that while our language may be strange, and our approach may be unusual, we are in fact talking about something they know very well. The Catholic heritage holds that God is encountered in and through nature, that the natural world is a valid, if inadequate, reflection of God, that for all their flaws, nature and society are still reflective of God's goodness and love, that this goodness and love are a guarantee of a happy ending and cause for joyous celebration, and that these encounters and reflections and celebrations are most likely to occur in our most intimate interpersonal networks.

Catholicism in the United States will be saved by Catholics—lay, clerical, and hierarchical—understanding their religious sensibility more explicitly and living it more fully in ecclesiastical policy and institutional life.

Part Three

POLICY ISSUES

Chapter 7
. . . .
SEX AS SACRAMENTAL EXPERIENCE

For many Catholics their day-to-day experience of the relationship of religion to life is still ensnarled in abstract theology, watered down in the often inept interpretations of parish homilists. As a result, they find little relationship between their hope experiences and what they hear proclaimed from the pulpits on Sundays. Nor do they see much connection between their religious problems and what they read in their daily papers about the statements of their bishops or the pronouncements of Rome. Though they may lead profoundly Catholic lives by the standards of what we have called the Catholic sensibility, they often are not even aware of it, and as they struggle on through the inevitable difficulties of life, they receive little help from the "wisdom" of the Catholic heritage.

Those responsible for ecclesiastical policy at every level of the Church will "save" Catholicism through a two-pronged approach. First, they must recognize the ways in which the Catholic heritage responds to the pressing questions of human existence in the modern world. Pastoral leaders must be committed to learning about the significance of the basic experiences of humans living at this time and in the various places of our modern world, and not rely on a priori conceptualizations. Second, Catholic leaders must apply the insights of the Catholic heritage to the experiences of their people.

We are not advocating moral directives that will "make" Catholics live according to a formula devised out of an interpretation of the Catholic heritage. Rather, Church leaders should construct a vision of what life means that is founded on the traditional genius of Catholicism.

As John Shea has observed, Scripture and tradition must "prosecute" our discovery of God in our experiences, and our experiences must "prosecute" the interpretations of the Scriptures and tradition. If the Church encourages its members to engage in this "prosecuting" process, it will elicit a response from those whose religious heritage is deeply Catholic, but who do not now see how this heritage can enrich their lives and the lives of their communities.

The Church must address itself to the basic areas of human experience—sex, marriage, the family, and the neighborhood/religious community—if it is to be successful in upholding the Catholic heritage. All these areas have been deeply affected by official teaching devoid of sensitivity to the components of the Catholic sensibility.

We begin our policy recommendations by considering each of these experiences from the perspective of the wisdom we find in the Catholic heritage. There are intrinsic links among the various aspects of the heritage, and all of them must be attended to in the development of policy. But the key to regaining Catholic credibility lies in emphasizing the sacramentality of sex, the analogical potential of woman, the comic aspects of marriage and family life, and the organic nature of human community.

Consider this scenario. It is election night, and a man and a woman, key members of the candidate's campaign staff, are with a small group of loyal workers in a hotel suite watching the returns. They have worked together for over a year trying to convince the voters that their candidate for mayor will turn the city around and restore it to its previous days of glory. A down-to-the-wire race has been filled with enormous tension, especially in the last weeks of the campaign. Shortly after the polls close, the candidate predicts a win by a narrow margin, and the toasting begins. Still, the newscasters vacillate and refuse to proclaim either candidate a winner. The group's drinking continues on a less merry note. Eventually a large block of precinct returns wipes out the opponent's small lead and puts the candidate in front. As the candidate moves to make an appearance in the hotel ballroom, the slightly tipsy staff members begin a round of jubilant embraces. Our man and woman hug and kiss each other and suddenly something happens. Their bodies, alive with sensation, cling together. Their embrace and kiss are filled with a passion unlike the embracing of other jubilant staff members. When they finally separate, both are somewhat shaken. As they move to congratulate the others, they ache to return to each other.

This man and woman have worked side by side in intense situations for over a year. Both are happily married. Indeed, their spouses are not present in the hotel suite because they are visiting with the enthusiastic throngs in the hotel ballroom. The man and woman eventually find themselves locked in a second embrace in a dark corner of the hotel suite desperately wanting to shut out the rest of the world while they share the warmth of their physical contact.

How might we characterize our scenario up to this point? Is it another predictable soap opera plot? A story that is commonplace now that women are more active outside their homes? Or could it simply be a modern-day version of the age-old story of the surprise of human passion? An even more important question for our discussion of the Catholic heritage is, What should the couple do?

The Catholic "instinct" about sex is the stubborn conviction that sex is good and indeed sacramental (it reveals God). This instinct has been loyal to the Catholic experience and imagination, despite the almost universal condemnation of sexual pleasure by Catholic theologians. It views the initial discovery of sexual attraction as a potential religious experience, an opportunity to discover something about the God who lurks in all human experiences, especially in those with an element of "mystery" about them. Our couple could more deeply appreciate the God who created them with a marvelous drive toward unity, a drive which, perhaps in the midst of the frenzy of a political campaign, had been ignored. They could view this experience as God's reminder of the need to be more conscious of the Divine gift (grace) of their sexual drive. Most important of all, they could understand that in moments of sexual arousal they are like the God who in Chapter 20 of Exodus describes himself as "passionate," using a Hebrew word that elsewhere in the Scriptures describes the sexual desire of a newly married man for his bride.

At this point our readers might wonder if we are familiar with all the Church pronouncements they heard in their youth, and often continue to hear today, about sins of passion and especially about sins of infidelity. Haven't we all heard about "occasions of sin"? Don't we know about "self-control"? Where were we when priests and sisters and Church statements warned about the dangers of passion? And how can we say that a couple in an adulterous relationship might claim that somehow God was responsible for their initial attraction to each other?

In fact, the scenario where a couple find themselves in an adulterous situation that is not in keeping with our understanding of the Divine plan for human sexuality highlights a major implication of the Catholic sensibility about sex. The body with its passion, its sexual attraction, its sexual drive, is a sacrament; Catholicism will be "saved" when Catholics—lay, clerical and hierarchical—appreciate the grace-filled potential of sex and passion. It is the "wisdom" of the Catholic instinct that we find God lurking within the passionate feelings that every human being experiences, and the passionate God thus offers us an opportunity to discover Her/His presence in both the ordinary and extraordinary occurrences of our lives as sexual beings. Our experiences of ourselves as sexual beings are meant to help us appreciate the ultimate goodness of life, a possibility that is realized as we learn to integrate our powerful drive toward unity into our ongoing life as social beings.

The sacramentality of sex emphasizes both the goodness of passion and the importance of commitment. In Exodus, Yahweh makes a personal commitment to His people. "I am Yahweh, your God." You may not have asked for me, you may not on occasion want me, but, like it or not, I'm your God and that's that. And then, just to make sure that the point has not been missed, He informs us that He is a passionate God and wants no other lovers cutting in on His time. (In one of the great idiocies of the history of Christianity, the word was translated as "jealous" for centuries, turning the generous passion of

God into nasty possessiveness. Yahweh is a passionately committed God—that is the essence of the Yahwistic tradition. All else is commentary and explication. When we are on fire with passionate love and committed to the one who has aroused our passion, we are most like God.

The story of a passionate, committed God is consistent with the understanding of passion developed by contemporary social science: commitment needs passion to sustain it over the long haul, and passion needs commitment if it is to keep its flame. Catholics who learn to appreciate the sacramentality of sex experience a continual call to be both passionate and committed. If Church policy applies these insights to the experiences of sexuality in modern society, the Church will once more be able to help people understand the meaning of a basic facet of human existence. Our understanding of sexuality needs an appreciation of the aesthetic, sensuously beautiful dimension of sex, too. Recognizing the sacramentality of sex lays the foundation for a spirituality that will encourage this aesthetic appreciation. Good sex, sacramental sex, needs the same nurturing attention that is given to developing a good prayer life.

Humans desperately need an explanation for their sexual activity that integrates it into the rest of their lives; meaning is required especially for the powerful surprises with which sexual desire assaults them and for the joy and the terror that come from such surprises. In the context of the Catholic imagination, this explanation is found in the story of a passionately playful and joyously committed God Who has fallen in love with us rather as we fall in love with each other. Our experience of falling in love parallels God's falling in love with us and reveals to us God's grace. God's love and our love correlate—they disclose each other.

Humans, alone of all the species we know, must explain to themselves the meaning of their own behavior. We are, as the anthropologist Clifford Geertz has often remarked, meaning-bestowing creatures. Our genetic programming is meager. We are born with relatively few charts to guide us through life. Rather we fashion our own charts by imposing meaning on the disorderly phenomena that assail our senses and by integrating them into patterned explanations that give order, direction, and purpose. Deprive a human of meaning for an area of behavior and the human is confused, disoriented, immobile.

Sexuality has baffled us since we began to reflect. It is essential for our species, extremely pleasurable, and often absolutely deadly. We have always been like poor Woody Allen, desperately confused about sex but not ready to give it up merely because of our confusion.

To develop the Catholic instinct about sexuality requires an understanding of this correlation between our experience of ourselves as sexual beings and the explanation of life's meaning presented in the Scriptures and interpreted by the Catholic heritage through the ages. The first step in this process of combining life and faith entails listening to the experience of sex.

The couple in our opening scenario were surprised by a physical attraction to each other that they had not experienced, or at least not acknowledged, during the intense campaign of the previous year. The key element in their story is its unexpected intrusion of a sexual attraction at a time when they believed that they had sex under "control." Who has not been surprised by an unexpected bodily attraction and/or reaction? When we are least prepared to feel "sexy," something happens. Perhaps an extremely attractive member of the other sex sits next to us on our way to school one morning. Or a co-worker, whom we never thought of in terms of his sexuality, communicates with us in such a way that we feel stirrings of desire. Or an attractive neighbor, who was always only "Little Joey's mother," decides to sunbathe in her bikini when we are working in the garden. Or a scene in a novel or movie causes a new string of fantasies.

We are caught up short, surprised by the intensity of the sexual drive that diverts our attention. We intended to study for an accounting exam on the bus that morning. We needed to concentrate on the information our co-worker was giving us. We wanted to hurry through the gardening and rush off to a game of tennis. We planned to do a critical appraisal of the novel or movie. Our ability to "control" our bodies is called into doubt.

We might react to such an experience with the same frustration that Delores, the heroine in Marilyn French's novel *The Bleeding Heart,* exhibits when she laments that her body continually betrays her, leading her into relationships her mind tells her to avoid. Or remembering admonitions heard in our youth, we might feel guilty because we cannot control our feelings or even angry because our bodies have caused us to experience such feelings. Or we might simply find the experience enjoyable and not be bothered by its significance.

Whatever our reactions are to what happens to us at these surprise moments reveals a significant aspect of human sexuality. We alone of all the primates are able to be "sexy" at times other than when the female is fertile. This would suggest that the reproduction needs of *Homo sapiens* required a different kind of sexuality than that of the other primates.

In the struggle for survival in a world of hunting and gathering, our species could allow its young a longer period of development in which to learn the non-genetically programmed skills of survival. Our ancient ancestors were able to do this because of the quasi pair-bonding function of human sexuality. The human female's interest in sex at times other than those necessary for conception allowed her to bind a man to her for that period necessary to assure his protection of her and their child. We experience surprise moments of sexual arousal because our ancient ancestors were genetically programmed with a readiness for sex. The archaeologist Richard Leakey sums up the thinking of many scientists when he says that it appears that very early on in human history a man and a woman entered into "an economic contract in which the product was children," which in time led to the forming of an emotional bonding. However, this bonding function of human sexuality was not genetically determined as it is in some species of birds. Again to quote Leakey, "We were conceived in an animal world but came to maturity in a self-generating culture." Our ability to assign different meanings to our surprise moments of sexual arousal springs from this, that we determine the meaning of these experiences. Though there is a genetic propensity toward bonding, how sex binds, whether it binds, when it binds, and why it binds differ from culture to culture and among individuals within cultures. What does not differ is the fact that humans, no matter what their cultures, may experience the power of their sexual drive at unexpected times and in unexpected situations, and this has vast implications for how human society orders its life.

Our attitudes today toward the meaning of our sexual drives and our resulting actions derive from cultural attitudes toward sex, some of which go back to prehistoric times. Every culture in human history has attempted to "explain" this dimension of life, most often with a religious interpretation. Society's reproductive needs require control of the sexual drive in the service of survival of the clan, tribe, country, or nation; the "will of the gods" dictates when, where, why, and with whom one engages in sexual activity.

Primitive cultures believed that the gods were present in an act of intercourse, and fertility rites to assure successful harvests were carefully controlled by religious leaders, who took no chances that the sexual drive would not be used in service to the community. More advanced cultures, patriarchal in orientation, considered sexual mores and sex-role regulation essential to assure the continuation of humanity. Despite the human propensity toward emotional bonding, most cultures emphasized the reproductive aspects of human sexuality.

Rules for sexual behavior developed in such cultures are not valid (at least not for the same reasons) in a culture that no longer considers reproductive survival a matter of overriding concern. We are freer than were our ancestors to explore the bonding potential of our sexuality. One mystery remains, however: the mystery of intimacy. Our powerful and surprising sexual drive impels us toward intimacy with others, yet we all fear the demands of intimacy. What means this paradox of attraction and repulsion?

Social scientists who study human growth emphasize the importance of developing a capacity for intimacy at the same time that they acknowledge how difficult it is to achieve it, especially over a long life with the inevitable ups and downs. One of the "mysteries" we encounter, one of those situations that we don't fully understand, is the seeming contradiction between our desire for intimacy and our desire for independence. But perhaps we are simply searching for appropriate ways to be "sexy," to acknowledge our genetic sexual drive and its propensity toward bonding. The hint of a potential for intimacy that is offered in every experience of sexual arousal was easily lost in cultures that needed to "control" the sexual drive for reproductive purposes; it can just as easily be lost in a society that fails to appreciate the link between sex and bonding. We have a genetic propensity for bonding, but this tendency needs nurturing if it is to overcome all the obstacles it will encounter.

The power of the sexual drive that intruded into our campaigners' well-ordered lives is a natural development of a sexuality "conceived in an animal culture but come to maturity in a self-generating culture." We might, at times, wish that we were not subjected to this erratic tendency of our body, but there is little we can do to suppress its influence on our lives, even when we have more or less successfully integrated it into a mature adult personality. Our sex drive retains its power of surprise.

David Tracy maintains that our sexuality is the last outpost of the extraordinary in our experience. We may, it is true, be moved by a beautiful sunset, terrified by an earthquake, or awed by the power of a roaring sea; we might even be led to think about the God Who we believe is responsible for all of Creation when we witness such events. However, we either understand what forces of nature are at work in these phenomena or at least know there is someone who does. But our experiences of ourselves as sexual beings continually confront us with challenges we do not fully understand, no matter how familiar we are with all the scientific studies of human sexuality. The bliss of falling in love, the sorrow of unrequited love, the ecstasy of a good experience of love-making, the frustration of an inability to communicate with a beloved, the surprise intensity of our attraction to another person's body are all experiences that lead us to want to understand more about why these things happen. We begin looking for answers, searching for explanations.

Our sexual drive propels us toward union with the person who excites us. Since it is impossible to obtain a response from every person who excites us, we come to learn that we are restricted in our ability to exercise our sexual potential independently. Sex makes us aware of the social dimension of human existence. We must in some fashion or the other "relate" to another (though in some instances only at the most minimal level) if we hope to enter even a limited sexual union. Our fellow primates, who only respond at genetically determined times, don't have to "figure out" how to live as sexual beings. We not only have to determine how to live as sexual beings, we must also spend a major portion of our emotional energies on this aspect of our existence.

Catholicism tells us that our sexual drive is a reminder of God's presence in our midst. It invites us to a union in which we will be a

113

reflection of the God in Whose image we were created, male and female. Every sexual stirring is a potential for increasing this awareness, even when it does not or cannot lead to a union. Scientists would call it a genetic propensity; the Catholic instinct would call it a gift of creation, a sacrament, a way in which we can discover more about our God and Her/His plan for human existence.

Since sex, passion, and the body are goods to be celebrated as sacraments, the sacramental understanding of sex offers a hint about how to live our lives as persons with a powerful sexual drive. The Catholic heritage's understanding of sex as good, as sacramental, suggests that we look to the "story" of God for hints about how to have a sex life that is sacramental, that helps us both to discover and to reveal God. We turn to the story not for an exact formula to give us specific directions for every question that arises in our experiences as sexual beings; rather, we search the story for hints of what sex might mean in our lives.

We often return to that story of Christmas for an understanding of the "why" of an experience. What stories might we return to when we are confronted with a "why" in our experiences of sexuality? What stories will serve as continual reminders of the sacramentality of sex? What accounts of God/human and human/human relationships might serve as a basis for a spirituality of sexuality? How might church policymakers use these stories to help "save" Catholicism?

The story of our falling in love captures the essence of how the sexual drive functions as sacramental. This human experience "correlates" with the story of God's falling in love with us and thus reveals the positive function sexuality can play in our life.

Do we fall in love?

Of course.

God falls in love, too.

Really? With whom?

With us.

Really? That's interesting. The same way we do?

A lot as we do—with passion and commitment.

No kidding? God's really like that?

No kidding. God is like us and we are like God, the more passionate and committed we are, the more we are like God.

Wow!

Perhaps we are with a long-time friend and the feeling that has been gradually developing suddenly surfaces in our consciousness, or we are with a virtual stranger and are struck as if by a bolt of lightning. Our heart races; our nerves tingle. We find ourselves wanting the other, not just for a night in bed, but totally and completely. Our reaction is physical, but it is more than sexual. We sense that there is so much "more" to the person than the beauty of maleness or femaleness and we want to explore that more. We are falling in love; if the feeling is mutual, we move into what we are convinced is a realm of existence different from that which those around us inhabit.

We feel a call to move beyond ourselves. Our beloved becomes the focus of our attention. Our self-complacency is shattered. Our independence is threatened. Yet we make no effort to resist the attraction. We delight in the discovery of this other person and experience a desire to be with her or him for the rest of our lives. We are overwhelmed by the thought that another person feels the same about us. Though we might not even be aware of it, when we fall in love we are involved in a deeply religious experience. Falling in love reveals for us the exciting possibilities in human existence. We are like Adam and Eve when they discover each other in the garden and are called to be the image (revelation) of God in Creation.

We know that life with our beloved will be so much richer and more exciting than what now appears to have been the dull existence of all of our past life. We begin to feel what it was like for the Israelites to be called from slavery in Egypt, convinced that their God would lead them into a land of milk and honey. We comprehend the experience of the poor fishermen called to walk the roads of Israel with the stranger who promises a new life. We understand the excitement that must have existed in the towns of the Gentile world when Saint Paul arrived with an exciting message about life "according to the Spirit." We have been touched by God.

In the glow of falling in love, partners rejoice in each other's presence; when the other is not physically present they experience her or his presence in a fantasy world that often causes friends and co-workers to realize that something is afoot—such bliss can only come from love. Those who are familiar with the partner might well be surprised at the description of her or his qualities, never having perceived such attributes in their encounters with her or him. Falling in love allows us to ignore another's shortcomings and allows the other to discover qualities in us of which we had been unaware. When others find our perceptions unreasonable we respond as Yahweh does in Paddy Chayefsky's play *Gideon:* "Passion has no reason."

For it is passion that is at the root of our experience of falling in love. It is passion that continues the feeling of bliss (even when we experience uncertainty about the depth of our lover's feeling about us). It is passion that makes falling in love an occasion for great rejoicing. Though our love is for the whole person of our beloved, we experience our initial attraction in the recognition that here is another with whom we can become "one flesh," another who is like us ("bone of my bones and flesh of my flesh," to quote Adam) and yet sufficiently different and exciting to make us eager to give up the isolation that has kept us safe from the demands of commitment.

Many psychologists are contemptuous of the "romanticism" of falling in love. It is adolescent behavior, unworthy of mature and sophisticated adults. But if it were not for the residue of adolescent desire that lingers in us at any age, the species might not have perpetuated itself, and most human intimacies would have withered away from boredom. More to the point, one ought not to judge behavior by its most superficial manifestation or by the harm it can cause when it is not guided by responsible intelligence. Like everything that pertains to human sexuality, falling in love can become destructive and demonic. But it must be judged by its wise and mature use and not by its shallow and destructive abuse. Precisely because it contains within it a strain toward permanence, a dream of "happy ever after," a propensity for commitment, falling in love strives for responsibility and maturity even when it is unable to achieve it.

Falling in love that succeeds in achieving commitment bestows grace, i.e., reveals what God is like and unites us with God's committed love. The experience of falling in love is like a great feast, perhaps a private feast shared only by the two lovers, but still a celebration in which normal patterns of living are suspended so the lovers may rejoice in their love. Like the lovers in the Song of Songs, most lovers revel in the delight of each other's bodies. Though we might use different imagery, who cannot appreciate the passion behind these descriptions:

Sex As Sacramental Experience

Behold you are fair, my darling,
Behold you are fair.
Your eyes are doves
Behind your veil.
Your hair like a flock of shorn goats
Streaming down Mount Gilead.
Your teeth like a flock of ewes
Coming up from washing,
All of them twinning,
None bereft among them
Like a scarlet fillet your lips,
Your mouth comely.
Like a pomegranate slice your brow
Behind your veil.
Like David's tower your neck,
Built in courses.
A thousand shields hung on it,
All bucklers of heroes.
Your breasts like two fawns,
Twins of a gazelle,
Browsing on the lotus . . .
You are all fair, my darling.
Blemish there is none in you . . .
You ravish my mind, my sister, my bride,
You ravish my mind with one of your eyes,
With a single gem of your necklace.
How fair your love,
My sister, bride.
Sweeter your love than wine,
The scent of your perfume than any spice.
Your lips drip honey, bride,
Honey and milk under your tongue,
And the scent of your robes
Is like the scent of Lebanon.

My love is radiant and ruddy,
Conspicuous above a myriad.
His head finest gold,
His locks luxuriant,

Black as raven.
His eyes like doves by waterducts,
Splashing in milky spray
Sitting by brimming pools.
His cheeks like spice beds,
Burgeoning aromatics
His lips lotuses,
Dripping liquid myrrh.
His arms rods of gold,
Studded with gems;
His loins smoothest ivory,
Encrusted with sapphires.
His legs marble pillars,
Based on sockets of gold.
His aspect like the Lebanon,
Choice as the cedars.
His mouth is sweet,
And all of him desirable.
This is my love, this is my mate,
O Jerusalem girls.

When we are in our lover's presence, assured of love, we again feel that life is meant to be like the feast we are experiencing, and we ask for a commitment that will keep this feast alive:

Set me as a signet on your heart,
As a signet on your arm.
For love is strong as death,
Passion fierce as Hell.
Its darts are darts of fire,
Its flames [the flames of Yahweh himself].
Mighty waters cannot quench love.
No torrents can sweep it away.

These verses from the Song of Songs capture the essence of falling in love. An experience, rooted in the genetic propensity of our sexual drive for a union with another, reveals a new dimension of existence. A passionate response to a beloved reminds us of the passion of our God. We become open to the possibility of commitment and experience the hope that our love will never be destroyed, not even by death. We are enriched by the positive qualities of this event. A body that can both attract another and be attracted to another is experienced as a most gracious gift, a gift which is like God, a gift that reveals God's grace.

When we fall in love, our sexual drive propels us toward unity in a creative way. We must now ask, How is it possible to live our lives as sexual beings with the same appreciation of the positive possibilities our bodies reveal when we fall in love? What does the wonder of falling in love tell us about how to nourish the commitment we are called to in this encounter? What is there about our sexuality when we fall in love that speaks to all of our experiences as sexual beings?

Playfulness and commitment are indeed polarities, but they are not contradictory. They require each other. The festivity of falling in love, the play of lovers playing at the "game" of being in love, offer a clue as to how one lives a mature sexuality. For lovers sex is playful, and their relationship exists in a different kind of reality than that of the mundane world. True lovers want commitment, believe that it is possible (often in spite of great obstacles), and are convinced that the game of love will go on forever. As a cynical Brazilian poet put it, "Undying love is impossible. It withers like a flame. Yet while it lasts, let it be eternal." Mature people realize the importance of playfulness for sexual fulfillment and strive to incorporate it into their understanding of sex.

Sacramental sex is sex that is playful, sex that is fun, and sex that is relational. Unlike the *Playboy* notion of sex as playful and noninvolving, the Song of Songs image of playful sex includes the desire for commitment. Scriptural scholars debate whether this book of the Bible is simply a collection of love poems or if it was written explicitly to explain the relationship between Yahweh and Israel; they also are not in agreement as to whether the couple is married. Whatever the reason for the presence of this book in the Bible, its writer or writers (the scholar Roland Murphy suggests that perhaps women had a hand in the writing of this book) viewed sex as contributing to the playfulness of the lovers' relationship, and understood that the joy of the world of falling in love demands a playful response.

Properly understood, the Catholic sensibility should encourage lovers to play together because they have discovered that life, despite its inevitable tragedy, is meant to incorporate the fantasy, festivity, and celebration encountered in the joy of falling in love. But sex as play does not mean the empty, noncommitted, nonrelational, impersonal sex of the *Playboy* ideal. On the contrary, the *Playboy* philosophy is destructive of play. By its very nature play is not casual; within the context of the game, play lays down indispensable norms that must be taken seriously. It is necessary for those who would "play together" to have shared some sense of what they mean by what they are doing. There must be some element of commitment in sex if it is to be playful.

The physical drive toward unity has a strong underlying current pulling the lovers toward commitment and intimacy. Even within the feast of falling in love, however, there remains another strong current of independence that pulls the partners apart. The pull toward intimacy is joyful; the counter-pull is caught up in the somberness of the tasks of everyday life, a somberness that many fear is an inevitable ingredient of commitment. Yet without commitment, the romance of falling in love fades as the lovers find the tension and uncertainty of the mundane world threatening to become part of the real world of being in love. It becomes difficult to be playful when one grows uncertain about one's partner's commitment to the game. Commitment is difficult; it is threatening. You can make a commitment only if you are convinced that the playfulness will continue despite all the other tasks of life, that playfulness will keep the mundane tasks from their interference with the world of the game, which is equally important.

In short, the playfulness of sex is resisted only at the price of losing its potential as a binding power in intimacy, and playfulness will survive only when it is rooted in the context of a long-term, committed, total relationship in which hope and love are real. Human dynamics rule out the possibility that noninvolved sex will ever be truly playful. Depth, richness, variety, and playfulness in sex require a partner with whom one is willing to explore, develop and grow, experiment, make mistakes, and persevere over a lifetime. Commitment, while not guaranteeing playfulness, is still the absolute prerequisite for it. Of course, as with the couple in our opening scenario, sexual desire may intrude surprisingly in instances where there is no possibility of fulfilling it. These experiences serve to remind us of the graciousness of the gift of our sexual drive, and this in turn should encourage us to embrace a playful—i.e., hopeful—attitude toward all of human existence. We can respond in this way when we allow our religious imaginations to recognize the analogical side of the sacramentality of sex.

The God we discover lurking in the power of our sexual drive is the God of falling in love. God is like a lover or like me when I am a lover. We who believe that our sexuality is a gift from the God who created us also believe that we are created "in the image of God, male and female"; we believe that we are an image of God, a mirror of the God who created us not as some disembodied spirits, but as sexual beings.

The correlation between the passionate and committed playfulness of God and our own passionate and committed playfulness has not always been evident to Catholic teachers. The same influences that sought to "control" the erotic and bonding potential of sexuality in order to assure reproductive survival also resisted the implications of Genesis, which is the source of our belief in the sacramentality of all nature. The ancient Israelite leaders seemed to have waged a continual battle with the attraction of the fertility cults, and frequently condemned their rituals. And many of their purity rituals give the impression that certain aspects of sexuality, especially female sexuality, were viewed as evil. Still, throughout Judaism and Christianity we find reminders that sex can reveal aspects of divinity. The God of the Covenant (Exodus, chapter 20) is like a passionate, committed lover, promising faithfulness and demanding it of the beloved, Israel. The prophets—especially Isaiah, Hosea, and Ezekiel—represent God as a spouse. The love that joined Yahweh to Israel is like the love of a married couple, with Yahweh remaining faithful even when Israel wanders. And both Jewish and Christian interpreters have seen the Song of Songs as an analogical interpretation of the love between Yahweh and Israel. If God is like even one of the partners in a sexual act, then it would seem difficult to maintain a condemnation of the act.

Saint Paul, who at times seems doubtful about the positive value of sex, still continues the reference to God as a spouse or lover; he views the image of a man and wife clinging together as representative of the relationship between Christ and the Church. Somehow Christ and the Church, both sacred symbols, are like a man and a woman who cling to each other so as to become "one flesh."

While Church authorities, at times begrudgingly, accepted the necessity of sex for reproduction, many thinkers also cautioned against enjoying sex, even with one's lawful partner. Manichean attitudes toward sex infiltrated the official level of the Church. Sex was seen as a distraction from things divine that drew one into the murky world of temptation and evil. In certain eras, cultural practices bordering on hedonism understandably led serious Christians to be wary of the abuses of the sexual life. Yet the sacramental instinct that said that all creation is revelatory ought to have protected Catholic thinkers from sweeping and obsessive denunciations of physical love. There were fortunately some Catholic thinkers who dissented from the conventional wisdom that sex was at best tolerable and at worst evil. One of the more sensitive of these dissenters was the medieval monk Richard of the monastery of Saint Victor.

More important, Thomas Aquinas saw through all the Manichean and Platonic nonsense and asserted the self-evident truth that sex was for loving. Aquinas's dissent is critical because, while he was only one theologian, he was the most influential one for at least a millennium. To its considerable embarrassment, the Church did not listen to him.

Despite Richard of Saint Victor and despite Aquinas, the Platonic and Augustinian suspicions of sex persisted. Even the decision at the Council of Trent (1545–1563) to consider marriage one of the Seven Sacraments was less than full endorsement of the sacramentality of human sexuality. Still, the instinct that sex was sacramental persisted as a minor theme, most probably influenced by the cultures with which the Church mixed and by the ordinary experience of lay people and married clergy who knew that their passionate love was not evil.

Another strain of Catholicism that continued to recognize the analogical power of human sexuality is seen in the writings of the mystics. For example, Saint Teresa of Avila reflects a strong mystical tradition in *Interior Castle* when she uses the metaphor of betrothal and marriage to describe the unique relationship between a personal God and His/Her human creatures. In the "Fifth Mansion," on the way to complete transfiguration and communion with God, Saint Teresa writes that one resembles a person who has encountered a lover and looks forward to a betrothal to the God Whose great love has so "completely subdued it that it neither knows nor desires anything save that God shall do with it what He will." In the "Sixth Mansion," Teresa recounts how "Our Lord treats those He makes His Brides," describing the Spiritual Betrothal in which the Spouse and Bride meet, and, as in the Song of Songs, He leaves her, disregarding the soul's ever-increasing "yearnings for the conclusion of the betrothal, desiring that they should become still deeper." Then, "moved by delectable desire," the soul is granted opportunities to praise God, even through painful afflictions and trials. The yearning of separated lovers is echoed by Teresa, addressing her God, "Lord, how thou dost afflict thy lovers." In the "Seventh Mansion," Teresa continues this analogy, seeing the union for which all lovers yearn achieved as "God has been pleased to unite Himself with His creature" and "will not separate Himself from her," giving her the assurance of his Presence at her side all of her life. God will never dissolve this spiritual marriage where, given the "kiss for which the Bride besought him," the soul enjoys peace, free from "the usual movements of the faculties and imagination."

In this account of the "transformation of an imperfect and sinful creature into the Bride of the Spiritual Marriage," Teresa affirms the sacramental possibilities of the experience of falling in love, using this experience as an analogy for the prayer life that will help the soul achieve its desire for union with God.

Saint John of the Cross, a contemporary of Teresa's, also imagines God as a Lover when he describes the experience of a soul achieving union with God by the way of spiritual negation. The Catholic imagination is seen as responding to the sacramental possibilities of the sexual drive with these words:

> *Upon a gloomy night,*
> *With all my cares to loving ardours flushed,*
> *(O venture of delight!)*
> *With nobody in sight*
> *I went abroad when all my house was hushed . . .*

> *Upon a lucky night*
> *In secrecy, inscrutable to sight,*
> *I went without discerning*
> *And with no other light*
> *Except for that which in my heart was burning . . .*

Oh night that was my guide!
Oh darkness dearer than the morning's pride,
Oh night that joined the lover
To the beloved bride
Transfiguring them each into the other.

Within my flowering breast
Which only for himself entire I save
He sank into his rest
And all my gifts I gave
Lulled by the airs with which the cedars wave.

Over the ramparts fanned
While the fresh wind fluttering his tresses,
With his serenest hand
My neck he wounded, and
Suspended every sense with its caresses.

Lost to myself I stayed
My face upon my lover having laid
From all endeavor ceasing:
And all my cares releasing
Threw them among the lilies there to fade.

Meister Eckhart also celebrates the power of love to take one out of oneself, seeing the soul as the "she" in a love relationship with God in these words:

> Oh wonder of wonders! When I think of the union of the soul with God! He makes the soul to flow out of herself in joyful ecstasy for no named things content her. And since she is herself a nature named, therefore she fails to content herself. The divine love-spring surges over the soul, sweeping her out of herself into the unnamed being in her original source, for that is all God is.

As in James Joyce's description of Stephen's encounter with the young girl on the beach at Clontarf, this mystical power of sex also works on the imagination of writers. Rosemary Haughton argues that Dante's original encounter with Beatrice had a significant impact on Dante's development as a Christian poet. According to Haughton, Dante's first encounter with Beatrice was for him what many lovers describe as an "Oh my God!" experience. It stirred the depths of his imagination and led him to appreciate the relationship between this "good" in his life and the "good" (God) of the eternal life toward which he was striving. His beloved colored everything in his life from then on. She even inspired him to speak of God the way he spoke of her. She was the "savior" because "she is also without attenuation, Beatrice, an 'everyday' young woman of most solid earthiness."

Those lovers who do not have the mystic's direct encounter with God or who lack the poetic imagination of a Dante or a Joyce still at times find that their "Oh my God!" experiences of a lover move them not only to be aware of God's presence, but also to think of God as a lover. Research on the religious imagination supplies evidence of three ways in which a positive sexual encounter can lead to behavior which suggests that these experiences have influenced the religious imagination of the lovers, even if only at an unconscious level.

First of all, the research indicates a positive correlation between a person's sexual satisfaction in marriage and his or her tendency to think of God as a "lover." Second, in those marriages where the husband considers the sexual relationship satisfactory, he is more inclined to engage in religious practices than a husband who does not have a sexually satisfying relationship with his spouse. Finally, statistics on the "angry" Catholic woman indicate that the image of God as a "lover" positively affects the Church attendance of this type of woman.

A number of policy recommendations can be suggested for Catholic sexual teaching:

1. The Church must encourage its members to become better lovers—more playful, more passionate, more skillful, more challenging. The better Catholics are as lovers, the more fully will they experience God and the more adequately will they reveal Him/Her.

2. The Church must sustain lovers through periods of difficulty and conflict. For the Catholic, the hope of lovers that their love will last forever is not doomed to tragic disappointment. The lovers in the Song of Songs recognize that their love will be strong as death when they keep the flames of Yahweh Himself (passion) alive. They do not deny the destructive possibility of death—either literal or figurative—

but they believe that Yahweh, who gave them this passion, will help them avoid destruction.

3. The Church must help lovers to renew their loves. Marriage is not a smooth curve drawn on the chart of life. It is, rather, a series of cycles, of deaths and rebirths, of old endings and new beginnings, of falling in love again. Marriage is a sequence of surprise love affairs with the same person. The Catholic sensibility confirms the hope of all lovers that playful sex will endure when passion and commitment are joined in a relationship of intimacy. It recognizes that the strain toward intimacy that is present in every sexual encounter is a strain toward the formation of an organic community capable of repeated renewal. It is never too late to begin again.

One strategy for a Church policy concerned to recapture the positive potential in our religious sensibility would be to use the theme of sexuality during Holy Week, demonstrating how we need to die to our abuse of sexuality in order to allow its sacramental potential to reveal that the Risen Lord is committed to us in the same way as a lover is committed to a beloved. The religious imagination of anyone who is familiar with the experience of falling in love undoubtedly would be stirred by such a technique.

The Catholic view of sex is comic. It refutes those suspicions that underlie the Manichaean tendency to view sex as evil because of its demonic potential. It accepts the fact that individuals and societies have caused physical and psychological harm to themselves and others because of failure to live sex sacramentally. Still, the comic story tells us that sex does not have to be lived in this destructive manner. And even when a person fails to appreciate the sacramentality of sexuality, the comic power of the sexual drive (the flame of Yahweh Himself) continually challenges him or her to understand its ultimate meaning. The strain of the sexual drive toward unity may be ignored, dousing the comic flames of Yahweh, but the sparks smolder, ready to burst into flame and burn away the resistance to intimacy.

This power of the sexual drive propels us to intimacy, to union with another, to the formation of a community rooted in love, which becomes a model of the committed, passionate love of God. Our religious sensibility helps us appreciate this power of the sexual drive to reveal how community should be lived if it is to be truly human, if it is to be "in the image of God." The comic union that is the goal of sacramental (revelatory) sex is a model from which we learn how to live all our human relationships—those among individuals, communities, religious groups, and nations. The intimate relationship of lovers, shored up by passion and commitment, sheds light on how to overcome the mundaneness that can eventually destroy any relationship or community.

The concern and respect for each other, the need to work together to overcome inevitable obstacles from within and without, and the willingness of both to give and to receive that characterizes those relationships that reveal God as Lover should be the hallmark of relationships within an institution committed to carrying on the task of revealing God to the world.

Our readers may wonder why we have not discussed the "real" issues of sex and sexual morality. How can any Catholic discussion of sex avoid the topic of morality? It is all well and good to talk about sacramental sex revealing a passionate God, but what does that have to do with the couple in the opening scenario and with the decisions we have to make in situations that excite our sexual drives? Or perhaps some will say that the claim that sex leads to hopefulness sounds good, but what about all the nonhopeful sexual activity in the world? How can we ignore the myriad forms of sexual exploitation, some of which mask as a way to sexual fulfillment? In short, what are the rules or at least the guidelines for how to act in light of a Catholic sensibility?

Sexual morality per se has not been discussed in this analysis for three reasons. First, the concern of this volume is not with morality or ethics but with religion. The Catholic sensibility is not concerned with sexual morality as such. Second, Church statements on sexual morality are in any case ineffective. Catholics who followed Church rules on sex in the past, because that was what a "good" Catholic did or because they feared hell, did not necessarily discover the sacramentality of sex. Most Catholics today no longer consider themselves bound to the rules the Church lays down for them about sex because they don't think the Church knows what it is talking about. The problem for the Church created by this attitude will not be solved by more rules but by re-establishing itself as a credible teacher. Finally, moral pronouncements on sexuality should follow, not precede, an acknowledgment of the sacramentality of sex. Then the Church will be in a position where it can invite *all* Catholics to be a part of the moral decision-making process.

The alternatives provided by the "new" Catholic sexual ethic, which many theologians have offered in opposition to the old traditional morality, disagree with the Church's traditional teaching on birth control, premarital sex, divorce, homosexuality, and other sexual behavior. But it is unclear that the followers of "permissive" or "situational" or "liberated" sexual ethics are in fact "freed" by the revolution. Premarital intercourse, for example, does not necessarily lead to marriages that are any more sensitive or durable. The problem is not in the rules but in the systems of meaning applied to sexual behavior. It is important to have rules, but they are no substitute for an overarching system of meaning that links sex to the ultimate purposes of life—religion, in other words.

The proponents of the "new" Catholic sexual morality, often indistinguishable from hedonists, seem innocent of the sacramental and revelatory dimension of sexuality. They share with traditional moralists the tendency to equate approval or disapproval of an activity with a religious understanding of the meaning of life. Codes, guidelines, and pronouncements especially relating to sex become a substitute for the challenge of finding meaning in human sexual experience.

A revolutionary change in the Catholic approach to sexuality was contained in Pope John Paul II's "Audience Talks." From September 1979 to April 1981, he presented a series of 56 Wednesday addresses on a theology of sexuality and the body. He argued that the "nuptial" meaning of the body—its sexual differentiation and its propensity for unity with the opposite sex—is sacramental, that it reveals the propensity of human nature for union in love with God. He also suggested that dealing with issues of sexual morality according to rules will not provide an answer to the basic question of the meaning of sexuality, a question he, too, sees as a prior question to that of whether certain behaviors are contrary to the law of God.

This chapter has been little more than a commentary on what the Pope said in these talks. He has a poor reputation on this topic—inaccurate reporting and the negative response to many of his other statements on sexual morality have led many Catholics to turn off when they hear that the Pope has spoken on sex. This is tragically unfortunate. The Pope's remarkable theories have at last repudiated the Manichees and the Puritans. Better late than never.

Chapter 8

. . . .

WOMAN AS ANALOG
OF GOD

The Catholic Church will not be able to bear witness to the sacramentality of sex until it rids itself of a deeply ingrained, and largely unacknowledged, bias against women. This bias not only rejects the personhood of woman but also fails to acknowledge the fullness of God, who is mirrored in creatures, male and female, made in the "image of God."

The Church can no longer be excused for its anti-woman attitude on the grounds that other institutions have a similar anti-woman tradition and that it will take time to adjust to women's newly discovered aspirations. The Church should be in the forefront of efforts to affirm the personhood of woman. This will require a concerted effort to eliminate all those ideas and practices that grew out of and continue to support anti-woman attitudes and behavior.

In addition, at all levels—from Rome down to the local parish—the Church must celebrate the sacramentality of woman's body as this idea has been nurtured in the religious imagination of the Catholic tradition. "Stories" of the femininity of God in the Bible, in the accounts of some mystics, and in the popular celebrations of the Mary myth, coupled with "stories" of the contribution women have made to the growth and development of Catholicism, need to be told and retold until they are integrated into the treasury of our religious imaginations.

Church policy would improve vastly if there were an increased emphasis on woman as an analog for God—that is, God is like a woman, but God is more than a woman. The shattering potential of this idea makes it the logical antidote to the Church's present paralysis on women's issues.

Five specific concerns of American women call for a Catholic response that considers the feminine experience in a positive light:

1. Women are questioning the "naturalness" of assigned gender identities and roles. Longer life, less time spent on child rearing, and technological aids in the home and at work have created opportunities for women that their ancestors would never have imagined possible. At the same time, the old models for "correct" womanly behavior no longer apply. Women are left to work out on their own how they might grow and develop without giving up what they feel is valuable in feminine experience.

2. Women are aware that their inferior status leads to exploitation. Many women in the past accepted their inferiority as "natural," as part of God's plan, but increasingly, women are rejecting obstacles to personhood and questioning the exploitation that accompanies this view. Wife abuse, rape, prostitution, unequal pay, lack of work opportunities, and other forms of discrimination are no longer accepted as inevitable burdens to be borne silently. (American women are not the only ones rejecting assigned sex roles. In a television special, "Journey to Survival," a primitive tribal woman complains how unfair it is that the women in her tribe must bear all the burden of the daily search for water. Why don't the men help with this exhausting task? And many women in the past have also rankled under oppression and expressed similar private complaints. Church officials who feel that the "women's issue" is only a problem for a handful of radical American nuns don't understand the deep effect on women of a history of "second-class" citizenship.)

3. Because femininity has been viewed as inferior, the movement of women into new positions of power has been accompanied by a

questioning of all feminine values. Many women choose to copy the male mode of behavior—modes of dress, aggressiveness, sex without strings. Some of this anti-feminine attitude is present in a different guise among feminists who reject attempts to celebrate the beauty of the feminine body.

4. Some women consider religion, especially institutional religion, to be the major source and perpetrator of their identity problems. This feeling is not limited to radical women who have rejected any hope that patriarchal religion will address their needs. Indeed, between a million and a million and a half Catholic women who would not consider themselves radical no longer attend Church regularly because they blame the Church for their current problems with role identity. In addition, many women who are active Church participants are upset and embarrassed by the behavior of Church officials who try to intimidate women in religious orders and who seem concerned that female acolytes will tarnish the celebration of the Eucharist.

5. Women are conscious of a polarity between the sexes that impedes intimacy. More and more, both men and women have felt helpless and angry—feelings that get acted out against each other all too often.

To nurture the Catholic sensibility on women's issues, the Church must, first of all, examine the strong element of mistrust, fear, and even hatred of women in its tradition; on the other hand, it should recall its own sensitivity to the Divine plan for human sexuality reflected in the story of the "beginning." The former must be rooted out; the latter will serve as a basis for positive policies.

We should not be surprised at anti-women attitudes in ancient Israelite writings. Mistrust, fear, and even hatred of women are understandable reactions in a culture that did not understand the mysteries of human reproduction. Women were set apart by their loss of large amounts of blood each month and by their ability to bear and nurse the next generation. These mysterious creators who were familiar enough to be powerfully sexually attractive, but nonetheless unlike, threatened men, whose physical powers allowed them to dominate.

The social condition of women described in the Bible is largely the result of these cultural factors, though, as Pope John Paul II observes, the domination of women is a "peculiar distortion of the original interpersonal relationship of communion, to which the 'sacramental' words of Genesis 2:24 apply." The way in which this distortion has functioned in the Jewish and Christian traditions gives testimony to the deep-rootedness of this "conflict between the sexes"—what the Pope refers to as a "relationship of appropriation" as opposed to a "relationship of gift."

Specific denigrations of women in the Old Testament include the "ownership" of a woman by a man, along with her inability to inherit; greater severity of punishment of women than men for sexual transgressions; divorce and polygamy for men only; and religious laws regarding the impurity of women.

Two of the many Old Testament texts that refer to women in a negative manner illustrate this point:

> I would rather dwell with a lion and a dragon than dwell with an evil wife. . . . Do not be ensnared by a woman's beauty, and do not desire a woman's possessions. There is wrath and impudence and great disgrace when a wife supports her husband. A dejected mind, a gloomy face, and a wounded heart are caused by an evil wife. Drooping hands and weak knees are caused by a wife who does not make her husband happy. From a woman sin had its beginning, and because of her we all die. Allow . . . no boldness of speech in an evil wife. If she does not go as you direct, separate her from yourself. (Sirach 25: 16-26)

> If a woman conceives, and bears a male child, then she shall be unclean seven days; as at the time of her menstruation, she shall be unclean.... Then she shall continue for thirty-three days in the blood of her purifying; she shall not touch any hallowed thing, nor come into the sanctuary, until the days of her purifying are completed. But if she bears a female child, then she shall be unclean two weeks, as in her menstruation; and she shall continue in the blood of her purifying for sixty-six days. (Leviticus 12: 2-6)

This Jewish attitude toward women, challenged only slightly in the Greco-Roman world, characterized the environment in which Christianity had its beginnings. It is not surprising that Saint Paul took an ambivalent, at times negative, approach that leaves his work open to a variety of interpretations on the woman issue. It is possible that he, along with other later New Testament writers, progressively more negative and misogynistic, became the source of Church doc-

trine on women. In his First Epistle to the Corinthians, Saint Paul
wrote:

> But I want you to understand that the head of every man is Christ,
> the head of a woman is her husband, and the head of Christ is
> God.... any woman who prays or prophesies with her head un-
> veiled dishonors her head—it is the same as if her head were
> shaven....For a man ought not to cover his head, since he is
> the image and glory of God; but woman is the glory of man. (For
> man was not made from woman, but woman from man. Neither
> was man created for woman, but woman for man.)

This Biblical element gave rise to negative positions on women
among the Fathers of the Church. Origen summarized the attitude of
the Greek Fathers when he wrote: "What is seen with the eyes of the
Creator is masculine, and not feminine, for God does not stoop to
look upon what is feminine and of the flesh."

Augustine, probably the greatest Father of the Church, influenced by
the dualism of the Manichaeism he had embraced before converting to
Christianity, troubled by his own sexuality, and having developed an ab-
horrence of women, found a religious basis for his negative view:

> Flesh stands for the woman, because she was made out of a
> rib.... The apostle has said: Who loves his woman loves him-
> self; for no one hates his own flesh. Flesh thus stands for the wife,
> as sometimes spirit for the husband. Why? Because the latter rules,
> the former is ruled; the latter would govern, the former should
> serve. For where the flesh governs and the spirit serves, the house
> is upside down. What is worse than a house where the woman has
> governance over the man? But that house is proper where the man
> commands, the woman obeys. So also is that person rightly ordered
> where the spirit governs and the flesh serves.

This negative view of woman persisted largely because the culture
of the times found the ideas acceptable. This same fear, mistrust, and
hatred have persisted in both Church and society up to the present
day. Legitimized in part by Saint Thomas's reflections on women, the
idea of the inferiority of women continued to influence Church teach-

ings and to be taught in seminaries. Though Saint Thomas might not have had a fear of a woman's body (given his views on sex), his thoughts reinforced the fears of men who had reason to distrust women.

This fear of women is at the root of much of the opposition among Church leaders to the ordination of women. Arguments that women cannot "image" Christ, who was a man, have the ring of masculine superiority and, at the same time, indicate a negative attitude towards woman's body. This claim is made not on the basis of the words of Christ, but on the basis of "tradition."

The clerical hatred for women—superbly portrayed, by the way, in Umberto Eco's *The Name of the Rose*—was integral to seminary training well into the middle of the twentieth century. Women's bodies were no longer portrayed as vile swamps designed to trap men or as painted tombstones, but nonetheless one was warned in the seminary to avoid the ballet (pronounced *ballot*, by the way) because of the indecent costumes women dancers wore. (One such condemnation was occasioned by the movie *The Red Danube,* based on Bruce Marshall's novel *Vespers for Vienna,* and the presence in it of a youthful Janet Leigh, considerably more dressed, be it noted, than her daughter Jamie Lee Curtis in movies today.) If the seminary's spiritual director feared that we would run off to the "ballot" to ogle women, he was quite unaware that Irish and Italian and Polish seminarians of that era would not have known where to find a ballet even if they wanted to. (And even the memory of Ms. Leigh in tights was hardly enough to make us want to.) But either the bodies of dancers are sacraments to be admired, within appropriate limitations, or demons from hell to be avoided. In a seminary of the 1950s, as in the monasteries of the 1350s, the option was for the latter choice.

Today's Catholic women are angry at what this tradition has meant for women in the past and continues to mean for them today. Undoubtedly women in the past rejected the idea of "ownership" by a man, but there was little opportunity for a woman to escape her "fate" or to question whether it was rooted in a divine will. Women spent most of their adult years (to live to 35 was considered an achievement) bearing and rearing children (until 200 years ago a woman had to have approximately ten pregnancies and seven live births to assure the survival of two children to the age where they could reproduce), which left them with little opportunity to question the prerogatives of the man who "took care" of them. Most probably their "imaginations" accepted the message of their inferiority that both their husbands and the Church supported.

Women today are angry precisely because of the effect this false tradition has on their imaginations. They don't hear the positive statements on the subject of women made by Church leaders in the parish and beyond; and even if they did, they would not be open to them unless they were rooted in a belief in the personhood of women. Nor are they hearing the "stories" of their religion that would help them "imagine" how to react creatively to the challenges they face. They know little of that element of our Catholic heritage that "imagines" God as feminine and women as persons.

If Catholicism is to be saved, Church leaders will have to reject all traces of the "false" tradition and begin to celebrate the positive understanding of women kept alive by the imaginations of those sensitive to "the beginning" and to the example of Jesus. The presence of this positive element within the tradition undoubtedly accounts for the contributions some women made to the Church and society in the past, and it affects the religious imaginations of those women today who seek to make Church leaders more sensitive to the Catholic sensibility.

We don't know exactly how individual women have come to acquire a Catholic sensibility on women, but despite official negative attitudes on women, the presence of this sensibility throughout our history cannot be denied. The roots of a positive, "true" tradition on women are found in biblical stories of women and of feminine images of God. This tradition continues in the activities of some women throughout the Church's history. As leaders of religious communities, mystics, and challengers of both secular and ecclesiastical authority, their lives refuted the idea of women's inferiority. In addition, the Mary myth preserved an image of the sacredness of women in societies that failed to acknowledge the sacredness of their own women. Though some radical women thinkers reject Mary as a positive symbol for women, her continued presence in the Catholic strand of Christianity has perpetuated an image of sacred femininity.

Beginning with interpretations of the story of Eve, we find that the perception of woman influences what we look for in the Church's tradition. Scholars in the past considered Eve's creation *after* Adam a sign of her inferiority; she was also weak when tempted, and caused Adam to sin because of her wily ways. But Pope John Paul II interprets the Creation story as a tale of the incompleteness of a solitary individual being, who is overcome with the discovery of another *person* ("Bone of my bones and flesh of my flesh"), making it possible for both to unite and become "the image of God." The story of the Fall then becomes the story of two persons who reject the opportunity to live together in a "relationship of gift" in which they reflect God, and choose instead a "relationship of appropriation," where they no longer respect each other as persons. In the Pope's interpretation, the personhood of woman—her equality with man despite the differences in their sexuality—is affirmed. Indeed her differences reveal something about God that is unclear when God is understood only from a male perspective.

In spite of the patriarchal culture, women in Old Testament tales exercised an influence strong enough to be acknowledged. Miriam, Deborah, and Judith were prophets through whom God spoke, akin to the women referred to in Joel: ". . . I will pour out my spirit on all flesh; your sons and your daughters shall prophesy" (Joel 2:28). The women of Tekoa and Abel resolved problems and Deborah acted as a judge. The Queens Athaliah and Salome Alexandra took over the thrones upon the deaths of their husbands.

In addition, "singing women" both created and transmitted the literary culture. (The presence of these women in the Jewish Bible leads some Scripture scholars to theorize that the Song of Songs is a collection of their works. Phyllis Trible goes so far as to interpret it as a midrash of Genesis 2–3: paradise, lost in Genesis, is regained in the Song of Songs. In any case, while celebrating the sacramentality of sex, the Song of Songs presents woman and her body in a positive light.) And even the stories of Judith, Esther, and Jael, often seen as emphasizing female stereotypes, show that women could be instruments of God's wrath against the enemies of Israel. These stories show an ambivalence about women, whose sexual attractiveness causes death to the enemies and reveals the difficulty in acknowledging the personhood of women.

Israel's religion had an ongoing struggle with the influence of goddess worship, leading it to speak of its transcendent God primarily in masculine terms. Still, a number of references to the feminine dimensions of divinity indicate that the "image of God"—the woman with her feminine characteristics—was seen in a positive light, at least some of the time and by some religious leaders.

In various places in the Bible God is portrayed as a Mother, giving birth, nursing and comforting her children, a theme obvious in Isaiah, for example:

> The Lord goes forth.... "Now, I cry out as a woman in travail, I will gasp and pant." [42:13–14]

> But Zion said, "The Lord has forsaken me, my Lord has forgotten me." Can a woman forget her sucking child, that she should have no compassion on the son of her womb? Yet even these may forget, yet I will not forget you. [49:14–15]

> For thus says the Lord: . . . "As one whom his mother comforts, so will I comfort you." [66:12–13]

In other places God is referred to as a seamstress, a midwife, and a mistress, all activities generally associated with women. Another theme in Jewish literature shows Wisdom as a personification of an attribute of God, a personification influenced by the very goddesses whom Judaism wanted to repress. The feminine grammar and the portrayal of Wisdom as a woman mean that any reader of the four books of the Wisdom literature (Proverbs, Wisdom, Baruch, and Sirach) would have been aware of the femininity of Wisdom. She is described in a variety of ways, in particular as a person with earthiness and sexuality.

As one commentator has observed, "Beginning as a personified hypostasis of God, Wisdom grew in stature and importance for the Jews from the fourth century to the first century B.C., until her power was virtually equivalent to that of any Hellenistic goddess. She combined in herself positive and some negative qualities, although she was often paired with another feminine figure called Folly... entirely negative in character."

But does this minor positive strain on women in the Old Testament make any difference to the Church's policy on women? After all, the more dominant strain we are all familiar with has been anti-woman.

Aren't we engaging in a needless exercise, trying to prove that women were regarded more highly than one might at first think?

No, it is not needless. The presence of this alternative attitude toward women is important because it achieved more prominence in the life of Christ and in the beginnings of Christianity. And Church policymakers need to be aware of the positive attitudes of Christ and the early Church for several reasons:

1. Some feminist critics maintain that Christianity is patriarchal and anti-woman at its very core, that it cannot accept the personhood of woman. If, in fact, Jesus and the early Church accorded women a status later denied them, the claim can be supported that the Catholic sensibility recognizes the sacramentality of all creation, including women.

2. If the evidence indicates that Christ treated women as disciples, then his expectations were for *both* women and men to "image" him. Those who oppose the ordination of women can no longer ground their opposition in "the will of Christ."

3. If Christ and the early Church recognized the validity of women's experiences, then the modern Church must follow their example. The insights of both men and women are necessary if the Catholic sensibility is to have an influence in today's world. A Church dominated by males certain that their domination is divinely ordained cannot hope to offer enlightenment to the issues of modern life.

4. Women need to know that they are essential in keeping alive the Catholic sensibility. If Christ expected both women and men to carry on his message of salvation, then women must hear his call addressed to them.

Before considering the evidence of a positive attitude toward women in the New Testament, we must remind ourselves that the Gospels are no longer considered accurate eyewitness accounts of the life and words of Christ. The Gospels are four different portraits of Jesus addressed to four different faith communities. They consist of written and oral material gathered together (scholars say "redacted") to show how the life and message of Jesus applied to the situation of the community to which each Gospel was addressed. Though not meant to be historically accurate, the accounts nonetheless give us information about how the teachings of Jesus took root. Scriptural scholars try to determine how these many-layered stories of Jesus can help us better understand what took place during the life of Jesus and the beginnings of Christianity.

Women were active followers of Jesus. They remained with him even after the male disciples fled in fear. They were the first to whom he appeared after His Resurrection. Accounts of their presence in His life confirm that a positive attitude toward women continued even in the primitive Church communities where women were much more active than we have been led to believe. One of the hallmarks of the earliest Christian communities was their openness to women. This openness eventually threatened the surrounding social structures, which opposed women's leadership because it had a negative effect on family ties. The vision of unity enunciated in the "beginning" and reiterated by Jesus could not be sustained.

Even when fiercely opposed by Church and society, the sacramentality of woman was too strong to be buried. The call that Christ issued to women for personhood and equality is so powerful that many women continued to respond to it, oftentimes unaware that by so doing they were being analogs for God. Even with the strong anti-woman bias of the official Church, women assumed leadership responsibilities and continued Christ's task at times better than their male counterparts.

Among the many who by their lives kept the Catholic sensibility alive were:

1. The deacons and deaconesses. Phoebe and Priscilla of apostolic times and the ordained deaconesses who followed in their footsteps were the "religious education coordinators" of their day. Their ministry, which after the apostolic age appears to have been only to women, undoubtedly contributed to the spread of the Church. Although deaconesses were still functioning in the twelfth century, statements from fifth- and sixth-century councils indicate a much earlier decline in their status.

2. The wives. Many woman converts to Christianity eventually converted their husbands, children, and sometimes whole households. In the early Church and in the barbarian kingdoms of the sixth to eighth centuries, these women often were the first to embrace the Christian faith.

3. The abbesses. Priests, monks, and nuns all took vows of obedience to some of these powerful religious women. The abbesses se-

lected their own priors, dispensing the license to preach, hear confessions, and serve various women's houses. The Abbess Jeanne-Baptise de Bourbon, of the Abbey of Fontevrault, was responsible for the payment of benefices to the forty rectories, chapels, and churches of her priors, and for the nomination of a hundred prioresses dependent on her. In tenth- and eleventh-century Germany, the abbesses of Quedlinburg and Gandershein had permission to strike coins bearing their own portraits. (The Abbess of Quedlinburg had a seat and a vote in the Imperial Diet.) And in twelfth-century England, abbesses were called to Parliament.

4. The Beguines. In twelfth-century Belgium these women lived in communities on the outskirts of towns, caring for the sick and the poor. They took no vows and supported themselves by teaching or manual labor. Unlike orders of nuns, each community was independent, with neither common rule nor general order but with a common purpose and worship. By the end of the thirteenth century practically every town in Germany, England, and France had at least one Beguinage. Many of the Beguinages became centers of mysticism and, at least in the Netherlands, often influenced the religious lives of people more than the monks and the secular clergy.

5. The "Doctors." Although thirteenth- and fourteenth-century theologians denied women the right to be depicted with the halo of Doctor of the Church, women had actually been engaged in scholarly teaching and continued to do so. Hildegard of Bingen was a "prophetess" with encyclopedic learning. Juliana of Liege was the inspiration behind the Feast of Corpus Christi and its liturgical splendor. Bridget of Sweden and Catherine of Siena were involved in politics.

6. The mystics. Perhaps their "inferior" status in the eyes of the official Church and society opened many women to mystical possibilities. Whatever the reasons, women mystics often moved from their mystical experiences into more vocal roles in the Church. Catherine of Siena, who for three years lived a life of solitude culminating in a mystical "espousal" of Christ, eventually felt impelled to serve the sick and poor and then to reform the corrupt Church. Teresa of Avila, whose entrance into religious life began because of family worry over her "frivolous behavior," lived a life of great religious turmoil, until at the age of forty she experienced a mystical encounter that changed her life. For the next twenty-eight years, until her death, she directed

her energies to reforming the Carmelite order, counseling the elite in both Church and state, and writing masterpieces of mystical literature.

7. Religious women of the Counter-Reformation Church. Activist women of the sixteenth century began religious orders somewhat parallel to the Jesuits and Vincentians. Angela Merici of the Ursulines and Louise de Marillac of the Daughters of Charity are examples. While these women adhered to the vows of poverty, chastity, and obedience, they initiated an alternative to the contemplative life of monastic communities, making a significant contribution to female education.

Perhaps the example of these women and others like them contributed to the survival of another theme of the Catholic sensibility, found in the Old Testament, continued in the New Testament, and surfacing in the Middle Ages: the femininity of God. Between the apostolic age and Julian of Norwich in the fourteenth century, the idea of the femininity of God—as Wisdom, as Holy Spirit—persisted in the apocryphal and gnostic writings; in orthodox writings of Augustine, Anselm, and Mechtild; and in Church art.

Jesus did not hesitate to compare God to a woman or to use feminine language Himself. In the three stories he told to the Pharisees who complained about the sinners and taxpayers who followed Him, the one of the woman and the lost coin (Luke, Chapter 15) clearly says that God is like the woman. And when Jesus mourned over Jerusalem He experienced a longing "to gather [her] children, as a hen gathers her brood under her wing." He compares Himself to a nursing mother, inviting all who are thirsty to come to Him and drink, applying to Himself the Scripture reference "from his breast shall flow fountains of living water." Nor did Jesus' behavior fit the masculine stereotype. He displayed qualities that are traditionally attributed to women, qualities which might, in part, be responsible for Julian's understanding of Jesus as Mother.

Julian of Norwich's portrayal of Jesus as Mother is particularly interesting because it raises the question of whether men and women imagine God differently, and it shows that even when the feminine dimension of God is not acknowledged in official circles, it is still experienced in the lives of those who participate in the Church. With theological precision, she applied the theme of the femininity of God to the relationship of the Trinity. Drawing on her own feminine experience, she described the motherhood of God in great depth, her mystical experience of the totality of God giving us a beautiful and original imagery:

> I understand three ways of contemplating motherhood in God. The first is the foundation of our nature's creation; the second is his taking of our nature, where the motherhood of grace begins; the third is motherhood at work. And in that, by the same grace, everything is penetrated, in length and breadth, in height and depth without end; and it is all in love.

Julian's ability to see God as feminine contrasts with the mystics who imagined God as a male lover: even for the male mystic, the human soul was the female half of the love relationship. But Julian demonstrates that a woman can apply her own experience to a description of God if she, in fact, views that experience in a positive light; and she can imagine God as lover.

But, we wonder, when a man is moved to realize that woman reveals God, and he wants to say something about God in light of that experience, what does he do? The movie *All That Jazz* offers one contemporary man's experience of God.

The filmmaker Bob Fosse had a close brush with death on the operating table during heart surgery. To his astonishment, death was not a terrifying figure, but warm and gentle and lovely—very like a woman, indeed like his wife and his mistress and, especially, his daughter. In the film based on his own life story, he raises the question of whether the reality he encountered might be God and hence whether God might not be like a woman, indeed like Jessica Lange.

"I never did anything important," Fosse's character says. "I never made a rose, for instance."

"Only God can make a rose," says the beauteous, filmily clad Angelique—and then in the next scene holds a rose.

Fosse gives us a choice at the end. The protagonist dies. In one conclusion he walks down a long corridor toward Angelique, dazzlingly attractive and waiting with open arms. In the other ending, his body is wrapped in a plastic bag to be brought to the morgue. Take your choice, Fosse tells us: either a fair bride or a cold slab.

Is God as sexy as Jessica Lange? She'd better be a lot more sexy. Or, to put the matter less facetiously, the beauty we see in the actress is a hint of the fascination of God's beauty. Her appeal is a faint clue of God's appeal.

When official images of God were all masculine, the human propensity to describe God as feminine surfaced in yet another form—in the honoring of Mary. The symbol of Mary continued to celebrate the femininity of God for both men and women, despite the Church's attempts to affirm the inferiority of women. She is an example of how woman's sacramentality cannot be completely denied. If we want to infuse a Catholic sensibility into the modern Church, we should look at how the Mary symbol continues to affirm this reality.

Great devotion to Mary has coexisted with disdain for all human femininity, but that does not mean that the symbol is meaningless for today's women. Women have shortchanged themselves by letting go of a symbol that, if correctly understood, would require the Church to acknowledge woman's sacramentality and would certainly serve to remind women of their ability to reveal God.

Mary has occupied the imagination of both the official and unofficial churches. She has captured the imaginations of liturgists, songwriters, poets, storytellers, artists, and builders. She has been the patroness of individuals, religious communities, churches, towns, and nations. She has been the subject of heated theological debate and the object of devotion bordering on magic. She is such a multivalent symbol that every new culture Christianity has encountered has been able to claim her for their own, in most instances simply substituting her for their chief goddess and turning all their goddess festivals into Marian feasts.

Through all this, she has remained very much a human being and very much a woman. Church officials who might have wanted to de-eroticize her, to rob her of her feminine body, could not do so and keep her as the mother who gave birth to Jesus Who is both human and Divine. As a mother she has a feminine body that bears and nurses a child. The Church has gone so far as to affirm that this female body is now in heaven, an affirmation that should, if logical thinking prevailed, put to rest all thoughts about the evil nature of the female body. The Assumption of Mary is a classic example of the Catholic sensibility surviving even among those who do not appreciate its full implications.

Our research among young Catholics has demonstrated that Mary is an enormously powerful religious symbol that correlates positively with sexual fulfillment in marriage, social concern, and a gracious image of God. Radical feminists may want to deny her this meaning, and saccharin-sweet Mariologists may equally want to deny it. The young, wisely, pay no attention to either.

The variety of manifestations of the Mary symbol challenges all Catholics to question why the sacramentality of woman is not readily accepted. How can a Church that celebrates Mary ignore the lack of respect for women that is at the root of their continued exploitation? How can the Church continue its hierarchical culture, excluding women's participation in decisions about how it can best reveal God in the modern world? How can a Church that should recognize the sacramentality of woman's body be so nervous about young women being altar girls? How can a Church that has benefited from the contributions of religious women justify its attempts to subject them to the authority of the male clergy? How can a Church hear the Wisdom of God when it continues to imagine God only in masculine terms? Perhaps the question is, Why does the official Church persist in behavior that reflects attitudes toward women that are no longer defensible on any grounds?

The fear, mistrust, and even hatred of women to be found at the core of societal and Church attitudes on women are a result of sexual differentiation gone amok and are also at the core of all opposition to women, past and present (relationships of appropriation rather than relationships of gift). This orientation to women threatens all human relationships, because it interferes with the ability of a man and woman to form a unity that reveals God. The attitude is contrary to the mission that Jesus articulated in His life and that He expects us to live in ours. The Church must learn to bear witness to a positive vision of woman, a vision rooted in the Catholic sensibility, a vision that proclaims that woman is a sacrament, that she is an analog of God.

Church policymakers who undertake to bear witness to this Catholic sensibility might consider what perspective it would give them as they clarify the women's issue at the forefront of today's Church. By bringing the Catholic sensibility to bear on these issues they also will be deepening their own appreciation of that sensibility.

To say that woman is a sacrament of God is to say that God may be experienced differently from the way God is experienced by men. To say that woman is an analog of God is to say that women are like God in a way different from that in which men are like God. Concretely, what do such statements mean?

One must start with the body, not because biology is destiny but because destiny begins with biology though it does not end there, and because the difference between men and women and between their experiences, however complex and elaborate, originates in their bodily differences, in the nuptial orientation of their bodies, to use John Paul's terminology.

A woman's body is designed by the evolutionary process to attract men, to conceive and give birth to a child, to nurse the child, and (probably) to care for the child (though not necessarily exclusively). At the raw level of what we might call primary sacramentality and elementary analogy, woman discloses the attracting, life-giving, nurturing, caring powers of the cosmos and has done so in almost every religion the world has ever known. She is also, therefore, seen as disclosing the tender, affectionate, protecting forces at work in the cosmos. The "madonna" image—known in many religions—sums up much of this symbolism: the mother affectionately nursing the newborn babe. God, the symbolism hints, might be like that mother.

We are not saying that a woman's "highest fulfillment" is to be found in bearing and caring for children. Quite the contrary. "Highest fulfillment" transcends the biological and it comes from the development of oneself in generosity and love as a complete human person. The ultimate sacramentality and the ultimate analogy of any human is to be found in that person's capacity for loving service. The God of love is best revealed by love.

Human love, the perfection of analogy and sacramentality, also comes in two fascinating packages, which reveal, equally but differently, the splendor of God's love. Is God male or female? God combines the equal perfections of both. Does God love like a mother or like a father? God loves in ways that are reflected equally by the two packages of human loving. Can we call God She? Every bit as much as we can call her He. As John Paul I of short but glorious memory said in one of his few audience talks, God is both a mother and a father.

What are some of the images of God that develop when we talk about God as a woman? How do we begin to imagine God when we explore this possibility? Bob Fosse has his Angelique, a bride and a lover constantly teasing him, enticing him to put away a life of pills and pressures and join her in an unknown world. For him, God is like a bride, a woman lover. God can also be envisioned as like a mother, a sister, a daughter, a grandmother, a nun, a girlfriend or any other womanly roles. If, at some time or the other, the beauty, gentleness, patience, loyalty, concern, fortitude, playfulness, nurture, or love of a woman move us to discover God, we will, like Fosse, be able to imagine God as "like a woman" with those qualities. Our images of God as Father are colored by the images of Father we have collected during a lifetime of encounters with the experience of fatherhood. The qualities of God the Father mentioned in Scripture help reinforce our personal images, perhaps at times alerting us to dimensions of fatherhood we had not ever considered. The same is true for our images of God as woman.

One image that captures many qualities traditionally considered the exclusive province of woman, and therefore not Godlike, is that of woman as housewife. For weal or woe, we have all been influenced by this image, and though it is considered objectionable, an attempt to keep woman "in her place," it reveals many of the attributes of human nature that have been nurtured by women throughout human history. It is possible, in other words, to discover something about "humanness" in the housewife's experience that cannot be discovered in man's traditional roles. If we permit these qualities of humanness to interact with our stories of the femininity of God, we will expand our image of God; in turn we shall have a spiritual incentive to nurture these qualities in our own lives—whether we are male or female, housebound or career executive.

The role of housewife evolved because a woman's body with its reproductive possibilities kept her attached to the home. The traditional housewife saw her home as sacred space. She was the priestess who, through the ritual enactment of housework, turned an ordinary, profane place into an extraordinary, sacred space. In the home family members could experience a sense of rootedness, sanctuary, containment, and mystery that allowed them to be "at home" with themselves. Thus the home became a symbol of ultimate concern.

What values did the housewife cultivate that helped her transcend the ordinariness of daily life and perhaps discover an insight into the ultimate meaning of human existence? What would the image of God as housewife say about how we are to live our lives?

The Scripture story of Martha and Mary points us toward the crux of Godlikeness in the "waiting" mode of existence as it was lived by the traditional housewife/priestess. Undoubtedly both Martha and Mary were traditional housewives. Many have considered Martha a symbol of secular concerns and Mary a symbol of religious concerns. (Some interpreters have even seen Mary as "like a man," disdaining the traditional "womanly" tasks.) But Mary is really a symbol of how all human tasks, if they are done with an attitude of openness to others, offer revelatory possibilities. Martha is the housewife whose concern over daily tasks blinds her to God's presence in her midst. Mary is the traditional housewife/priestess who made her space sacred by having a concern for others as persons.

Thus we can say that God is like a traditional housewife/priestess. She is concerned about each of us personally and wants us to feel "at home." She creates a world for us "to come home to" in the midst of the chaos of daily existence. She gives us the sense of containment we need when buffeted by the inevitable trials and tribulations.

Since a woman's reproductive possibilities no longer tie her to the home, the creation of a sacred space of the home is a task that now falls on all family members. People still need a "place to come home to." They still need a place where they can feel "at home." Both men and women need to cultivate the human, Godlike quality of concern for others that was the hallmark of the traditional housewife/priestess.

To address again the five problems raised at the beginning of this chapter:

1. The Church must begin to celebrate the various lifestyles open to women. Church policymakers, at all levels, must stop seeing women as two-dimensional creatures—mothers and wives. Motherhood is wonderful, and the Church should certainly continue to affirm the

parenting role that women have always performed. But it must also recognize the need for shared parenting and encourage both men and women in it. Shared parenting could give children an opportunity to learn that God is like both Daddy and Mommy, both of whom are of equal importance to the child.

Church policymakers must realize that the major portion of a woman's life (in terms of both time and energy) is not dedicated to child-rearing, at least not in advanced technological societies. The Church has models of womanly behavior unrelated to child care; policymakers should encourage women to explore the modern meaning of these models.

The Church needs pastoral theologies for women. Any pastoral theology develops from the interaction between experience and faith. The Church will be able to encourage women only when its pastoral leaders understand their experiences well enough to bring about this interaction.

2. The Church must take strong stands against all forms of the exploitation of women. Church leaders must speak out against wife abuse, rape, enforced prostitution, unequal pay, and other injustices as loudly as they do against nuclear warfare and injustices in the Third World. Exploitation of women casts a pall over attempts to help people experience the nuptial meaning of the body; it is the result of relationships of appropriation, from which Jesus sought to free us. Catholics must recognize the harm caused by these injustices against women.

The Church must acknowledge that the fallacy of its own attitudes toward women has contributed to the acceptability of exploitation of women. If the Church truly accepts the personhood of women, it can no longer countenance any attempt to justify exploitation on the grounds of its past teachings, no matter how well-intentioned they might have been.

3. The Church must validate the feminine experience, including the experience of women's bodies. Back when we were in school, nuns worried about the female body as an occasion of sin for young men; young girls were cautioned against fashions that might be too revealing; parents who allowed their teenage daughters to wear strapless formal gowns were often given stern lectures on the evils of this form of dress, which, it was believed, caused young men to have unwanted

fantasies. Today, some feminists campaign against any adornment of the body that might enhance its sexual appeal. While Susan Brownmiller worries over her desire to have bigger breasts, to be shorter than the man she is dating, to have long, flowing hair, South American revolutionary women celebrate the disappearance of advertisements that use woman's body as a sign that the revolution has been successful.

We doubt that the young boys' fantasies were unwanted. Men both young and old will have fantasies about women no matter how they are dressed or undressed, and vice versa. The sacramental possibilities of the human body make this inevitable. While we certainly don't approve of advertisements that have their sole appeal in an exploitation of sexual desire, we think that many Madison Avenue businessmen recognize the sacramental potential of the unclothed body more than Church leaders do.

Church policies rooted in an appreciation of the nuptial meaning of the body should lessen any "guilt" women might feel regarding their own desire to be feminine, to be sexy. While it is true that this desire can become demonic, the repression of it can be equally demonic. Stories of the femininity of God and stories of Mary, reinterpreted for our modern world, would provide an impetus for the celebration of femininity.

The "Lovely Lady, dressed in blue" to whom we prayed as an intercessor for us before God was a Mother whose femininity was both lovely and powerful. May crownings, which affirmed the queenship of Mary, might have disintegrated into popularity contests among potential "crowners," but the symbol of Mary as Queen suggests the potential for leadership that women are beginning to rediscover. We can ask, what kind of leadership does the Queen of May suggest for women? And we can ask the same questions about her motherhood, her role as wife, her religious status both as a Jew and as a member of its reform movement begun by her son. The Mary myth, reexamined in light of modern women's experiences, is filled with great potential. We wholeheartedly recommend that Church policymakers explore it.

4. The Church must bear witness to the sacramentality of woman and her role as analog for God. The problems surrounding women's role in the Catholic Church will not disappear overnight, even if the

Church were to be suddenly put in the charge of bishops who recognized the need to address the issue, which is not the case at the present time. But new policies can encourage priests, husbands, and mothers to recognize that they can be a positive influence on a woman's religious imagination. The nuptial meaning of the body requires women's full participation in Church life and the decision-making processes. Short of this, the Church will continue to be its own worst enemy when it comes to women.

Though women must be allowed to be ordained if the Church is to bear witness to the full implications of the sacramentality of woman and her analogical power, this will not automatically bring about the change necessary to make this witness truly effective. As experiences of women ordained in other churches have shown, the anti-woman bias is strong not just in the clergy but among the laity, including some women. Other means must also be used to reach those who, consciously or unconsciously, resist woman's analogical power.

Church policymakers must affirm the challenge of God's plan to discover the meaning of existence through the "image of God," male *and* female. God cannot be comprehended adequately by a people who use only masculine imagery of God. A Church cannot continue adequately the task of Christ when it uses only male experience as the basis for its understanding of its task. The Church must use its full resources—men and women—not just as ordained ministers and altar servers, but at every level of Church activity.

The Church must help men and women to face and resolve the problems of trust and intimacy they encounter in their lives. The Church, as the continuing presence of Christ in the world, must constantly re-issue the call to unity and provide the "stories" of the meaning of life that will inspire both men and women to risk a response.

Is God really like a fair bride? Does She really care for us like a mother who has brought us into the world? Does She really nurse us at the breast? Does She really seduce us like an attractive lover who has determined to make us Her own? How can anyone who is Catholic say "No"?

Chapter 9

. . . .

MARRIAGE AND FAMILY LIFE: INTIMACY AS COMIC STORY

The Catholic sensibility is incurably romantic. It believes that sustained intimacy is possible in marriage. It also believes that intimacy must grow and develop if the marriage is to be sacramental. In other words, the capacity of a marriage to "give" grace to the couple and to the world resides in its ability to nurture the intimacy for which the human sexual drive longs. Furthermore, when a marriage provides the environment in which playfulness and commitment interact, then the "comic," hopeful Catholic story is told and retold, influencing other family members who "see" it. If Catholicism is to be saved, its policymakers must discover how to nurture the capacity for intimacy in marriage.

Many Church policies that consider fidelity the key sacramental ingredient of marriage fail to recognize that fidelity without hope for intimacy cannot reveal Divine love. Even as the rejected lover in the prophets' stories of Israel, Yahweh continued to hope that He and

Israel would once again achieve intimacy. And Church pronouncements on marriage and family life fail to understand the interplay between sexual, psychological, and religious elements in the development of sacramental intimacy. It is as if these were written in a vacuum, ignorant of modern research on human growth and development. Perhaps Church officials fear that the research on intimacy will undercut marriage's sacramental possibilities, though in fact, the research shows that for most people attempts at intimacy are experiences of mystery, at least some of the time having a sacramental potential.

Policymakers might better appreciate how true fidelity requires intimacy if they examine Pope John Paul II's analysis of Matthew 5:27–28—"You have heard it said: You shall not commit adultery. But I say, too, everyone who looks at a woman lustfully has already committed adultery with her in his heart." The Pope regards the faithfulness demanded by the commandment against adultery as much broader than mere physical fidelity. His reflections should lead to Church policies rooted in an understanding of the multidimensional character of marital intimacy.

Distorted understandings about sex and women constitute two of the major obstacles to intimacy in marriage. But even when these obstacles are diminished, the tension between the desires for intimacy and for independence must be seen in a proper perspective (be "saved") if intimacy is to flourish. The hopefulness of the Catholic story—especially the stories of Christmas and Easter—provides the incentive for marital partners not to settle for a mundane existence but to strive for growth in intimacy.

The secrets of success in intimacy need to be shared with others, especially with the family that grows out of the intimacy of marital partners. Children learn the basics of intimacy from their parents, and couples refine their intimacy skills not only with each other but with their children. In short, marital intimacy creates the environment in which the Catholic imagination can grow. It gives the grace that makes a family also a church.

An example illustrates how the quest for marital intimacy is at the core of marriage and family life. As we write this book, the first of the next generation of our family to marry is planning a wedding. Some of the bride's "worldly" friends assure her that within a year, "all that glow will wear off; you won't be so excited about being around him." But Irish temper, Irish romanticism, and her Catholic sensibility encourage her to reject this cynicism vehemently. She and her fiancé believe that romance will continue throughout their married life. They say that they believe this because they have seen romance stay alive in the marriages of some of their elders and they still see "romance" in their parents' marriages. These are not unrealistically naïve young people (they are probably more mature than their parents were in similar circumstances). They claim they know there will be bad times as well as good times. Still, they continue to hope that the good times will outweigh the bad and that love will see them through.

The hope of this young couple (romance will stay alive) and the experience in which it is grounded (romance is still alive in some marriages after 30 years) shows how the Catholic sensibility can be hopeful about marital intimacy and what effect this can have on the life of the Catholic community, how the religious tradition might inspire and encourage them, how the Church can speak to their religious imaginations. They should realize that they are creating Church, in its most basic sense, when they commit themselves to a continuing journey of marital intimacy.

Our primary interest here is in marriages that have the potential for intimacy, which makes it possible for a marriage to be sacramental. This is not an Ideal, a "perfect," marriage. Rather, two fallible human beings, beings who live in what the Pope calls "historical time," may be able to "imagine" God's presence by equating their journey of marital intimacy with their journey toward God.

Certain social science findings will guide our examination of how the Catholic story enriches the marriage story and how the marriage story, properly lived, enriches the Catholic story:

1. Increased life spans mean that couples marrying today can expect fifty or more years of marriage. In most cases today couples will spend at least twenty years without the presence of children. Past patterns of marital and family intimacies simply do not apply in these new circumstances.

2. Consciousness of selfhood, a characteristic unique to humans, makes the depth of any human relationship dependent on the choices

of two people, each of them self-determining. Individuality, self-reliance, and development of human potential, plus a decreased acceptance of role stereotypes, are factors in the search for growth and development. It is crucial that each partner have a sense of self-worth, but some of the goals of selfhood may set up barriers to intimacy.

3. The human sexual drive is a powerful force for overcoming a tendency to isolation. This force, which assured the survival of our species, is the basic fact of human existence and will influence how humans act in all their endeavors, not just those activities with obvious sexual implications.

4. Sexual intimacy is an art that must be cultivated. The sexual drive propels us toward a unity that will renew the race, but if this unity is to renew individuals, they must learn how to satisfy each other's sexual needs. Like any other game, the game of sexual intimacy can be "played" by amateurs, but to be "good" at it, partners need practice. Also, the human ability to give sex meaning implies that the practice must take place between two individuals who are seeking intimacy. No matter how "experienced" either partner is prior to the game, if they want to be successful at intimacy, each must learn the other's rhythms, fantasies, and needs.

5. Studies indicate that there is a cyclical pattern to our growth and development through life. A basic theory maintains that the overriding psychological development pattern responds to three questions: Who am I (identity)? With whom will I share the "I" that I discover (intimacy)? And whom or what shall I create (generativity)? Women may go through these stages in a slightly different progression and with somewhat different intensity than men. And neither a sense of identity nor the capacity for intimacy is a static trait, acquired once and for all somewhere along the road to adulthood. Their dynamism means that at times in our adult life, times that Gail Sheehy dubbed "Passages," neglected aspects of our personality will force us to reflect and re-evaluate.

6. Expectations about marriage are deeply related to one's parents' experience of marriage. Two marriage "stories," sometimes quite different, join on a wedding day. Although the goal of the marrying couple is to write a "new" story, characters and events from the other stories influence the "new" story—sometimes without the awareness of the authors.

7. Finally, a spouse is a powerful influence on the formation of an individual's religious imagination and on his or her religious behavior. Social science research on religious behavior has discovered that one of the strongest influences on an individual's religious behavior is the religious behavior of the spouse. Moreover, studies indicate that a husband's positive religious images may diminish the effect of negative images of Church and woman in the imagination of his wife, images formed as a result of her mother's religious behavior.

We recommend a spirituality of marital intimacy as an antidote to the pessimism of those who see marriage as a tragedy. We do not deny the tragic possibilities of intimacy, but there is also a transcendent possibility. The God who created humans with a drive toward unity is also present as a couple journey along the path to genuine unity, a path that will make them the "two in one flesh" who are "in the image of God." God's presence on the journey challenges the couple to behave in ways that enrich the intimacy and enlarge the hope that love will triumph, despite disappointment, failure, and even death.

The Catholic sensibility encourages us to examine how the sexual, psychological, and religious dimensions of the human personality interact in marital intimacy. A spirituality solidly based in this interaction will give us the means to "imagine" marital intimacy as a comic story. The theme of death and rebirth in the Catholic religious story and the theme of cycles in human growth and development can be connected spiritually. The "story" of marital intimacy, a continuing saga of ups and downs—falling in love, settling down, bottoming out and beginning again, repeated over and over—shows a generic pattern that allows us to "retell" the story with the promise of a comic ending. The religious perspective shows how people can avoid the trap of monotonous repetition of stages. Intimacy as "comic story" suggests that each stage is an opportunity for growth and development.

People might question this close attention being paid to the sexual dimensions of intimacy. There are those who hold the Church responsible for most of the sexual problems of married couples and want the Church to "get out of the bedroom," while others are tired of what they see as the continual emphasis on sex as the cause of marital difficulties. But the Church *does* belong in the bedroom, not as a policeman but as an inspiration, encouraging partners to discover the God who is the third partner in their sexual intimacy. Since we humans are only quasi pair-bonded, we need a constant reminder of the bonding call of our bodies. One can never say too much about the sacramentality of sex. And the grace of the sexual drive can help overcome what often seem like insurmountable problems. Marital partners should be encouraged to be "sexy" because their desire for a renewal of intimacy is part of the grace of the human body. The tone of sexual intimacy should be a joint effort to develop an openness to the grace-filled possibilities of sexiness.

When we turn to the comic story of marital intimacy, we begin with the experience of falling in love when it has reached the point where the individual partners decide that they both want this to be a "long haul" relationship. Romantic love, reinforcing sexual desire, frees them to hope they will overcome obstacles to their goal of lifelong happiness. The grace of their sexual drive allows them to "risk" commitment. Like Adam and Eve, they have each found God by going outside of themselves and joining with another, not just for the moment, but so as to "cling to each other" permanently. It is a deeply religious moment when they "imagine" their life together as a comic story.

The willingness to risk, to see a beloved in a positive light, to hope that together they can overcome all obstacles puts a couple in touch with what Pope John Paul II calls the time of "original innocence," when Adam and Eve were filled with a grace that freed them from experiencing the obstacles to intimacy, when they were "naked and not ashamed." The grace of falling in love that inspires the decision for marriage is a valuable resource for the religious imagination. If partners use this experience as a touchstone during their married life they will find that recapturing their feelings and attitudes at the time can help them overcome what seem like insurmountable obstacles, whether psychological or sexual. It is probably not possible to live a whole lifetime in the excitement of falling in love, but the memory of the excitement can help one move out of the depths in which partners periodically find themselves.

In such interludes, lovers grow bored with the routine of the garden and are ripe for temptation. Bottoming out, the antithesis of falling in love, occurs when one or both partners can no longer tolerate the feelings of rejection, the hurts, and the unsatisfied needs that accompany a lack of continual growth in intimacy. The partners are like Adam and Eve hiding from Yahweh, because they are "naked and ashamed." They are like the frightened disciples on Good Friday, missing the obvious message of Jesus in their excessive concern for where they fit in the scheme of things. They are like Israel in captivity, cut off from the Promised Land. Spirituality at this time should be prophetic, challenging the couple to acknowledge how they have hidden from the grace of sexuality and reminding them of God's presence, available if they will only search for it. Spirituality should focus on discovering how the grace of the sexual drive offers hope that partners can "risk" forming habits that will help them be "naked and not ashamed." Positive habits of sexual intimacy, coupled with the images carried over from falling in love, will help them avoid the tendency to take each other for granted.

Partners in this stage have three options. If they see no possibility of recapturing their original dream, they generally choose to end the marriage. If they fear the challenge of the original dream and are content with a static existence, they remain together and find their "romance" elsewhere—in work, affairs, parenting, or even sickness. The final option, taken when one hopes that things could be different, is to fight, to confront the spouse with one's built-up anger and run the risk of total rejection—a possibility in any fight—if it will end the stagnation.

If during the darkest moments of bottoming out, a partner hears the command to "love your spouse as yourself," he or she might find the courage to fight for a renewal of the original love. Ironically, fighting, which is so painful, gives the partners the opportunity to mourn over their individual hurts and to acknowledge their mutual loss of intimacy. Like Jesus they weep over their loss, but they also are the mourners "who will be comforted."

As mourners, wounded by the exchange of hurtful insults but comforted by the "comic story," partners can begin again. Once their grief has been penetrated, perhaps by renewal of sexual attraction or by the persistent apology of one partner or maybe by a moment of shared laughter, they discover they have survived. They are like Jacob after his battle with the night visitor. They are wounded, but they are better for it because now they know that even the hurtful insults of their fighting could not destroy them.

Just as they needed a language to express their grief in bottoming out, now the partners need a language of reconciliation to heal the wounds. Though relief comes with the realization that love has prevailed, partners know that they must now take steps to protect their intimacy. They must discover what barriers led to their frustration. Since each usually feels that he or she was both the "hurter" and the "hurtee," they must start, as it were, to negotiate, letting each other know what they feel, desire, fear, dream. They need to die with Christ to their sins against marital intimacy, so they can rise with Him to a deeper appreciation of the sacramentality of marital intimacy. They need a spirituality that continually repeats the comic story.

Euphoria, somewhat similar to the "walking on air" of falling in love, accompanies the realization that intimacy is still possible. The partners are like Adam and Eve when they are promised a redeemer, like Israel when she is allowed to return to the promised land, and like the disciples on Easter. The Catholic sensibility invites them to celebrate the Resurrection. They are comforted and want to "sing a new song."

Beginning again reminds the couple of the wonder of sexual intimacy. Even if sexual relations continued through the dark period, they lacked the playfulness of sacramental sex and were often a frustrating reminder that something very good had turned sour. Now there is a chance to share more of the needs, desires, and fantasies that fuel their imaginings about sexual intimacy. The gift of sexual intimacy once again inspires hope. Partners can again risk being "naked," both psychologically and physically.

This retelling of the story of marital intimacy with emphasis on its religious dimension only hints at the happy ending. After completing one cycle of marital intimacy, a couple learns that their quest for genuine intimacy will be a lifelong task. With the help of a spirituality gauged to the problems and possibilities of each stage, marital partners can come to appreciate how God, who helped write their story when S/He created their sexual drive, also offers them many reminders of His/Her continuing presence in their story. S/He also promises a happy ending to the story.

A renewed hopefulness, grounded in the actual experience of survival, increases the ability of marital intimacy to be sacramental, to reveal both for the couple and for others the presence of God. According to John Paul II, marital intimacy is the continuing model for all human relationships that we find in Genesis 2:23–24—"two in one flesh" as a relationship of gift. If they want to respond to the sexual attraction of their bodies so they can be "naked and unashamed," physically and psychologically, partners must learn the skills of the various stages of marital intimacy. These stages then offer a model for the psychological "nakedness" that is essential for all attempts at intimacy.

The definition of a sacrament in catechism terminology—an outward sign, instituted by Christ to give grace—declares what actually occurs in marital intimacy. When marital intimacy is lived as comic story, partners "give" to those who see their story the grace that has been given to them by God's presence. This passing on of grace is most apparent in the way parents teach intimacy by example to their children.

Church policymakers need to understand how the religious experience of marital intimacy influences the religious behavior of family members. Although there are Church statements about the family as a "domestic church"—statements from the Second Vatican Council and *Familiaris Consortio,* the statement from the Synod on the Family—there does not seem to be any practical recognition of this truth. Perhaps Church leaders are unfamiliar with the research on family influences on religious behavior. Many of their statements seem to imply that the religious-education function is bestowed on the family by the larger Church, not recognizing that the family, by its very nature, forms religious attitudes.

Again, some facts will serve as a basis for our analysis of how marital intimacy affects family intimacy and creates the family church.

1. Research in archaeology and anthropology indicates that fairly early on in human history an emotional bond formed between those who entered an "economic contract in which the product was children." An emotional bonding inevitably leads to experiences of mystery, giving the union the potential to create grace-filled moments.

2. The family—not the educational system—has the greatest influence on an individual's religious formation. The best predictors of religious behavior are the family of birth and the family of choice. Any formal religious education merely reinforces the values, attitudes, and behaviors acquired in the home.

3. The pre-school years, when the child's major contacts are with family members, are the most formative of an individual's personality. It is from the family structure, or how the child interprets this structure, that the child first learns about role identity and intimacy.

4. Our religious imagination is affected by our parents and our spouse. There is evidence that "warm" religious images—i.e., God as lover, God as woman—are related to the degree of sexual satisfaction in a marriage.

5. Grown children who believe their parents had a happy marriage are more apt to be religious than children who considered their parents unhappily married. This is true even when the happily married parents were not regular churchgoers or the unhappily married parents attended church weekly.

We acquire our first images of religion, informally, from the way our parents behave toward each other and toward us and not from their commitment to formal church structures. If our parents appreciate life as a comic story, they leave us open to finding the comic story of Catholicism meaningful. Adult anger at the Church is often the result of negative images we formed of it based on the model of intimacy (a model of grace for us) we experienced as a child. When there is no intimacy in a family, silent messages of hopelessness abound. When marital intimacy is comic story, hopefulness encourages positive religious images.

The failure of Church policymakers to recognize how marital intimacy helps to create the family Church is obvious in Pope John Paul II's exhortation prohibiting divorced and remarried Catholics from receiving Communion. If the couple must stay together for the "sake of the children," he suggests, then they must avoid sexual intercourse. But if the research facts are correct, a family sustained for the "sake of the children" demands parents who are truly intimate and can be a model of intimacy for them. Here Pope John Paul II does not seem to apply his theological insights into sexuality to a pastoral situation. He obviously sees sexual union as the sacramental center, but in *Familiaris Consortio* he fails to recognize that without this sacramental possibility the marriage will not be able to "give" grace to the next generation.

Parents fall in love, settle down, bottom out, and, inspired by hope, begin again many times over as their children grow to adulthood. If parents are truly intimate together, they will manage the inevitable crisis that comes with the child's need to be "on my own." If children are cheerfully hopeful about life because they have observed the hopefulness of their parents' intimacy, they can risk adulthood and learn to begin again in an adult relationship with their parents.

Just as falling in love is the touchstone of marital intimacy, the joy experienced at the birth of a child is a model for how parents should sense their relationship with their children. The father in the story of the Prodigal Son shows the excitement of rebirth in a parent/child relationship and offers hope that barriers will always be surmountable.

Also, parents need to re-examine how, in the settling-down stage, the habits they developed toward a child when the child was young should be modified or even abandoned as the child matures. The example of Yahweh in the Garden, giving Adam and Eve the freedom to err, should suggest a way to give maturing children the right to make their own choices (something they will do anyway, even over parental objections). Ultimate hopefulness helps parents through what often seem like total disasters in their children's lives. They can give their children freedom when they remember the parables of the man who finds a pearl and goes and sells all that he has so that he can buy the pearl; having found something greater than what he has, he sells his possessions to gain it. Maturity is the great pearl parents want for their children, and they must give up unwarranted expectations so as to allow the children the freedom they need for maturity. "Letting go" is not easy but it is essential to the comic story of intimacy. Respect for the personhood of the child demands that parents keep their control to the minimum necessary for each stage of growth.

For children, the challenge of intimacy with their parents requires that they learn to forgive their parents for the real or imagined mistakes made during their childhood. Unfortunately, one of the hardest things for a child to do is admit the fallibility of a parent. The equivalent of the falling-in-love stage for a child is filled with images of a "perfect" parent. As children mature this image fades, and the disappointment often colors their attempts at intimacy, at least until they can come to terms with their anger at the parent's imperfections.

If, as children enter adulthood, they can recapture the positive moments of their relationship with a parent and at the same time recognize the parent's good qualities, hopeful intimacy becomes possible. Children who learn to forgive their parents can risk admitting their own shortcomings.

Church policy needs to acknowledge these inevitable ups and downs in parent-child relationships and challenge and encourage everyone to hopefulness. Families are the continuing presence of God to each other, and together with other families they "give" the grace of intimacy to others beyond the home. Family members who want to keep a Catholic sensibility alive can see how they must cultivate intimacy in the family if they hope to bear witness to the sacramentality of marriage and family life. Family members who tell the comic story by the way they relate to each other deepen their appreciation for the meaning of the hopefulness in the Catholic heritage.

The Catholic sensibility is incurably romantic because it refuses to believe that the tragedy is the final answer. The Church must recognize that marital intimacy gives the grace to form the family Church, which in turn nurtures the religious imagination. Once it does, Church policymakers should:

1. Re-evaluate their approach to marriage education. The Church must gear its policies to both the problems and the possibilities of each stage of marital intimacy. Marriage guidelines that ignore the grace of falling in love separate the official Church from one of the most powerfully graced moments in human life. Understanding and appreciating that moment and its significance should be primary.

2. Stop issuing statements on sexual morality in marriage until they understand the significance of sexual intimacy in the overall comic story of marital intimacy. Statements issued a priori, with little evidence to back them up (such as "Support natural family planning as *the* way to grow in marital spirituality"), only reinforce the general view that church policymakers are ignorant of the true story of married life.

3. Encourage a spirituality of marital intimacy that will be supported at every level of the Church. There should be a continuing affirmation that intimacy constitutes the sacramentality of marriage. This approach would challenge Catholic married people to see the

importance of marital intimacy and also encourage them to believe they can grow in marital intimacy.

4. Recognize that one of the primary tasks of family ministry should be to help families appreciate the influence they have on religious imagination. Much family ministry today is crisis-oriented, serving the needs of those experiencing family tragedies. This approach often overshadows the need to encourage ordinary, stable families. Celebrating the ongoing journey of marital life is a way to remind people of the constant presence of God (grace).

5. Encourage the study of marriage and family intimacy at all levels of the Church, so that pastoral leaders will not follow the "wisdom" of the secular culture and question whether the family is a meaningful institution. Since marital intimacy offers a model for all human relationships, the Church should better understand how to imitate marriage as the model, and call other social institutions to discover its wisdom.

6. Train local churches to encourage and support the family-as-church. Our next chapter will develop this point at greater length. Local churches are where families come together to celebrate, challenge, be nourished and challenged.

If Church policymakers follow these suggestions, people might begin to call them incurable romantics.

Like Jesus of Nazareth.

Chapter 10

. . . .

THE PARISH AS
ORGANIC COMMUNITY

Catholicism will be saved when we all realize that the local church—
be it a parish, a college Newman Center, or a young-adult religious community—is the heart of the Catholic Church for most Catholics. Rome, or the National Conference of Bishops, or the diocesan
chancery office might represent the bureaucratic, institutional Church,
but these centers influence individual lives only when they encourage
or discourage thriving local churches.

In the United States, the urban parishes of the immigrant neighborhoods and the suburban parishes of their children and grandchildren are unique examples of organic religious community. The original
leaders of these parishes recognized the importance of maintaining a
religious base in a local community. A parish was—and still is—
successful if it is able to tell the religious stories that respond to the
needs of the people, if it helps people appreciate the sacramental
moments of life, and finally if it links its members with the world
beyond. A successful parish is one in which laity and pastoral leaders
(especially the pastor) share a vision of its meaning, when the com-

munity works together to continue God's presence in its time and place.

There are both sociological and religious reasons why parishes have been so important in the North American Church. Church policy-makers would be well advised to examine the successful urban and suburban parishes, which are excellent models suggesting how local churches can foster an appreciation of the Catholic sensibility. The Church will be saved when its policies encourage pastoral leaders with a Catholic sensibility.

This is not to deny the importance of the universal Church. Centered in Rome, the universal Church is a continual reminder that localism carried to an extreme can lead to sectarianism. One of us had a vivid reminder of the tension between universality and localism in Catholicism during a Holy Week visit to the Eternal City. During church services at home on the Palm Sunday prior to my departure with my family, I thought, regretfully, that we would miss celebrating Holy Week in our parish community, a local church where for more than twenty years we had gathered with many of our neighbors for this most solemn week in the Church's liturgical year. But then, as we stood in the carnival-like atmosphere of Saint Peter's Square during the Easter Sunday liturgy, listening to people from different countries respond to Pope Paul VI's blessing to the city and the world (*urbi et orbi*), we could vividly sense the significance of the universal religious community. The balloon men hawking their wares may have made the liturgy less than solemn, but the excitement of all those people from all over the world, responding to a blessing in their own language, created a unique Easter event, reminding us of the wide variety of parishes that celebrate Easter. So we returned to our own parish more conscious of our link with other local churches.

This healthy tension between the local parish and the universal human community has been part and parcel of the experience of successful urban and suburban parishes in the United States. Yet many North American bishops, theologians, and pastoral workers who are busy proclaiming the wonders of the *comunidades de base* (small-base communities) consider the parish an obsolete institution, not worthy of serious study. They dismiss it as a remnant of ghetto Catholicism that has alienated large numbers of Catholics and that is ill-equipped to address the religious issues of the contemporary world.

Mind you, they base their conclusions on the portrayal of parish in the writings of a few alienated Catholics and on some personal experiences of parishes that seemed to inhibit rather than encourage growth in Christian life.

We happen to be among a much larger segment of American Catholics who have a benign view of the parishes. We have been told that our experience of parish life in Chicago—both as children and as adults—is not typical and that we cannot claim that it offers a model of effective localism. Though it might not be replicated exactly in other geographical areas, and though there are plenty of parishes in Chicago that are not successful "storytelling communities," the failure of some parishes does not merit dismissing the significance of parish life in general. Localism is both a sociological phenomenon and an important ingredient in the Catholic sensibility.

Parishes have been and continue to be important in the North American Church because they are the religious counterpart of neighborhoods. The critics of parishes often consider neighborhoods obsolete as well. However, the Catholic sensibility understands that the neighborhood parish is a natural outgrowth of our human need for community. There are at least four social science research findings that explain why neighborhoods—or at least neighboring—persist, even in suburban areas where some people think they have given up the "narrowness" of the ethnic areas of their youth, and why the Unconnected Person, uninterested in community, or neighborhood or parish, is a myth:

1. Primary groups and informal friendship groups continue to have enormous influence, even in our highly technological society. With the advent of instant communication, rapid transportation, mass media, and world community, some social commentators predicted a "future shock" society where we would live an anomic, unconnected existence as isolated individuals in isolated family units. Though we do have a greater number of formal, stylized, specific relationships than our ancestors did, these have not developed at the expense of the informal, casual, diffuse ones of the past.

Beginning with sociological studies in the late 1920s, evidence has accumulated to demonstrate that friendship groups continue to be important in situations as diverse as the assembly line, the combat squad, the marketing group, and the doctor's lab, all highly technical situations. The majority of American families live within a mile of at least one grandparent, and siblings and cousins are the people whom Americans visit most frequently. *Gemeinschaft* persists.

2. Humans have a territorial propensity, rooted in our nature as embodied, pair-bonding, friendship-forming creatures. The study of territoriality by ethnologists, sociobiologists, and comparative primatologists leads to the conclusion that, like our sexuality, human territoriality is rooted in the animal world but came to maturity in self-generating cultures. That is to say, we are neither determined to a specific place nor free from the need for a place of our own, a place we can share with those with whom we are intimate. We defend our turf because of the meaning it has for us and for those with whom we share our place.

3. Humankind is a cooperative and gregarious species. For psychological and emotional convenience, we form relationships with those who are most like us; for physical convenience, we generally form relationships with those who are physically closest to us. In order to avoid a situation where we would be a "cognitive minority"— embracing attitudes, values, and behaviors unlike those of the majority surrounding us—we seek out "our kind of people" in the places we live. Often we choose where we will live on the basis of how similar we are to the people who are already there.

The neighborhood offers us an extended "place to come home to." The concept of the "defended neighborhood" developed by Gerald Suttles understands neighborhood as a place on the massive urban checkerboard where we and our family and friends feel "safe" as we live with "our kind of people." Though the forms of neighborhoods may change from urban to suburban areas, the need for a place where we are with our own kind persists, especially if we live in a family situation. The basis of neighborhood—the process of neighboring— persists.

4. Finally, the primary "value-socialization" that takes place within a family is reinforced in a local community or neighborhood. William McCready has theorized that, just as families are the organism in which individuals learn the social meaning of certain values, local communities are the context in which families are socialized to values. Socialization takes place in situations where there is both permanence

and longevity. Local communities, especially neighborhoods but even new suburban developments, create the impression of permanence, even for newcomers. They quickly develop a "story," a history of how the community was in the beginning and of where it is going. A child, a teenager, a young adult, a parent, and a grandparent all benefit from interaction with others who support their values, challenge them to be true to them, and invite their contribution to a communal sense of value. People in a neighborhood socialize each other, especially at key moments in growth and development cycles. Again, the neighborhood supports *Gemeinschaft*.

So, unlike the European emigrants who wanted to discard their peasant ties when they moved from rural areas into the urban centers of their own countries, the immigrants to the big cities of North America tried to recreate the community spirit of their European peasant villages. In the neighborhoods, living with their own kind of people, they found a place where they belonged. Perhaps a man was a "dumb Polack," a "greasy Wop," or a "shanty Irishman" to his co-workers; but he was accepted as "one of the family" when he came home to the neighborhood. The neighborhood offered a sanctuary somewhat akin to the "place to come home to" created by the traditional housewife/priestess. The neighborhood was a sacred space. Pastoral leaders who recognized the religious significance of this need for a sacred space helped create neighborhoods when they established churches as the sign of the continuing presence of the sacred within the community. Parishes were the logical outgrowth of the need for local community.

In cities like Chicago, the neighborhood/parish gave a sense of identity—religious, social, cultural, and political—to the immigrant. Parish and neighborhood became interchangeable for Catholics, and they used the parish name when they told someone where they lived. Religiously, the neighborhood/parish created a sense of a shared faith rooted in a sacramental system that offered the hope of salvation. The validity of this faith was guarded by the priest, who had some link with a broader church community but was principally, for most parishioners, the chief representative of God in the community. Few immigrants ever left the Church because of something the Pope, a bishop, or a theologian said, but many who left did so because of a disagreement with their parish priest.

By the 1940s and 1950s, the successful parish neighborhood was so integral to the Catholic and American identity of the urban immigrants' children and grandchildren that they never thought to question what it meant in their lives. They simply took it for granted. They assumed that no matter where they moved they would find a parish that would be pretty much the same as the one they grew up in. Those for whom the local parish was the religious, social, cultural, recreational, and political center of their lives thought it inconceivable that there might be places where they would not find similar communities. Even though there were ethnic differences among various parishes, the idea of the parish as the center of neighborhood life was strong almost everywhere.

The static, Counter-Reformation mentality of the official Church during those pre–Vatican II days supported the idea of a united Church, its oneness symbolized by the Latin Mass. On the other hand, parishes of vastly different cultural backgrounds allowed for a pluralism of approaches to interpreting the meaning of unity. Indeed, the pluralism of the North American experience required that the Church acknowledge a pluralism of interpretations of the faith. Polish parishes, German parishes, and Italian parishes offered the immigrants the opportunity to preserve cultural traditions that might otherwise have been lost. The push for Americanization, with its demand that the immigrants give up their foreign ways, might have been more successful if it had not been for the neighborhood parish.

As it is, the model of parish that survived the immigrants' movement up the economic ladder was the Irish model. Ellen Skerret's study of Chicago parishes shows that the Irish had little Irish religious culture to bring with them when they came to this country. The English had effectively wiped out nearly all traces of the Irish language religious tradition. The religious leaders of the Irish immigrants brought with them a form of the Latin/Roman religious traditions that, along with their English language, made it easy for them to set up parishes that seemed in line with the established American culture. The descendants of other immigrant groups, as they moved up the economic ladder and out of their ethnic communities, felt they "fit in" this type of parish.

Actually, the Irish neighborhood/parish showed how organic community encourages the positive identity so necessary for religious growth. The Irish instinct for political organization, developed out of the Irish need to band together against oppressors, flourished when they were able to support each other in neighborhood parishes—as they were better able to do in North America than in Ireland.

In this environment families were socialized. Individuals within families as well as families as a whole were able to experience a reinforcement of values, attitudes, and behaviors that were important to the family but often scorned by the established American culture. And in unofficial or quasi-official neighborhood/parish activities, parish members often experienced powerful if pre-conscious intimations of Catholic sensibility. In most instances neither the clergy nor laity fully understood why these activities were such deeply religious moments, for the official Church's mentality did not encourage a celebration of the sacramentality of experience. Still, the wisest of pastors knew that the sacraments celebrated in community called for an embrace of all community life with its sacramental potential.

In Chicago, the Irish parish model continued to emphasize the importance of localism for the children and grandchildren of all immigrant groups in the 1940s and 1950s. Young people who had positive experiences of a neighborhood parish then moved to the suburbs later in the 1960s and 1970s expecting the parish to provide the same positive sense of community. Most likely, they had never bothered to analyze that positive sense. Yet, when they were unable to repeat it, they knew they had lost something of great value. When they were in a position to help create a new parish, the model they most often emulated was the parish of their youth.

The common characteristics of successful modern neighborhood parishes show that the localism of the immigrant neighborhood parish continues to be important. These parishes offer their members centers where they can appreciate the sacramental potential of various dimensions of their lives. Though the dynamics of parish life have changed as a result of the Second Vatican Council and a better educated laity, the modern parish's roots in its predecessors can be seen in at least four ways:

1. The successful modern neighborhood parish is an important social center.

Our immigrant predecessors needed a place to come home to, a place where they belonged, to give them an identity in the midst of the hostility of the alien world. Membership in a neighborhood parish meant more than simply going to church on Sunday. It also meant belonging; it meant being part of a social group. Family members needed help as they lived out their roles within the family. The Altar and Rosary Society, the Holy Name Society, and the High Club of the 1940s and 1950s gave social support to acceptable patterns of behavior for men, women, and teenagers.

Flourishing modern parishes offer opportunities for people to develop social contacts with others of similar interests. The Council of Catholic Women (a modern version of the Altar Society), the Men's Society, the Youth Club, the Christian Family Movement, Marriage Encounter groups, programs for divorced and separated Catholics, the parish school and religious education programs, Great Books, Girl Scouts, Boy Scouts, the choir, ministries to the sick and bereaved, Alcoholics Anonymous meetings, senior citizens gatherings, and other groups all bring people with the same interests together. The quasi-religious atmosphere of some of these groups gives the impression of a religious significance to the social bonding.

The Catholic sensibility's celebration of the community aspects of belief—belief in the God who wants humans to live in relationships that reflect Divine love—acknowledges the goodness of the God-given drive for human unity. Parishes that encourage a recognition of the religious significance of our socializing nature affirm that we experience God in our encounters with fellow human beings. If a parish encourages positive social bonding at the neighborhood level and sees this as a religious experience, it is helping people appreciate what must be done in all attempts at human unity. The social life of a parish community teaches its members about our social God. Parish policymakers must help people appreciate the God present in their social activities.

2. The modern neighborhood parish offers the opportunity for parishioners to recreate together.

Closely linked to the parish as a social center is the ability of a parish to offer its members the opportunity to play. Immigrant parishes that offered some recreational opportunities attracted many more active members than those that did not. Basketball courts and a basketball-playing assistant pastor, along with High Club dances, picnics, and variety shows, helped to keep teenagers "off the street" and in a place where parents "knew" they would be safe (parents didn't know about the drinking that went on before and after these events, but at least the parish-centeredness kept the level of drinking down). A parish plant was much more than the Church building where people went for prayer and sacraments.

In a successful modern neighborhood parish the parish center also serves as the place where many groups play together. Volleyball leagues for all ages, basketball tournaments for school-age children, Friday night open gyms for the members of youth clubs, dances, and adult and teenage variety shows are just some of the activities that go on in many parish halls. In addition, parishes often sponsor golf and bowling leagues, bridge and pinochle groups, opportunities to play tennis or racquetball. Parish picnics and ice cream socials bring parishioners of all ages together.

Though many people may never experience the religious significance of playing, the modern Catholic parish that encourages its members to recreate together is performing a deeply religious function. The playful God that can be encountered in these activities also calls the people to playfulness in their own relationships. People will better appreciate the sacramentality of all their experiences when they learn to appreciate the sacramental possibilities of playing.

Does this mean that a community that wants to be a religious center must also hold dances and sports events and picnics and encourage its members to play? It is difficult to imagine a parish in touch with its Catholic sensibility that wouldn't want to do this.

3. In a modern neighborhood parish, parishioners are encouraged to contribute to the political and cultural life of the community and of the world beyond.

The immigrants who adjusted best to their new American world were those who learned how to use the neighborhood parish as a power base. Family and neighbors with "clout" saw to it that newcomers to the community got jobs and places to live. Relationships developed that later helped some members of the community to take on influential political roles, which in turn benefited the community. At the same time, the parish schools educated the children not only to be better Catholics, but also to be better citizens, better Americans. By the time the immigrants' children and grandchildren went to parish schools in the 1940s and 1950s, the youngsters had little doubt that they were both good Catholics and good Americans. They never heard the stories of how their elders had been considered a threat to the American Way of Life, so they never realized how far they had come or how the neighborhood parish helped them. The socialization of children to the values their parents cherished was carried out in a formalized manner in the schools. At the same time children received a hidden message about the religious significance of developing skill and talent. God was somehow connected with the process of education. If that process was a good experience for the student, God came out looking good.

Many of these children eventually made their way to college and moved up the economic and social ladder at a rate oftentimes surpassing others who had been in America much longer than they. The Catholic school, which its opponents considered inferior and divisive, had in fact far exceeded the expectations of its founders.

The successful modern neighborhood parish continues to recognize the importance of the parish school. It was a fashionable practice among post–Vatican II intellectual elites to dismiss the Catholic schools as inferior (despite research evidence to the contrary). Critics also argued that the money a parish spent on educating its young would be better spent on education for the adults who would then teach their children in the home, with some help from the Confraternity of Christian Doctrine (CCD) or Parish Schools of Religion (PSR) classes (despite the fact that most adults were not really interested in adult education or in being formal religious educators). The critics claimed that if the parents didn't understand their faith (since they didn't always agree with the elites, it was supposed they obviously *didn't* understand it), there was no point in trying to educate their children in the faith.

But Catholic schools not only reinforce values taught in the home; they also build on these values with additional strength of their own. And it is in any event not true that parents have to have a sophisticated understanding of their faith to give their children the values of the Catholic sensibility. When the parish as a whole reinforces these values in a formal setting, it indirectly contributes to a deeper appreciation of the faith by everyone. And a good parish school makes an important contribution to the development of potential political and cultural leaders with a Catholic sensibility. Though some parish schools have been poor, when a community decides it wants a good parish school, and the research evidence indicates that most Catholic parents want this, it can find a way to provide it.

Unfortunately, pastors and bishops often fail to give the leadership necessary to establish a parish school. Bishops who decree that no more schools should be built in their diocese or pastors who decide that a parish "learning center" meets their flock's educational needs often fail even to seek the opinion of the parishioners. Catholic laity who have made great financial sacrifices to sustain parish schools have a greater sense of the localism of the Catholic sensibility than many of their religious leaders.

Neighborhood parishes that encourage a religious appreciation of the educational process also can encourage parish members to be concerned about political, social, and cultural questions within the community and beyond it. Though there is much talk about the Church's mission to the poor in the underdeveloped countries of the world, outside of making financial contributions there is not very much that most ordinary parishioners can contribute to these missions. However, as Mother Theresa observed in a stirring address to a National Catholic Education Association convention, there are many hurting people right here among us who can benefit from the loving support of their neighbors. The Catholic sensibility, with its sense of structures "no bigger than necessary," suggests that caring for these people is a challenge for the local religious community. At the same time, a neighborhood parish can encourage its young people to pursue the qualifications necessary to contribute to decisions about the large-scale problems of peace, justice, and poverty; it can also challenge its members to an in-depth study of the problems of human relationships in the modern world. Scholars with a Catholic sensibility, nurtured in the local neighborhood parish, are sorely needed by both the Church and the secular society.

We are often told by critics that the notion of a healthy neighborhood parish and what it can do is unrealistic, that it wasn't that way in their parish, and that indeed their pastors were or are authoritarian dictators who pervert the Catholic message.

Our response is usually that of our teenage friends: "Tell us about it." We can match horror story with horror story. And we know that some parishes are bastions of racial and religious hatred. We are not defending all parishes or even the typical parish. Rather we are attempting to understand the attraction, the appeal, and the success of the neighborhood parish at its best. And we quickly add that Catholics educated in Catholic school are substantially more likely to be in favor of racial integration and tolerant of members of other denominations than are public school Catholics. They are also no less likely to have close friends who are not Catholics.

A neighborhood parish, aware of the sacramentality of all experience, ought to encourage an appreciation of the arts in its people, both young and old. Thus far this has not been an important priority in the modern local organic community, but the neighborhood parish has the potential to develop a taste for the arts. Church policymakers need to see this as the next step in the educational process that has been an important component of successful neighborhood parishes.

4. Finally, the modern neighborhood parish is *the* religious community for most of its members.

In the old days the parish church was the locus for the celebration of the major sacramental events of the immigrant's life. The parish priest was the dispenser of the grace that came with these sacraments. The immigrant was assured that there would be a better world beyond the grave if she or he remained in "the state of grace," obeyed the Ten Commandments, and followed the precepts of the Church. The official sharing of a common faith by all the members of the neighborhood parish reinforced the sense of belonging with one's own kind. At the same time the celebration of religious holidays created the opportunity for the telling of the "stories of faith" in the home, often emphasizing customs the immigrants had enjoyed in the lands of their birth. The static, formal structure of the official Church, with its emphasis on catechism answers, took on softer tones when it was interpreted through ethnic customs and family stories.

The immigrant neighborhood parish integrated religion and the life of the local community. It supplied the religious dimension of the socialization to values within the community. It supported, encouraged, and challenged its members in their social, recreational, political, and cultural life. The parish priests, the nuns in the school, and the parish plant with its Church all reminded the immigrants that God was present with them. The religious flavor of the neighborhood parish contributed a sense of hope in the midst of an often dreary and mundane existence.

Until a quarter of a century ago, the neighborhood parish continued to be both an official and unofficial reminder of the religious dimension of individual, family, and community life. The priests in the rectory and the nuns in the school were the official representatives of Catholicism and their explanations of the meaning of Catholicism were taken as true. Although people were reminded of the Pope through periodic stories in the newspapers and of the bishop when there was Confirmation, the day-to-day or week-to-week practice of religion—the "heart" of their religion—took place within the parish. The parish Church was the center for both official religious practices (Mass on Sunday, Easter Duty, confession, First Communion) and private devotions (novenas, Benediction, May crownings). People who had positive experiences of such parishes generally still have a positive image of Church and have managed to weather the turmoil of the post–Vatican II years with a minimum of bitterness.

While family experiences are the foundation of religious images, research evidence indicates that a relationship with a parish priest can diminish the negative impact of certain family experiences. The parish priest on the basketball court or at the High Club dance with the teenagers often helped the adolescents develop positive religious images that might not have emerged from their family experiences. Sometimes seemingly nonreligious activity in a neighborhood parish had a significant religious impact.

The successful modern neighborhood parish is the religious center for most of its parishioners for many of the same reasons. The parish continues to be a reminder of the religious dimension of life. It officially celebrates the presence of God in individual, family, and community experiences; it challenges, encourages, and supports its members as they try to live Christian lives at home, at work, and in the community. The neighborhood parish tells the stories of God that give people a sense of hope. In addition, in the period following the Second Vatican Council, when the "Rock" of the Catholic Church was felt to be crumbling, the neighborhood parish mediated the changes as they occurred. Neighborhood parishes that are successful today are those in which pastoral leaders and laity together interpret the new understandings of faith that emerged from the Council.

In summary, the neighborhood parish, throughout its history in the United States, has been the social, recreational, political, cultural, and religious center of the lives of most Catholics. In its best moments, it has been and continues to be a manifestation of the localism of the Catholic sensibility. Even in its less-than-perfect moments, the neighborhood parish is a sign that the Church exercises enormous religious influence. Church policymakers must design policies that encourage local religious communities to be centers of people's lives. These policies must recognize the importance of joining individual, family, and community experiences in a social, recreational, political, cultural, and religious context.

Some critics of the parish argue that it is wrong to have policies that make the parish, rather than the home, the center of religious life, and that the parish allows people to compartmentalize religion and life by limiting God's presence in the community to His or Her presence in a church building. These critics overlook the community-forming propensity of human nature. The parish celebration of the sacramental life of the community is just one more sign of the importance of community affirmation of the religious experiences of the family; families need the support and challenge of a larger, local group in touch with the religious moments of family life. In any case, the neighborhood parish actually fosters an integration of religion and day-to-day life. Obviously, some parish members will compartmentalize religion, limiting it to church on Sunday, but the parish's broad communal scope discourages this. The neighborhood parish says God is present in everything we do and everywhere we go.

At this point, our readers might well ask, If the neighborhood parish is a manifestation of the Catholic sensibility, how come most Catholics are unaware of this sensibility? Why is it that most Catholics have to struggle through the crises of their lives unaware of how their Catholic heritage speaks both to the crisis and to their day-to-day experiences?

First of all, the genius of the men who began the urban neighborhood parishes was that they appreciated the organic community of the Catholic sensibility, even though they may not have articulated how this was a logical correlate of the official Church position. The dichotomy between the doctrinal and the experiential made it difficult to explore any broader ramifications of the Catholic sensibility. But at some level they recognized the sacramentality of all experience and the religious role of the family. Their neighborhood parishes were designed to acknowledge the religious dimension of the experiences of the community. Although some of them might have been taught that their task was to emphasize the supernatural as opposed to the natural, what they actually did was help people discover the supernatural in the midst of the natural. Karl Rahner has said that parish is Church if all of its activities flow from the Eucharist, the Mass. The founders of neighborhood parishes would have claimed a link between their activities and the Eucharist, and most probably would also have maintained that the community needs a Eucharist to help "tell its story" more fully.

Since an organic, storytelling community is the logical conclusion when one understands experience as sacramental, imagination as analogical, and story as comic, we believe that these dimensions of religion were also present, to some degree, in the neighborhood parish. The Catholic sensibility has never been lost completely; sometimes it simply has not been recognized. Even if this level of religious experience was not tacitly acknowledged, the parish model of integrating religion and life suggests that Church policymakers can best encourage a Catholic sensibility in the context of the local church. Church policymakers must encourage the development of communities modeled on successful neighborhood parishes—organic local communities where issues of sex, women, and family intimacy are of pressing concern.

Catholic sensibility probably flourishes in "successful" neighborhood parishes—that is, those which are organic, storytelling communities, those which have appreciated the richness of the tradition of the neighborhood parish, even if they do not consciously encourage an appreciation of this sensibility. Unfortunately, not many post–Vatican II parishes have made the successful transition from the static Counter-Reformation mentality to a more dynamic, collegial understanding of Church. The post-conciliar Church lacks the local leadership that can respond to the local needs as the founders of the immigrant neighborhood parishes responded to the immigrants' needs. These pioneers were very much in touch with the experiences of their people; and though their approach to faith might seem primitive to a modern pastor, their ability to listen to the concerns of their people is not matched by most pastors who claim a "people of God" understanding of the Church.

A Catholic sensibility will emerge in American parishes where pastoral leaders, who have a more sophisticated understanding both of faith and of human community than the pastors of the past did, can link together the stories of faith and the stories of people's lives. They must be willing to listen to the stories of the community and be well-versed in the stories of God. They, like the artist, must be able to see God's presence in the most unlikely places but especially in people's experiences and in the life of the community; and they must have the skills to bring this presence to community awareness not only in liturgical celebration but also in the social, recreational, cultural, and political life of the community.

Even though this is the "age of the laity," the pastor still controls the direction of the neighborhood parish (and a priest or pastor-substitute leads other types of local communities). So church policy-makers should be concerned about educating priests in both the art and the skills of pastoring. At the same time, others who perform pastoral roles, as well as those who hope eventually to move into pastoral leadership, need this same ability.

The pastors who are successful and who offer a model for all pastoring are the "hopeful, holy men who smile." They are the leaders who walk the streets of their neighborhoods, both literally and figuratively, in order to hear the presence of God in people's lives. They are on good terms with the grammar-school kids, the teenagers, the young marrieds, the middle-agers, and the senior citizens of their communities. They are the shepherds who want to lead their people to an appreciation of the Divine Presence in their midst, rather than to rule over the community's religious life. They are the organizers who work with the people, formulating a vision of parish that inspires all the activities of the community, which wants to be the continuation of Christ in its time and place. They lead both by what they say and by what they do, preaching the pre-eminence of love and acting toward all the members of the community in a spirit of love. They are the example of forgiveness and reconciliation, as they welcome back all who express a desire to be a part of the Church again without demanding that they go through rigorous, legalistic examination. They know the key religious moments in individual and community life and try to celebrate these, inviting everyone (those in the religious community, those who no longer consider themselves part of it, and those who only observe it) to consider the meaning of these celebrations. They tell and retell the comic story of the Catholic tradition in formal liturgy and in a variety of other ways that appeal to the diverse groups within the community.

These are the pastoral leaders who can move the members of their communities to a deeper appreciation of the Catholic sensibility. These are the pastors who can dare to celebrate the sacramentality of sex, the analogical power of women, and the hopefulness of family intimacy. Their numbers should be legion. Unfortunately, there are very few such leaders in the Church today.

Anyone who doubts the control (either positive or negative) a pastor exercises over his community, even in this modern "people of God" era, has not studied the dynamics of community leadership and has not examined either parishes or other local religious communities. Critics might argue against one person having the sole claim to leadership in a religious community. But the facts of the matter are that both by virtue of his role in the institutional Church and because of the expectations of most parishioners, the pastor is the leader of the neighborhood parish. How he chooses to exercise this role will determine how "successful" the community will be. When there is a change of pastors from one who is the "hopeful, holy man who smiles" to one who has neither the art nor the skills of pastoring, the parish is generally splintered, unable to function as the religious, social, cultural, and political center of the community.

Unfortunately, the system of the official Church, which has spawned a "clerical culture," does not support pastors who appreciate the importance of organic community and know how to pastor a local church. Both clergy and laity fall into the trap of equating leadership with ownership and tolerate priests who are unresponsive to the needs of a community. When a pastor who sees himself as the person with ultimate responsibility for the parish (most often meaning accountability to the chancery office) begins to think of the parish as "my" parish, then the vision of the parish depends on his wishes and the approach to community activities is that which he thinks important. The liturgy fits what he wants.

We have argued that our sexual drive, a gift of our Creator, leads us to strive for unity, a unity that insists that we recognize the personhood of woman and a unity that hopes for playful commitment. This same drive for unity is at the root of humanity's social nature and is the basis for the religious potential of local community.

When Church policymakers establish policies that encourage hopeful, holy men and women who smile, who bring a Catholic sensibility to their work, their policies will nurture that sensibility. They might begin this process by encouraging the development of the religious imagination of future priests, awakening them to the Catholic sensibility of their religious heritage. It just might be possible that a "grass roots" movement of local churches will be the impetus for a Church aware of its Catholic sensibility.

Chapter 11
. . . .
WORSHIP:
THE CORRELATIVE KEY

The key that will help Catholics discover the true riches of the Catholic heritage is worship. Worship calls forth the God lurking in all human experiences, reminding us that life's mysteries are hints about the God who created us. Through worship we can be encouraged to imagine God as like our experiences. In worship we can tell and retell the comic stories of our faith. And worship allows us to join with others and celebrate life and the God who created all life and continues to sustain it with Her/His presence. Given the sad state of both formal liturgies and private devotions in the 1980s, it is little wonder that the Catholic Church does not spark the religious imaginations of its members. If the Church is to be saved—if Catholics are to be encouraged to develop positive images of God and Church— then policies are needed that promote worshiping communities with a Catholic sensibility.

Worship can function as the correlator, linking the experiences of life and faith so that both are enriched. Worship can be the basis of the spirituality of the community, throwing light on life's stories from the perspective of the Christian story and, in turn, discovering new depths to the Christian story. When worship awakens an appreciation for the sacramentality of all experience, its influence spreads beyond the particular place where people publicly acknowledge they are engaged in a religious task. Good worship—worship that sparks the religious imagination—will underscore the value of sex as sacramental, woman as analogical, intimacy as comic story, and the local church as organic religious community.

Present liturgical practices should be studied to see why they do not promote a Catholic sensibility, and suggestions for future liturgical reform should be measured against its criteria. A major revamping of our worship is essential.

An irony of the post–Vatican II Church is that the liturgical movement—which helped make the Council the Church's entry into the modern world—has not created liturgies that help people discover God's presence in that world. The Council's concerns were primarily theological and institutional, and it paid little attention to how people might actually correlate life and faith from day to day. This religious (as opposed to theological or institutional) concern, which may have motivated the liturgical reformers at the Council, was not operational for those who implemented the new liturgical policies. Liturgical commissions in Rome, at the national level, and in dioceses set policy with little regard for how or whether it encourages meaningful worship. And in some parishes we have liturgical purists who believe that any practice of the early Church is automatically good liturgy, and who don't think they need to know anything about the experiences of the people before instituting new liturgical practices.

We now know that in the excitement of liturgical reform following the Council, many reformers threw out the baby with the bath water. The liturgy in English, which would make the Eucharist (the Mass) the center of Christian worship, was going to help "create" community. People would no longer need private religious devotions and nonliturgical practices (Benediction, May crownings, novenas, etc.) in order to worship God. If they joined in a communal Sunday Mass, they would discover how God was present in other people and not in a private "God and me" situation. Our lives became our "prayer," as we were told that the Sunday liturgy should inspire us, in the words of the final bidding of the Eucharistic celebration, to "Go in peace to love and serve the Lord."

But is the new liturgy, even in English (according to research findings, most people rate this positively) and with its community emphasis, living up to original expectations? When the Mass fails to link the people's life and faith and when there are no other opportunities to experience correlative worship, people experience a void. Criticism of sermons (most Catholics rate the homilies they hear as inferior) springs from the priest's inability to link the life of the community and the stories of the Catholic tradition. Most people attend Sunday liturgies, not because the liturgies are inspiring or because they fear eternal damnation if they are absent, but because they sense the importance of some act of worship, no matter how poorly their ministers serve their need.

Looking back on our experiences growing up in Saint Angela's parish on the West Side of Chicago, we realize there were many opportunities to worship that are no longer present and for which there are no substitutes. The seminarian had to attend daily Mass, and the little sister tagged along. The weekday Latin Mass offered little opportunity for participation (except for the altar boys)—people either followed along with the priest, using a missal with an English translation on a facing page, said private devotions, or prayed their rosary. But ironically, through these practices, many did their own linking of life and faith, perhaps incorrectly, perhaps superstitiously, but still with a sense that God was more than someone thought of only on Sundays.

The seminarian had to make a daily "visit" for a period of mental prayer. The nuns encouraged the schoolgirls, too, to "make a visit" regularly. When churches were open from six in the morning till nine or ten in the evening, these were not difficult to arrange. Certainly, we know that one doesn't have to go to Church to meet God, and we knew that even then; but still, the open church allowed us to remember the presence of God more vividly than "my life is a prayer" may allow.

Saint Angela's had innumerable community worship celebrations that emphasized the sacramentality of everyday life, and they reminded parishioners that they shared a common vision. Our memories of First Communions, Confirmations, graduations, May crownings, Holy Week morning liturgies, Sunday afternoon Benedictions, the Saint Anne's novena, the parish mission, and of being in the choir and being an altar boy at Midnight Mass on Christmas, of saying Lenten Stations of the Cross and of attending Forty Hours' Devotions remind us that the community of Saint Angela's was very busy worshiping together. And the practices of the liturgical seasons—the fasts of Advent and Lent, the celebrations of Christmas and Easter, the Ember Days and Holy Days of Obligation, the months set aside to remember the Holy Souls, to honor Mary, the Rosary, and the Sacred Heart told us that the story of our God was related, in diverse ways, to the stories of our lives. We can't help suspecting that our religious imaginations were positively influenced by many of the worship practices of our neighborhood parish.

Obviously, we didn't hear anything about sex as sacramental, or woman as analog for God (save indirectly in Marian devotions). Still, the worship at Saint Angela's pointed us toward an appreciation of the importance of organic community and, in many ways, was closely tied into the experiences of family life. It offered us opportunities to hope that, with God's help, life could be better. The Catholic sensibility was quietly exercising its attraction.

Unlike the parishioners in communities like Saint Angela's, the modern Catholic finds himself or herself with limited options. The main, and in many local communities the only, worship event is the Sunday Mass. Despite all the expectations of the liturgical reformers, the Eucharist generally is not an exciting celebration in which God is made present to the community in such a way that the members go forth enriched and able to live the Good News. Now and again a Eucharistic service, connected with a major life event—a baptism, marriage, anniversary, funeral, or Christmas—will be celebrative; but, for the most part, Sunday Mass is a poor substitute for the rich worship opportunities of the past. In the hope of emphasizing the centrality of the Eucharist, the reformers lost sight of the fact that its affirmation of the sacramentality of all life should be an incentive to acknowledge the worship potential of *many* life experiences.

The Eucharistic liturgies of the post–Vatican II Church are not, in most instances, grace-filled moments that touch the religious imaginations of the congregation and help people see the links between what is being celebrated (however poorly) and their lives. In other words, correlation is not occurring in most liturgies. There are at least five reasons why this function of worship, an inevitable requirement of the liturgy of the Catholic sensibility, is not taking place:

1. Most liturgists, from the members of Roman commissions down to members of parish liturgy teams, don't appreciate the necessity of correlation. They design lectionaries, write Eucharistic canons, set rules for liturgical ministers, and write comments and prayers of the faithful—all in a vacuum. Even when they are well versed in the stories of faith, they do not see that for liturgy to be true worship it must link these stories with the stories of people's lives. The gap between abstract ideas on faith and the religious-imagination experience of God continues to bury the Catholic sensibility.

An example of how the liturgist can actually inhibit worship occurred in one "successful" parish. A specific concern centered on the Sunday Masses, which, though well attended, were neither the community-building nor community-celebrating events everyone had hoped they would be. When the pastor retired and the associate pastor was assigned elsewhere, the community asked the diocesan personnel board for replacements who would address this particular concern. The personnel board sent an associate with a degree in liturgy who called himself a liturgical "purist" and a pastor who was considered a liturgical expert. Within a month of their arrival, and with no sense of the experience of the community, these liturgists "reformed" the liturgy. They initiated one-minute pauses between scriptural readings, lengthened the homilies by five minutes, and decreed that the visiting priest whose homilies were popular with the community had a different theology than they and had to be replaced. Then they could not understand why, when the masses were fifteen minutes longer than they had been, people began to leave early. They took to the pulpit to denounce this behavior as "scandalizing to the children" and took to the doors of the church to frown their disapproval at the leave-takers.

And that was only the beginning. They were convinced that the community's liturgical problems prior to their arrival were due to an overemphasis on the Word and not enough attention to Ritual. They turned their attention to new ways to highlight the rituals of the liturgy. All of these changes took place before either of them had any real sense of the experiences of the parish, and obviously neither of these men understood the Catholic sensibility. At least the less-than-dynamic liturgies under the previous pastor had been recognized by everyone as in need of improvement. But the new leaders can't understand why the parishioners are unhappy. Needless to say, the liturgical experts did not create community-building or community-celebrating liturgies.

Although these men were liturgists, they were not liturgical artists. Father Patrick Collins suggests that good liturgy requires liturgical artists, who can create "mystery moments" in liturgy that relate to the moments of mystery in our lives, people who know both the stories of faith and the stories of the community, people who can adapt directives from liturgical commissions to local needs. The liturgical artist is one who "sees" the big picture, who knows what experiences of a community are potential revelations of God, and who can design a liturgy that allows the people also to see what they would not see without the insights of their religious heritage. John Shea once suggested that anyone interested in being a liturgist had to have "it"—"it" being the artist's and poet's ability to reflect for others the significance of their experiences as well as the presence of God (the mystery) in these experiences. The liturgical artist must be a part of the community but also must be able to step back from the community and criticize, challenge, and encourage it. Like all artists, the liturgical artist lives on the figurative fringes, at least some of the time.

Church policymakers who want to promote worship that will appeal to the religious imaginations must begin by putting liturgical artists in charge of liturgy at all levels of the Church. The first step would be to identify those who have the right potential—people who have "it"—and then encourage them to develop it.

2. The quality of most preaching is poor. Since at least the early 1970s, research data from the National Opinion Research Center have indicated that Catholic laity rate the caliber of preaching as inferior. In the ten or more years since this evaluation there has been little indication that the priests have responded to the criticism. Most preaching, both at Sunday Mass and at other important sacramental occasions, continues to be poor. Little if any effort is made to change this situation either on the part of the individual preacher or by church policymakers.

More than likely, Catholic preachers are no worse now than they were in the pre–Vatican II era. The harsher view of the homilies is probably the result of a better educated laity, with higher expectations, and a vernacular, community-centered liturgy billed as more "relevant." Poor homilies are an insult to the intelligence of the congregation, especially when they make little attempt to touch the religious imagination of the listeners. And when ritual, which was somewhat mysterious under its Latin wraps, becomes a mere repetition of familiar noncorrelative prayers, people expect preaching to perform the correlative task. And for the most part they are disappointed.

Unlike Protestant ministers who, knowing the central importance of their preaching, spend many hours preparing their Sunday sermons, most Catholic priests do little homily preparation. Many rely on a stock set of ideas largely unrelated to issues important in the lives of the congregation. Even some priests who do spend time preparing their homilies do so in a vacuum. For them, revelation is one-dimensional, the Church and Scriptures its sole source; people are exhorted to love God, to be followers of Christ, to preach the Kingdom, but there is little mention of how this is to be done.

Perhaps priests do not believe they can accomplish much in only ten minutes on a Sunday morning. Yet beyond that ten minutes, most Catholics have little contact with the message of their religious tradition. While it is undoubtedly hard to link the three Scripture readings (an abomination of the new liturgy) and the community experiences in such a short span, a skillful preacher can do so, even if he makes only one basic correlative point. But if people are able to gain fifty-two new insights into their lives and into their faith in the course of a year, a priest can be content. At the present time, most people don't feel they gain even one new insight in the course of a year.

A preacher who understands the correlative nature of preaching is continually listening for new understanding of both the stories of God and the stories of the community. He is constantly searching for new ways to tell both these stories so they will touch the religious imaginations of his listeners. He is never content with the mere repetition of ideas he acquired in his seminary days. He recognizes the importance of the ten minutes he has each Sunday and prepares for them as carefully as any Protestant minister, who might have four times as long to get his or her message across.

Church policymakers should also reconsider the requirement that only the priest preach the homily. At certain times, other members of the liturgical community might be well qualified to address a revelatory moment in the community's life. Women, married people, even teenagers can sometimes, if they have the skills, preach a correlative message more effectively than a priest.

Until the official Church recognizes preaching talents of lay people, it is incumbent on a priest that he consult with the laity about his interpretation of their experiences before he incorporates his ideas into a homily. For example, there is nothing more frustrating than to hear a homily describing the Eucharist as a family meal and urging families to return to the good old days when family dinners were the center of family life, when your family consists of one pre-schooler, a pre-teenager whose piano lesson comes in the middle of the dinner hour, and a teenager whose friends invariably wait until the family sits down to dinner before they begin to telephone. Perhaps the Eucharist is somewhat like those times when everything goes right at a family meal—or maybe like a joyful holiday feast—but a priest had better get his facts straight before he begins to use such analogies.

Are we suggesting that the ten-minute homily in the hour-long Sunday Eucharist is important? Do we really think that better homilies could have a good effect on the religious imagination of the participants? Are we claiming that a homilist with an appreciation of the Catholic sensibility would not dare preach an inferior homily? Indeed we are. Both Church policymakers and priests have their work cut out for them.

3. The vernacular ritual tends to be a boring re-enactment of the central event of our faith. If it is to create a sense of mystery, ritual must be written by artists and retold by artists. If ritual is not art, especially when it is in one's own language, people will not discover God's presence either in the story it reenacts or in their own stories. Ritual must move people out of ordinary time and into the time of the gods, the mysterious time that sheds light on everything that happens in ordinary time. Ritual must add romance to the love affair between God and His/Her people. The best ritual, like good theater, catches the imagination of the participants. But good ritual is more than theater because the members of the audience are active participants.

At the present time few liturgical events create this sense of participation in a Divine drama. Vernacular ritual has not created a sense
of participatory theater, of drama at its best, of God as the Storyteller
who invites us to be actors in the Divine drama, modeling the role
first played by Jesus Christ. More often than not, the priest is the
only actor and he does not get good critical reviews. Instead, ritual
is a mundane repetition of words, most of which seem boring to the
listeners. As one priest observed, "I can see them turn me off and go
into their own little worlds, especially as we move into the canon."

The priest, who as the convener is the "director" of the liturgy,
must be an artist who strives to have each player in the drama attuned
to what is occurring. Only then can the God who lurks in the coming
together of the community make Him/Herself present. Too often the
story is retold so that no one ever realizes that God is present.

Perhaps part of the reason the post–Vatican II ritual is not more
successful than its predecessor (and at times might not even be as
successful at reminding people of the mystery of life) is that too much
emphasis is placed on the priest as the image of Christ. When the
priest gives an unenthusiastic, monotone recitation of the ritual prayers, no one is inspired to "imagine" Christ as an exciting, God-giving
presence in our midst. While the celebrant does not have to have the
skills of a Shakespearean actor, he certainly must be aware of the
need to draw all those present into the story and realize that they,
too, are images of Christ. He (and she, when Church policymakers
realize that "imaging" Christ is not a talent reserved to men) shouldn't
have to resort to gimmicks.

Some critics of the new liturgy sense that it fails partly because
most liturgical gatherings are too large. They claim it is impossible
to experience mystery in a crowd the size of a Sunday congregation.
There may be some validity to this argument, but one should not
dismiss the significance of the Sunday communal gatherings, which
most often represent a cross section of the community that reminds
all participants of the need to unite diverse groups—to emulate the
union of two different representations of a human body, male and
female, in one flesh.

And even in the midst of a large group at Midnight Mass or at the
Easter Vigil, the mysterious presence of God can be experienced.
Many liturgists criticize these events because there are too many

"Christmas and Easter only" Catholics present. Yet these services are often highlights of people's lives. Perhaps liturgists should learn that they cannot define how God will make Himself/Herself visible. They should assist in the process of making God present, and not limit how or when.

One suggestion to counteract the mundaneness of large Sunday liturgies is to provide smaller liturgical experiences in which the potential of ritual reenactment can be appreciated in a way that will create the proper mindset for participation in larger liturgies. Small liturgical gatherings—home Masses, celebrations of special events with a group of family and friends in a parish church or a university chapel, the gathering of the members of a resort community in a clubhouse or in the open countryside, teenage Masses, late Sunday night liturgies in college dorms—are all potentially correlative events. First of all, at these gatherings the priest can have a precise sense of the experiences that must be correlated with God's story so as to make God's presence more visible, and he is in a better position to touch the religious imagination of the participants through the Word. In addition, if he is a good director, he tries to make the ritual one of participation. He can interpret the ritual prayers more forcefully than is often possible in a larger congregational setting. But then the liturgies for large congregations must also reflect to the community the God present in its midst, and similarly inspire the people. When ritual becomes correlative, God's presence will be discovered both in the liturgical gathering and in all the mystery experiences of individuals, families, and the community. The romance of the Catholic sensibility will brighten our love affair with God and with our fellow humans.

4. Liturgical music fails to contribute to the sense of mystery, to the extra-ordinary dimension of life that liturgy must call to our attention. Very few Catholics are satisfied with the music of the post–Vatican II liturgy, used as they were to another kind of music as *the* Church music. In theory, the new diversity of musical approaches is positive; it acknowledges that there is a pluralism of musical tastes, a variety of ways in which to stir the religious imagination through music. In practice, however, the requirement that liturgical music, like all of liturgy, should contribute to the sense of mystery celebrated in liturgy has not been met by many musicians. Church policymakers

must encourage the creation of classical music within the various musical styles; by "classical" we mean music that, though in a particular style, has such power that it can be experienced as uplifting even by those who are unfamiliar with its style or who have not enjoyed it under other circumstances.

Another problem is that despite the post–Vatican II emphasis on congregational singing, most Catholics do not sing during liturgies; the music does not move them to do so. Some claim that the difference between the poor singing in Catholic churches and enthusiastic Protestant singing is often given that Catholics aren't used to singing. But nearly twenty years is enough time in which to get used to it. The problem is more than that of not developing the habit. Rather the music does not encourage us to sing. When the music is correlative, it will inspire people to participate. Then even those who, like the authors, are tone-deaf will at least be uplifted by the heavenly music of people worshiping the God they meet in both liturgy and life.

5. Too few devotional practices provide ongoing reminders of the correlation that should, at least theoretically, take place in the liturgy. Liturgies and para-liturgies were supposed to meet the worship needs of all the individuals in the community. But now it is admitted that perhaps some of the devotional practices of the pre–Vatican II Church should be reinstated. Perhaps some of them need to be reinterpreted so they no longer appear to be magical attempts to manipulate God, though even when they did, they still functioned as reminders of God's presence for those who engaged in them.

The Eucharist as the center of Catholic worship demands a recognition of the sacredness of all life. Devotional practices are a continuation of the Eucharistic theme in day-to-day life, the sacramentals that recall the story that is retold in the Eucharist. They are not substitutes for the Eucharist, but they allow for more direct correlation than can often take place in a liturgy.

For example, we cannot imagine a community attuned to its Catholic sensibility that would not have Marian devotions. Marian devotions acknowledge the sacramentality of a woman's body and the analogical power of women. The Catholic sensibility demands that we celebrate the power of Mary as a reminder of the femininity of God. Local communities that are concerned about touching the religious imaginations of their people with the images of God as Lover and God as Mother can begin by celebrating Mary as a symbol of the Love and the Motherhood of God. Mothers and lovers will be helped to discover God's presence in their experiences. All of us will be encouraged to be more like God by recognizing how Mary reveals God.

In a similar way, devotional practices connected with the liturgical seasons can support the comic story of marital intimacy. One of us once suggested that the theme of Advent services be "Be a Better Lover by Christmas," since certainly the rebirth of Love in the Christmas Child calls us all to be better lovers. So, too, we have suggested that a good Lenten practice for marital partners would be to make the sacrifices necessary to be sexy for each other. Thus the Eucharistic theme of preparation for birth and resurrection can be correlated more specifically throughout the year.

Blessings are another devotional practice that should be reinstated. We remember blessings of our car (we should be careful drivers), the blessing of our house as our family was dedicated to the Sacred Heart, a betrothal blessing, a blessing for a new mother, and the blessing of Easter baskets—all reminders that these things, places, and events were sacramental. Along with Advent wreaths and Christmas cribs, these blessings celebrate the presence of God in our midst, helping us to appreciate the importance of our experiences. A renewal of devotional practices, along with the institution of new practices that reflect the insights of the Catholic sensibility, will serve to remind people of the sacramentality of all experience. The stage will then be set for a deeper appreciation of how the Eucharist tells of the story on which all our stories are based.

Surprisingly, dissatisfaction with liturgy has *not* been the cause of decreased Church attendance, and it appears that unless Catholics have other reasons for being angry at the Church, they will continue to attend Sunday Mass. Although most Catholics do not experience liturgy as correlative, they still sense an importance to worship and participate in the principal worship of their religious tradition.

Some years ago Father Hans Küng gave a lecture in Chicago entitled "Why Sunday Worship?" One of his admirers—an anti-clerical woman whose distaste for poor homilies had led her to attend weekday but not Sunday Mass—was certain that he was going to shatter another tradition and advocate that we discontinue our emphasis on the Sunday obligation to attend Mass. We assured her that Father Küng was not the flaming radical the press made him out to be and was undoubtedly going to explain why Sunday worship was important. We're not sure if she changed her opinions on Sunday worship after listening to Father Küng, but the three reasons he offered in support of Sunday worship are in fact the reasons why most Catholics continue to attend Sunday Mass in spite of the liturgical deficiencies:

1. The individual *needs* the once-a-week reminder of God's presence.

2. The members of the community need one another's presence as a sign that theirs is a community of shared faith.

3. The world beyond the community needs Sunday worship as a sign that there is a religious dimension to life.

Perhaps in pre–Vatican II days Catholics attended Sunday Mass out of a fear of hell as punishment for nonattendance. Indeed the drop in Church attendance that is not directly attributable to the birth control issue—the principal reason for disaffection from faithful attendance—is probably explained as a result of the belief in a loving God who is not keeping track of records in attendance at Mass. We taught our young people about this loving God, and most of them go through periods where they do not attend Mass with no fear that this will result in eternal damnation. Still, the Catholic sensibility exercises an influence on those who voluntarily attend Mass. They "know"—though they might not always know why—that worship is necessary; they sense its importance for themselves, their family, and the religious community. At times, they even realize that they are making a statement about God's presence in the world to those who do not share their religious beliefs.

In the Catholic Church in the 1980s, people flock to church each Sunday, searching for an explanation of life, for a map to help them through the ups and downs of their daily lives. Their experiences supply one component of correlative worship. Their religious heritage supplies the other component. The liturgy should provide the link between the two. When Church policymakers, at all levels of the Church, appreciate the importance of worship, they will trigger the religious imaginations of Catholics so they can in turn recognize the sacramentality of all experience, including sex, the analogical nature of their images of God, the hopefulness of their religious story, and the importance of local community.

The liturgical reforms of the Vatican Council have been both the biggest opportunity and the biggest failure of the last twenty years. Failure they need not remain, and opportunity they still are. The rearticulation of the Catholic sensibility will occur for most Catholics only in and through liturgy.

Chapter 12

. . . .

CATHOLICISM
AND ART

I f the Catholic Church is to be saved, it must rediscover the historic link between its heritage and the fine and lively arts. It must realize that art is not a luxury to human life and religion, but a necessity; it must support and encourage the best of artistic efforts; and it must demand the highest standards of professional craftsmanship.

At most times in the history of Catholicism these premises would be so self-evident that it would not be required to pronounce them. It is a measure of the problems of the Catholic Church in the United States today that they are not at all self-evident and that, indeed, most Catholic leaders would presume they are false.

Art is by definition sacramental; it seeks to capture the essence of an experience and share it with others. It flourishes in the pre-conscious—the locale of experience, image, and story. It seeks to illumine the good, the true, and the beautiful as they are experienced and to share that illumination with others. Art heightens experiences, enriches symbols, generates stories, and binds communities together.

A sacramental religion like Catholicism cannot escape art even if it wants to. Its fundamental insight that God lurks in creatures requires it to realize that art, however unconsciously, searches for the lurking God, for Being both hidden and revealed in beings. The artistic act is in its very nature sacramental because it seeks to reveal, to disclose, to illumine. In creations of art the God who lurks in the creation of nature is especially likely to be discerned. All other things being equal, the better the art the more sacramental it will be and the more revealing of God. Since art reveals God and indeed tells, one way or another, stories of God, the best of artistic activity is none too good for God. And poor artistic activity is an insult to God.

Even in the New Testament art was at work. Saint Mark's Gospel is now perceived to be a masterpiece of narrative technique and Saint John's Gospel to be deeply influenced by the techniques of Greek drama. Saint Paul's Epistles are filled with allusions to early Christian hymnody. The early Church did not forge its alliance with art because of an explicit policy decision; rather it assumed that art revealed the God who was working in the world and revealing Himself, especially through Jesus. The Church without art, and especially without a concern for the finest of artistic effort, was unthinkable for most of Catholic history. The loss of this implicit and unassailable awareness of the importance of art in religion is one of the great tragedies of Catholic history. A sacramental Church unconcerned for artistic excellence is almost a contradiction in terms.

The Catholic Church in the United States will not be "saved" without a recapture of understanding about the nature of art as religious activity and a rediscovery of the Church's role as enthusiastic patron of the best in art. There is no stronger instrument for facilitating religious experience, strengthening religious imagination, telling religious stories, and creating religious community.

A good measure of the state of the Catholic religious sensibility at any given time and place is the relationship of the institutional Church to religious art and indeed, to all art—painting, sculpture, architecture, music, poetry, and storytelling. And there is no opposition between the Church's concern for art and the Church's concern for scholarship. On the contrary, the two have usually gone hand in hand and are, in fact, both the product of the analogical imagination; if God is experienced sacramentally and described analogically, then both art and scholarship reflect God, are occasions for God's self-disclosure and a legitimate object of religious concern. When art is rejected as religiously irrelevant, it is almost inevitable that scholarship will be rejected, too.

One historical era produced Notre Dame de Paris, the *Divine Comedy,* and the *Summa Theologica.* Another era produced tasteless immigrant churches, the Baltimore Catechism, and a profound suspicion of the arts as "too sensual." Those who complain (perhaps with reason) that emotion and feelings are replacing intellect in seminary training and parochial religious education may well be making a valid argument, but what passes for religious "feeling" in many classrooms and Confraternity of Christian Doctrine programs is devoid of the analogical imagination and artistic sensitivity. The "feeling" of the pop psychologists is undisciplined and insensitive emotion. The sensibility of the skilled artist is disciplined by training and practice.

In its best moments, the Catholic heritage has always believed that scholarship and art cannot be separated, or, to use the terms in this book, that sensibility and rationality cannot be separated. The latter depends on the former for power and for raw data, and the former depends on the latter for clarification, discernment, and philosophical reflection. The Catholic religious sensibility, in its most flourishing eras, has never separated itself from rationality. If pseudo-Catholic religious sensibility in the post–Vatican II era has divorced itself from rationality, then it is once more a case of the Catholic sensibility being found hard and not tried rather than being tried and found wanting. "Let it all hang out" emotionality ought not to be confused with the traditional Catholic religious sensibility. What has replaced stern intellectual discipline in Catholic seminaries (to the extent there ever was any of it) is not an excessive interest in the fine arts but pop psychology and shallow pragmatism. It is not that at one time seminarians were required to learn theology and now spend their time on art and music and painting and literature. It is rather that at one time they were required to memorize theology manuals and now aren't required, in many seminaries, to learn anything at all.

If one believes that God's self-disclosure occurs in and through the natural and human world, then obviously the work of the human intellect, with all its limitations and imperfections, is one of the principal sacraments of God's loving goodness. If one's religious experience is sacramental and one's imagination is analogical, one must necessarily be committed to rationality. If the Church's commitment to rationality at any given time and place (as in the United States today) is defective, it is for the same reason that its commitment to the arts is defective: the Catholic religious sensibility—imagination, image, story, and community—are not valued highly enough by the institutional Church and its clerical elites.

There are five different ways the Church can relate to art:

1. Art is good in itself.

2. Art is a way of showing the power and importance of the Church or Church persons.

3. Art is a useful tool for religious education and instruction.

4. Art is a useful option but hardly essential and not necessary in difficult circumstances.

5. Art is dangerous because it leads to both pride and sensuality.

So if art is storytelling, we find five different responses at various times in Catholic history:

1. that storytelling is good in itself, though, like everything else, subject to abuse—because it is a way of sharing experiences, especially experiences of goodness (or of truth or of beauty);

2. that an effective story told by a Catholic raises the prestige of the Church (or of the churchman who funds the story, as with the Borghese Pope who gets central billing above the façade of Saint Peter's while Saints Peter and Paul are shoved off into the left-hand corner);

3. that storytelling is important to the Church because it is a way of driving home points of Christian doctrine for religious education;

4. that storytellers are useful, but not necessary, and indeed, at times when the Church is under siege (and it is almost always under siege) perhaps may be dangerous because they may lead the unenlightened faithful astray;

5. that storytelling in and of itself is almost always dangerous, both because it will lead the storyteller to pride, if people like his or her stories, and the people to sins of sensuality if they listen to them.

Only the first attitude is acceptable to the sacramental experience and to the analogical imagination. Whether the story is formally or explicitly religious (as, for example, Graham Greene's *The Power and the Glory*) or only implicitly religious (as for example, Shakespeare's

Macbeth), it is sacramental if it attempts, even if only in a very minor way, to share an experience of grace. Admittedly, some stories are written with other intentions, and their grace experience is minimal or even perhaps nonexistent; in still other stories, the experience is one of negativity, disintegration, destruction: not a tragedy in the Greek or Shakespearean sense, even in the sense of Camus, but rather one of utter meaninglessness (the plays of Pinter, for example). Still, the story as such must be judged by the experience that is being shared and by the craftsmanship with which it is shared, and by no other standards (which is not to say that ethical principles are irrelevant, but only that they are not operative when one is judging the story *as such*).

Abbot Suger suggested that the sacramentality of his church should be judged by the craftsmanship with which it is built. If the craftsmanship was such that light was revealed, then the church was a good church. Suger did *not* say that the church is a good church if it is a useful tool for backing up or illustrating the doctrinal proposition that Christ is the light of the world. Doubtless he realized that a church in which the light artistry was successful would surely reveal Christ as light of the world, but it was the craftsmanship that mattered and not the religious educational implication. The sacramentality of a work of art is structured into the work itself and is not added on from the outside because preachers or teachers are able to use it as an apt illustration. What counts is the experience the work of art produces and not the philosophical or homiletic lesson that may be derived from it. It would not have occurred to Suger, or indeed to any of the patrons or artists of the High Ages of Catholic art, that a work of art, including a work of religious art, should be judged by any other criterion than its craftsmanship.

In the present era such an attitude is practically nonexistent among Catholic Church elites in the United States. There is not even as much "class" among most American hierarchs as there was with the Borghese Pope who wanted to be memorialized in the world's largest basilica. Pastors and bishops do indeed build monuments to themselves, often big monuments, but unlike the Borghese Pope they are quite incapable of distinguishing between size and beauty.

The characteristic response of the clergy and the hierarchy to art in the United States could be summarized as follows: we don't have time for art; we're too busy protecting the faith of the simple or liberating the oppressed or following the inspirations of the Holy Spirit to devote our time to it; at its worst, art can give people dirty or proud thoughts and at best it may be a useful tool for religious education, but it's no substitute for the teaching (often by rote) of sound religious doctrine; maybe later, when we have the time and the money to devote to it, but right now art is a cross between a danger and a useful but expensive luxury. Building stained-glass windows in the Middle Ages was of course a religious and a priestly exercise, but that was a long time ago and we don't have the time or resources to act as though novel-writing and filmmaking are similar priestly activities today.

There are three reasons for this network of attitudes, which violates and perverts the historic Catholic religious sensibility: a false moralism, a false pragmatism, and a false romanticism.

The moralistic impulse equates religion with morality. It has no notion of experience, imagination, story, or community as aspects of religious experience. Catholicism is seen essentially as a set of moral rules, clearly stated and rigidly applied, and especially moral rules governing human sexuality. No one perhaps will say it out loud, but the preoccupation with sexual ethics of the Vatican and of many clergy is conclusive evidence that an implicit equation is made between religion and sexual morality, that the Catholic heritage is sexual ethic, and that salvation is achieved by obeying all the negative sexual regulations.

In this frame of reference a work of art, of whatever sort, is judged solely in terms of its ethical content, and particularly in terms of what it says or does not say about sex. If a painting depicts a human body, the measuring stick is pulled out and the painting is judged by how much human flesh, male and especially female, is revealed. A novel or a short story is judged by the sexual behavior of its characters. If they violate in any way the explicit sexual code of contemporary Catholicism, then the story is evil and even more evil if their sexual violations are described with any realism. Even good sexuality, between husband and wife, for example, must not be portrayed in any but the most indirect and obscure terms, lest immature readers (always lurking around to pick up a book) be given "bad thoughts." Moreover, it is the actions of the characters themselves, formally considered, that matter. Fornication is in and of itself a moral sin, so if fornication is committed in a story, then the story is immoral.

One might argue that even the ethical and moral theological manuals of the pre–Vatican II Church took into account the circumstances of an action and concluded that objectively grave sins could be substantially less than that in a given set of circumstances that included an understanding of the weakness, frailties, and passions of the characters. Moralistic judgments about a story do not admit of such nuance. But a moralist does not permit an author to put his characters in circumstances where their freedom from grave moral evil is severely impaired, nor does he permit the author to describe actions of which he himself does not approve. For that matter, he does not even permit the author to depict God as drawing straight with crooked lines and turning human sinfulness into His/Her own game of human salvation (hence the alcoholism and sexual sins of Graham Greene's whisky priest in *The Power and the Glory* make that novel immoral, whatever Greene's intention might have been to explore the crooked lines of God).

This may sound like a caricature of the Catholic response to art in the pre–Vatican Council era. But it is still the dominant and prevailing attitude among the clerical and hierarchical elites in America. One of us began writing explicitly theological novels a couple of years ago, convinced that the novel was an appropriate way of talking about God in the contemporary world. The stories were explicitly, formally, deliberately, blatantly theological. But with one or two exceptions, the possibility that these stories were religious or theological was not even addressed by Catholic reviewers. It was unthinkable to them that a novel could be about sacraments of grace and analogical images—despite an explicit statement that they were.

A priest wrote the following indictment:

1. Corruption and politics in the Church—do you mean to give the impression that the majority of bishops and cardinals are irresponsible with money, are homosexuals or are profligate?

2. That all rich women have loose morals except your mother—surely you have encountered people who blended wealth and goodness nicely?

3. That all young people are automatically hopping in and out

of bed every chance they get—what impression did you intend to convey?

4. That all priests have a secret sex life to compensate for the Church rule of celibacy. Here you have reinforced our weak-ego-strength priests that they are not so bad after all. We missionaries are the ones to give witness.

5. That the priests in Rome are all selfish, power-hungry and corrupt politicians. I met some excellent order men there.

It is hard to explain why a priest would want to air so much dirty linen that would soil the Bride he has chosen to serve instead of picking up the positive qualities of the sinner who learns to love through a forgiving mother's help. My married friends go further; they maintain you are experiencing the sexual escapades you describe so well. I tell them you learn this in counseling, but they will not accept it. As a diocesan priest you are entitled to make money but it should not be tainted money which sells books but lowers the dignity of your Bride.

The priest obviously was sincere and, moreover, a dedicated and hard-working man, yet just as obviously he had not read a novel for a long, long time and was not likely to read one again. He'd read *The Cardinal Sins* because it was a novel by a priest and he felt he ought to read it. He was horrified. It was not an "edifying" book, it presented sinful priests, it depicted sex outside of marriage, it implied that most priests were unfaithful to their vows and that all Vatican officials or most Vatican officials were corrupt. The laity would be shocked and scandalized, the clergy would be disgraced, the moral code of the Church would be flouted and possibly, indeed probably, the author was celebrating his own sinfulness.

For such a sincere though patently uneducated cleric, the statement at the beginning of the book that the story was not autobiographical or historical was impossible to accept. The distinction between the narrator and the author, a commonplace of literary analysis, was one which he could not comprehend. The distinction between a story and a book of piety on the one hand or of sociological analysis on the other was also one he could not fathom. Piety edifies, sociology depicts averages, and stories tell of sin and redemption, of God's grace overcoming human evil. A story about good people who are paragons of virtue and do nothing wrong, a story about priests, all of whose behavior is edifying, would not be a story at all. One may only write pseudo-stories in which grace is not required because redemption has already happened.

The moralistic criterion would, of course, if systematically and rigidly applied, ban much of the Old and the New Testaments. The Gospel stories surely would have to go, because all but one of the priests depicted in the Gospel is a coward or a traitor (it escapes us why the New Testament writers were permitted to portray the apostles with all their weaknesses and limitations but why a contemporary writer has to depict priests as perfect). Many of the books of the Old Testament would also have to go, but especially the Song of Songs, which is explicitly, and indeed appealingly, erotic. Most of the parables of Jesus would also fall victim to the moralistic censor's blue pencil, for the characters in the parables are very rarely edifying.

Surprise is the essence of any good story. The parables of Jesus are filled with surprises. The greatest surprise of all is that sin is forgiven, that grace overcomes justice, and life overcomes death. If one does not write stories about those who are liable to sin and to justice and to death, then there is no possibility of surprise. But the moralist does not want surprise, he wants universal and triumphant virtue, even at the beginning of the story. At the end of the story he wants, not a hint of hopefulness, which is the best we get in the human condition, but mathematical certainty.

In an ecclesiastical institution dominated by moralism all art becomes impossible. The clerical and hierarchical elites of American Catholicism assume that their moralistic criteria are beyond challenge. Under such circumstances, art and the Catholic sensibility have no chance. Even the story line of a marriage as a series of love affairs with the same person, as we described it in a previous chapter, would be intolerable to the Catholic clerical moralist, because the role of sexual attraction in binding a man and woman together would almost certainly give readers—especially young and impressionable readers—"dirty" thoughts. Yet try to write a story about constantly renewed marital love in which sex is left out!

The claim here is not that the work of art is free from ethical judgment but, rather, that the judgment about craft must be made first and that ethical judgment is no substitute for it. When ethical judgment is substituted for artistic judgment, artistic expression of the analogical imagination cannot occur. Moreover, if the ethical criterion, applied after a judgment about artfulness has been made, is that the work of art must not "harm" the young and impressionable, then art also becomes impossible. In any case it is not altogether clear who the young and impressionable are these days; teenagers seem less likely to be shocked than their parents, if anything. If parents cannot keep materials that might scandalize them out of the hands of their teenagers, then the young people are much more likely to find truly scandalous materials in nonreligious works. If the artist/painter/writer is not permitted to address his work to mature individuals, then she or he might just as well find a job as a director of religious education or a youth minister or a head usher—all harmless and frequently useless activities.

"But why do you have to have sex in it?" asks the moralistic critic. Or "Why couldn't you put more clothes on that body in your painting?" (a question that led one Pope to mutilate many of Michelangelo's paintings). The answer is that sex is part of the human condition, and the human body is good and beautiful, and both are sacraments of God's love. Eroticism in art and music and literature and dance may be pornographic but it need not be. If the line is hard to draw on occasion (and while it also may vary with time and place), that line ought to be drawn by mature, self-possessed adults who understand the nature of the artistic enterprise and not by nervous and anxious clerics of the sort who covered up the genitals on figures in Michelangelo's *Last Judgment* in the Sistine Chapel. Unless the American Catholic Church, as an institution, is ready to make artistic judgments first and then ethical judgments, and to leave the ethical judgments to the mature and self-possessed, then it will continue to pervert the Catholic religious sensibility and to destroy whatever artistic capabilities may exist among those who are subject to the discipline of its authority.

In the years since the Second World War, and especially since the presidency of John F. Kennedy, American Catholics in massive numbers have moved into the population groups that produce, support, and "consume" the fine and the lively arts. Irish, Italian, and Polish names are now easily recognizable in the rosters of orchestras, dance groups, and opera companies as performers, sponsors, and even on occasion directors (the Lyric Opera of Chicago, even as we write this, produced a new version of *Aïda* with the funds coming entirely from two Catholic donors). Catholic novelists abound; new ones seem to be appearing every year. More and more Catholics are engaged in both the performance and the production and management of radio and television and newspapers. The Church ignores them, pretending that like the new generation of Catholic scholars they do not exist.

Several years ago the Lyric Opera of Chicago, along with La Scala of Milan, commissioned an opera based on John Milton's poem *Paradise Lost*. The composer was the great Polish musician Krzysztof Penderecki, perhaps the greatest living Catholic musician and a close personal friend of John Paul II (so close, in fact, that when the opera was performed in Rome, the Pope attended and gave a small talk— reproduced faithfully in *L'Osservatore Romano*—about the opera). In Chicago, the premiere of *Paradise Lost* went totally unnoticed by the institutional Church. As one prominent Catholic associated with the opera remarked, "Who would have expected Cardinal Cody to give a damn about opera?" The great medieval and Renaissance churchmen, who may on occasion have gone to the other extreme in their patronage of art, would simply have not been able to understand the mentality behind this lack of interest. (Of course, for the first forty years of this century priests in the Archdiocese of Chicago were forbidden to attend the opera under pain of suspension. Everyone knew, didn't they, that operas were erotic? One wonders, somewhat dyspeptically, if anyone has ever had an erotic thought during a performance by the Lyric Opera.)

Even when the moralistic criterion has been overridden—and despite the enormous changes over the last forty years, Catholic moralism seems to be every bit as strong as it was when Graham Greene wrote *The Power and the Glory*, *The Heart of the Matter* and *The End of the Affair*—the criterion of pragmatism takes over. It is much to be doubted that ecclesiastical authority now thinks that opera is erotic and evil; now it merely dismisses it as pleasant, perhaps, but irrelevant. How many souls will a priest save by a night at the opera? Wouldn't it be better for a priest to stay home and prepare his sermon instead of going to the opera? (Opera here is an example of high culture, not necessarily entertainment to be urged on everyone.)

First of all, God saves souls, humans don't, and how God goes about that process is beyond our comprehension. If the alternative on a given night was indeed opera or sermon, then of course the priest should attend to the sermon. Most priests have time to do both, however, and in fact do neither. The pragmatist's artificial opposition between the cultural activity and the work of the ministry is a dishonest dodge rather than a real dilemma. The pragmatist sees no value at all in "entertainment" (though he may well spend a good deal of time watching baseball or NFL football on television). Entertainment does not save souls, it does not create justice in the world, it does not provide a practical program for parish renewal, it does not design a CCD instruction course for you. It may be tolerable as recreation, i.e., as an escape from which you can return to the work of the ministry with renewed vigor, but life is too short and there are too many things that have to be done to "waste" much time on entertainment.

Thomas Aquinas wrote that life without pleasure becomes impossible. He did not suggest that pleasure was an "escape," but the pragmatist has no more time for exploring the subtle philosophical distinctions of Aquinas than he has for pursuing "entertainment" in the fine or the lively arts. At the end of a hard day he barely has the energy to watch the late-night news or the movie or *Mash* reruns after it.

The pragmatist with a little more education than most may well admit that a painting or a statue or a story or a song is a great religious education gimmick and hence may, under certain circumstances, be useful. When there is time, he will have someone he knows draw a picture or even maybe write a song for a religious education class or a parish renewal program. He may even try to begin each Sunday sermon with a story. He justifies these hasty and perhaps halfhearted attempts at art not because art is a good thing in itself, an activity in which there is special opportunity for the self-disclosure of God, but because they are programmatically useful as long as they don't take too much time or cost too much money. That's what the pragmatic hierarch or cleric or religious wants—the quick, useful, and efficient program: high-falutin' ideas are not relevant unless they lead to immediate and detailed programs. The history of the American Catholic Church since the Second Vatican Council has been a history of quick-fix programs, generally discovered in summer workshops that last no more than two weeks (and often only two days), applied with all the verve and enthusiasm, all the drive and energy characteristic of American Catholicism.

A typical clerical pragmatist in the years after the Vatican Council wanted to learn as much as possible about the new theology, the new Scripture, the new psychology, the new whatever. The learning consisted of a couple of books or a course or a workshop or two and the acquisition of a few summary sentences in which he could quickly account for the whole subject. Having thus mastered the complexities of theology or biblical studies or psychology or world politics, the pragmatic priest was ready either to develop his own program or to acquire, sometimes at considerable cost, someone else's pre-packaged program so that there would be something new and exciting and fashionable in his parish the following September.

One can even imagine such workshops and pre-packaged programs on the Catholic religious sensibility. The perspective expressed in this volume could become merely the newest clerical fashion and its conclusions reduced to next year's (spoken trippingly on the tongue) clerical jargon.

To tell the pragmatist that works of art are good in themselves, that they expand the personality and enrich the character (though they do not necessarily produce virtue) is for him to speak utter nonsense. To say that God's self-disclosure can take place through the fine and the lively arts because they are especially designed to be sensitive to the sacramentality of the world is to convey an idea that is dangerously close to blasphemy. To say that the Church should support the very best in the arts because the better the art the more likely it is to be an effective sacrament is to introduce a totally unintelligible concept. To tell him that the well-crafted work of religious art can be a more powerful sacrament of God's goodness and a more stimulating challenge to the analogical imagination than any parish program that mixes simple propositions and simple-minded psychological manipulations is to speak so-called intellectualist idiocy.

He will respond that art is entertainment. One must yield the point to him. Any work of art that is not entertaining in some fashion to someone fails as art. And if you agree with that point, the pragmatist feels that he has carried the day. Entertaining realities are in one category of being, and important realities in another. The Church is interested in the important, the pragmatist will contend, not the entertaining. One builds a church in order to house a Sunday congregation, to provide that congregation with light and an effective sound system and heat in the winter and air-conditioning in the summer. One must consider the flow of people in and out of the church and the flow of cars in and out of the parking lot. Of course, one must be sure that the roof doesn't leak and that the tuck-pointing costs that the church is billed for are not too prohibitive. If there is enough parish money, one may also want the church to be large and constructed with some kind of white stone veneer, thus to impress parishioners and non-Catholics in the community and perhaps to create a monument or memorial to the pastor who built it. But all that is really required is the basement of the parish school, a simple assembly hall which later, after the church itself is constructed (as the last part of the parish "plant"), can be used for parish meetings and musicals. One must calculate carefully what the heating and lighting bills will be and how deeply one must go into debt to construct the church, but beauty . . . ? Well, that's the architect's job. He seems to know what he's doing. Abbot Suger and the Borghese Pope would think such a pastor to be mad, perhaps dangerously mad.

Where the moralistic imagination dominates, creativity becomes impossible because craftsmanship is abolished as the primary intrinsic criterion for a work of art. When pragmatism dominates, creativity is necessarily excluded, because the beautiful—i.e., the sacramental— is considered without purpose and merely an unnecessary expense. Where moralism and pragmatism dominate the ethos of ecclesiastical culture, the Catholic religious sensibility is truncated beyond recognition. It persists, of course, for it is strong in the tradition, passed on from mothers to children and through such phenomena and events as the Christmas crib, the May crowning, First Communion, Midnight Mass, and the Easter Vigil. But the moralistic, pragmatic churchperson has no time for the Catholic sensibility, no understanding of it, and contempt for those of us who try to speak about it. Do we know, after all, what it's like to try to get a thousand cars out of a parking lot on Sunday morning when you only have twenty minutes between Masses?

This description of the moralistic/pragmatic ethos, typical of American Catholicism in the years immediately before the Second Vatican Council, is not a caricature. It is appalling, however, that despite the changes accomplished through the Council the ethos does not seem to have diminished.

The major change in the Catholic attitude toward art during the last several decades is the expansion of the romantic fallacy from ecclesiastical administration, where it has always been strong, to scholarship and art. The romantic fallacy says that one needs to have no special skill or craft or training or professional perspective to do a work of art. Just as at one time anyone could be an ecclesiastical administrator, and more recently anybody could take a "survey" for catechitical directories or to counsel the psychologically disturbed (after a course or two or an M.A. at the most), so the romantic fallacy now says that to the extent that the fine or the lively arts are required by the Church, they involve works that any priest or nun can achieve without any particular training, experience, discipline, or skill.

This romanticism is the logical conclusion of pragmatism. If something is worth doing at all, it can be done simply and quickly and easily and cheaply: doing it well, doing it to high standards—the contemporary American ecclesiastical mind cannot comprehend the possibility, much less the necessity, of this.

How moralism, pragmatism, and romanticism came to stunt the Catholic religious sensibility in the United States is a question the complete answer to which is far beyond the scope of this book. The doctrinaire mentality of the Counter-Reformation, the worry about protecting the faith of immigrants in a hostile society, the rigidities of seminary education after the Americanism and Modernism controversies at the turn of the century are all contributing factors. Whatever the explanation, the fact remains that the people in the pews on Sunday now have much better artistic taste and much greater awareness of the importance of art in human life than their religious leaders. Catholic lay people are much more likely to understand our theme about the Catholic sensibility as experience, image, story, and community than the clergy or the religious or the hierarchy, still trapped in a spider's web of moralism, pragmatism, and romanticism. Moreover, Catholics active in the fine and lively arts in the United States today are for the most part resigned to being ignored by their Church— it is, of course, much better than being condemned as they would have been twenty or thirty or forty years ago.

One is forced to make the candid admission that it is practically impossible to think of a decent painting, sculpture, building, musical composition, dance, story, film, song, or television program that has been made under the auspices of the Roman Catholic Church in the United States in the last half century. It's a long way from Notre Dame de Paris to Notre Dame du Lac and most of that way has been downhill, and an equally long way from Saint Peter's to the Touchdown Jesus.

One could, for the sake of the argument, challenge the pragmatist on his own grounds. Demonstrably, the most important creative thing a priest does is his Sunday sermon. Yet the Sunday sermon is above all the work of the creative imagination, a work that stirs up images, recalls experiences, links stories of individual experience to stories of the overarching experiences of the tradition. The creative imagination is developed both by contact with works of art and by practice in exercising one's own. Therefore, it is important that the homilist and the future homilist receive intensive and systematic training in the works of the imagination and the development of their own imaginations.

That only slightly complex syllogism is probably unanswerable, but most seminary rectors will cheerfully admit that the homiletics course is the poorest in the seminary and most homiletics professors would be hard put to see the connection between the creative imagination and Sunday homilizing. The suggestion that one of us made a number of years ago, not altogether facetiously, that no one should be ordained who hadn't written a novel or a dozen sonnets or four short stories was dismissed by homiletics professors and seminary rectors as absurd. Preaching, they say in effect, is not a work of creative imagination, and it is hardly necessary to be concerned about the development of the creative imagination of priests and future priests.

In a clerical culture in which disciplined intellect is of minor moment, one can scarcely expect developed imagination or disciplined creativity to be important. One does not need to be able to think or to judge, to imagine or to create. One merely needs a few quick sentences to summarize the latest fashion, the newest program book for the most recent surefire technique. If someone like our colleague and friend John Shea writes a book about the theology of story, one will either make up stories as part of the new program or buy a program book with pre-packaged stories. Anyone can tell stories, can't they? You're not claiming, are you, that someone has to experience a fundamental restructuring of their personality, redevelop their imagination, and acquire new skills and disciplines just to tell stories?

The raw materials for the salvation of Catholicism in America can be found in the Catholic religious sensibility—sacramental experience, analogical imagination, comic-story telling, and organic local community. Should the Church leadership, as seems unlikely, be persuaded by the thesis of this book (and if they are we shall check with both Lincoln Park and Brookfield zoos to see whether the other leopards are changing their spots), then they will have to undertake a profound and systematic and comprehensive reeducation of their clergy.

The Catholic religious sensibility survives despite the clergy, of course, because after a couple of millennia it is too durable and too attractive to be destroyed by moralism and pragmatism and romanticism—and stupidity. Its revitalization occurs not because the bishops understand them or the priests and religious want them, but because a new generation of laity demands them.

And refuses to pay the bills unless it gets them.

Chapter 13
. . . .
SOCIAL THEORY AND NATURAL LAW

The Catholic sensibility has articulated two traditional perspectives on human society and human nature—a "Catholic social theory," which emphasizes, as against both capitalism and socialism, the importance of localism and pluralism; and natural law, which stresses the need for empirical investigation of the nature of human nature. While Catholicism has no monopoly on either, they are both important dimensions of its heritage and can be the source of important contributions to the ongoing human dialogue as well as resources of internal strength for Catholicism in crisis. Tragically, both are ignored by the Church, precisely at the time when other people are raising questions to which the Catholic sensibility has an excellent opportunity to respond.

The distinguished sociologist James Coleman remarked recently that the end of this century would be a time of reconstruction of microstructures. By that he meant that intellectual fashions would shift back to a recognition of the importance of the closest of human relationships and to the development of the human person—family, home, neighborhood, local community, classroom, work group. The assumption that we live in a mass society dominated by the mass media in which the individual person does not have or does not need these "micro" relationships is being abandoned. Second, social policy will increasingly focus on reestablishing those microstructures which were, either from indifference or deliberate design, weakened during the past decades. Social policymakers will realize that government programs can only work when they solicit the active cooperation of the smallest groups in society. Billions of dollars invested in education, for example, will have little effect unless the funds are concentrated on improving the dynamics of the classroom experience—the teacher-student, student-student relationships.

The irony in Coleman's prediction, with which there seems to be little reason to disagree, is that Catholicism's traditional social theory is a microstructure theory (though the phrase was never used). At the precise time when the rest of the world begins to discover the importance of the smallest groups in society, whether in classroom dynamics for improving education in the United States or in village dynamics for improving agriculture in Africa, Catholics suddenly discover that they hardly know that their own theory of social structure—with clear social policy implications—exists.

At the very moment that the rest of society has decided in theory that massive bureaucracies do not accomplish social change and is searching for nonbureaucratic or less bureaucratic social policies, most Catholics who are committed to social change have embraced that most bureaucratic of reform movements, Marxism. Precisely at the time when Catholics ought, in light of their own social theory, to make a unique and special contribution to the discussion of how social injustice can be eliminated, Catholic social activists are content to parrot warmed-over versions of either Left Liberalism or Pop Marxism. While one might not endorse all the social policy recommendations of the late E. F. Schumacher, it nonetheless was clear that his theory and policy were remarkably similar to that espoused by Catholic social activists before 1960—indeed Schumacher, after developing his own theory and policies, became a Catholic because it was the religion most compatible with his view of the nature of society. Ironically, and in our view tragically, Catholics who have graduated from colleges or universities since 1965 do not see the similarity between Schumacher's "Small is beautiful" and their own traditional Catholic social theory—in great part because they have never heard of the latter.

If Catholicism is to be "saved," then traditional Catholic social theory must be rediscovered, re-explored, and reinterpreted in practical policy recommendations based on those disciplines that are especially pertinent for social reform—economics, sociology, political science, international agriculture. Anyone can scream class conflict slogans. One does not need Catholic activists for that purpose. Not everyone has a social theory and a tradition of social policy perspectives that acknowledge the fundamental and essential importance of microstructures.

Four social theories have dominated the debate in the Western world since the beginning of the nineteenth century. Two of the theories are bourgeois, capitalism and socialism; both originated in the French Revolution and in the bourgeois thinking that shaped it and implemented its reforms, especially on the Continent but also in the British Isles. The two other social theories, Catholicism and anarchism, are anti-bourgeois; both rejected and continue to reject the destruction of the old social order by the bourgeois outcome of the French Revolution. One need only read the statements and the documents of the early nineteenth century anarchists (recently summarized in a remarkable work by William Sewell of the University of Arizona) or the great anarchist thinker Proudhon to realize that however radical and destructive the anarchists might have sounded, they were in fact reactionary: they yearned for an old social order that they thought once existed. The anarchists wanted—and still want, to the extent that they exist—a "corporate" society, i.e., a society organized from the grass roots up in corporate organizations like the medieval guilds, destroyed in France by the Revolution, which sought to organize life downward. The anarchists were like the American Revolutionaries, who turned against an ever more powerful central government of London, not in terms of and in the name of new freedoms and new rights, but rather in the name of the old and traditional rights of free citizens of England.

Educated as most of us are to believe that the French Revolution was a great liberalizing phenomenon, we seldom ponder the other side of the coin, or consider that the revolution merely continued the centralizing tendencies of French absolute monarchy more rationally and more effectively, in effect depriving the communes and the guilds, the local communities and decentralized structures of traditional freedoms they were already losing to Versailles and Paris. All revolutions, the great sociologist Max Weber once remarked, lead to more centralized control rather than less. It was against the centralized control of post-Napoleonic France that the anarchists revolted, and their criticisms of bourgeois liberal capitalism are virtually the same as the criticisms of the Catholic social encyclicals of the nineteenth and twentieth centuries. Liberal capitalism destroys freedom because it wipes out the microstructures of society—in the name of freedom and rationality, perhaps, but in fact for the profit of the bourgeois capitalists. Napoleon and his successors believed that to create a new world you had to wipe out all traces of the old one. Their bold attempt to restructure society according to a centralized and rationalized model did not work. The present government in France has slowly begun to reverse the process, delegating more power where it belongs—to the regions and communes and smaller communities of France.

The similarity between capitalism and socialism in this matter can be seen in the way the two social systems approach economic development. Both of them assume that one can move into a "lesser developed" society, ignore the local communities and social structures, and build either big factories or massive farms—collective farms in the socialist model and technology-intensive farms in the capitalist model. If there is one lesson that the world has learned in the years since the end of the Second World War, it is that neither strategy works. One does not have to take a stand against either factories or modernization of agriculture to say that any attempts to impose drastic social change on a society without taking into account the customs and cultures, the patterns of relationships, the hopes and the fears of the local communities and their structures and leaders is doomed to failure.

To the extent that the new nation-states of Africa have any economic success, it is not because they have overcome the traditional structures of the African village but rather because the extraordinary persistence and durability of the village sustain enough agricultural production to avoid famine, despite the failures of the nation-state. Julius Nyrere, the saintly Catholic leader of Tanzania, thought that he would improve the lot of the people in his dreadfully poor country by taking them away from their small peasant plots and concentrating them in large collective farms, not unlike those of Russia or China (for all his saintliness, he did not seem to have read about the failures of collective farming). The reform seemed to make sense—it was to eliminate inefficiency, maximize collective efforts, impose discipline on the workers, stir up enthusiasm and commitment for the goals of a new and better life, and increase agricultural production, enabling Tanzania to become more self-sufficient in its food supply. Of course it didn't work. The nineteenth century anarchists could have told him it wouldn't work, and so could the social theorists of his own Catholic Church, if someone had explained in terms that made sense for his problems.

You don't destroy the local structure. Rather, you seek its cooperation, you integrate it into your plans, you listen to its wisdom, you cooperate with its leaders, you serve the peasant village, and you help it to increase its well-being. Or, in the case of the United States, you don't destroy the neighborhood school in the name of racial integration; rather you develop systems and techniques in which the neighborhood school is preserved and becomes the tool *for* racial integration.

The argument here is not necessarily in favor of small farms or small factories, much less in favor of parochial racial bigotry. The argument, rather, is that you help people to change their ways and you improve the condition of society by enlisting the microstructures on your side instead of making enemies of them. The family, the neighborhood, the work group, the classroom will not go away because social planners or the social reformers, armed revolutionaries or executives of multinational corporations, pretend they do not exist or even try to abolish them. The microstructures will continue to exist, perhaps in truncated or corrupted form, because it is in the nature of human nature to form microstructures. You put two perfect strangers together, next to each other working on machines, and in the course of a few hours or a few days they become a microstructure. You move a group of perfect strangers into a classroom and in the course of a couple of weeks they become a system of microstructures. The theorists and planners and bureaucrats may pretend such structures don't exist, but they do so only because of bureaucratic blindness. Moreover, in most cases, a bureaucracy does not encounter a collection of unrelated individuals but a pre-existing network of structures. Thus young people who come to a classroom already have friendship groups, cliques, alliances. The social structure of school normally ignores these clusters even though the school administrators were taught in their graduate courses that the level of classroom achievement is set by friendship groups, and not by teachers.

There are four choices: one tries to destroy the microstructures and usually fails; one tries to ignore them and must then contend with their hidden influence; one co-opts them and manipulates them, which is dangerous, since microstructures are resistant to manipulation; or one cooperates with them, treating them and their members as social assets instead of liabilities, as resources instead of obstacles, as sources of wisdom instead of sources of resistance.

Urban planners and advocates of social change often rail against neighborhoods because their irregular and messy patterns on a city map obstruct desirable social change. In Chicago, neighborhoods are damned as tools of racial segregation though even critics will admit that strong neighborhoods prevent the total re-segregation of a metropolitan area in which the city is mostly black and the suburbs mostly white. The appropriate stance, from the point of view of Catholic social theory, is neither to damn neighborhoods nor to praise them but to accept their inevitability (for minority groups establish neighborhoods of their own that are also resistant to invasion, either by other minority groups or by lower-class members of their own minority groups) and to ask under what circumstances they might facilitate racial integration and under what circumstances they impede it. In Chicago, for example, legislation requiring city employees to live within the city boundaries has been a much more powerful force for racial integration than all the social activism of religious leaders. Yet many religious leaders, including Catholics, show little sympathy for this social policy. It is not "idealistic" enough or "moral" enough and is not developed by marching on picket lines or protesting or other forms of religiously approved activism.

The conflict between the two kinds of social theory—the one that wishes to sweep away microstructures, and the one that accepts their inevitability—is more a conflict of imagination than of ideology. A certain kind of imagination cannot picture society any other way but as a network of networks, too powerful to destroy and too important to endanger. Another kind of imagination pictures society as a collection of mostly autonomous individuals caught up in corrupt patterns of behavior that must be eliminated. The anarchist and Catholic social theories, with their emphases on localism and pluralism are, in fact, exercises of the analogical imagination. Capitalist or socialist social theories, desiring in the name of either profit or ideology to remake society on totally new and more efficient models, are exercises in the dialectical imagination. Liberation Theology and other forms of Catholic "peace and justice" radicalism have abandoned the analogical imagination and become convinced that social reform means social revolution, wiping out the old in order to create the new. In effect, they are arguing that the microstructures and microcultures that shape the contemporary world are so evil and corrupt that they are beyond redemption, and only the most drastic kind of change offers any hope to alleviate human suffering.

One can deal with such an argument on two levels. One can argue factually, pointing out that revolutions always mean more centralized control and more oppression rather than less (at least since the French Revolution); one can contend that in most revolutionary societies, the last state of the ordinary people is worse than the first and while there might be some temporary alleviation of misery, that usually diminishes after a few years of bureaucratic incompetence. (Cuba, one of the countries most admired by the Catholic radicals, is the only other country in the world beside Cambodia where the standard of living has declined in the last twenty years. Admittedly, the health services are better now than they were before Fidel Castro, but as the increasing mortality rate in the Soviet Union demonstrates, after a time even socialist health services deteriorate.) There is no socialist experiment in the world—in Eastern Europe, in Africa, or in Asia—that has not been a social and economic failure, given sufficient time.

Catholic radicals, particularly those who work in poor countries, respond that anything, even Marxism, has to be better than the situation in which the ordinary people of their country are now living. One has to be sympathetic with their concern, though it is not altogether clear that ordinary people would freely choose Marxism. But in fact, as many in Eastern Europe or China would quickly testify, it is simply not true that anything would be better than the present situation or that nothing could possibly be worse, as the South Vietnamese found, once the corrupt Saigon regime was replaced by what turned out to be the equally corrupt and even more incompetent Hanoi regime. Things can and do get worse under Marxist governments.

One can also observe that the microstructures and the microcultures do not go away. The culture of Mandarin China, for example, does survive in the Communist state as does the ordinary style of social interaction among people in China. The traditional microstructures are converted into more deadly, sometimes even demoniac, institutions of social control and repression—and also mechanisms of stolid, stubborn, silent resistance to oppression. Revolutions, one can argue against the Catholic radicals, simply don't work. The only effective means of social reform is more gradual and organic development that respects a society's structures and cultures.

But Catholic radicals want change and want it now. They want freedom and dignity and prosperity for the people with whom they are concerned and cannot wait for developmental change. One had merely to attend a meeting of the Catholic Committee on Urban Ministry at Notre Dame during the heyday of that "peace and justice" organization in the 1970s to realize that Catholic social activists then were angry, manic enthusiasts with whom reasoned discourse about social structures, microcultures, and the technicalities of rural agriculture and economic development was impossible.

Thus on the level of objective factual evidence, the radical position can be refuted. However, one can also concede the possibility that revolution or revolutionary action can be successful and yet also observe that to support class conflict and the destruction of the existing microstructures is to abandon the Catholic heritage. The Catholic social tradition does indeed acknowledge the existence of competition and potential conflict among various groups in society, old and young, men and women, white and nonwhite, capital and labor, affluent and poor. But it also adds—and Catholic radicals do not always seem to hear this—that while the various social classes may be in competition and even conflict, they still depend on one another, and unless the conflict occurs within a larger framework of overall cooperation for the common good, the social organism is torn apart. Pope John Paul II's criticism of Catholic Marxists in Latin America insists on this truth above all others, but somehow he does not seem to be heard. The Pope's position merely articulates and develops the Catholic imagination, which is perfectly willing to acknowledge that social structures can often distort and corrupt (in Marxist societies, be it noted, as well as capitalist) but also insists that the solution is to reform the microstructures instead of destroying them. The structures, however corrupt they may become, are still basically good and indeed, revelatory of God.

It may well be true that patriarchal family structures (in the most micro of micro relationships) produce intolerable oppression of women and children, but the solution, self-evidently it seems to the Catholic imagination, is not to destroy the family, a human relationship that is sacramental and revelatory of God, but to reform it. Moreover, the Catholic imagination insists, returning to the first argument, even if foolishly you try to eliminate the family in order to end oppression, the family won't go away. You must either cooperate with existing families in order to reform family relationships, or you crusade for social change and no matter how noble, or how passionate, or how zealous, or how Christian, it won't occur.

Many Catholic radicals (and most "peace and justice" advocates in the American Church are Catholic radicals in this sense) would be singularly unconcerned if they were told that they have abandoned their own heritage and the instincts of the Catholic religious sensibility. Social change is important, not the heritage, they would say. They would insist on strongly questioning the commitment to social justice of those who wish to explore the implications for social change of the Catholic imagination. In their minds the measure of one's commitment is the intensity of one's radicalism. The more vigorous and even violent one is in one's demands for social change, the more one is committed to "liberating" the poor and the oppressed. To question whether a particular kind of social change will work or to insist that advocacy must be intelligent if it is to be worthy of the Catholic heritage is to them conclusive evidence that one is indifferent to misery and suffering. Our old friends, moralism, pragmatism, and romanticism, are all involved in this judgment. They believe that a moralistic concern for justice is all that is required to serve the cause of justice; programs for the immediate elimination of injustice are the only possible evidence of social commitment; and anyone, no matter how ill-informed or how unskilled, can legitimately advocate such programs as long as such a person is filled with moral fervor.

How Catholic social theory, taught enthusiastically in colleges and seminaries before 1960, could have disappeared from consciousness so quickly is an interesting question. Perhaps it was never fully understood. Surely we do not have sufficient historical studies to understand how it emerged and developed. The romantic radicalism of the Berrigan era in the late 1960s seems to have released many Catholic social activists from any need to be concerned about such ideas. Moreover, some of the social encyclicals of Paul VI seem to have been drafted by men who are much more interested in debating with Europe's Marxist intellectuals than understanding their own heritage. Finally, the leaders of the American Church have surrounded themselves with staff personnel who are well-meaning and enthusiastic but incompetent liberal leftists (of the sort who could equate American and Russian social systems in the first draft of the Nuclear Weapons Pastoral).

Hence the interesting irony that at precisely the time when Coleman's prediction about microstructures seems to be especially true of those who wish to reform American capitalism and make it more responsive to human needs and hence more effective, the Catholic hierarchy is apparently preparing (with the aid of a staff that seems to know very little about economics) to launch a full-scale attack on American capitalism, an attack that will be devoid, if one is to believe what one hears, of any sense of the traditional Catholic social theory of personalism, pluralism, and localism. In other words, just at the time that intelligent, well-documented rearticulation of Catholic social theory might have great impact as a critique of the present condition of American capitalism, the leaders of the American Church will condemn American capitalism from the perspective of Pop Marxism and European anti-American Left Liberalism (and with no realization at all, if the reports are to be believed, that condemning unemployment in the American steel industry on the one hand, and advocating help to the Third World, including nations such as Brazil and Trinidad and Korea, which directly compete with the American steel industry, on the other, is not only inconsistent but monumentally ignorant).

To say that concern for microstructures is a concrete application of the Catholic social theory of personalism (the conviction that society exists to promote the welfare of the individual person and not vice versa), pluralism (a healthy society has a wide variety of diverse overlapping groups between the individual and the state), and localism (nothing should be done by a larger or higher organization that can be done as well by a smaller or lesser) is not to end the challenge but to begin it. Perhaps the greatest fault of the Catholic social tradition in the last twenty years is that no research has been done in the social and economic disciplines that might lead to programs and policies implementing Catholic social theory as an alternative to socialistic and capitalistic social theories—no research about microstructures, in other words, done under Catholic auspices or by Catholic scholars that might lead to social reform and reconstruction. To save Catholicism, in the sense the words mean in this book, will absolutely require that such research be undertaken. It will also require a much higher level of intelligence and professional competence in the "peace and justice" staffs of the American hierarchy, both nationally and locally.

A related dimension of the Catholic heritage that also demands rejuvenation is the "natural law" tradition. To most people "natural law" means rigid, unchangeable, aprioristic moral rules inherited from the past and applied without any sensitivity or nuance to the present.

In fact, however, in the natural law tradition the emphasis has always been much more on "nature" than on "law." For Aristotle and Cicero and Aquinas, the search for natural law was an empirical investigation of the nature of human nature. There were, it was believed, three levels of natural law—the most general principle of doing good and avoiding evil, the intermediate principles forbidding lying, theft, adultery, and so forth, and the third level of principles illustrating how the first and second levels should be applied. For this third level Aquinas always argued that it was necessary "to go to the *gentes*," that is, to the people. For Aquinas, *jus gentium*—law of the peoples—is derived empirically. One searches among the nations to find out how they apply the first two levels of principles and then after the search one tentatively states the practical and concrete norms.

Obviously this traditional understanding of natural law has been forgotten, mostly, we suspect, because whenever there have been serious debates about the third-level decisions, the teaching authority of the Church has preempted the debate by going to the "deposit of faith" (which one suspects, in the mechanical way it is used, may very well be a check-cashing center in the basement of the Vatican or perhaps adjoining the Vatican Bank). If faith can solve questions of philosophical debate before the debate itself settles the issue, then there is no reason for debate and no reason for any serious natural law scholarship. The teaching authority will resolve the question at hand without scholarship.

Obviously the teaching authority of the Church has the right to settle questions of morality for Catholics, but unfortunately there seems to have grown up an inability to distinguish between matters of morality on which faith has the ultimate word on the one hand, and issues of philosophical and empirical debate on the other. Philosophy, as Aquinas pointed out long ago, is distinct from theology. Similarly, natural law is distinct from faith. But not in the minds of many, indeed most ecclesiastics, for whom the distinction sounds very strange. Unfortunately, while co-opting natural law and equating it with faith may seem the logical and natural thing for Church leaders to do, it is a process that ultimately demolishes the natural law tradition of free and empirical investigation, a tradition that Aquinas would have thought ought to be protected if only to provide important raw material for theological decision making.

Not only has the natural law tradition been weakened to the point of destruction, but its weakening has precluded the possibility of the Church's making its own contribution to the fierce debate raging in the scholarly and scientific world today about the nature of human nature, a debate in which both Catholic theology and natural law philosophy would come down very heavily on the side of those who are more optimistic than pessimistic. Indeed, many of the participants are themselves Catholic, particularly among the younger generation of scholars, but they have only the vaguest awareness that they stand as heirs of a tradition that has said many important things about human nature, that is flexible enough to absorb the new learning on human nature (in the case of Aquinas, one must say that he would have been eager to absorb the findings of the empirical disciplines), and whose basic outlook has been substantially confirmed by the human scientists.

Pope and bishops and Church leaders pay lip service to the importance of the human sciences, but when push comes to shove they don't listen, probably because they think they know already what the human scientists have said, without reading the literature seriously or listening to the scholars. It is clear from a number of empirical disciplines—comparative primatology, paleontological anthropology, social biology, for example—that you can reproduce a higher primate with a good deal more convenience and a good deal less stress than is to be found in human reproduction. Alone of all the primates humankind is sexually preoccupied all the time. The scientists hypothesize that the reason for this in the evolutionary process was to establish a "quasi pair bond" between male and female to keep them together long enough to raise their offspring; the sophisticated mental and cultural development required a long period of parental care. The bond between male and female—found in none of the other higher primates (with the possible exception of one species of small monkey)—is reinforced by the permanent sexual attraction between the male and the female and the affection that grows up in the context of that attraction. The family—understood as a propensity to quasi pair-bonding—was a necessary prerequisite for the evolution to *Homo sapiens*. The family, in other words, was a pre-condition in the evolutionary process.

Now there are four pieces of good news for Catholicism in that finding and perhaps one piece of bad news.

The good news is:

1. The Church's perennial concern about the family is completely appropriate. There's a built-in bias in the human organism toward family—not necessarily toward the patriarchal family, but at least toward family.

2. The Church's emphasis on the permanence of marriage is supported. While there is not a biological inevitability in the quasi pair-bonding between human male and female, there is still a strong strain toward permanence in bonding, a strain that can be ignored only by not paying attention to the kind of creature we're dealing with.

3. The Church's emphasis on microstructure is also sustained. It is the most intimate of human relationships that are the most important to the species. And, according to many paleo-anthropologists, another and related factor required for the evolution of *Homo sapiens* is the development of the biological propensity to share food, thus reinforcing the notion of the fundamental goodness of human nature over against those scholars who see *Homo sapiens* evolving from the human propensity to hunt and kill.

4. Against Manichaeism and Puritanism, both of which tend to think of human sexuality as the most depraved part of a fundamentally depraved nature, the Church's position that sexuality is good and sacramental (revelatory of God) is validated. The pervasiveness of human sexuality as opposed to the episodic nature of the sexuality of other primates is a sign not that we are depraved but merely that we have a propensity to bond with those with whom we have sex—a propensity, in other words, to love.

The bad news is that whatever is specifically human in human sexuality, in comparison with the sexuality of the other higher primates, is ordained toward pair-bonding and not procreation. All the other primates procreate nicely without the intensity of sexual behavior and relationships that marks the human species. The Church's conviction (not shared by Aquinas, by the way) that sex is primarily for procreation and only secondarily for the "fomenting of mutual love" simply cannot stand against the test of the empirical sciences' present knowledge. However, the Church has gradually abandoned that position, first saying that the two ends were co-equal, and then more recently saying that the primary end of human sexuality is the common life, the interpersonal sharing between male and female. If we were listening to the human sciences, or perhaps one should say, if we were capable of listening to the human sciences, we would have made this adjustment more quickly and more easily.

The implication of this for the birth control debate is obvious. Since that which is specifically human in sexuality is there primarily for creating the bond, it does not seem to follow—not from the natural law tradition, at any rate—that every single sexual act has to allow for procreation; this was the position taken by the majority on Pope Paul VI's birth control commission, a majority which he overruled. One may, from the perspective of faith, still require that every act of sexual intercourse be open to the possibility of procreation, but one cannot, it would seem, do so in the name of natural law.

A re-evaluation of the purpose of human sexuality with the aid of the empirical disciplines, a re-evaluation which by and large reinforces most Catholic positions (though not the fear and hatred of women, which has long marred the Catholic religious sensibility), might well be the occasion to reconsider birth control teaching, especially since married couples have testified that strict observance of the Church's birth control teaching makes sexual intimacy in marriage virtually impossible. Pope John Paul has said that married people have a unique and indispensable contribution to the Church's understanding of sexual matters, from the "charism" of the sacrament of matrimony. We are not suggesting, in this context, a change in the Church's birth control position. We are, rather, pointing out that the Church's own natural law tradition, properly understood, might provide the occasion to re-evaluate much of the Church's thinking about sexuality, a re-evaluation in which the Church has much to gain, and open up the possibility of reconsidering the birth control decision. We have made this suggestion repeatedly to priests, bishops, theologians, and other Church leaders and have usually been greeted with a total lack of comprehension. They have never heard, it would seem, of this understanding of the natural law tradition (though it can easily be found in Aquinas's *Summa Contra Gentiles*), and they're utterly unaware of the current human nature debate and apparently fail to perceive its implications for the natural law tradition in the Church's sexual teaching.

But merely rediscovering the natural law and social theory traditions of Catholicism will not be sufficient. Both must be linked with the best theories and research findings and programmatic practices currently available from the human sciences—a program, as we've said before, frequently endorsed by Church people but never vigorously pursued. The "peace and justice" activists may summarily reject the contribution of scholarship, but those who preside over a tradition that created Europe's medieval universities can ill afford to do so, at least if they are to be true to their own tradition. Hence to our third conclusion: it will be pointless to rejuvenate the social theory and natural law elements of the Catholic heritage without, at the same time, rejuvenating distinctively Catholic scholarship.

Langdon Gilkey has argued that one of the strengths of Catholicism has always been its rationality. But this rationality is not merely aprioristic but involves, as does the natural law tradition in Thomas Aquinas, a considerable passion for empirical evidence. Yet, in fact, while there are scores of institutions in the United States that claim to be both Catholic and universities, Catholic scholarship is almost as invisible as it was thirty years ago, with the single possible difference that thirty years ago the leaders of influential American Catholic elites

deplored the absence of a scholarly tradition and the lack of distinguished Catholic scholars, while now, when Catholics are at least as
likely to be scholars as other Americans, the institutional Church has
not caught up with the emergence of a Catholic scholarly intelligentsia
and most Catholic social activists would condemn the work of such
an intelligentsia as irrelevant and useless.

The excuse given for this deplorable lack of Catholic scholarship
is that the Catholic universities are concerned primarily with the education of undergraduates. Indeed, that was the explanation offered
in the October 1983 issue of *Notre Dame Magazine* by the director
of that university's graduate program in response to a study made of
American universities by the Conference Board of Learned Societies
in which the ranking of the graduate programs at Notre Dame on
the average was barely "adequate" (and Notre Dame was the highest
of the Catholic universities). In fact this excuse simply won't work.
First of all, while one may be well prepared to admit, as we are, that
undergraduate education is the most important thing a university
does, an institution has no legitimate claim to be a university unless
it is also engaged in serious scholarship. This was how a university
was defined by Catholicism in the Middle Ages, and it is what a
university must still be.

There is no empirical evidence that scholarship and teaching undergraduates are mutually exclusive. While doubtless some publishing
scholars are poor undergraduate instructors, so it is also the case that
some college professors who never publish a thing are also dismal
instructors. The excuse used by an individual faculty member that
she or he does not publish because of a commitment to undergraduate
instruction is simply given the lie by the considerable number of
distinguished scholars who are superb undergraduate instructors. For
the individual professor it's an excuse, and so it's an excuse for the
university.

Moreover, if someone makes the argument that, precisely because
they are not burdened with scholarship, the teachers at Catholic universities provide *better* undergraduate instruction, the argument surely
demands proof and, as far as we're aware, no one has offered it or
even seriously attempted to find it. Would anyone seriously argue
that undergraduate students at Harvard are not as well instructed as
undergraduate students at Notre Dame?

Nonetheless, it is a researchable subject. The large data bases collected by Professor Alexander Astin at the Higher Educational Research Institute at the University of California at Los Angeles make such investigation possible. Holding constant both educational ability and family background, do graduates of the so-called Catholic universities perform better on various measures of academic achievement than do graduates of comparable private universities, with less endowment than Notre Dame (for example) and higher scholarly ratings? Would the graduates of Notre Dame, for example, score higher than the graduates of Southern California or Vanderbilt or Brown or Brandeis or Syracuse? If they do, then the argument that scholarship must to some extent be sacrificed to undergraduate instruction in the Catholic universities might have some validity. Until such evidence is produced, the alleged commitment to undergraduate instruction that impedes Catholic universities from what they maintain is the less important task of scholarly research must be dismissed as a poor rationalization and an abject excuse.

According to the director of the graduate program at Notre Dame, his university has no ambition to make it one of the top ten universities of the country in scholarly quality. One wonders why not. Notre Dame now has the endowment funds to make such an ambition achievable. Doubtless it would take a long time. But with effort, Notre Dame (or Georgetown, for that matter) would have some departments in the top ten within a decade and an average rating in the top twenty by the end of the century. Mediocrity of ambition reveals mediocrity of performance and imagination.

If Catholicism is to be "saved," it must rediscover its traditions of microstructure social theory, of empirical natural law searching to discover more about the nature of human nature, and of rational and scholarly respect for learning. The magnitude of the task ahead can be judged by the near total absence of awareness in the leadership of the American Catholic Church of all three of these traditions.

Chapter 14
. . . .
ANGELS, DEMONS, SAINTS, AND HOLY SOULS

Catholicism seems to have given up on angels at the precise time that the lively arts have discovered them. The Catholic heritage's conviction that there are creatures of mystery intervening between us and God has become a commonplace on *Star Trek* precisely at the time that the poor guardian angels have vanished from the Catholic schools.

Today the most important theologian of angels is filmmaker Steven Spielberg. In *Close Encounters of the Third Kind* he has confirmed our intuition that we are not alone in the universe by sending us on a vast flying saucer with cherubic little creatures of light who intend to do us only good. In *Poltergeist*, the forces of good manage to rout the forces of evil, despite the enormous supply of hellfire that seems to be available to the latter. And finally, in *E.T.*, one of the cherubic creatures of light comes back and is marooned temporarily on the planet earth but finally manages to rout the powers of evil with the assistance of ingenious earthling children, and to exorcise evil finally with high comedy. Spielberg knows what many Catholic teachers and theologians have forgotten: the cosmos we live in is a mysterious one in which there seems to be a war between good and evil, light and darkness.

All religions have their good spirits and bad spirits. Among the religions of Yahweh, angels and demons exist even in the high traditions and, of course, play a major role in folk traditions. Angels are relatively inactive in Protestant piety, but in some denominations the devil is still alive and well. However, from the very beginning, Catholicism has been a religious tradition in which lesser spirits abound and have far more influence in popular and elite piety than they do in any of the other Yahwistic religions. Superstition, financial corruption, trading in relics and other holy objects, devotions that are often silly and sometimes perhaps even pernicious are the price Catholicism has paid for its angels and its demons, its saints and its holy souls. But Catholicism is ready to pay that price because in its heritage, the "intermediaries" are in fact "sacraments," revelations of God. The Catholic stories of angels and demons and saints and holy souls are another way of saying what the Catholic theologian Karl Rahner meant when he said, "Grace is everywhere." Superstitious and naïve stories of God, told as stories of angels and saints and demons and poor souls, may well need to be reinterpreted so as to be freed from ignorant and superstitious piety, but they are too important a part of the Catholic tradition to be cast aside as outmoded and useless in an ecumenical and scientific age.

To put the matter differently, you may not particularly like the popular Catholic pious tradition that each of us has a "guardian angel." But if you reject the loving intimacy between God and His/Her creatures for which the guardian angel stands, and if you fail to comprehend that the guardian angel story is a marvelous way of revealing that intimacy, then you are turning your back on what has always been an important element in Catholic religious sensibility.

There are a number of reasons why the "intermediary" or "revealing" spirits abound in the Catholic tradition. Most important is the Catholic sacramental experience of grace everywhere. The intermediaries abound because of the Catholic analogical imagination, which sees God reflected in creatures, and the Catholic sense of organic community, which believes in a network of intimate relationships, not only with those who share the world with us but also with those who have gone before us. The "revealing" spirits are an almost inevitable consequence of such a religious sensibility.

For weal or woe, depending on your viewpoint, Catholicism was not afraid of adapting for its own purposes the good and useful popular pieties of the pagan world. The Neo-Platonic philosophy of the Second Temple era and early Christian Platonic thought, especially as articulated outside the Church by Plotinus and inside the Church by a theologian who pretended to be Dionysius the Aeropagite, taught a worldview in which God acted through "emanations," beings of lesser importance who emerged from truth, goodness, and beauty, and descended in gradual progression of importance and dignity and intelligence until finally the progress of emanation descended into the material world and humankind appeared. Angels, archangels, cherubim, seraphim, thrones, dominations and powers, and the nine choirs of angels were a Christian version of the descending order of beings that resulted from divine emanations. We were created by and ruled over by the lesser spirits, who in turn were presided over by the greater spirits. In some heretical versions of this worldview, Jesus was one of the great angels, the most important of the divine emanations. In a culture where such a worldview was dominant, it was inevitable that in some kinds of theology and in most kinds of piety, angels would assume tremendous importance.

Why are spirits, good and evil, so important in the religions of the world, and especially in the nature religions of which Catholicism absorbed so much? They're important because they are "stories" or "models" that fit the data. There is much unexpected goodness that happens in our life that seems above and beyond the goodness of individual humans or groups of humans, and there is also much evil in the world that seems to transcend individual human malice. Our ancestors, searching for explanations, attributed the goodness—the order of the seasons, the fruits of the fields and the flock and the tribe, unexpectedly bountiful harvests, unexpectedly good wine, unexpectedly rewarding sex—to the good spirits. The excessive evils—the southwest wind that in Babylon could wipe out the crops in an afternoon, hailstorms, floods, invasions, epidemics, early death—were attributed to the evil spirits. There was mysterious good and mysterious evil in the world; how explain both? Demons and angels were the answer.

We are a good deal more sophisticated than our ancestors. We can explain the order of the seasons without the need to imagine angels presiding over and enforcing this order. The four basic forces of contemporary physical science models—gravity, the weak force, the strong force, electromagnetism—are sufficient to explain what goes on in the universe without the need to postulate intelligent beings that make these forces operate. Now we know that meteorological disturbances, such as the El Niño "current" of the winter of 1982–83, are responsible for bad weather, and we don't have to blame malevolent spirits who stir up the wind and the snow and the ice and the cold.

Nonetheless, there is still something wonderful about the coming of spring and something terrifying about the winter storm. Only the insensitive and the unimaginative lose their sense of awe and mystery and fascination with the physical world because they have available the latest scientific explanations (which themselves are often at least as awesome and wonderful and mysterious as are the angels and the demons of yesteryear).

Moreover, there are surely forces and energies operating in human society that transcend or seem to transcend the malice of individuals. A mean and nasty little man like Lee Harvey Oswald could change the course of human history with a few bullets and make the late 1960s and early 1970s one of the most evil periods through which the American Republic has ever suffered. Two bland, insignificant men, Hitler and Stalin, presided over the mightiest nations in Europe in the 1930s and 1940s and were responsible for the deaths of more than 50 million people. The outcome of their own personal malice so far exceeded that malice as to make it look tiny by comparison. The ingrained evil in such places in the world as Palestine, Lebanon, and Northern Ireland, for example, is much greater than the individual evil acts of the terrorists and gunmen and assassins. One need not postulate personal devils to realize that we do struggle against principalities and powers, dynamisms and energies of evil that far exceed our own individual capacities for wrongdoing. The demons are symbols developed by the human imagination to explain the mystery of evil in the world. Even if we reject demons, we are not any closer to any explanation of evil than were our ancestors who believed in them.

We also realize that the dynamisms and energies of evil and obstruction have not yet eliminated kindness and gentleness and tenderness and affection and loyalty and nobility and patience and sensitivity and love in the human condition. Good survives despite evil, always on the defensive, always threatened with elimination but still somehow surviving. Our ancestors believed that the good angels were responsible for the fact that evil has not yet won its final victory over good. Even if we no longer believe in the existence of good angels today, we are no closer to an explanation than were our ancestors for the mystery of good in the universe.

This is not to argue that personal demons or personal angels exist. The questions are both theologically and scientifically open. Rather, the Catholic imagination, with its stories of angels and devils and saints and holy souls, has a sensitivity to the mystery and power and awe and wonder of the war in heaven between good and evil, which exists both in the cosmos and in our own individual personality; this is an asset to the Catholic tradition and not a liability. You may have to reinterpret the angel and devil stories to explain them to the modern mind, whatever that may be, but explaining what angels and demons mean is much more helpful, religiously and humanly, than trying to explain away the enormous energies and powers of good and of evil that we experience every day in our lives.

If grace is everywhere, God can be experienced in and through anything. If the created world and its events and phenomena and persons and objects are revelatory, and if stories in which good wins out over evil, comedy over tragedy are finally the best explanations we have of what life is all about, then there is certainly room in our imagination and our storytelling for agents of God who restrain the lunatic energies and dynamisms of evil that are at work in our world. One can dismiss as ignorant and superstitious piety the old Catholic childhood prayer, still said by many Catholic adults:

> *Angel of God,*
> *My guardian dear,*
> *To whom God's*
> *love*
> *Commits me here,*
> *Ever this day*

> *Be at my side*
> *To light, to guard*
> *To rule and guide.*

Or one can see in the prayer a simple expression of faith in a God Who lurks in our world, Who reveals Herself/Himself through the world, Who can be imagined as being like the protective persons who take care of us in our life in the world and Who presides over stories of our life whose ending finally will be happy. There is enough flexibility and imagination in the Catholic tradition to rehabilitate the angels.

Do they, however, in fact exist? We both rather hope they do and find attractive, if not thoroughly convincing, the argument of the medieval Franciscan theologian that angels have to exist for aesthetic reasons: a universe in which there are no created pure spirits somehow seems less attractive than one in which such beings do exist. Most contemporary scriptural scholars would agree that the references to angels and demons in the Bible do not settle the argument either way. They point out, for example, that in such a late work as the Book of Job, Satan was one of God's angels and not the chief of the demons, and that much of the demonology of early Christianity was borrowed from Persian religion. All the Scriptures can be interpreted as saying is that God works in the world. The "Angel of Yahweh" is merely Yahweh insofar as S/He operates on earth. Many if not most Catholic theologians today would argue that the conciliar definition of angels need not be interpreted differently from the scriptural references to them. If one is prepared to concede the point to the scholars and theologians, all we have established is that there is no compelling proof in Scripture or in Catholic tradition of the existence of angels. That scholarship, however, does not prove that angels do not exist.

Is it not possible that those interventions of seemingly rational creatures, recorded in the Scriptures and in the tales of most religions, are in fact the intervention of created beings, like ourselves, perhaps even with material bodies like our own, who for one reason or the other have appeared intermittently throughout history on the planet earth? The German scientist Hoimar Von Ditfurth notes, apropos of the evolutionary process:

> There must be many places in the cosmos . . . where evolution
> for various reasons has made more headway than here on earth,

places where it has by now pressed its efforts beyond generating life, consciousness and knowledge to new heights, enlarging the realm of subjectivity by annexing regions of which we are still ignorant. . . . these creatures would be equipped with brains which would help their owners to a much larger share of that mind which has just now begun to shed some light, though as yet a relatively faint one on our own heads. . . . we ourselves may have descendants as genetically distant from us as we are from *Homo habilis*. . . . we might constitute a bridge to nonbiological descendants of an entirely different sort. . . .

Von Ditfurth's speculations do more than raise the possibility of the evolution elsewhere in the cosmos of biological creatures whose organisms are so different from ours as to be imperceptible by our senses, and it is surely not totally out of the question that if such creatures have evolved in processes far more mature than our own, they have also developed the skills required to visit our planet and might be among us, either permanently or intermittently. To speculate about the possibility of such development, of course, is not to assert that it has indeed occurred, much less to endorse the wild speculations of Von Daniken and others in books like *Chariots of the Gods*. There is no scientific evidence that such creatures have ever visited earth, though if they were sufficiently beyond us in the evolutionary process they might also be clever enough to cover their tracks. Admittedly there is a touch of science fiction about such speculations, which doesn't necessarily mean that they are untrue, but merely unproven.

The point of such speculations is that one closes off the possibility of "E.T." intelligences, some of which might be very much like our traditional images of angels, only if one is committed to a rigidly closed universe in which there is no room for wonder or mystery or surprise, a universe that might have fit the scientific paradigms of a quarter or a half century ago but certainly does not result from contemporary scientific paradigms. The more we know about the Gulf Current, said the oceanographer Cousteau, the more we know that we don't know. If such a judgment can be made about an ocean current, it can a fortiori be made about the cosmos. Skepticism is the proper attitude of the person who respects science—skepticism about dogmas that assert confidently without proof, for example, that extraterrestrial intelligences do exist, and equal skepticism about dogmas that assert the impossibility of their existence.

However, it is not our purpose here to try to persuade the reader of the truth of our own convictions that angels do exist (perhaps the conviction could be stated even more strongly: we feel that they had better exist) but merely to contend that the angel stories are true religiously, whether they actually exist as disembodied spirits (or, in Von Ditfurth's view, quasi-disembodied spirits) or not. The story of the angel Raphael protecting the devout lover Tobias and his bride from the demon of objectifying and depersonalizing lust or the story of Gabriel coming to visit Mary in Nazareth are comic stories about a sacramentally experienced and analogically imagined God of enormous religious power and importance whose impact and religious authenticity do not depend on whether Raphael and Gabriel are actual creatures (as we hope they are). Whether there really exists a Raphael or a Gabriel or not, the Catholic religious sensibility knows that there is a God who loves us and is intimately involved with us and whose loving concern is represented and revealed by these stories.

By way of transition to a discussion of saints, we should also note our conviction that there is, after all, a Santa Claus. Parents who finally confess the "truth" to their children that it is they who bring the Christmas presents and not Santa Claus misunderstand the story entirely. Saint Nicholas of Myra (and Bari and Manhattan, as one scholar calls him) may never have existed, and his Santa Claus persona may well owe more to nineteenth-century New York, and the Clement Moore poem "'Twas the Night Before Christmas," and the cartoonist Thomas Nast's drawings than it does to any ancient Christian tradition. Nonetheless, Santa Claus as the patron of little children can be imagined as revealing and representing God's loving concern for all of us and especially for children, a loving concern and generosity that, in the ordinary course of human events, is exercised through parents. There is no need to demystify Santa Claus. Loving concern need not live in the North Pole and ride in a sleigh pulled by reindeer (one of whom may or may not be known as Rudolph).

In his own modest way Santa Claus might well represent what the great scholar Paul Ricoeur calls the "pilgrimage from the first to the second naïveté." In the first naïveté we accept religious symbols literally and uncritically, either as children or as adults, or in earlier eras with little scientific knowledge or critical spirit. Then we enter the critical or analytical phase in which we "unpack" the image, the symbol and the story, discover where it comes from and what it means, and what purpose it serves in our religion. Then, as we approach the second naïveté, we "repack" the symbol, now understanding its origin, its purpose, its function, and commit ourselves to the religious truth for which the symbol stands. Santa Claus is such a delightful person that he really ought to be unpacked and repacked and served up once again as a marvelous representation, at Christmas time, of parental love, both Divine and human.

The souls in purgatory represented, and not so long ago, a wonderful story in the Catholic tradition. They were pictured as being those who had died but who had not yet gone to heaven and were located in a place of temporary, if intense, suffering while they earned admission to heaven. It was also believed that those who were still alive were able to help them since probably they were not able to help themselves. Thus, one prayed for them, did good deeds for them, and especially offered one's sufferings up for them.

Undoubtedly, there were superstitions and corruptions in the "holy souls" story involving indulgences and purgatorial societies and such things, of which the less said the better. But the idea of suffering for others was extraordinarily useful for Catholics, whether the sufferer was a little kid in the dentist's chair or a person with terminal cancer. Souls in purgatory gave us a chance to make our suffering meaningful because they were a way of our understanding that vicarious suffering—suffering for others—was possible. The "poor souls" or the "holy souls" seem to have disappeared from popular Catholic piety, save for older Catholics, but the instinct of prayers for the dead is one that is very hard to give up, as is the instinct that we can suffer, somehow, vicariously for others. If theologians and religious educators and other wise persons are going to deprive us of the souls in purgatory, then they're going to have to find another religious story every bit as good, which will convey the two important truths that our prayers do help the dead and that we can offer our sufferings vicariously for others. Unfortunately they are often content to destroy the old story without consideration for the need to replace it—or, what would be far more intelligent, to provide a new interpretation for the old story.

The Catholic doctrine of purgatory as a theological teaching emerged as an outgrowth of the practice in late Judaism and early Christianity of offering prayers for the dead. Since obviously one did not need prayers if one was already happy with God in heaven, it seemed that there was some intermediate place of purification between heaven and earth where prayers and even vicarious suffering could still help. In popular piety the holy souls were often confused, particularly in Northern Europe, with the spirits of the dead that wandered about at the beginning of winter on the Celtic Feast of Sahmaintide, the most morose and spooky of Celtic feasts. Christianity tried to adapt the custom, with only limited success, by making November 1 the Feast of All Saints and by suggesting that we should pray especially hard for the souls in purgatory on the Eve of All Saints (All Hallows' Eve, or Halloween) in order that they might make it into heaven in order to celebrate the festive day with the other saints.

Popular piety quickly suggested that the spirits of the Holy Souls wandered about the world on All Hallows' Eve, and tried to persuade those who could still help them by their prayers to do so quickly. The church fought this interpretation by creating the Feast of All Souls in Purgatory on the day *after* the Feast of All Saints. Undaunted popular piety said it was a feast for those whose machinations on Halloween were unsuccessful. The end-of-October, beginning-of-November festival, then, is a not-altogether-successful merging of Christian and pagan feasts that asserts the fundamental unity of all Christians— those in heaven, those on earth, and those somewhere in between, a unity that is very important to the Catholic religious sensibility. The wide-eyed youthful trick-or-treaters on Halloween are actually supposed to represent the temporarily liberated souls in purgatory!

Purgatory has slipped out of contemporary Catholic piety and religious education, but like many other hastily abandoned products of Catholic religious sensibility it has been discovered by non-Catholics. Thus, in one of the few major works on life after death written by an English-speaking scholar in recent years, John Hicks, an English Free Church theologian, makes purgatory the central theme of his presentation. In his brilliantly imaginative book, *Death and Eternal Life,* Hicks says that it is eminently reasonable to suppose that the development of our personality that does not take place in this world must take place somewhere else before we are ready to enjoy eternal happiness with God. Since most of us have relatively undeveloped personalities at the time of our death, obviously our life must go on elsewhere while we attempt to become the fuller, richer, better persons we are capable of being, indeed which we must become before we can cope permanently with God's love. Hicks believes that what in fact happens is a reincarnation in other times in other spaces but, unlike the reincarnation doctrine of Eastern religions, a reincarnation with memories of our previous existences. As imaginative and as creative as Hicks's vision is—a mixture of Christianity, Eastern religions, and science fiction—it is something less than completely persuasive. But Hicks's instinct that our contemporary knowledge of the psychology of human personality development demands an opportunity for continued personality development after death seems most reasonable.

The same instinct is brilliantly described in the "Coda" of D. M. Thomas's magnificent novel *The White Hotel*, in which the heroine is "transported" to Israel, but not the Israel of this life but rather a new Israel, a new Zion, frequently described in allusions to Dante's Purgatory. In this new Israel, it appears that Paradise/Heaven is created in part by human effort. Freud, for example, who treated the heroine earlier in her life, is present, still suffering from facial cancer, but the doctors are making progress in curing him. However, the principal effort in Thomas's purgatory is straightening out the conflicts and the twisted relationships of our lives and making peace with our parents, our siblings, and our children. The heroine has made sufficient progress against her sinful habits of anger and conflict to volunteer to work in the hospital helping more recent immigrants, a gift of herself that is both generous and mature. As she walks through the soft night air toward the hospital, the hysterical symptoms that have plagued her life cease. As our friend John Shea suggests, she is entering Paradise.

We find Thomas's purgatory eminently persuasive and would not be surprised at all if the real purgatory is rather like the one he describes. However, we write about Hicks and Thomas, not to endorse their explanations, but to lament that a Catholic theological doctrine that can prove meaningful to a Protestant theologian and a secular novelist can be ignored in Catholic religious thinking and teaching.

Purgatory is a good and useful idea and a wonderful story, one that asserts that death does not end the unity of all human kind. Catholic theologians have abandoned it as they've abandoned concern about eschatology, because they are convinced that emphasis on the life to come minimizes the concerns of ordinary people for the life that is now. Implicitly they accept the old claim that heaven is pie in the sky when you die. It may well be advisable to oppose that kind of Catholic piety that detaches the salvation of the individual soul from social and ethical and human obligations in this world. And it may certainly have been the case that Catholic popular interpretations of heaven, purgatory, and hell tended to minimize and de-emphasize secular responsibilities. It may also have been the case, in some popular Catholic teaching in years gone by, that the terrible tragedy of death was minimized, papered over, obscured. But though these abuses did indeed occur, it does not follow that the instincts of the Catholic religious sensibility about death and judgment and purgatory and heaven were wrong and should be rejected. Rather, they must be interpreted anew. The Catholic instincts about prayers for the dead, vicarious suffering, and the unity of the living and the dead (formalized under the doctrine of the Communion of Saints, which proclaimed the unity of the Church Militant here on earth, the Church Suffering in Purgatory, and the Church Triumphant in heaven—warfare models if there ever were) are all fundamentally right and can be readily articulated in "second naïveté" stories about holy souls.

Finally, there are the saints, that most uniquely Catholic contribution to religious sensibility, that vast array of legendary, half-legendary, and real personages in the tradition of Catholic popular piety that stand as intermediaries and go-betweens, pleading our case before God.

Very few Catholic theologians have written in recent years about the saints except for the Austrian Karl Rahner, in one of his theological investigations, and the American Lawrence Cunningham, in *The Meaning of the Saints*. Such neglect is curious, especially in view of the enormous importance saints have had in Catholic piety (consider the number of American cities, for example, with saints' names).

There are two important issues that must be faced in any attempt to revitalize and reinterpret the Catholic imagination about saints, to make the journey on the subject of saints from the first to the second naïveté. The first question is whether saints are more important as miracle workers or as examples of the Christian life, and the second question is whether the great tradition of Catholic saints is served by the present canonization process.

The first Catholic saints were the martyrs. Catholic devotion to them was developed in the very early Church out of the practice of honoring those who had given their lives for the faithful. It is doubtless true that patron saints replaced patronal deities in many Christian countries (the pagan goddess in Ireland became the Christian Saint Brigid without any of her responsibilities—poetry, spring, storytelling, new life—changing). Nonetheless, in the Roman tradition, devotion owes more to the practice of honoring the martyrs than it does to baptizing lesser pagan gods and goddesses.

The martyr cult, beginning with the practice of offering Mass at the tomb of the martyr on the day of martyrdom, soon developed the custom of asking the martyr to intercede to God for those who honored the martyr—a logical and natural development. Roman society knew what it meant to have patrons and go-betweens and influential friends with "clout." The martyr, because of the heroism of his or her death, was assumed to have clout with God, and therefore to be capable of obtaining favors for the devotee whose life was much less impressive and who therefore could be expected to have less clout with God.

This notion of the saint as a person with clout has persisted into the present and has made one of the principal ecclesiastical concerns with sanctity the question of whether the clout has been proved by miracles. It is assumed, of course, that the saint would have led a good and holy life, but that is not enough; before a person can truly be considered to have lived a life worthy of imitation by the Catholic faithful, that person must have established sufficient influence with God to have worked four miracles.

Hence the present elaborate and juridical canonization process in the Catholic Church is a very careful investigation of, first of all, the holiness of the person's life but then, secondly, the proof that miracles have in fact occurred. As Cunningham points out, the result of these rules are rational and sensible, given the assumptions. The men and women who have been canonized in the present era (more men than women, of course) are often people of unquestioned probity of life but with little capacity to illumine and direct the lives of the ordinary faithful or to prove a striking example of what Christianity means to those who are not Catholic. All too often, the saints are either heads of religious orders or persons who have won the favor of important ecclesiastics or special groups within the Catholic community, all of whom are able to sustain the costs and the efforts of bureaucratic canonization. The saints may provide names for new Catholic suburban parishes but rather little else in the way of inspiration for and illumination of the Catholic life. For the good of the Catholic life, might it not be much better to choose for saints those who perhaps have not worked miracles, but whose lives are challenge and inspiration, illumination and mystery?

While the saint seems to be declining in importance in the Catholic tradition, he or she is still a subject of fascination to writers and filmmakers: Dostoyevsky, Silone, Greene, and Kazantzakis have all tried to explore in novels the meaning of sanctity, though usually their saintly heroes and heroines are so radically different in their circumstances and personalities from the rest of us that it's not clear whether they are any more of an inspiration than some of the obscure Italian saints who have been canonized by recent popes.

Cunningham makes a good case for what we ought to consider a saint to be in the contemporary world:

> [Saints] will exemplify what it means to be a Christian in a con- sciously new way. . . . they will reveal the past/future dimen- sion. . . . By their life, they will show that the Christian tradition has come to a new understanding; and in that recognition, they will become a standard against which others in the future will be judged. In short, their lived-out consciousness will be the instrument for teaching others.
>
> It is precisely because the saint is one who in his or her life shows the deep possibilities of what it means to be truly religious that we call a saint "holy" (compare the Hebrew KDSH, set apart)—one who is "separated" or "set apart" by the presence of the Divine. The saint sets forth the meaning of God in the living out of her life. True hagiography should be an ideal locus for what Sallie TeSelle calls "intermediate theology," that is, seeing in the lives of another not merely a consistency with certain doctrinal formulations, but a resonance and a depth that reflect back on the reader or observer of that life in such a way as to illuminate or clarify. In that sense,

the life of the saint should act like a parable: It should shock us into a heightened and a new sense of God's presence (and judgment) in our own life.

And John Henry Newman, a century before, said almost exactly the same thing:

They [that is, the saints] are the popular evidence of Christianity, and the most complete and logical evidence while the most popular. It requires times, learning, the power of attention and logical consecutiveness and comprehensiveness to survey the church in all ages and places as one, and to recognize it (as to the intellect, it is, and must be distinctly recognized) as the work of God alone; to most of us it is the separate and in one sense incomplete, portions of this great phenomenon which turn one's mind to Catholicism; but in the life of a saint, we have a microcosm, or the whole work of God, a perfect work from beginning to end, yet one which may be bound between two boards, and mastered by the most unlearned. The exhibition of a person, his thoughts, his words, his acts, his trials, his features, his beginnings, his growth, his end, have a charm to everyone; and where he is a saint they have a divine influence and persuasion, a power of exercising and eliciting the latent elements of divine grace in individual readers as no other reading can have.

Professor Cunningham asked the very pointed question of why the Franciscan male gentile Maximilian Kolbe was canonized whereas the Carmelite Jewish woman Edith Stein has yet to be canonized. Doubtless Kolbe (who was guilty of using language on occasion that today we would equate with anti-Semitism) was a heroic martyr, but how is it that Edith Stein, clearly an extraordinarily holy woman before her death and a deeply mystical person, has not been canonized?

There is no reason to abandon the "clout" or intercessory role of the saint. The saint, like the Blessed Mother, simply reveals (is a sacrament for) one of the aspects of God's goodness, an aspect of the goodness that we find especially appealing or consoling or useful in our own spiritual life. However, it does seem that in the present world, the exemplary role of the saint is more important than the intercessory role, and it is precisely the exemplary role that makes the saint a sacrament of God. Under such circumstances the wonders a saint may or may not have performed are of less importance than the saint's ability to challenge, to illumine, to summarize, to reveal.

If this aspect of sanctity is important to rejuvenate the Catholic tradition of sanctity in our time, then there obviously must be more women saints, more married saints, more saints who are not heads of religious orders, and even more saints who are not martyrs and who do not have to suffer enormously for their faith, save as that suffering is required by the demands of everyday life. Canonize Maximilian Kolbe and Edith Stein, of course, but don't forget that in canonizing Saint Thérèse of Lisieux the Church honored her teaching of the "Little Way" to sanctity, that is, the path to great holiness through excellence in daily life. Such excellence is, for our time, it would seem, a more important miracle than a marvelous cure of a sick person.

Or, to put the matter differently, if we are to bring the statues of saints back into Catholic churches, they must be statues of recognizable persons and not twisted coils of metal or other forms of abstractionism that, however artistically sound, are not much use for storytelling to little children. Let us bring into the church statues of saints with which the men and women, and especially the little boys and the little girls of our era, can identify, saints who are a challenge and an illumination, not because they are so unlike us but precisely because they are so like us.

There is a tendency in some contemporary Catholic discussion of sanctity to equate holiness with dedication to political and social causes. Dorothy Day and Mother Teresa of Calcutta are cited as modern saints, quite unobjectionably, as far as we can see, and Dag Hammarskjold's name is added to the list, somewhat ambiguously, because though Hammarskjold was certainly a good and holy and mystical man, his explicit Christianity was rather thin. Then one hears that Martin Luther King, Jr., was a modern saint, as are some of the revolutionary priests who died fighting with Marxist guerrilla bands in Latin America, and occasionally even someone will suggest that Fidel Castro is a saint.

It seems to us that goodness and social and political commitment are not quite enough to be a saint in any sense the word has traditionally possessed. The goodness of the saint, the quality of the saint's life, is after all what really counts, and that quality must not only be good but overwhelmingly, startlingly, disconcertingly good, and it must touch all aspects of life, not merely one's political and social commitments, however important these may be. In the modern world, indeed, the person without some kind of political or social concern, appropriate to time and place and age and status in life, cannot possibly be even considered as a potential saint. Sanctity requires social commitment, but social commitment, not even of the most extraordinary variety, is not enough for sanctity.

The saint, in the Catholic religious imagination, plays a role like the angel and the holy soul and perhaps the demon. The saint represents mystery. The saint is a sacrament of God's love, a revelation and an illumination, a concretization in a human life of the power and the passion of God's love, a revelation of God's love through the effectiveness of one particular person's response to that love. The saint is a creature of the analogical imagination that is able to say that God is like the saint and the saint is like God and the saint's story is a comic story, a story in which good triumphs over evil, a story in which through the power of God's love a happy ending does indeed reveal itself. The saint may work miracles, the saint may have special clout, the saint may have died a heroic death—or the saint may have done none of these things—but the saint must stand as a sign of mystery. The statues of the saint in church provide an opportunity to tell all children, young as well as old, stories of mystery, stories of wonder, stories of the enormous power of God's love.

We Catholics have messed up many of the most marvelous elements in our tradition down through the centuries. None have we messed up more than our tradition of saints. Excessively pious hagiography has dehumanized the saints, turning them into automatic miracle workers, immune from human emotion and feeling and passion. We have made them models of pious edification but precisely because they are so edifying, they have become hopelessly uninteresting, not a part of the human condition and hence no more challenging to us than the horrendously "pretty" religious art by which they are often represented. Moreover, in our hagiography and our private devotion, we have smoothed over the fact that many of the saints were ruthlessly persecuted by the Church or by their own religious orders—Saint John of the Cross was imprisoned and beaten every day by Carmelite monks, the works of Saint Thomas Aquinas were burned at Oxford,

247

Joan of Arc was burned at the stake. We have ignored the fact that the Church, like every other bureaucratic institution, has a hard time knowing what to do with a person who really takes its teaching seriously.

If Catholic devotion to the saints has survived, it is despite both theological neglect and hagiographical abuse—and also despite incredibly bad religious art, whether it be art in which women look like men and men look like women or art in which more recently nobody looks like anybody. The Catholic tradition of sanctity does indeed seem to have survived among ordinary Catholic people, many of whom still light vigil candles whenever they can. We used to be appalled every Sunday afternoon when the money from the vigil light collection boxes in the parish church had to be removed and we felt then that the vigil light was a horrendous abuse; but it is probably true that lighting a votive candle is a more important form of religious devotion, because more intelligible and more symbolically meaningful, than trying to recite a mostly unintelligible Psalm verse between the first two readings at Mass.

One may debate about vigil lights, but if one is committed to the Catholic heritage, one cannot debate about angels and saints and holy souls as signs of wonder and of grace, of love and of comedy, signs that are still important to many Catholics and that, properly reinterpreted and newly understood, could be of much more importance. The obstacle to the rehabilitation of angels and saints and holy souls is to be found in both the secularist theology that devalues mystery and the pietistic devotions that turn mystery into superstition.

From which the saints deliver us!

Conclusion

Our work in this book is concerned with a problem and a paradigm, and then with possibilities and policies. It is not concerned with programs and projects.

The problem, originally posed to us by a very wise editor, is whether Catholicism can be saved when it seems to be becoming like every other religion. What is more or less unique about Catholicism that can be offered as its distinctive contribution to the human enterprise?

Catholicism consists of deeper phenomena than the Latin Mass, clerical garb, absolute obedience to authority, and fish on Friday. Social science data indicate that the Catholic Church in the United States has responded to the traumatic changes of the post-conciliar era with remarkable resilience and vigor. The continuing loyalty of Catholics to their heritage, despite the difficulties and frustrations of the current transitional era, gives us a hint of what the distinctive Catholic contribution is. The special Catholic perspective will suggest Church policies appropriate for our present transitional crisis.

Conclusion

The paradigm grows out of the converging wisdom of many different academic disciplines in which humans organize and direct their lives according to a set of meaning systems. These meaning systems are networks of "pictures" against which the multitudinous phenomena of daily existence are compared and interpreted. Such "pictures" result from our experience of life, shape our further experiences, and provide us with "stories" that serve as road maps for our journeys through the complexities of life. What is special, we asked, about the Catholic experience, picture, and story, and about the Catholic community in which these stories are told and passed on to succeeding generations as archetypes for shaping their experience?

The Catholic experience is sacramental. More than any of the other religions of Yahweh (and probably more than any of the other great world religions), it experiences God as lurking in and disclosing Herself/Himself through the objects, events, and persons of the world. Alone of the great world religions, Catholicism has dared (perhaps foolishly, it will seem to many) to absorb absolutely everything it could from the pagan nature religions. It worries only on secondary reflection about not maintaining a radical enough disjunction between God and World. The central sacrament is Jesus. The Church is a sacrament of Jesus in its preaching His Word and administering the Seven Sacraments. But because Jesus is an incarnate being, then the whole world in which He took on flesh and everything in it is also sacramental—disclosive of God's love.

The Catholic imagination then must necessarily be analogical. It must see God as similar to the objects, persons, and events of the world, different from them, of course, profoundly and radically different, but not totally different, not so different that we do not learn something of God from the objects, persons, and events of daily life. The Catholic "picture" sees the sacred potentially everywhere and thus all things as potentially sacred.

The Catholic story therefore must be comic, it must have a happy ending. We work out the stories of our life in fear and trembling, perhaps, but also in confidence and hope because the world in which we live and the God at which it hints suggest in their best moments that we are involved in a romance that will have a happy ending. It is in the very nature of hope to postulate some kind of happy ending. Believing that the world is fundamentally good, if often fragile and easily perverted, Catholicism has always felt that hope must be taken with full seriousness. Life is too important ever to be anything but life. Love is stronger than hatred. Good is stronger than evil. Life is stronger than death. The Boy born in the manger grows up to die and be laid in the tomb.

But He and His Mother have the Last Laugh.

God is experienced in the objects, persons, and events of daily life, is similar to those realities, and blesses them as comic stories. Therefore we must tell our stories and pass them on in the context of our daily life, in the most intimate relationships in which we experience love and life and hope. Thus the Catholic storytelling community—however global its overarching structure—is local and organic. We hear the stories and pass them on to others first of all in the family and the local community. When the family and the neighborhood (or the neighborhood surrogate) turn to God, they become Church.

We then turned to possibilities and policies as they might be illumined by the use of this paradigm. It is possible, we said, to deal with some of the Church's most serious problems—and seize some of its best opportunities to make its unique contribution—by considering sex to be sacramental, woman as an analog of God, the Catholic story to be one of a continuously renewed romantic love affair, and the storytelling community in our country at any rate to be a development of the genius of the immigrant neighborhood parish that appealed to as many different dimensions of human life (sacraments) as it possibly could.

To take advantage of these possibilities, it seems to us, the Church must understand that worship (liturgy) is the situation in which the stories of the members of the community interact with the correlative overarching stories of the tradition. Liturgy—including preaching, which is an essential part of it—is fundamentally a work of correlation.

Moreover, the Church must reclaim its passionate involvement in art and scholarship because both are sacramental: both seek out wonder and surprise in the world. It must rediscover its own traditions of natural law and of social order, which are deeply rooted in its experience of revelatory organic local community. And it must reevaluate its angels and saints and holy souls, all of whom play important parts in the ongoing Catholic story. Especially it must renew its imagination of the Mother of Jesus in whom experience, image, story, and community all converge with enormous artistic and liturgical power.

To some this will seem like a reactionary agenda. We would not deny the charge if by it is meant that our agenda refuses to write off everything that happened in Catholic history before 1965. We do not seek a return to the past whether it be the past of 450, or 1250, or 1950. If we are reactionaries and traditionalists, we are not Catholic Traditionalists of the sort who wish a return to the Tridentine Latin Mass; we have no objection to it on occasion and we strongly support it for congregations of fourth-century Romans.

It is impossible to re-create the past, but it is necessary to learn from it. The tradition ought not to be mindlessly reimposed, but neither should it be mindlessly rejected.

Unfortunately the tradition, the Catholic sensibility, in the first half of the present century was all too often ossified, dessicated, frozen. When the hurricane of Pope John's council hit the Catholic elites, they were unequipped emotionally and intellectually to understand the riches of their own tradition. They felt only what they took to be the oppression and the irrationality of some of the forms of the tradition. Instead of imposing it, as they had done, they disposed of it. They rejected the tradition without re-examining it.

They threw out the baby, in other words, with the bath water.

And the baby's Mother too.

We asked Father Edward McKenna, the distinguished Chicago church musician, when he thought Gregorian chant would return to the Church (after a university cocktail party in which an FM station seemed to be playing chant music all night long). He said it would not happen till after the year 2000. There had been so much bad, mindless, dull, deadly, horrible Gregorian chant for so long that the whole tradition had been jettisoned without a thought to what it might contain that was good, true, beautiful, and useful.

We do not advocate a return, heaven save us all, to the Missa de Angelis. But we do advocate a reconsideration and re-evaluation of plainsong as an important component of our heritage, not a dead artifact to be restored as a museum piece but a living component on which to develop a living tradition of church music.

If that position sounds reactionary, then we hasten to point out that our suggestions that sexual passion is a sacrament of God's passionate love, that a woman's body is an analog of God's tenderness, and that life is a continuously renewed romantic love affair—all, it seems to us, highly compatible with the Catholic sensibility and profoundly rooted in it—will be considered in certain Catholic circles to be dangerously radical.

Something, we trust, to offend all ideologues.

And something, we hope and pray, to excite all nonideologues.

We have deliberately avoided particular programs and for two reasons: the time is not yet ripe for them. Much research, thought, discussion, reflection, and imagination must be done before anything more than ad hoc and experimental programming can be attempted. The American Catholic Church is program happy: develop a plausible program, get it on the summer school circuit, and sit back to watch it become this year's hottest fad. Even if it is a good program, it will quickly wither because it has been deracinated from the thought and reflection (and perhaps research) on which it is based. Our old friends' pragmatism and romanticism will destroy the best of projects if they are given half a chance. New ideas or, in our case, renewed ideas must be protected from the mindless, rote imitators.

Rather, we challenge readers to develop their own insights—hopefully pre-programmatic—in response to our arguments. Stop to think and reflect and imagine before rushing to the Xerox machine.

A single example, a "ferinstance," to illustrate what we mean:

Lent is supposed to be a time of penance, of suffering for our sins. Would not an excellent Lenten penance for married people be a renewal of their romance? To re-ignite the love affair with your spouse is an arduous and difficult task. It requires humility, patience, sensitivity, timing, persistence, vulnerability, forgiveness, determination, gentleness, courage. Few enterprises are more difficult, few psychological deaths more painful. The potential payoffs are, of course, very great. But also uncertain. Resurrection, as Noele Farrell observes in *Lord of the Dance,* is not supposed to be easy.

Renewing the romance with your spouse is a perfect Lenten parallel to death and resurrection. When the candle is plunged into the Holy Water at the Easter Vigil, and we are told in image and story that

Easter is the marriage of Jesus and his Church, it would be especially appropriate to our own married lives to be in one of their most passionate phases.

We don't insist on this as *the* spirituality. It is only a possibility that ought to occur easily to a Catholic sensibility that has become fully and articulately aware of itself. And it certainly ought not to offend such a self-conscious and articulate sensibility.

Yet most priests would be afraid, we think, to use it in an Ash Wednesday sermon. And many laity would think it strange, if not offensive. Ought not the priest to be warning of the dangers of too much sex, especially during Lent, instead of encouraging it?

Many other laity, we are quite sure, would think it a great idea. Lent as a time of more and better sex? Wow! Right on! Only do we really have to work hard at it?

You'd better believe it. And expect to fail at first. Resurrection of a romance isn't supposed to be easy.

The challenge of this book is simple and straightforward: the Catholic sensibility must become more self-aware and self-consciously articulate. Simple but not easy. You don't bring back from the dead a self-conscious awareness easily either.

It is hard to be sanguine about the prospects for our proposal, especially if it depends for its success on the work of the hierarchy, clergy, and religious. Two examples of objections we have heard illustrate the problem.

A priest rose up immediately after the completion of a talk to castigate one of us for not discussing nuclear weapons. It is the most serious problem the world faces. Why talk about imagination when we are threatened with destruction? The only possible answer was that the lecture was not on disarmament, that the Church hierarchy had dealt with the subject at great length, and that other speakers were doubtless making presentations on that subject. But this answer, of course, did not satisfy our adversary. Disarmament was his agenda for the year. Nothing else was tolerable. (One might have asked where he had been during the other thirty-three years since 1950.) Any other subject, no matter how interesting, had to be abandoned under pain of being charged with responsibility for a nuclear holocaust. Is there not room to talk about both? The answer was no, there was not. In the shadow of the Bomb we must talk only about the Bomb.

Since the Vatican Council cracked open the certainties of many priests and nuns, there has been a frantic search by many of them for new certainties to replace the old. Last year it may have been the rights of gays; the year before, the ordination of women; the year before that, the "Third World"; the year before that, the Charismatic Renewal. Next year it may be the rights of the unborn. All these issues are taken, while they are fashionable, to be uniquely compelling. Those caught up in this fad approach to every situation want only to know whether their Issue is going to be discussed. If it is not, as Righteous Guardians of the Only Agenda they will rise up to smite those of us who are not so morally sensitive. For such personalities, and they are legion in the clergy and religious, only simple certainties will suffice. Any proposal that departs from that format is rejected because by definition it is morally inferior.

The other questioner demanded to know whether the speaker thought Mary had sexual relations during her life. The response was an affirmation of the Church's teaching and a reference to a theological book that discussed the meaning of the virginity of Mary: in the Scriptures the virginity of Mary is proposed not to make an argument against sex but to emphasize the absolute uniqueness of Jesus. How then, demanded the questioner triumphantly, can Mary serve as a symbol of the sacramentality of sex?

If the nuclear weapons question demonstrated the hyper-seriousness of some clerics, the Mary question demonstrated the frivolity of others (and alas, the two can exist together). The power of a symbol is dependent not on a single historical, not to say gynecological, fact. A college student with an introductory course on metaphors knows as much. The Mother of Jesus was a female member of a sexually dimorphic species and as such sexual in every cell of her body. Whatever may be involved in her virginity, she still was a sexual person and lived in the world as a sexual person—very sexual indeed, we should think.

Intercourse does not guarantee sexiness and the absence of intercourse does not impede it. Why, one wonders, is it necessary to say that? Probably because of the half-educated pop Freudianism that permeates the Catholic elites and that, with vulgar Marxism, acts as the principal ideological prop of many priests and nuns.

Doubtless, Mary has been used by some of the Mariologists as a symbol of sexual repression and denial. But the origins of the symbol are different as is its operation in the Catholic imagination even today (a warm image of Mary correlates positively with sexual fulfillment in marriage). Why must we be paralyzed by the misuse of the symbol? Why cannot we rediscover its basic function and reinterpret that for our people?

Because it's hard, that's why.

Not all clergy and religious, not even a majority perhaps, are victims of either hyper-seriousness or pseudo-sophistication. But those two qualities sufficiently permeate Catholic elite culture so that serious discussion of even moderately complex proposals like ours is almost impossible.

The Catholic sensibility says "both/and," not "either/or"; both sexual virginity and married love, both concern about disarmament and concern about the future development of the Church. And its power is such that eventually, we are convinced, it will impose its own agenda. The resiliency of the Catholic sensibility is enormous. It is absorbed by Catholics in great part in the early years of their lives and in the environment of family and neighborhood. It is transmitted unself-consciously and without the need of deliberate intent. If we have you for the first six years of your life, then the odds are overwhelming that your religious sensibility will be Catholic no matter what else happens. You may be a lapsed Catholic, but you will never be, no matter how hard you try, an ex-Catholic.

The Mary image has survived centuries of distortion into a triumphalistic, pietistic, cloyingly sentimental, anti-sex symbol. It has also survived twenty years of pseudo-ecumenical neglect. The image of Mary among young Catholics, according to our research, is warm, powerful, and strongly influential in their lives even though they may never have said the rosary, or heard a Marian sermon, or attended a May crowning.

The symbol survives intact both because of the power of its story (God loves us as a mother loves a newborn child) and because it is transmitted from generation to generation without the need of much attention from ecclesiastical elites. So too the Catholic sensibility: it will survive and be vital despite the hyper-seriousness and pseudo-sophistication of the elites. The challenge is not to save it but to rediscover it, rearticulate it, and reinterpret it for our time.

One cannot expect this to be done by hierarchy, clergy, religious educators, Catholic-college faculty, Catholic journalists, or other institutionally influential persons (with some exceptions, of course). They ride on a powerful and surging ocean and think they are walking across a desert. Where will the "resurfacing" of the Catholic sensibility take place? Mostly, it will occur among those on the fringes of the institutional Church who are striving to rediscover and re-examine their heritages—artists and storytellers often rejected or ignored by the Church, Catholic teachers on secular university campuses, Catholic writers who are part of the mainstream marketplace, young Catholics who want to recover what their parents seemed to have lost, older Catholics who say, "Hey, there was something good in the old neighborhood that we lost."

We do not see how even the most mindless misunderstanding by the clerical and clericalist elites can prevent this from happening. The vital issue is not "whether" but "how soon?" The question is not "Will it happen?" but "How much must we suffer before it does?"

Mary is the litmus paper, the touchstone. She represents the genius of the Catholic sensibility and also the pre-1960 ossification and dessication of it. She also represents the power of the sensibility to survive the madcap faddism of the post–Vatican Council era. The elites may not notice her. They may abhor rosaries and May crownings. Yet Mary is alive and well in the Catholic imagination. And when she is rediscovered, we will know that everything else has been rediscovered too. In John R. Powers's play *Do Patent Leather Shoes Reflect Up?* the second grade stages a May crowning. The actors begin to sing "Bring Flowers of the Rarest." At the chorus, the night we attended, the entire theater broke into "O Mary, We Crown Thee with Blossoms Today, Queen of the Angels, Queen of the May." Afterward we asked Powers whether it happened often.

John shook his head in astonishment. "Every single night from the very first performance."

Precisely.

When the tune, or perhaps much better music written for the same purpose (with singable melodies, however), is heard again in Church we will begin to believe that the power and the richness of the Catholic sensibility are being rediscovered—especially if a decent homily precedes the song, explaining that Mary represents God's life-giving, nurturing, caring, tender love.

Or, as an alternative to "Bring Flowers of the Rarest," the ancient Gregorian "Salve Regina":

> *Salve, Regina, mater misericordiae;*
> *Vita, dulcedo et spes nostra*
> *Salve!*
> *Ad te clamamus,*
> *Exsules filii Evae.*
> *Ad te suspiramus,*
> *Gementes et flentes*
> *In hac lacrimarum valle.*
> *Eia ergo, advocata nostra,*
> *Illos tuos misericordes oculos*
> *Ad nos converte.*
> *Et Jesum, benedictum fructum ventris tui,*
> *Nobis post hoc exsilium ostende.*
> *O clemens, O pia,*
> *O dulcis Virgo Maria!*